GHOST OF A CHANCE

ARCANE CASEBOOK 2

DAN WILLIS

Edited by Stephanie Osborn

Cover by Mihaela Voicu

Published by

Dan Willis
Spanish Fork, Utah.

1

THE SAPPHIRE ROSE

Waves of heat rose off the ground under the August sun, distorting the piles of garbage that made up the Brooklyn landfill. Alex Lockerby took off his hat and mopped his brow, lowering the spade he carried in his left hand. Putting his hat back on, he reached into his vest and pulled a battered brass compass from the pocket. The little needle trembled but kept pointing onward through the piles of stinking rot and refuse left over from the world's largest city.

As he stepped over the shattered remains of a wooden crate, the ground gave under his foot with a wet, squishing sound. The stench of rotting vegetation, spoiled meat, and sour milk assaulted him, and he had to repress the urge to gag.

"How do you let yourself get talked into this?" he said out loud, mostly to keep his mind off his surroundings.

He knew very well what had brought him here, of course. Money.

Or rather, the lack of it.

It had all started that morning when a well-dressed Brit named Gary Bickman came to see him at his Mid-Ring office. Bickman worked as a valet for some swell named Atwood who had a fancy Core address. A brooch worth more than Alex would earn in a decade went missing, and suspicion fell on the lady's maid, Bickman's wife. Both were immediately fired, and Atwood was pursuing criminal charges against his former employees.

Bickman insisted that his wife was innocent and offered Alex a C-note if he could prove it. The easiest way to do that was to find the brooch. The police had searched Atwood's house and the couple's living quarters but had found nothing. Since Bickman and his wife were the only people with access to the room where the brooch was kept, naturally they were the only suspects.

But Alex had methods the police didn't.

He had the best finding rune in the city.

Alex reached into his pocket for a cigarette, but found it empty. He swore as he remembered that his last few cigarettes were locked in his desk back in his office.

Eleven short months ago he'd been paid a grand for helping the government recover a deadly man-made plague and now, here he was, chasing down a lead in a garbage dump without even the comfort of a cigarette to blunt the smell. Most of that money had gone to his training as a runewright. The special inks and equipment needed to master the craft didn't come cheap, and while he was good, Alex still had a lot to learn. Thinking back, he remained amazed the cash had gone so quickly, leaving him owing his secretary Leslie back pay, and Alex behind on rent and short on smokes.

Garbage dump or not, a C-note would go a long way toward putting him back in the black.

"Once more unto the breach," he sighed, quoting the Bard. His mentor, Dr. Ignatius Bell, late of His Majesty's Navy, insisted that he learn more than just rune magic as part of his training. Extensive reading was also required. Alex had complained at first, but as time went on, he began to like it.

Not that he'd be telling Iggy that any time soon.

Watching for any more wet spots on the ground, Alex pushed his predicament out of his mind and moved on. After a dozen more yards, the compass needle began spinning in lazy circles. He lowered the spade, pushing it gently into the garbage at his feet. Taking off his jacket, he draped it over a broken crate nearby that didn't look too dirty. Depositing his dark blue fedora on top of his coat, he picked up the spade and began gently removing trash from the area.

He tested each shovel full of debris by holding the compass over it, just to make sure he hadn't removed the brooch. Ten minutes in, the compass turned and pointed toward his latest shovelful of garbage. Carefully, Alex picked through the damp pile until he found a wadded-up bundle.

It was a lady's handkerchief, lacy and delicate. Alex could guess why it had been thrown away, as it was tattered around the edges.

Being careful not to tear the fabric, Alex unwrapped it. Inside lay the most expensive thing Alex had ever held in his hands, the *Sapphire Rose*. The brooch had a platinum setting with dozens of little diamonds around a blue flower in the center. The flower's petals were made up of small, blue sapphires with one as big as a robin's egg in the center. Their color was perfect, a deep, lustrous blue, and it sparkled in the afternoon sun.

"Hello, beautiful," Alex said with a grin. "I know some folks who will be very happy to see you."

"OH, GOD," Leslie Tompkins exclaimed as he trudged wearily through the door of the fourth-floor offices of Lockerby Investigations. Leslie immediately covered her nose with the back of her hand. "What happened to you?"

A former beauty queen, Leslie had worked as Alex's secretary for years. She was in her early forties, but time hadn't slowed her down any. Tall and statuesque, she had strawberry blonde hair and hazel eyes that looked blue when she wore blue, and green when she wore green. Today she had on a white blouse, so they were gray. Leslie was the business side of Lockerby Investigations, booking Alex's clients and making sure the bills got paid while Alex did the actual detective work.

"Long story," Alex said as Leslie threw open the window behind her desk despite the August heat.

"Cut to the chase," she said, still covering her nose. "Did you find it?"

Alex grinned and dropped the handkerchief on Leslie's perennially organized desk. He opened it, revealing the brooch.

"Wow," Leslie said, looking at the brooch as it glittered in the afternoon light. "That's really something. Is that little trinket really worth twenty Gs?"

Alex nodded.

Leslie wanted to get closer and examine it but as she moved, her hand came back up to her face.

"Where did you find it?" she gasped. "You smell like a fish market at closing time."

"It was in a dump in Brooklyn," Alex said. "Don't worry, though, I've got a cleansing rune in my office."

"Good," she said, stepping back toward the window. "Just don't use it in here."

"Yes mother," he said with a grin and trudged toward the door marked, *Private*.

ALEX ENTERED his office and pulled out his rune book, a pasteboard volume with a red cover that he carried in his suit jacket. This was where he carried the runes he needed for work, so he'd have them when he needed them. The pages inside were made of volatile and delicate flash paper so he turned them gently until he found the one he wanted. It bore the symbol of a triangle with circles at each point, drawn in silver ink. Delicate lettering ran around the inside of each circle and along each edge of the triangle.

He carefully tore the vault rune from his book, licked the edge of the paper, and stuck it to the wall of his office. The outline of a door had been painted on the wall complete with a keyhole in the exact center. Taking a paper matchbook from his pocket, Alex lit one and touched the flame to the flash paper. It vanished in a puff of flame and smoke, leaving the glowing, silver rune behind, hanging in the air by the wall. After a moment, the rune seemed to melt into the wall itself, then a cold steel door appeared. Alex took a heavy skeleton key from his pocket and used it to open the door to his vault.

Vaults were extra-dimensional spaces where runewrights could keep valuables or supplies. Alex's vault was bigger than his entire office, encompassing a large workspace with workbenches, shelves, and storage for all the tools of his trade.

Entering the vault, Alex left the spade in a rack of tools along the wall, then moved to the tall, angled drafting table against the back wall. Several papers were strewn about the table on the floor, testaments to the difficulty of his work. Many runes were simple to draw but costly to create, requiring inks infused with precious metals or gemstone. Cleaning Runes, on the other hand, were cheap to make, requiring just an ordinary pencil, but the rune was excessively complex, needing meticulous attention to detail to get right.

Still, Alex was used to writing complex runes. This time the delicate lines and symbols of the cleaning rune eluded him for a different reason. Last year he'd teleported the floating castle of New York sorceress, Sorsha Kincaid, out over the Atlantic Ocean. It had cost him decades of his own life to power the magic required to move such an enormous mass, but since a Nazi spy was trying to drop the castle on the city at the time, Alex reckoned it was a good trade. Ever since that event his brown hair had turned completely white, and recently — his hands had begun to tremble.

Alex reached for the sole paper on the table, his lone success after hours of work, but the memory of his shaking hands made him stop. The tremors weren't enough to notice except when he was trying to write delicate symbols, but he rubbed his hands together anyway. He felt like he could force them to stop if he only squeezed them tightly enough.

Grinding his teeth at the futility of the gesture, he picked up the paper and stuffed it into his pocket. He turned to leave, but stopped beside a long shelving unit against one wall to retrieve an electric desk fan made of brass.

Dropping the rune and the fan on the desk in his office, Alex unlocked his desk and took out his last pack of cigarettes. There were only three left, so he tucked the pack into his pocket after withdrawing one. Lighting it with the touch tip on his desk, Alex took a satisfying drag and let it out. That act alone helped his trembling hands and he felt better. Especially since he'd soon have spending money to buy ciga-rettes again.

Shaking off his euphoria, Alex opened his office window, letting in a blast of heat. One of the few nice things in his life was the fact that his office was always cool thanks to the small coldbox mounted above the door.

A coldbox was basically a box lined with asbestos that had an opening in the top and a fan on the front edge. When the power was turned on, the fan drew air through the box and over three metal disks that had been enchanted to remain cold for up to six months. The disks were the work of the Ice Queen, Sorsha Kincaid. Despite Alex dropping her castle in the North Atlantic, Sorsha had offered Leslie new cold disks whenever she wanted them, so Alex's offices were always cool, even in the summer.

With the window open, Alex was almost ready for the rune. Cleaning runes were finicky magic, and they had the potential to simply redistribute filth rather than removing it. He plugged the desk fan into an electrical socket, pointed it at the window, then turned it on. The motor hummed as the brass blades of the fan began to pick up speed.

His preparations complete, Alex stood in front of the fan, facing the open window. Licking the edge of the paper, Alex stuck the cleaning rune to the brim of his hat, then touched the lit end of his cigarette to it. The paper burned away in an instant and Alex felt a tingling sensation wash over him. He held his breath until a puff of dust-like particles leapt away from him, catching in the wind from the fan and swirling away out the window. Alex knew from experience that you didn't want to breathe any of that. If you did, it took days to get the taste out of your mouth.

With the dirt and the smell of the landfill stripped away, Alex shut the window, then returned the electric fan to his vault. When he emerged back into his office, the coldbox was already beginning to return the room to a comfortable temperature. All in all, Alex reasoned, this had been a good day's work.

LESLIE'S FACE did not mirror Alex's enthusiasm when he went back into the outer office. She sat at her desk, staring at the Sapphire Rose with a stern look on her face.

"What's the matter?" he asked.

She looked up with a grim expression.

"Did that butler pay you for this job yet?" she asked.

"No," Alex admitted. "He kept his money in his employer's safe and the jerk refused to give it to him. He'll have to once I bring this back."

Leslie's expression soured even more.

"I doubt it," she said. She stood and handed Alex the brooch. "It's a fake."

Alex held the brooch up to the light, but the stones looked real enough.

"How could you know that?"

Leslie took the brooch back and turned it over so Alex could see the back of the setting where a long straight pin and hook would keep it in place when worn.

"Here," she said, indicating the seams where the pin had been attached to the setting.

Alex looked closely, but aside from a bit of tarnish on the silvery metal, he saw nothing amiss.

"I called the Atwood's insurance company while you were out," she said, picking up a note pad from her desk. "According to them," she said, consulting her notes, "the Sapphire Rose is a brooch made of seven small sapphires, one large sapphire, and sixteen diamonds in a platinum setting."

Alex turned the brooch over and did a quick count of the stones. All were present and accounted for.

"I still don't get it."

Leslie turned the brooch to the back again.

"Platinum doesn't tarnish," she said, indicating the tarnished area again. "This is silver, which means it isn't the original setting."

Alex felt a lump form in the pit of his stomach.

"And if the setting's a fake—" he began.

"Then the stones are sure to be fakes too," Leslie finished.

Alex just stared at the bit of tarnish on the bottom of the brooch.

"This means we aren't getting paid, doesn't it?" Leslie said. "I mean, if you take this to Atwood, he'll just say the butler had it made."

"Valet," Alex corrected absently while his mind was working overtime. Leslie was right; Atwood would claim that Bickman had the fake made, either to clear his name or to cover for the theft. He had to prove that the fake came from Atwood.

Unless he didn't.

"Who is the Atwood's insurance company?" he asked, puffing absently on his cigarette.

"Lloyds," Leslie replied. "And if we're not getting paid, you could at least let me have one of those," she said, pointing at the cigarette. "It's been almost a week for me."

Alex grinned and tossed her the nearly-empty pack.

"Save me the last one," he said, heading back to his office. "And call Bickman. Have him meet me in front of Atwood's place in an hour. Then call Danny and have him tell the detective on this case to do the same."

"CALLAHAN BROTHERS PROPERTY," a perky voice came through the phone once Alex's call connected.

"Arthur Wilks, please. Tell him it's Alex Lockerby."

The perky voice asked him to wait. Alex met Arthur Wilks while chasing down some stolen diamonds. He was a former cop turned insurance investigator with an extensive network of underworld informants.

"I thought I told you not to call me," Wilks' gruff voice rumbled at him.

"No," Alex corrected. "You told me not to come back, which you'll note I haven't. How are you, Wilks? Catch any jewel thieves lately?"

"I've got things to do, Lockerby," Wilks growled. "What do you want?"

"Do you know anybody at Lloyds of London?"

"It's a small industry," he said.

"Do any of them owe you a favor?"

"Lockerby, quit wasting—"

"Would you like them to?" Alex cut in.

The line went quiet for a long moment before Wilks answered.

"What did you have in mind?" he said with a conspiratorial smile Alex could hear.

———

ALMOST AN HOUR LATER, Alex got off a crosstown crawler right in front of Empire Tower. Crawlers were the brain child of John D. Rockefeller, former industrialist and now one of New York's six resident sorcerers. They had the upper body of a double decker bus but from the wheel wells down, they had thousands of glowing blue legs made of pure energy. To Alex, they looked like a cross between a centipede and a snail.

Formerly called the Empire State Building, Empire Tower had been converted into a magical battery that radiated power to most of the Island of Manhattan. The closer you were to the tower, the better the power reception got, so naturally New York's well-to-do built their townhouses right up against the tower in an area known as the Core.

The home of Ernest and Linda Atwood was styled after a Grecian temple, with marble columns and friezes under the eaves. Ernest was second-generation money, his father Marvin having made millions providing textiles to the growing nation's clothing manufacturers.

Marvin was widely reputed to be a workaholic who spent his days in the office making deals and, more importantly, money. Ernest was a man of leisure who, as far as Alex could tell, had never worked a day in his life.

Alex's clients, Gary and Marjorie Bickman, were waiting for him on the sidewalk outside the elaborate gates that led up to the Atwood home. A police detective Alex didn't know stood with them, wearing a brown suit and a sour look on his face. He was average height with brown hair, a strong nose, and tired eyes.

"You Lockerby?" he said, barely containing the sneer in his voice.

Alex put on his most affable smile. He was well used to police detectives looking at him like something nasty on their shoe.

"Call me Alex," he said, offering the detective his hand.

"Marcus North," he said, not shaking. "I'm only here because Detective Pak vouched for you, but if you're wasting police time, I'll bring you up on charges."

Alex's smile didn't even hint at slipping.

"Did you find anything, Mr. Lockerby?" Bickman asked in his proper, British accent. He stood with his arm around his wife, who looked like she might faint at any moment. Gary Bickman was short and slim with a slight build and black hair that he wore slicked back. He was dressed in a tuxedo, which Alex assumed was standard attire for a rich man's valet. His wife was pretty and blonde with a plump face and round figure in a tasteful floral dress.

"I think I've got good news for you," he said, looking around. "We just need to wait for — ah, here they come."

A sleek black sedan eased up to the curb and a woman in a form-fitting silk dress got out. She was about Leslie's age, but time had not been as generous to her as it had been to Alex's secretary. Her face was lined and her hair had started to gray, but her eyes were sharp, even shrewd.

"Which one of you is Lockerby?" she declared as she mounted the sidewalk.

"Here," Alex said, tipping his hat. "Are you from Lloyds?"

"Greta Morris," she said, holding out a hand.

"If this is everyone," Detective North growled, "let's get on with this. Some of us have work to do."

"I couldn't agree more," Alex said.

"Do you have it?" Greta asked.

With a dramatic gesture, Alex reached into his jacket pocket and pulled out the fake *Sapphire Rose*.

"That's it," Marjorie gasped, collapsing against her husband as she began to cry.

"Good show, Alex," Bickman said.

"Where did you get that," North asked.

"I found this in the Brooklyn landfill," he said, passing it to Greta.

"How did it end up in a landfill?" Detective North asked.

"If I had to guess," Alex said as Greta pulled a jeweler's loop from her pocket and used it to examine the brooch. "I'd say Atwood threw it in the trash."

"Why would he do that?" Bickman asked.

"Because this brooch is a fake," Greta said, tossing it to North.

The detective caught the brooch deftly and held it up to sparkle in the sunlight.

"You sure?"

Greta favored him with a stern look.

"Detective, I've worked for Lloyds of London for twenty years," she said. "We're the most prestigious insurer of high-end jewelry in the world. I know fake jewelry when I see it."

"That can't be," Marjorie Bickman gasped. "Lady Atwood only wears it on special occasions. The master keeps it in his safe."

"When was the last time she wore it?" Alex asked.

"They went to a party last week, at the Astors," Bickman said. "A picture of the Lady Atwood wearing the brooch was in the Times."

"Convenient," North said, turning the brooch over in his hands. "I think I see where you're going with this."

"Based on what Mr. Wilks of Callahan Brothers Property told me, I've made a few enquiries," Greta said. "The Atwoods have sold off quite a bit of their art collection over the last year."

"That's true," Bickman said. "The elder Mr. Atwood was the collector. The master said he disliked art."

"I suspect it's more that he likes money," North said.

"Or rather spending it," Alex added. "When was the last time you got paid?" he asked Bickman. "I mean in cash."

Caught off guard by the question, Bickman took a moment to answer.

"Most of our needs are taken care of as part of the household," he said. "The master usually just puts my salary in his safe for me. I think the last time I needed money was about a month ago when I took Marjorie to a picture show."

"What's this about?" Marjorie asked, her fearful look back with a vengeance.

"Your boss is broke," Detective North said. "He got rid of this so he could collect the insurance."

"I suspect they sold off the stones in the real brooch a few at a time," Greta supplied. "Eventually even the setting. I have a colleague trying to track them down as we speak."

Alex chuckled at that. Wilks might be a jerk, but he was very good at his job. If the Atwoods had sold off the stones on the black market, Wilks would know about it by breakfast.

"My God," Marjorie gasped, clinging to her husband. "If the Atwoods are broke, what about our money?"

"How much do they owe you?" Detective North asked.

"Sixteen hundred and twelve dollars," Bickman answered immediately. "It's supposed to be in his office safe."

"I'll look into that," North said. "But if they're trying their hand at insurance fraud, I wouldn't hold my breath."

Mrs. Bickman made a sobbing noise and buried her face in her husband's lapel.

"What are we going to do?" Bickman asked, his face ashen. "That money is all we have and until the accusations against my wife are cleared up, no one will hire us."

Alex looked at North, but the detective just shrugged.

"I've got some questions for the Atwoods," he said, pocketing the fake brooch. "I'll lean on him about your money."

"Thank you, detective," Bickman said, somewhat woodenly.

"I'll go with you," Greta said to North as the detective headed toward the enormous house. "I have some questions of my own."

Alex watched them go as Marjorie sobbed into Bickman's tuxedo jacket. He pulled out his rune book and tore out a minor restoration rune, passing it to the diminutive valet.

"This will get the stains out of your jacket," he said.

"Thank you," Bickman said in the same wooden voice he'd used with Detective North.

"Do you have a place to stay?" Alex asked.

Bickman nodded after a moment.

"Marjorie's sister lives in the city."

"Good. Take your wife there." Alex hesitated. He really didn't want to go on, but the sight of Bickman's lost expression and Marjorie's sobbing drove him on. He sighed and resigned himself to the course of action in front of him. "Call me in the morning," he said at last. "I might be able to help."

"Thank you, Mr. Lockerby," Bickman said, his face brightening a little. "I'm sorry...I only have my pocket money right now. I can't pay you."

Alex didn't even grimace when the valet said it. Of course he'd known it was coming, so it wasn't such an incredible accomplishment.

"I know," he said, putting a comforting hand on Bickman's shoulder. "You'll pay me when you can."

2

THE MIDNIGHT SUN

Alex regretted promising to help the Bickmans almost as soon as the words were out of his mouth. They were nice enough people, sure, and they'd been dealt a bum hand, but helping them would mean calling *her*. He didn't even want to think about that.

He did, however, really need to get paid. He had about thirty cents in his pocket and that was pretty much it.

To avoid making the dreaded call, Alex crossed town to *The Lunch Box*, a diner a few blocks from the brownstone where he rented a room from his mentor, Dr. Bell. Iggy would be making dinner soon, but Alex hadn't had anything to eat since breakfast. He hadn't really been up to food after his encounter with the landfill.

"Hey, sugar," the waitress said as Alex sat down at the counter. "Haven't seen you in here in a while. What'll it be?"

A faded tag on her blue apron read, *Doris*, but she was such a fixture at the diner that she didn't really need a name-tag. Alex wondered if *The Lunch Box* even had another waitress.

"Coffee," he said.

Hungry or not, he wasn't about to insult Iggy by eating right before dinner. Besides, he didn't have enough money to spare for even a poached egg.

"Anyone leave a copy of the Times lying around?" he asked.

"Just this," Doris said, handing him a folded paper before putting a coffee cup in front of him.

As she filled the cup, Alex turned over the paper. It was thin and square instead of the regular newspaper shape, and its masthead bore the title, *The Midnight Sun*. A massive headline took up almost the top third of the paper, declaring; *Ghost Killer Strikes Again*.

Alex resisted the urge to groan. *The Midnight Sun* was a tabloid, devoid of any actual journalism, and full of salacious rumors and celebrity stories that appealed to the gossip-hungry masses. Still, Alex knew Iggy would want to discuss the news of the day over dinner and it had been a while since Alex had read anything Iggy didn't already know.

As he drank his coffee, Alex scanned the article. According to the author, one Billy Tasker, the suicide of an elderly man in a fashionable Inner-Ring home matched a pair of suicides in the last few weeks. In all three cases, the victims were found alone in a locked room. Tasker claimed that he had inside knowledge of the coroner's report, saying that each victim was stabbed twice in the chest by a long, thin blade. The mysterious part was that no weapon was found at any of the crime scenes.

Of course, Tasker's conclusion was that this was the work of a vengeful spirit, murdering people who had undoubtedly slighted it in life. Alex tossed the paper away in disgust, reminding himself that the last time he saw a copy of *The Midnight Sun*, it had claimed that runewright magic was actually the language of Atlantis.

"There you are," a familiar voice said from behind him.

Alex turned to find Police Detective Danny Pak standing just inside the door. He was in his late twenties, only a few years younger than Alex's thirty-two, with black hair, olive skin, and dark eyes. His features reflected his Japanese heritage and were made more prominent by the fact that he always had an infectious grin. He was also one of Alex's only close friends.

"What are you doing here?" Alex asked, picking up his hat up from the neighboring stool so Danny could sit down.

"Danny comes here all the time," Doris said, setting a coffee cup in front of the detective. "You want the usual, hon?"

"Yes, please," Danny said as he sat.

Alex raised an eyebrow. He'd been to Danny's apartment and it was on the other side of Central Park from *The Lunch Box*. There wasn't any reason for him to go this far out of his way for dinner.

He shifted his gaze to the kitchen. About a year ago Alex had met Mary, a pretty girl working a lunch counter who wanted to be a full-fledged cook. Alex sent her here and she'd been working at *The Lunch Box* ever since.

"It's not like that," Danny said, reading Alex's expression. To his credit, he didn't blush at all.

"Then you must have come to see me," Alex said. "Lucky you caught me, since I don't usually eat dinner here."

"I did want to see you," Danny said, ignoring Alex's innuendo. "I need your help."

"What's the trouble?"

"You heard about the rash of thefts we've been having?"

Alex shrugged. New York was a big city with over a million people; someone was always getting robbed somewhere.

"A bunch of deliveries have been hit," Danny added.

"Any pattern?"

Danny shook his head and sighed.

"No," he said. "That's the frustrating thing. The stuff that got taken is random. Some of it makes sense to steal, but the rest is just junk. A whole truckload of dungarees went missing, along with a load of paper napkins bound for Delaware."

Doris set a pastrami on rye in front of him and he paused to take a bite.

"People are pretty desperate these days," Alex said while Danny chewed. "Maybe they're just stealing whatever they can get their hands on."

"Maybe," he said. "I just can't seem to catch a break on this. I figured if you could use one of your finding runes to locate any of the stolen property, that might be the only shot I've got."

"I'd need something that links to any of the missing items."

Danny nodded and took another bite of his sandwich.

"I thought of that," he said with his mouth full. "I've got some leather from the machine that made a missing crate of work boots."

Alex shook his head.

"That's not going to do it," he said. "They probably made a dozen pairs of boots from that one piece. The rune will only have something to lock on to if the boots are still together in the same place, and that's assuming they all were in that one missing shipment."

"That's not likely," Danny admitted.

"Alex," a new voice said.

He looked up to see Mary emerge from the kitchen. She was a slim girl with brown hair and freckles on her nose. When she saw him, her face lit up in a smile.

"You haven't been by in a long time," she chided him. "Why didn't you tell Doris to say hello?"

"Sorry, Mary," Alex said, feeling a bit guilty. "Too busy with my own problems, I guess. How's the work?"

Mary beamed.

"I love it," she said. "Max says business has tripled since I started. He gave me a raise."

"That's great," Alex averred.

She turned to Danny and slipped her apron off, over her head.

"Mario is already here," she noted. "So, I'm officially off-duty." Alex raised an eyebrow and Mary smiled. "Danny is taking me dancing."

"Is he now?" Alex asked with a smirk. Danny had an eye for the ladies and Mary was a real looker. Alex had wondered how long it would take him to ask her out.

"If I get you a list of what was stolen," Danny said, as if he hadn't heard Mary, "would you look over it?"

"Sure," Alex said, standing up and putting on his hat. "Drop it by for Leslie in the morning." He tossed a dime on the counter, five cents for the coffee and five for Doris, then winked at Mary. "You kids have fun."

THE BROWNSTONE where Alex lived belonged to his mentor, Dr. Ignatius Bell. It was a four-story, Mid-Ring building just six blocks from Central Park. When Iggy retired from His Majesty's Navy and moved to New York, he'd found Alex selling runes on a street corner. Since the Brits only used runewrights for military doctors, Iggy took Alex under his wing and trained him to be a proper runewright.

He'd also trained Alex to be a detective.

Iggy hadn't been entirely honest with Alex when he took him in. He had been a doctor in the Navy, but he'd retired decades earlier, become a writer, and written the most famous detective in history.

Sherlock Holmes.

Iggy, or rather Arthur, hadn't wanted to leave his home and his family, but he'd done one other thing while he served in the Navy: he'd found the Archimedean Monograph. Originally written by Archimedes of Syracuse, the Monograph contained some of the most powerful and dangerous runes in history. It was a book many people sought, some of them perfectly willing to murder to get it. So Arthur Conan Ignatius Doyle became Ignatius Bell and moved to New York for the safety of his family.

The brownstone didn't look any different from its neighbors, just a row house of tan brick, but it was protected by powerful runes and wards. As Alex approached, he pulled out his battered pocket watch and flipped open the cover. As part of his training with Iggy, Alex had written small, delicate runes on the inside of the lid. These allowed him to open the front door by simply twisting the knob. Without the watch and its runes, a whole gang of men couldn't have opened that door with a battering ram.

"You're early," Iggy said when Alex came through the inner door of the brownstone's vestibule. "Dinner's not quite done yet." Cooking was a serious hobby that Iggy had picked up during his navy days.

Alex hung up his hat and moved through the front library to the kitchen. Iggy stood at the range, stirring something in a steaming pot. He was tall and slender with wavy silver hair and a bottle-brush mustache to match. Though he was well into his seventies, Iggy had the energy of a man half his age.

"Don't mind me," Alex said, picking up Iggy's issue of the New

York Times from the sideboard and sitting down at the kitchen table. "It's been a long day."

"Did you see the story about those robberies all over the city?"

"No," Alex admitted. "But Danny mentioned them. Supposed to be completely random so it doesn't sound like the work of a gang, just desperate people."

"How is Danny?"

"Out dancing with Mary," Alex said, paging trough the paper as fast as he dared.

"He'd better not break her heart," Iggy said, taking his pot off the burner. "I'll never forgive him if she stops cooking at the diner."

Alex chuckled at that.

"You're all heart," he said.

"I eat lunch there almost every day," Iggy admitted.

"It says here that the government of Spain is suing some American over a museum exhibit," Alex said, changing the subject.

"Phillip Leland," Iggy supplied. "The adventurer who found the treasure of the Almiranta. She was part of the 1715 treasure fleet that went down in a hurricane. Only the Almiranta made it out. Leland found it sunk off the coast of North Carolina."

"Paper says the treasure is worth almost one hundred million dollars."

"Which is why the Spanish government wants it back. They're claiming that the Almiranta and everything on it are still the property of Spain."

Alex flipped back to the article and scanned it.

"What does that have to do with the Museum of American History?" he asked.

"Leland loaned most of the treasure to them," Iggy said. "It's been on display there for a month but they've had to take it down until the case is settled."

"Do you think Leland will have to return it?"

"No." Iggy shook his head. "Salvage laws are hundreds of years old. The Spanish are grasping at straws."

"So what do you think about this ghost killer?" Alex asked, hiding a grin behind the paper.

Iggy groaned.

"Not you too," he said in an indignant voice. "Does everyone read that disreputable rag?"

"Doris had a copy," Alex explained. "How did you see it?"

"I played pinochle with Doctor Anderson down at the coroner's office this afternoon," he said. "He always reads that trash. But, since you bring it up, tell me what you think of these deaths while you help me set the table."

Alex put the paper aside and went to the cupboard for plates and silverware.

"I'm going to go out on a limb and say the victims weren't killed by a ghost," Alex said, fighting not to grin.

"Please," Iggy said in a wounded tone as he set out the bread and butter. "Don't indulge childish fantasy at my dinner table."

"If the details in the story are correct, the victims were all found alone in locked rooms," Alex said. "The police had to break in each time."

"What does that tell you?"

"Locked rooms mean suicide," Alex said with a shrug.

"You don't sound sure."

"According to the story, the victims were all stabbed twice in the chest," Alex said, filling two glasses with water. "I can't imagine someone killing themselves that way, let alone three people. Most people just turn on the gas and stick their head in the oven."

"A graphic, but accurate description," Iggy said, setting a tureen of stew on the table. "What about the absence of a murder weapon? Wouldn't that indicate that someone else was there?"

Alex nodded as they both sat down. He waited until Iggy said grace before continuing.

"Well, you've always said that if you remove the impossible, then whatever remains, however improbable, must be the truth," Alex said. "If there's two stab wounds and no weapon, it has to be murder. Someone is managing to get into and out of those locked rooms."

"How?" Iggy asked, serving the stew. "Are there secret passages?"

"No," Alex said. "Two of the murders were in upscale homes, but one was in an outer ring tenement house. Besides, the police would have checked for that; they're not idiots."

"Then how is our murderer doing it?"

Alex thought about that while he ate. There were only so many ways a crime like this could have been committed, and without examining the rooms in question, it was hard to draw a conclusion.

"A runewright could do it with an escape rune," he said at last.

Iggy thought about that for a few moments, then shrugged.

"It's possible," he admitted. "But that seems like a long way to go for something as easy as murder. The killer would be shaving months off his own life every time he used a rune to escape the locked room. Not to mention the cost."

Alex nodded. Escape runes could cost over a hundred dollars when you factored in the exotic inks.

"That would make these murders the most expensive in history," he said. "In dollars and life."

They passed ideas back and forth for another half-hour while they ate, but nothing felt right. In the end, Alex suggested that the tabloid had probably got the details wrong and these were three unrelated suicides.

"That paper needs to go out of business," Iggy said at last. "I hope the mayor's wife takes them down."

"Who?" Alex asked as he began clearing the table.

"The mayor's wife is suing *The Midnight Sun*," Iggy explained, lighting a cigar as he watched Alex. According to their arrangement, Iggy did the cooking and Alex did the washing up.

"Why?"

"They've been out to get her for months," Iggy explained, puffing out a cloud of aromatic smoke. "You can't open that rag without reading something salacious about her."

Alex hadn't known that, but he didn't even know who the mayor actually was, to say nothing of his wife.

"Well," Iggy said, rising, "I believe I'm going to the library to read for a few hours. Come join me when you're done."

That actually sounded like a great idea. Alex hadn't had time for pleasure reading in weeks.

"Sorry, Iggy," he said as he scrubbed his plate. "I've got to make a phone call."

"Oh well," Iggy said, heading off toward the library. "Suit yourself."

It was eight o'clock when Alex finally got upstairs to his room. The room, like most of Alex's life, was plain and simple. A metal framed bed stuck out from the back wall, flanked on either side by an end table, one empty and the other bearing an alarm clock, a telephone, a shot glass, and a mostly-empty bottle of bourbon. A dresser and a desk stood against one wall, one on either side of a large window. The opposite wall had two doors, one to his clothes closet and the other to a tiny bathroom complete with a stand-up shower. A comfortable reading chair stood alone with a small table next to it with a plain, brass lamp on it.

He took off his coat and poured himself a shot of bourbon from the bottle on his bedside table. His telephone sat right next to the bottle, but he studiously avoided looking at it.

After ten minutes and another shot of the bourbon, he finally pulled his red rune book out of his jacket and sat on his bed. He turned to the back of the book, just inside the back cover, where a pouch had been sewn. Inside, Alex kept business cards and anything important he might need with him.

He pulled a crisp, white card with sky blue printing on it out of the pouch. There were only two words on the card, along with a phone number.

Sorsha Kincaid.

Alex had met Sorsha in her capacity as an FBI consultant. She was the most incredible woman Alex had ever met, beautiful, sensual, and most important, dangerous. Sorsha was one of the New York Six, the six sorcerers who made their home in the greatest city in the world.

It was Sorsha that Alex had helped recover the missing plague last year. He'd thought she disliked him, but when Alex traded most of his life force to keep her floating castle from crashing into the city, she'd been very upset. The last time he saw her, she declared that she never wanted to see him again.

At the time, he'd thought that was a fine arrangement, but lately, he'd found himself missing her. He felt a connection to her that he could neither justify nor explain.

He sighed and picked up the phone, giving the operator the number. A moment later a cold, contralto voice slithered down the wire and into his ear.

"Hello?"

"Sorceress," he said, in his most annoyingly cheery voice. "It's been a long time."

"Alex?" Her voice changed; it held none of the disdain he had expected. She seemed almost happy to hear from him. Alex suddenly became very aware of his own heartbeat.

"You do remember," he said, trying to keep his voice easy and relaxed.

"I remember telling you never to call me again," she said, her voice back to its usual imperious chill.

"Actually," Alex said, a smile spreading across his face. "You said you never wanted to see me again. This doesn't count."

He didn't know why he felt the need to antagonize a woman who had once threatened to freeze him solid, but it was an urge he simply couldn't resist.

"This counts, Mr. Lockerby," Sorsha said, her formal speech patterns reasserting themselves. "But since you've already interrupted me, why have you called?"

"I need a favor."

Sorsha didn't sigh, but Alex could feel her rolling her eyes through the phone.

"You are without question the most brash annoyance I've ever known," she said. "And that's saying something. What makes you think I have the time or the inclination to do you a favor?"

"It isn't for me," he said, then he explained about Bickman and his wife and their predicament.

"So, if I understand you," Sorsha said once Alex finished, "you need help finding these people employment so they can pay you?"

Maybe that's why he liked the sorceress so much — she saw through him so easily. That didn't really make sense, but Alex couldn't resist the thought.

He cleared his throat and forced himself to smile even though the sorceress couldn't actually see him.

"That's not exactly how I would put it," he said. "These people need help and you're the only person I know who travels in the circles that might need their services."

The line went silent for a long minute and Alex could almost feel the chill on the other end seeping through the phone.

"As it happens, I might be able to help," she said at last. "Tell Mr. Bickman to come by my office in the Chrysler building tomorrow afternoon. I'll see him then."

"Thanks, doll."

"Don't push your luck, Mr. Lockerby," Sorsha said, then the line went dead with a loud click.

Alex replaced the receiver on the phone and looked around his room as if he expected there to be an audience.

"That went well," he said to the empty air.

A knock at his door made him turn. Before he could respond, Iggy pushed it open.

"Are you finished?" he asked from the door.

"You heard?"

"Sorry, lad," Iggy said. "I didn't mean to eavesdrop. How is Ms. Kincaid?"

"Chilly," Alex said with a grin. "What can I do for you?"

"You have a visitor," he said. "From the police," he added at Alex's confused look.

"Wow," Alex said. "Danny must really have blown it."

"It's not Danny," Iggy said with a serious look. "It's the Lieutenant."

"Callahan?" Alex asked. Frank Callahan was Danny's boss on the police force and definitely wasn't Alex's biggest fan. "What does he want?"

"I suppose he wants your help," Iggy said. "Apparently the ghost has killed again."

3

THE TRAIL OF THE GHOST

Half an hour later, Lieutenant Frank Callahan's car pulled up in front of a tidy Inner-Ring house just outside the Core. Unlike the Atwood mansion, this house was a tasteful Victorian, complete with a veranda. The only thing off-putting about the house was the number of police cars clogging the street in front of it. The coroner's van was parked in the driveway, and half a dozen officers milled about outside. Alex could only imagine the mess they had already made of the crime scene.

"Okay," Alex said, taking in the scene. "We're here; are you going to tell me what this is about?"

He turned to Callahan and found the big man lighting a cigarette. He seemed cagey, like he didn't actually want to tell Alex why he'd dragged him across the city after dark. Callahan was the quintessential police detective, big, square-jawed, and good at his job. Like most cops, he also actively disliked private detectives, so the fact that he came to Alex at all meant something important was going on.

"This is the home of David and Anne Watson," Callahan said at last. "Earlier tonight, Anne called the police because her husband had locked himself in his study and wouldn't answer her when she went to get him for dinner. When the responding officers got here, Anne had crawled through the vent duct from an adjoining room and found David dead."

"Let me guess," Alex said. "Two stab wounds to the chest?"

Callahan looked surprised and then a mask of disgust covered his face. "Does everybody read that rag?" he muttered. "Don't tell me you believe it was a ghost?"

Alex laughed at that.

"Of course not, Lieutenant," he said. "Everyone knows that ghosts strangle their victims."

Callahan blinked as if he didn't know whether or not to believe Alex, then Alex smiled.

"Funny," he said without any trace of humor in his voice. "The guys who caught this case think it's a copycat," he went on. "They think the wife killed her husband and tried to pass it off as the ghost."

"Any servants?" Alex asked, his mind shifting into gear.

"Just a maid," Callahan said, "but she had the night off." He puffed on his cigarette.

"Can I have one of those?" Alex asked.

The lieutenant rolled his eyes and held out his pack so Alex could extract one.

"You need a real job, Lockerby," he said, flipping open his lighter. "I know you could pass the detective exam in your sleep; why don't you come work for me?"

Alex lit his cigarette and sat back. He was about to say something sarcastic, but he stopped himself. Callahan hated private dicks and he didn't much care for Alex personally, but the fact that he'd offered Alex a job was a sign of his respect for Alex's skills.

It was flattering, and Alex resisted the urge to make a smart remark. He owed Callahan that.

"You wouldn't want me working for you, Callahan," he said at last. "I break too many rules. Besides, the official policy of the department is that magic doesn't have any practical application in law enforcement."

"We both know that's crap," Callahan said.

Alex nodded at that and took another drag on his cigarette. He'd been economizing so long that two in one day felt like luxury.

"So the wife was alone in the house," Alex said, getting back to the murder. "Why do you think she killed her husband?"

"Not me," Callahan said with a sour look. "It's not my case. Third division caught it."

Alex had never been too clear about how the police department allocated their resources. He knew that all the detectives for Manhattan worked out of the Central Office of Police near the park, but there were six different divisions. Callahan was the lieutenant over division five.

"It's not your case," Alex said, a light finally going off in his head. "That's why we're sitting here in your car instead of going inside."

Callahan grimaced and nodded.

"But you think the wife is innocent and that's why I'm here," Ales went on. "So is she an old girlfriend or something?"

The lieutenant's gaze narrowed.

"Current girlfriend?" Alex pressed with a raised eyebrow.

"You're right," Callahan said. "I wouldn't like you working for me. I don't know Mrs. Watson at all."

"Then why do you care?"

"Listen, Lockerby," Callahan said, jabbing his finger at Alex and sending ash flying from his cigarette. "Someone is killing people. This makes four and we've got nothing to go on. Nothing. That's why you're here. Maybe you can find something we missed. Maybe whoever is doing this is using magic to kill these people. Either way, that's why we need you."

Alex nodded, feeling a bit embarrassed. He tended to have the same opinion of cops that they had of him and he regularly forgot that some of them were just as driven and dedicated as he was.

"So the wife is my in," Alex said. "Has she been arrested yet?"

"I don't think so," Callahan said, tossing the stub of his cigarette out the window. "They were still questioning her when I left to get you."

As if on cue, someone stepped up to Alex's side of the car.

"One of my boys said they saw you parked out here, Callahan," the newcomer said. He was short and stocky with thinning hair and a crooked nose. "What are you doing back?"

"You still think the wife did this?" Callahan said, without answering the question.

"You bet," the man said. "She obviously read that article in the Sun and used it as cover to kill her husband."

"Why do you say that?" Alex asked.

The man turned his gaze to Alex. He had a round face and a crooked smile to match his nose. He wasn't large, but he had an imposing sort of air about him.

"I don't believe we've met," he said.

"Lieutenant Detweiler," Callahan said. "This is Alex Lockerby. Alex, Lieutenant James Detweiler, Third Division."

"I've seen you around the Central Office," Detweiler said. "You're a friend of Callahan's boy, Danny."

Alex nodded.

"You've got a good eye, Lieutenant. So, what makes you think the wife did it?"

Detweiler clearly wasn't used to being put on the spot. He held Alex's gaze for a long moment as if considering whether or not he could safely reveal his thought processes.

"Simple," he said. "There's a copy of today's Midnight Sun in the kitchen trash," he ticked that off on his finger. "Second, the wife is almost fifteen years younger than her husband."

"So?" Alex asked.

"She obviously married him for his money."

"But why kill him?"

"He was only sixty," Detweiler said. "He might have lived another twenty years. She obviously got tired of waiting."

"Does she have a man on the side?" Alex asked.

"Who cares?" Detweiler said.

"Well, Lieutenant," Alex said with a smile. "If there's no boyfriend then why bump off the husband? Was he blowing through their money? Did he have a girlfriend? Did he threaten to cut her out of the will?"

Detweiler glared at Alex.

"Let me clarify," he said. "When I said, who cares, what I meant was, why do you care?"

28

Alex pulled one of his business cards out of his shirt pocket hand handed it over. Detweiler's face soured when he read it.

"Mrs. Watson asked the Lieutenant here to find her someone to investigate her husband's death," Alex said with the biggest smile he could manage. "If you don't mind, I'd like to see my client now."

Detweiler threw the card back in Alex's lap and stormed away. Callahan chuckled as he and Alex both got out of the car.

"You're right, Lockerby," he said. "Right now I'm really glad you don't work for me."

ANNE WATSON SAT at her kitchen table rubbing her hands together absently. She was in her mid-thirties but looked even younger with high cheekbones, a perky nose, and full lips. Chestnut brown hair flowed down over her shoulders and framed her face perfectly. Alex thought she would have looked quite pretty had her makeup not run down her face from crying — and if her shirt weren't stained with blood.

In addition to the blood, her clothes were grimy and dirty. Alex remembered Callahan saying she'd crawled through a vent to get into the locked room where her husband's body had been found.

"Mrs. Watson?" Alex said, sitting down at the table opposite her. "My name is Alex Lockerby."

"I've answered your questions," she said, her voice ragged and weary. "I want to call my lawyer now."

"I'm not a policeman," Alex said, handing her his card. "You asked a Lieutenant Callahan to find someone to help you find out who killed your husband. He sent me."

Her hands started trembling as Alex spoke. She was holding in so much and Alex represented a lifeline. Tears filled her eyes and ran down her face.

"Can you really help me, Mr. Lockerby?" she asked, struggling to stay in control.

Alex put on his most reassuring smile and nodded.

"Call me Alex, and I do this kind of thing all the time," he said. "But I'm going to need something from you first."

"Of course," she said, wiping her eyes. "I'll get my handbag."

"No," Alex said with a genuine smile this time. "Let me look around first, and make sure I can help."

She looked confused then sat back down. "What do you need from me then?"

"Permission," Alex said. "The police are pretty much done, but they won't let me look around unless you insist."

She met his eyes, searching them for signs of deception. Alex recognized the look: she wanted to believe him, to believe in him, but so much had happened in the last few hours she simply didn't know what to believe.

"Let me look around, Mrs. Watson," Alex began.

"Anne," she said.

"Let me look around, Anne," he amended. "If I can't help you, I'll tell you and you'll owe me nothing. If I think I can help, I'll tell you what the next step is, and we can go from there."

She closed her eyes and after a minute, she nodded. Alex pulled out his notebook and pen and passed them across the table.

"Write a note that says I can look around as much as I want," he said.

She flipped to a blank page and began writing.

"What do I do if they arrest me?" she asked, clearly getting to the topic she'd been avoiding.

"Don't worry about that," Alex said. "Do you have a lawyer?"

She passed the book and pen back.

"I've never needed one," she said, "but James did."

"Call him," Alex said. "Tell him to get over here right away. He'll make sure you're okay if the cops decide to arrest you."

At the word 'arrest' Anne's hands started shaking again, but she nodded.

"It's going to be all right," Alex said, putting his hand on hers. "I'll go look around; you sit tight."

DAVID WATSON'S body had already been taken away by the time the police let Alex into the room where he'd been killed. It was a study that would have made Iggy proud. Shelves lined one wall, filled with books of every description. A glass cabinet on the opposite wall held curios and knick-knacks of all kinds. A polished oak desk stood in front of a large window, loaded down with papers and files, and a green carpet covered the wood floor. In the center of the carpet an oddly shaped red stain showed where the dead man's body had laid.

A brass vent cover about a foot high and two feet wide lay on the carpet as well. Callahan said that Anne claimed to have gotten into the room by crawling through a vent. A smear of dirt on the wood floor under the glass case revealed the opening. Alex knelt down and looked through the small duct. It ran to the next room, under the glass case, and was about three feet long.

Alex set down his kit, a leather doctor's valise, and opened it. Inside were his tools for investigation and the various special papers and pens he might need to make runes. Reaching in, he withdrew an egg-shaped, brass lantern with glass lenses on each of its four sides. Three of the lenses were covered with a leather cap, blocking them off.

Alex set down the lantern and withdrew a round oil reservoir with a cotton wick sticking out of the top from his kit. This one had the word *Ghostlight* stamped into a metal plate on its curved side. Inside was a special mixture of alchemical oils and some ingredients Alex had made magical with runes. He opened the lantern, revealing runes etched into the metal on each side. The burner clipped into a round slot in the bottom of the lamp and Alex fixed it in place.

Reaching into his kit again, Alex took out what looked like an over-sized leather eye patch with a short telescope mounted into it. The telescope had several dials, like the focus adjustments on a camera lens, and four colored lenses could be moved into the field of view. Once in place over his eye, the oculus would allow him to see things revealed in the lantern's light. With the ghostlight burner in place, the lantern would reveal magical residue. If anything magical happened in David Watson's study, the ghostlight would show it.

Alex took a paper matchbook from his pocket to light the lamp.

"What did she say?" Callahan's voice interrupted him.

Alex turned to find the lieutenant leaning against the door frame.

"She's scared," Alex said, closing up his kit bag.

"I know that," Callahan said. "What did she say about her husband?"

"I didn't ask," Alex replied. Iggy taught him never to question a suspect until he'd first looked at the scene.

People lie, he'd say. *Evidence never does.*

"You didn't ask her if she killed him?"

Alex chuckled at that. As if Anne would have admitted it if she had murdered her husband.

"I didn't need to ask her," Alex said. "She didn't do it."

Callahan laughed at that.

"How do you figure?" he asked. "The husband didn't have any defensive wounds on his body, just the two stab wounds, one on either side of his chest."

"You're saying he knew his attacker," Alex said. "But that doesn't mean it was the wife."

"It damn well makes her a suspect,' he said. "What makes you think she's innocent?"

"Did you see the blood on her clothes?"

Callahan nodded.

"Yes, what about it?"

"According to her story she crawled in through there and found her husband already dead," Alex said, pointing to the open vent.

"She could have killed him first," Callahan pointed out, "Then gone around and crawled in to make her story look believable."

"You're right," Alex admitted. "She could have done that, but if she did, the blood on her clothes would be under the dirt from the vent. It wasn't."

"How do you know that?"

"Some of the grime scraped off her shirt when she was sitting at the table," Alex said. "The shirt beneath didn't have bloodstains."

Callahan looked as if he wanted to protest, but stopped and nodded.

"If she'd killed him first, she'd have gotten blood somewhere," he sighed. "Stabbing someone is messy."

"You seem disappointed," Alex said. "I was under the impression you didn't think she did it."

"I asked her and she said she didn't kill him," Callahan said. "I believed her but it's always nice to have it confirmed."

"You probably ought to tell Detweiler," Alex said. "I've got work to do here."

"Right," the lieutenant said, turning to go. "It's not like he'll believe me, but I'll tell him anyway."

Alex waited until Callahan's footsteps faded away, then took a matchbook from his pocket and lit his lamp. A greenish light began to emanate from the uncovered lens, glowing brighter as the wick began to siphon oil from the little reservoir.

Strapping the oculus over his right eye, Alex closed his left and began shining the lantern around the room. Several of the objects in the glass case had magical residue, signs that at one time they had been enchanted. None of them glowed brightly though, so whether they had been made magical by a sorcerer or with a spent rune, none of the magic was recent.

Behind the desk was a small liquor cabinet. Several of the bottles glowed, but they were brands which Alex knew contained alchemical ingredients. Other than that, there wasn't any magic in the room.

Satisfied that Mr. Watson hadn't been killed by magic, Alex blew out the ghostlight burner and returned it to his kit, replacing it with one labeled *Silverlight*.

This time when he lit the lamp, a purplish-white light shone out from it. Alex took the caps off the other lenses in the lantern and placed it on the desk. The light shone all around the room and everywhere it touched, things began to glow. Fingerprints stood out on the shelves and the glass of the cases. Ink stains covered the top of the desk where it had been spilled or splashed over the years. A stain on the carpet revealed where a drink must have been spilled and the dark stain of Mr. Watson's blood was clearly visible.

Alex spent the next hour examining every glowing site in the room, but came away with nothing. Every fingerprint and stain seemed to have a reason for being where it was.

Defeated, he put out the light and returned his lantern and oculus to his kit. He was sure that Watson hadn't killed himself but if anyone else had been in the room with him, Alex couldn't find any evidence of it.

"Done?" Callahan's voice cut through the static in Alex's mind. He was sitting in a chair in the hall and Alex found it disturbing that he had no idea how long the big Lieutenant had been there.

Alex nodded.

"Find anything?"

"Just that Mr. Watson made his money in land," Alex said, pointing to one of the glass cases with a display of surveying equipment, land maps, and pictures of enormous, beautiful homes.

"So, nothing?" Callahan said, coming into the room.

"Not nothing," Alex insisted, packing up his kit. "You said it yourself, he had no defensive wounds, so Watson clearly knew his attacker."

"Or someone surprised him," Callahan countered.

"And the wife didn't hear anything?" Alex said. "She was in the house the whole time."

Callahan thought about that for a moment, but didn't seem willing to concede the point.

"Speaking of Anne," Alex said. "I should probably let her know what I've found."

"Her lawyer got here about an hour ago," Callahan said. "He had her go to a hotel for the night."

"So Detweiler didn't have her arrested?"

"No," Detweiler's voice came from beyond the door. A moment later he sidled around and into the room. "Her lawyer is a real son-of-a-bitch. Said if I arrested her on such thin evidence, she'd sue for police harassment."

"He's right," Alex said. "Didn't you check out the blood on her clothes?"

"Yeah," Detweiler sneered. "Callahan told me about your little theory. What if she stabbed her husband, then crawled through the vent, then held her husband's body as a show for the officers?"

Alex shrugged, admitting that Detweiler's theory was possible.

"Did you take her blouse as evidence?" he asked.

"Of course we did," Detweiler said, irritation in his voice. "You seem to think we're idiots."

"Did you turn the shirt inside out and check it?" Alex asked.

Detweiler's irritation shifted to confusion.

"Why?"

"Because," Callahan interjected. "If she got any blood on the blouse before it got dirty, it would have soaked through to the inside."

Detweiler thought about that and shrugged.

"We'll look into it," he said. "Since you don't like the wife for this, Lockerby, why don't you tell me who you think did kill Mr. Watson."

Alex glanced at Callahan but the Lieutenant just shrugged.

"I think a ghost killed David Watson," Alex said with a grin.

Detweiler's face screwed up in anger but before he could explode, Alex hurried on.

"One from his past."

Callahan hid a smile behind his hand and Detweiler growled.

"Consider the way he was killed," Alex explained. "Stabbing is an up close and personal way to kill. Intimate even. Whoever did this wanted Watson to know who it was that killed him, to look into his eyes."

"That could be anybody," Detweiler said.

"Not really," Alex said. "How many people have genuine enemies? Ones who want them dead badly enough to do something about it? Mr. Watson is the fourth victim of this killer; whoever is doing it is trying to make a point."

"What point?" Detweiler asked.

"No idea," Alex admitted. "But I suspect if you dig into James Watson's life, and the lives of the ghost's other victims, you'll find a connection. That will give you your killer."

"Gee," Detweiler said, his voice dripping with sarcasm. "We detectives never would have thought of that. Thanks, Lockerby."

"You're welcome, Lieutenant," Alex said as sincerely as he could. "Glad I could help. Let me know if you need anything else."

"You wait by your phone, Lockerby," Detweiler said with a sneer. "We'll be sure to call you."

He turned and left the room. Alex looked at Callahan and the big lieutenant was shaking his head and chuckling to himself.

"What?" Alex asked.

"Nothing," he said innocently. "I'm just really glad you don't work for me."

4

THE MISSING MAN

Alex arrived late to his office the next morning. Callahan had given him a ride home the previous night, since he didn't have the money for a cab, but he still didn't get to bed until well after midnight. Then, in the morning, Iggy had wanted the full report about Alex's findings in the matter of the ghost killer. He agreed with Alex's conclusions but had nothing substantive to add.

"You're late," Leslie said as he walked in. She stood in front of her desk, smoking Alex's last cigarette. He was about to chastise her but something was off. Leslie was usually dressed immaculately. Her beauty queen days had given her a keen eye for fashion. Today, however, she wore a light blue blouse with a green, knee-length skirt. Alex was no expert, but they didn't seem to go together.

"What's the matter?" he asked. His danger sense was telling him to tread lightly.

"Oh, this?" Leslie said, indicating her ensemble. "These are the last clean clothes I own," she said, her voice hard. "It's been three weeks since I've been paid, and I can't afford to get my laundry done." She regarded him with a hard stare. "The Bickman job was supposed to solve all that. I don't suppose there's any chance they'll be paying you soon."

37

Alex put on a smile and moved over to where Leslie was fuming. He had the distinct feeling that he was stepping inside a tiger's cage.

"Mrs. Bickman is off the hook," he said. "But they're still fired."

Leslie's eyes went hard and he could hear her grinding her teeth.

"But there is some good news," he went on quickly. "I may have got them a new job."

"Can you get one for me?" Leslie asked, no trace of humor in her voice. Alex knew she wasn't serious, but he hated the fact that she was suffering for his problems.

"Take it easy," he said, putting his arm around her shoulders. "Call Bickman and tell him to go over to Sorsha Kincaid's office after noon. She says she knows someone who's looking for help."

"Wow," Leslie said, a sardonic smile creeping onto her face. "Things must be bad if you called the Sorceress for help."

"Funny," Alex said. "I was just looking out for you and your laundry," he continued. "I can't have you looking anything but your best; after all, you represent me."

She elbowed him in the ribs, hard, and he winced.

"How much does your laundry cost?" he asked.

"Three-fifty," she replied.

"I've got a few bucks at home. Call Bickman and I'll go home at lunch time and bring back enough for your laundry and two packs of smokes for you."

Leslie glared at him.

"Better bring me a fiver," she said. "I'd like to eat this week, too."

Alex nodded.

"A fiver, two packs of smokes, and an invitation to dinner at the brownstone this week."

Her glare finally cracked, and the ghost of a smile crossed her face.

"Now was that so hard?" she asked, slinking around her desk.

"After you call Bickman, call around to the Inner-Ring hotels west of the core."

Leslie picked up her notepad and pencil.

"Who am I looking for?"

"Anne Watson," Alex said. "Her husband was murdered last night."

"And she wants you to find out who did it?" Leslie asked, her ghost of a smile widening into a warm grin.

"Yes, but I don't think there's much I can do." Alex explained about Lieutenant Callahan's visit and his investigation. "I'm not going to take her money for a job the cops are going to do anyway," he finished.

"But she does owe you for the work you did last night," Leslie pointed out. "Those oils you burn in your lantern aren't cheap, you know."

"I was there about two hours," Alex said. "Charge her my usual rate and let her know I'll come by to see her this afternoon and answer any questions I can."

"Will do, boss," Leslie said, sitting down. With the prospect of some money coming in the door, she was much more chipper.

Alex ducked toward his office. He knew he was behind in paying Leslie but he should have known that she hadn't been paid in three weeks. It was Leslie who handled the money, and the fact that she hadn't paid herself meant that their situation must be particularly bad. He flirted with the idea of staying on the Watson case for a few days, just to pad out the bill, but he wasn't desperate enough, or enough of a heel, to skim money from a grieving widow.

Not yet, anyway.

ONCE IN HIS OFFICE, Alex pulled out the morning paper that he'd stolen from Iggy earlier. One reason the doctor insisted he read the paper every day was that, if a detective were desperate, he could always try to drum up work from the paper. In the classifieds, there was always someone seeking something, or someone, they'd lost, and the police blotter held news of people who'd been robbed. Such folk were excellent prospects for a detective with a good finding rune, and nobody had a better finding rune than Alex.

He read the classifieds, but nothing jumped out at him. One woman was seeking a man she'd met in the Great War, but she had no idea where he might be living. Alex's rune was good, but he could usually only find things that were still in the city. The lady's lost love could be anywhere.

Lost dogs were his go-to backup, but for some reason all of New York's dogs decided to stay home this week. He shrugged and put that section aside. Leslie would have combed through it already anyway, looking for the obvious jobs.

He had just turned his attention to the police blotter when there was a knock at the door and Leslie let herself in.

"You find Mrs. Watson?" Alex asked.

"Not yet," Leslie said in a quiet voice. That usually meant there was a client in the outer office. "There's a Mrs. Hannah Cunningham outside who says her husband is missing."

"What does she look like?" Alex asked. It wasn't a pleasant fact, but husbands with plain wives had an annoying tendency to look for greener pastures. Alex hated those cases because they always ended badly. Still, he was in no position to be picky.

"Young," Leslie said. "And she's a looker. Seems pretty upset."

Alex pulled out his red rune book and checked to make sure he had a finding rune prepared. He had two.

"Send her in," he said.

Mrs. Hannah Cunningham looked like she was still in her teens, but something about the way she carried herself made Alex peg her age at twenty-one or twenty-two. Leslie had been right; she was quite pretty, with delicate features, deep blue eyes, and hair a shade or two darker than strawberry blonde. Alex decided it was more the color of ripe wheat. Hannah wore sensible, working class clothes, a cream-colored blouse and a black skirt with navy flats. It was clear she wasn't wealthy, but she had a beauty that made her appearance rich. The only detraction to her look were the tracks of tears that traced down her cheeks.

Alex rose as she came in and offered her the comfy chair in front of his desk.

"How can I help you, Mrs. Cunningham?" he asked once he'd taken his own seat.

"Didn't your secretary tell you?" she asked. Her voice was pulled tight with worry.

"She did," Alex admitted. "But I find it's always good to hear a client's problems from her own mouth. Saves misunderstandings."

"Oh," she said, more quietly. She wrung her hands together, nearly tearing the handkerchief she clutched in half. "I don't know what to do, Mr. Lockerby," she began. "My husband Leroy has been missing for three days."

"Have you been to the police?"

She nodded.

"They say there's nothing they can do beyond telling their officers to keep a lookout for him." She leaned forward in the chair and clutched the edge of Alex's desk. "I know something's happened to him," she said. "He would never just leave and not tell me where he was going."

Her face had a desperate, anxious look, as if the next words out of Alex's mouth had the power to save her or destroy her. He reached into his desk and pulled out a pair of shot glasses followed by his nearly empty bottle of bourbon.

"Here," he said, pouring two-fingers' worth into a glass and passing it to her. "This will calm your nerves."

She took the glass and downed it in one gulp. Alex refilled it, then poured one for himself.

"What does Leroy do for work?" he asked.

"He's a draftsman for Milton and White," she said. "They're an architectural firm on the west side. He also goes to school at night to become an architect himself."

"Have you called his office and the school?"

She nodded.

"I called every day, but neither one of them have seen him."

"How long have you and Leroy been married?" Alex asked.

"Three years," Hannah said. "We met right after he moved to the city to go to school."

"Where did he move from?"

"Coaldale," she said. "It's in West Virginia. Leroy grew up there."

"Do you know if your husband had any enemies?" Alex asked, scribbling the details in his notebook. "Anyone who might have wanted to hurt him?"

"No," she gasped. "Everybody loved Leroy."

"Does he gamble, or have debts?"

She shook her head.

"You're not rich, are you?" Alex asked.

She shook her hand again, tears blooming afresh in her eyes.

"I'm sorry," she said, setting the glass back on Alex's desk. "I guess I made a mistake. I though you could just find Leroy with magic."

"I can, Mrs. Cunningham," he said, offering to fill her glass again before he realized the bottle was empty. "But the magic works better the more I know about the person I'm looking for, and why he might have disappeared."

"Oh," she said. "I'm afraid I'm not being much help."

"You've been a big help," Alex lied to her. "Do you happen to have anything that belonged to your husband, or something he was attached to?"

Hannah started to shake her head, but stopped. She pulled a small silver ring off her finger and passed it over.

"This belonged to Leroy's mother," she said. "He gave it to me when we got married. It's kind of a family heirloom."

The ring was a simple band of silver, dented and scraped from years of wear, but it was clean and lovingly cared for.

"This will do," Alex said. "I charge fifteen dollars to cast a finding rune."

Hannah nodded and took a wad of faded and rumpled bills from her bag. Alex guessed she had raided the coffee tin or wherever they kept their emergency money. She counted out a five and ten ones, most of her stack, then returned what little remained to her handbag.

Alex pocketed the money, then removed the glasses and the empty bourbon bottle from his desk, stowing them back in the drawer where he'd gotten them. He then rose and moved to the filing cabinet in the corner. Opening the top drawer, Alex took out a rolled map of New York and a cigar box.

"What are you doing?" Hannah asked.

Alex put the map down on the desk.

"This is how I'm going to find Leroy," he said.

Unrolling the map, Alex placed the cigar box on it to keep it from rolling back up. Opening the box, Alex took four small figurines from inside; a wolf, a jaguar, a rhino, and a horse. Each figure was about the same size, rendered in dark green Alaskan jade, with a rectangular base.

"What are those for?" Hannah asked, her fear for her husband momentarily forgotten.

Alex picked up the wolf and smiled an enigmatic smile. He rolled the map out to its full size and placed the figurine on the corner.

"Weight," he said.

Hannah couldn't help herself and snickered while Alex placed the other four figures on the other corners of the map.

With the map fully open, Alex took a battered, brass compass out of the cigar box, then set the box aside. The box also contained chalk, candles, and special powders that he could use to draw a stabilizing symbol around the map that would make the Finding rune work better. Here in his office, however, he didn't need them. Alex had a permanent stabilizing rune cut into the wood floor under the room's faded red rug.

He took out his rune book and tore out one of his two remaining finding runes. The rune had an octagon as its base, with diamond shapes at each corner, and a symbol in the center that looked a bit like a dragon reclining on a chaise lounge. Carefully, Alex folded the paper into quarters and then placed it atop the brass compass. He put the compass in the center of the map with the silver wedding ring on top of the rune paper.

"We're ready," Alex said, shifting his gaze to Hannah. "I'm going to activate the rune and the compass will be linked to your husband."

"What does that mean?"

"It means I can use the compass to find him," Alex said. He removed the metal match in the touch-tip lighter on his desk and pressed it down on the sparker. The match caught and flared to life.

"Now, I need you to think about your husband," Alex said, bringing the burning match close to the rune paper. He closed his eyes for a second and mentally reviewed everything she had told him about Leroy Cunningham, architecture student from Coaldale, West Virginia. Opening his eyes, he lit the flash paper and it vanished in a puff of smoke and fire. A sound like a miniature gunshot erupted from the space where the paper had been, and the silver ring was sent rolling across the map. Alex had been expecting this, and he intercepted the ring before it could roll off the table, dropping it into his pocket.

In the space above the compass, an orange copy of the finding rune appeared, spinning in the air over the compass. As Alex and Hannah watched, the needle on the compass began to spin in parity with the rune. As the needle came up to speed, the rune began to slow down until their speeds matched, then rune and needle slowed to a stop.

"That way," Alex said, following the direction indicated by the north end of the compass needle. The indicated direction moved away from the compass toward the east side of Manhattan.

"So, Leroy is somewhere along that line?" Hannah gasped.

Alex slid the compass along the map in the direction of the needle. He didn't lift it up; that would break its connection to the map. Eventually, the needle began to spin in lazy circles. Alex pulled the compass back to see what was directly beneath it. The spot was near the east side docks. At this scale, it was hard to tell exactly but it looked like a small, private marina.

Alex knew the place. Rich folks kept their boats there. It didn't seem like the kind of place to keep a kidnap victim, but he'd ask them about it when he found Leroy.

"Is he there?" Hannah Cunningham asked, fresh tears blossoming in her eyes.

"Yes," Alex said.

Hannah leapt to her feet.

"Then let's go," she said. "Hurry."

"Easy," Alex said, motioning her back into her chair. "Would Leroy leave and not tell you where he was going?"

"N-no," she stammered, not understanding Alex's hesitation. "But, we need to—"

"You need to go home," Alex said in a firm voice. "If Leroy didn't go there on his own, someone took him. Whoever did that is likely to be dangerous. I'm going to go over there right now and check it out. If I can get Leroy out safely, I'll do it."

"What if you can't?" Hannah asked, fear rising in her voice.

"If I can't," Alex said, coming around the desk to put a comforting hand on her shoulder, "then I'll call the police and they'll go in and get him. Either way, I'm not going to put you in harm's way."

He didn't say that having an emotionally involved spouse on the site of a rescue was likely to get him and Leroy killed. He hoped he didn't have to explain that.

"What if he's not there?" she asked.

Alex picked up the compass and its connection to the map vanished with a small pop. The needle swung around and pointed off to the east.

"The needle is linked to your husband," Alex said. "If he moves, I can follow. Now go home and wait. I'll call you as soon as I know anything. Okay?"

Hannah hesitated for a long moment, then she nodded.

"Thank you, Mr. Lockerby," she said, rising. "Please bring my Leroy back."

Alex promised that he would, and Hannah left.

"She seemed happier," Leslie said, entering the office once Hannah was gone. "I take it you found her husband."

Alex grinned at her.

"Best finding rune in the city, remember?"

"Did she pay you?" Leslie said, trepidation in her voice. This was clearly the reason she'd come in and Alex didn't blame her a bit.

He pulled the bills from his pocket and handed the singles over, then presented the fiver to Leslie.

"As promised," he said.

She started to turn away, but he stopped her and picked up two of the ones.

"Cab fare," he explained.

"Take a crawler," Leslie said, reaching for the money, but Alex put it in his pocket.

"I think I might need to hurry this time," he said, rolling up the map.

"Why?" Leslie asked. "You know where the husband is, right?"

Alex nodded as he returned the figurines to the cigar box, and put it and the map back into the filing cabinet.

"Something just doesn't add up about this," he said. "The husband has no money, nothing they could use to ransom him."

"You're worried the kidnappers will figure that out and kill him," Leslie finished. "What are you going to do when you find him?"

Alex opened the second drawer down in the filing cabinet and withdrew his Colt 1911 in its holster, slipping it over his shoulder.

"I'll convince whoever took him that Leroy Cunningham isn't worth keeping," he said.

5

THE LEAK

A little over half an hour later, Alex got out of a cab in front of a quiet little boatyard on the eastern edge of Manhattan. A wooden sign hung, suspended over the entrance with the words, *Sunrise Marina*, painted on it in gold letters. Beyond the entrance, a short paved road ran down to a small wooden building beside a concrete boat ramp.

A long wooden dock stretched out over the water from the far side of the building. From there, other docks branched off the main one to either side. Boats of every description, from tall sailboats, to boxy cabin cruisers, and even the occasional sleek speed boat bobbed in neatly arranged slips. At this time of the year many of the slips were empty, their owners having taken their boats out on the water.

Alex consulted the brass compass and found the needle still pointing vaguely east. It had changed as the cab moved through the city, so he was sure it was still linked to Leroy Cunningham.

The marina was the only thing to his east, but Alex decided to be cautious. Stepping into the cover of an alley between a naval supply shop and what smelled like a fish market, he pulled out his 1911 and checked the magazine. This one had a small cross drawn on the bottom in red ink and he swapped it for the spare kept in his holster.

The Spellbreaker runes on the bullets in the first magazine were hard to make, especially with his trembling hands.

Spellbreaker runes were just what they sounded like, magic designed to destroy other magic, like shield spells. He didn't figure he'd need them against a normal group of kidnappers. Still, even ordinary thugs could be dangerous, so Alex cocked the pistol, clambering a round, and stuck it back into his holster with the safety on.

Satisfied he was suitably prepared, Alex crossed the street and began walking along the marina's fence. As he moved, the compass needle turned, indicating a spot out toward the edge of the marina.

Alex pocketed the compass and walked down the paved road to the wooden building. It was a small office with a room above for the care-taker, a white-haired man with a bushy beard, an island shirt, and deck shoes. He sat, reading a paper and smoking a pipe in a comfortable-looking chair with a view of the bobbing boats through a massive bay window.

"You in charge?" Alex asked as he entered.

The old man glanced up over the top of his paper and ran an appraising eye over Alex, then returned to his reading.

"S'right," he said, slurring his words lazily. "Wha'cho want?"

"Name's Lockerby," Alex said, stepping up beside the man. "I'm a P.I. A rich lady hired me to find her deadbeat husband; apparently he's hiding out somewhere on his boat."

"I ain't no snich," the man said. "Run along, sonny."

Normally, this was when Alex would have to drop a fiver to loosen the man's tongue. Unfortunately he only had two bucks on him, so he was going to have to do this the hard way.

Alex pulled the paper out of the man's hands with a quick move-ment. The caretaker tried to stand, but Alex pushed him back into his chair with enough force to make his point.

"Listen, friend," he said. "The guy took their kid. It's part of some messy divorce that you don't want any part of, so either you answer my questions, or I call the cops and tell them the kid might be here."

The man's angry look faded to one of irritation. The kind of people who parked their boats in private marinas tended to like their privacy. Ever since the last mayor dumped all the slot machines into the east river, a lot of Manhattan's wealthy had moved their poker games to places like this to avoid the law. Alex was betting the caretaker didn't want the cops crawling around looking for a missing kid.

"Fine," he said after a long moment. "What's this feller's name?"

Alex shrugged.

"He wouldn't be hiding under his own name," he said. "Is there anyone here living on their boat?"

"Sure," he said. "Lots of folks do that. Prob'ly five or six here right now."

"Anyone acting cagey, you know, nervous? Staying out of sight, only coming and going at night, that sort of thing?"

The old man shook his head.

"Nothin' like that," he said. "But folks round here like to keep to themselves."

Alex resisted the urge to swear and thanked the old man instead.

"Mind if I have a look around anyway?" he asked, heading for the door.

"Help yourself," the caretaker said, picking his paper up off the floor and going back to it.

Alex made his way slowly down the dock. The sun shone brightly on the water and he had to squint to see clearly. He pulled the compass from the pocket of his jacket and consulted it.

This time he did swear.

The needle of the compass was pointing north.

There were plenty of boats on the north side of the marina, but the needle was pointing right down between a row of berths, right at the open water. He took a few steps back, but the needle didn't even waver. The magical link was gone.

It wasn't pointing at Leroy Cunningham anymore.

Alex took a deep breath and reined in his anger. Lots of things could cause magic to fail. Sometimes spells simply ran out of energy and expired, or the subject could have moved too far out of range. In the case of water, if Leroy had been on a boat out in the ocean, the presence of that much water could block the spell, even if he were relatively close by.

Looking around and finding himself alone, Alex knelt down on the

49

dock and pulled the last finding rune from his rune book. He folded it quickly and put it atop the compass, adding Hannah's silver wedding band from his pocket. The paper matchbook in his pocket only had three matches left and he lit one and touched it to the rune.

This time the silver ring went rolling right for the edge of the dock and Alex had to throw himself at it to keep it from being lost. When he turned back to the rune, he found it spinning aimlessly over the compass. The needle in the compass wasn't moving at all.

He sat there, staring at it in stunned silence. The rune had failed to lock on to Leroy, yet Alex was certain the previous spell had traced him right to the marina.

Standing, he scanned the horizon out to sea. If Leroy had been on a boat that was already underway when Alex got here, it was possible he was now too far out for the spell to find him. As he looked, however, there were no boats to be seen. He didn't think it was likely that he would have missed a boat leaving the marina when he arrived.

He resolved to go boat by boat and search, but realized the caretaker would call the cops on him if he hadn't already. Plus, if Leroy was here somewhere, searching could end up getting him killed. Alex knew he couldn't go to the police; they'd never take the word of his seemingly unrepeatable spell as cause to search a marina full of rich people's boats. He was going to have to figure out another way to find Hannah's husband.

"Hold on, Leroy," he whispered to himself. "I'm still coming."

ALEX DECIDED to save his money and took a crawler back to his office. The trip took him almost an hour and by the time he arrived, he had no better idea what had happened then he had standing on the dock at the *Sunrise Marina*. He'd never had a finding rune fail once it had made a connection with its target, and that bothered him.

"Did you find the husband?" Leslie asked when he walked into his office.

Alex shook his head in disgust and explained.

"Well, the wife called twice while you were out," she said. "What are you going to tell her?"

Alex hadn't thought about Hannah. He owed her an explanation and he wished he had one.

"I'll call her," he said. "But first I'm going to try another finding rune, just to be sure. Hold my calls," he said, heading for his office.

AN HOUR LATER, Alex sat at the drafting table in his vault. A half dozen discarded sheets of flash paper littered the ground around him and he tore the one he'd been working on from the clip that kept in in place and threw it after the rest.

"Damn it!" he should, throwing the pen he'd been using after the rune.

Finding runes weren't that hard. He'd written over a hundred of them in his career. Now he'd just wasted an enormous amount of expensive, ruby-infused ink to make seven pieces of avant garde art on rectangles of flash paper.

The trembling in his hands was getting worse.

He'd thought that last one was good, but as he finished it, he couldn't feel any magic flowing into it. That was how runes worked. When a runewright drew one, he served as a channel for the magic of the universe, infusing it through the pen and into the ink and the symbol it formed. Alex didn't know what was wrong, but he could tell that last rune had no magic at all.

He forced himself not to think about it. If he thought about it, it would scare him to death.

"Is something wrong?" Leslie's concerned voice came from behind him.

He turned to find her standing at the open door of his vault.

"I don't know," he said. He hadn't told anyone about his hands, but the weight of the knowledge overwhelmed him and he explained it to her.

"I think..." he said, his mind going down the dark alley he desperately wanted to avoid. "I think I might be losing my magic."

"Let me see," she said, crossing the floor of the vault to his table.

Alex held out his hands and she took them in hers. Leslie's hands were smooth and warm as they glided over his fingers and palm. She took him by the right wrist and held his hand up, noting the tremors in his fingers.

"It doesn't look too bad," she said.

"Yesterday I drew one good cleaning rune out of five," he said. "Today I couldn't manage a finding rune, and they're ten times easier than a cleaning rune."

"Have you told Iggy?" Leslie asked. "He is a doctor, you know."

Alex shook his head, kneading his hands together.

"I think it's because..." he began.

"Because of the life rune," Leslie finished. She always could see right through him. "You think it's another side effect of all that life energy you lost. Like your hair."

He nodded again, his hands trembling now from the fear of having that thought said out loud.

"If that's the case, I doubt Iggy will be able to do anything about it," he said. "Doctor or not."

Leslie fixed him with a hard stare.

"You won't know until you ask," she said. "It might be nothing."

"Or it might be something," Alex said. "What if I *am* losing my magic?"

"Is that even possible?" she asked.

"Think about it," he said. "That would explain why my finding rune lost its connection to Leroy, and why the next one failed."

"Or he could have been on a boat, like you said," she reminded him. Leslie crossed her arms and fixed him with a hard stare. "You're good at what you do, Alex. One of the best. I refuse to believe this is how you go out."

Alex just shrugged.

"We both know I don't have much life-force left," he said. "What if this is it?"

Leslie's jaw tightened. Alex could tell she was fighting the urge to be scared. She was too tough for that, and a moment later her hard look came back.

"Is your brain trembling?" she asked, crossing her arms. "Or is it just your hands?"

"What's that supposed—"

"You're still a detective," she cut him off. "And a damn good one, so if you don't use magic, get your sorry ass out there and find Leroy Cunningham the old-fashioned way."

He looked her in the eyes and found her blue eyes hard, but earnest.

"You're right," he admitted at last, smiling at her. The tension in his chest began to ebb away, leaving just a tiny mote of doubt behind. "I'm done feeling sorry for myself. I'll go home and have Iggy look at my hands and make me some new finding runes, then I'll track down Leroy."

"You might want to look at this before you make any plans," Leslie said. She reached under her arm and pulled out a folded-up newspaper, depositing it on his drafting table.

Alex opened it, revealing the masthead of today's issue of *The Midnight Star*. The large headline read, *Ghost Killer Claims Fourth Victim*. A subheading declared that the police were baffled and had called in a P.I. runewright to help solve the case. When Alex read that, he groaned.

"Oh, it gets better," Leslie said with a sardonic smile. "Read the article."

Alex did and he began to feel sick in the pit of his stomach with every word.

"This makes the police sound like bumbling incompetents."

"Uh-huh," Leslie said. "And it makes you sound like you've come in to show them how to do their jobs." She pointed to one particular paragraph. "He calls you the Runewright Detective."

Alex rubbed the bridge of his nose, pinching hard. This was not good.

"Detweiler is going to assume I talked to this rag," Alex said. "He's going to blow a gasket."

Leslie picked up the paper and turned to leave.

"I suggest you get over there before someone shows him a copy," she said.

Alex followed her out, shutting the door to his vault.

"Did you find where Anne Watson is staying?" he asked.

"Not yet," Leslie said. "I'm going for lunch then I'll get back on that."

"If you find her, tell her I'll call her when I can. I'm going by the Central Office to try to smooth things over with Detweiler, then I'm going home."

THE NEW YORK CITY CENTRAL OFFICE OF POLICE was a ten-story building in Manhattan's inner ring a few blocks south and west of the park. It was early afternoon when Alex walked through the front doors and headed for the elevators in the back. All six of the detective divisions were on the fifth floor and he had no desire to take the stairs after the day he was having.

"You!" Detweiler's voice assaulted him as soon as he exited the elevator on the fifth floor. Before Alex knew what was happening, the portly lieutenant was right in his face. "You've got a lot of nerve showing your face here!" he yelled.

"Me," Alex yelled right back. He'd decided on the way over that the only chance he had to convince the lieutenant that he had nothing to do with the story was to be offended himself. "Somebody on your team has a mighty big mouth!" Alex yelled, shoving Leslie's copy of the tabloid at Detweiler.

"My team?" he yelled back as detectives from all over the floor began to drift out into the hall to see what the commotion was about. "It was you who talked to this rag, why else would they make you sound like some master detective come to save us keystone cops?"

"You think that's good for me?" Alex rejoined, lowering his voice a bit. "This hack makes me sound like some all-powerful sorcerer. What happens when clients come to see me expecting miracles I can't deliver? Word will get around I don't have the juice. It'll ruin my reputation and my business."

"Don't try to make yourself out to be the victim," Detweiler said. "No cop would say these things about a fellow cop, it has to be you."

"Yeah?" Alex spat back. "And what about those details in the paper from yesterday? What about the stab wounds? Someone leaked that before I was even on the case."

"That's no big thing. That doctor you live with is chummy with the coroner. You could have learned that from him."

"And then what?" Alex said, addressing the assembled crowd for the first time. "I got myself involved? How? Anyone think I put Callahan up to it? He brought me in, remember?"

Apparently Detweiler had forgotten that point because he opened his mouth to answer and abruptly shut it again. A murmur of agreement rumbled through the onlookers. Most of them wouldn't have peed on Alex if he'd been on fire, but no one believed that Callahan could be bullied into anything.

Alex had guessed that if it came down to a choice between believing Detweiler or believing Callahan, the detectives would go with the latter. Everyone who knew the big Lieutenant knew he was a tough, honest, son-of-a-bitch. Not the kind of guy someone like Alex would be able to leverage.

Alex may not have though much of Detweiler, but the man wasn't stupid. He sensed the shift in the audience instantly and his face screwed up into a look of fury. He understood the corner into which Alex had backed him.

He rushed Alex, grabbing him by the front of his waistcoat and slamming him into the wall of the hallway.

"All right, scribbler," he said in a low voice only Alex could hear. "That was pretty smart of you, but don't think I've changed my mind. You've been talking to that hack from the Sun and if anything you've told him ruins my case, I'll have you brought up on an obstruction charge."

Alex looked him right in the eyes without blinking.

"Wasn't me."

"I don't believe you," Detweiler growled. "Now get out of my building and stay out of my case. If I catch you anywhere near this, I'll have you arrested."

"For what?" Alex asked, a smile creeping across his lips.

Detweiler smiled too.

"Obstruction," he said. "Interfering with a police investigation, jaywalking, and anything else I can think of."

"That won't stick and you know it."

Detweiler shrugged.

"Maybe not," he said, "but I can hold you for forty-eight hours without charging you with anything. Now get out."

He let go of Alex and stepped back, smoothing out his jacket.

"Get back to work, you mugs," he said to the hallway, and he and the other detectives disappeared, leaving Alex alone by the elevator.

Alex straightened his own jacket and turned to the call button. His gamble had paid off, so he wasn't in jail, but he was off the case. The more stubborn part of his mind wanted to tell Anne Watson that he'd keep working just to spite Detweiler, but that was asking for trouble, and he really didn't have any meaningful way to help her anyway.

He sighed as the elevator doors slid open.

"That went well," he said to the empty hallway.

6

THE DOCTOR'S VAULT

"Let me see your hands," Iggy commanded once Alex got back to the brownstone and explained his day.

Alex held out his hands and Iggy took them, each in turn, squeezing them and feeling the bones and tendons in the fingers.

"How long has this been going on?" he asked, feeling the trembling in Alex's fingers.

"A few weeks now," Alex said.

Iggy gave him a sour look.

"You should have told me," he said.

"Why?" Alex said. "It's because of the life rune. The only thing you can do about that is worry, and we both know it." Iggy glared at him, but Alex didn't relent. "Right now I'm doing enough worrying for the both of us," he went on.

"Firstly," Iggy said, fishing his green-backed rune book from his jacket pocket. "This tremor might not be related to the Incident."

The Incident was Iggy's nickname for Alex's teleporting Sorsha Kincaid's floating castle out over the Atlantic.

"Secondly," Iggy went on, "you don't need to spare my feelings. I'm not some frail old man." He tore a vault rune from his book and pasted it into a barely visible door frame painted on the wall of the kitchen.

"I'm sorry," Alex said as Iggy touched the lit end of his cigar to the rune and it vanished, leaving a heavy steel door in its place. "But I'm not dead yet either. We agreed we'd just keep going as usual for as long as I've got left."

Iggy looked at him somberly before he pulled open the heavy door to his vault. Alex knew that look; he'd seen it in the mirror plenty of times. It haunted him on the nights when he couldn't sleep, which was more and more often these days. That look had only one meaning.

Your days are numbered and there's not a damn thing anyone can do about it.

Seeing that look on Iggy's face, a man he owed almost everything, pained Alex in a way he didn't want to dwell on. The sorceress had known that look was coming and removed herself from Alex's life before it became a reality. He didn't blame her for that. If he was honest with himself, he would have hated seeing that look on her perfect features almost as much as he hated it on Iggy's craggy face.

Iggy sighed.

"We'll soldier on," he said. "It's all we can do. Now come inside."

Alex stopped, flat-footed for a moment. He'd never been allowed inside Iggy's vault before. Stepping around the door, he entered a vast space, much bigger than his own large vault. The central area was a round room, laid out as doctor's surgery. It had an examination table under a cluster of magelights in the center, and cabinets, cases of medical supplies, and racks of alchemical solutions along the curved edges.

To the right an arched doorway led into what looked like a runewright's workshop, with a large, well-lit writing desk, and shelves and shelves of inks and components.

On the left, another archway ran into what looked like a study, complete with a comfy chair, shelves of books, and a perpetual fire in a grate.

Above him, the ceiling was vaulted, rising up to a dome. Intricate images covered the ceiling and Alex recognized some of them as Michelangelo's work on the Sistine Chapel. Other were frescos from other great masters. A wide spiral stair ran up along the back wall to a vaulted opening overhead. From his vantage point below, Alex couldn't see much, but the top of a four-poster bed stuck up just enough to be recognized.

"Sit on the table," Iggy instructed as he went to one of the glass-doored cupboards and began looking through a shelf of stoppered vials made of dark glass.

Alex sat on the table, admiring the smooth, painted walls and the tile floor.

"How did you do all this?" he asked as Iggy came back with three of the alchemical vials.

"Drink this," he said, shoving one into Alex's hand.

Alex peeled away the lead that was used to seal the cork stopper to the bottle, then opened it. A pungent aroma assaulted him and he almost gagged.

"Better hold your nose when you drink that one," Iggy added.

Alex did as he was told and managed to get the noxious liquid down. It burned in his gut and made him feel sick.

"You didn't answer my question," he said, trying to take his mind off his churning gut.

Iggy looked around at his vault.

"You'd be amazed what you can do if you put your mind to it," he said.

"Why do you have a bedroom in here?"

Iggy chuckled.

"There's plenty about vaults you still don't know," he said, enigmatically. "I can close the door to this vault and it will disappear from the outside. No one can get in unless I open it from in here."

Alex whistled.

"Sounds like a good place to hide if people are looking for you."

"Or if you're traveling," Iggy said. "Just open the door on the back wall of a train station or a general store in any town you might visit or any stop along the way. You've got a place to sleep without having to pay for a room."

"What if you need to go to the bathroom?" Alex asked. "Or eat."

Iggy shrugged.

"I've got a bathroom in here," he said. "Shower and all, and I've got a little kitchen with tins of food. Plus, there's a diner in every town in America where you can grab a bite."

Alex was stunned. He had no idea most of this was even possible.

"But, how do you get water in here for the shower?"

Iggy picked up Alex's hand and checked the trembling. Alex had been too busy to notice, but the trembling seemed to be a tiny bit better.

"Now drink this," he said, handing him the second vial.

This one had a rubber stopper and no lead seal. It also tasted better, like licorice. Alex hated licorice, but it was still better than the first elixir.

"You have got to teach me this," Alex said, looking up at the domed ceiling.

"Later," Iggy said, checking Alex's hands again.

"Hey," Alex said as Iggy felt each of his fingers in turn. "How come you used our kitchen table as an operating theater when you have this place in here?"

Iggy chuckled as he put down Alex's right hand and picked up his left.

"I added this room last year after you kept getting shot and bringing other wounded people here to the house." He let go of Alex's hands and picked up the last bottle. "Blood is the very devil to clean off the kitchen floor."

He walked back the open cupboard and put the last vial back on its shelf.

"We won't be needing that one, I think."

Alex held up his hand and examined it closely as Iggy disappeared into his runewright lab. It looked steady, with almost no sign of trembling at all.

"What did you do?" he asked.

Iggy came back a moment later carrying a wooden crate lined with hay.

"I gave you a nerve tonic," he said, putting the crate down on the table beside Alex. It was full of glass jars and beakers like the kind the university had in their lab.

"So I'm cured?" Alex asked hopefully.

"Unfortunately no," Iggy said. "The tonic will suppress the symptoms for a little while. You're going to need something specially formulated and you're going to have to take it on a regular basis."

"Is it expensive?"

"Very," Iggy said.

Alex looked at his temporarily-steady hand and sighed.

"In that case, I might need you to write some finding runes for me in the foreseeable future."

Iggy opened his green rune book and tore out three pages.

"Here," he said, setting them on the table. "On the house. And don't get discouraged about the tonic," he patted the crate full of glassware. "That's where this comes in."

In answer to Alex's questioning look, he reached in and pulled out a round-bottomed beaker with markings along its neck indicating measurements. He rotated it so that Alex could see the back where several runes had been etched into the glass.

"I have an arrangement with an alchemist here in town," he explained. "I put runes on her equipment that help with more efficient and faster brewing. She trades me for the medical elixirs I keep on hand."

Alex had wondered how Iggy always seemed to have the alchemical supplies a British navy doctor would need. Iggy pulled a folded slip of paper from his pocket and handed it to Alex.

"Her name is Andrea Kellin," he said. "Her address is on the paper. Deliver this crate to her and tell her I need a batch of the tonic listed there." He pointed to the bottom of the paper where a long, Latin formula had been written out.

"Thanks, Iggy," Alex said. He felt more relieved than he had in days.

"Nothing to it, lad," Iggy said, tamping out the stub of his cigar. "Now you'd better get going, Andrea closes promptly at six."

Alex got up from the table and picked up the crate, being careful not to jostle the glass. He followed Iggy out of the magnificent vault and back into the brownstone's kitchen.

"Now don't dawdle on your way home," Iggy said, shutting his vault doo. "I want to hear if you've dug up anything new in the ghost case."

"All I did on that today was get yelled at by the Lieutenant in charge," he said with a chuckle. "Guy named Detweiler. You should read the story they wrote in that tabloid though. It'll give you a laugh."

"If you didn't work the ghost case, why do you need finding runes?" Iggy asked.

Alex nearly dropped the crate. He swore.

"Language, lad. You're a professional."

Alex quickly explained about Hannah Cunningham and her missing husband as he put down the crate on the kitchen table. He used Iggy's painted door frame to open his own vault and retrieved one of his maps of Manhattan.

He unrolled it and laid out his compass, the silver ring, and one of Iggy's finding runes. His hand trembled as he lit it, but he supposed that was from nervousness.

The rune popped, but the ring didn't go rolling across the table this time, It spun on its edge like a coin and as it spun it moved in a wide circle around the map.

"I don't get it," Alex said. "You sure that was a finding rune?"

"Of course I'm sure," Iggy said. "I'm not senile."

Alex looked up and found his mentor studying the spinning ring carefully.

"Iggy," he said, drawing the doctor's attention up to him. "This is the second time a rune I cast hasn't locked on, but didn't just fail. Is it possible..." He took a breath and tried again. "Is it possible that I'm losing my magic?"

Iggy thought about that for a long minute, his mustache twitching the whole time.

"No," he finally said. "There's no precedent for a runewright losing their abilities. I'm seventy-five and my magic is just as strong as it's ever been. Stronger in some ways. This," he indicated the spinning ring that hadn't seemed to have lost any momentum yet. "This must mean something else."

"I'm open to suggestions," Alex said. "Otherwise I've got to call Hannah and try to explain to her how I found her husband and then lost him again."

Iggy considered the map. Alex had no idea what he was looking for, it looked exactly as it had before, with the silver ring spinning around it in circles.

"Why is the ring doing that?" Alex asked.

"Look at the compass needle," Iggy said.

Alex shifted his gaze and found the compass spinning in time with the ring, following its progression around the map.

"I think the spell is trying to find Leroy," Iggy said. "But the link is so weak it can't fully connect."

"What could cause that?"

"Oh, any number of things," Iggy said. "He might be too far away."

"No," Alex said, pointing to the map inside the orbiting ring. "I don't think that's accidental. Leroy must be somewhere inside that circle."

"Could be," Iggy agreed. "If he's underground or shielded somehow, that would explain it."

"If that was the case, the spell wouldn't connect at all."

"Well it isn't that you're losing your magic," Iggy insisted.

Alex held out one of the two remaining finding runes.

"You want to try?"

Iggy gave him an irritated look.

"You know that's not how it works," he said. "You met with the wife, you heard about Leroy from her, you've got a basis for a connection. All I know is his name; it would never connect for me."

Alex sighed and caught the spinning ring. It resisted him for a fraction of a second, then the magic dissipated with a small popping sound.

"Looks like Leslie was right," he said, pocketing the ring and his compass. "I'm going to have to find Leroy the old-fashioned way."

"I have faith in you, lad," Iggy said with a grin. "You were trained by the best, after all."

"If you do say so yourself," Alex added.

Iggy put a hand on his shoulder and looked him square in the face.

"One thing you learn at my age, lad, is that you have to toot your own horn when you get the chance. God knows no one else is going to do it for you."

"All right," Alex said, feeling better in spite of himself. "I've got to call Hannah and try to tell her why I haven't found her husband, then I'll go see your alchemist."

Alex moved to the phone on the kitchen wall. He thought about going upstairs to his room to make the call, but Iggy already knew about everything that had happened and he was too tired to trudge all the way up to the third floor for some unnecessary privacy.

"Hello, Mr. Lockerby?" Hannah's frightened voice came through the receiver at him the instant the call connected.

"It's me," he confirmed.

"Did you find Leroy?" she gasped, the tension in her voice squeezing the words into frightened squeaks. "Is he with you?"

"No," Alex said. "When I got to the marina, my rune lost contact with him. I cast another rune, but it couldn't connect with him either. I think they might have moved him somewhere underground."

"Mr. Lockerby," Hannah said in a small, desperate voice.

"Alex."

"Alex," she amended. "I can't pay you for the second rune. I had to raid our savings to pay for the first one."

"Let me worry about that," Alex said. "Just because I can't find him with a rune, doesn't mean I can't find him. I'm just going to have to do some investigating."

"I can't pay you for that either," Hannah said. Alex could tell she was crying now. Alex was tempted to let that stand, but he felt like too much of a heel. He suppressed a sigh as he made his decision.

"I told you that I'd find your husband and that's what I'm going to do," he said.

"But how?" There was desperation in that voice, but Alex detected a tiny trace of hope as well.

"I'm pretty sure he's still alive," he said. "That means whoever took him needs him for something. If I figure out why they took him, I'll know where to start looking."

"Thank you, Alex," she whispered. "Please find my Leroy."

"Have faith, Hannah," Alex said, passing on the favorite saying of Father Harry, the priest who helped raise him.

Hannah promised that she would, and Alex hung up.

"You're a good man, Alex," Iggy said from the kitchen table, where he sat sipping a cup of tea. "You'll go broke, but you're a good man."

"Let me worry about that," Alex said.

"You don't worry about money at all," Iggy chuckled. "That's your problem. If you didn't have Leslie around to run your business, you'd have been bankrupt years ago."

"That reminds me, Leslie's coming over for dinner this week. When's a good night?"

Iggy raised an eyebrow at that.

"You know the rules, lad," he said. "No dinner guests unless they're extremely easy on the eyes."

Alex nodded, understanding.

"So Leslie is welcome any time."

"Exactly," Iggy said.

"I'll set it up for tomorrow then," Alex said, picking up the crate of glassware for Iggy's alchemist friend.

ALEX HAD to set the crate down to shut the outer door to the brownstone. He didn't have to lock the door, of course. Only someone with the right combination of runes could open it, and there were only two sets of those in the city.

He picked up the crate and turned to walk down the steps to the sidewalk. As he did, he noticed a long, black sedan that was parked against the curb. An enormous mountain of a man leaned against the fender reading a paper in the bored manner of someone waiting for a bus. Another man stood further up the street, loitering by one of the streetlights.

Alex felt suddenly exposed. He'd left his 1911 in his vault before he left his office, not wanting to have it on his person during his confrontation with Detweiler. Retreating back into the brownstone was an option, of course. These men were big, but they weren't anywhere near big enough to force their way past the protective runes and wards Iggy had put on the door.

Still, Alex wasn't too alarmed. He doubted anyone with murderous intent would try to grab him off the street in broad daylight. So what were they here for?

He made his decision and proceeded down the stairs and turned toward the crawler station.

"Are you Alexander Lockerby, the runewright detective?" the man by the streetlight asked as Alex approached.

Alex suppressed a groan, recognizing the name the tabloid had given him.

"Who wants to know?"

The man reached into his jacket and Alex tensed, but he came back with a business card.

"Andrew Barton would like a word. Now."

Alex knew the name. Everyone in the city knew the name. Andrew Barton was one of the New York six, the sorcerers who made the city their home. Known as the Lightning Lord, Barton was the man who electrified Empire Tower and pushed out wireless power to most of Manhattan. Arguably one of the most powerful, and therefore dangerous men in the world.

And he wanted to see Alex.

"I guess I can make the time," Alex said with a smile.

7

THE LIGHTNING LORD

Empire Tower stood on the south side of Manhattan and radiated its magical energy over the island. It used to be a commercial building, but Barton had bought it and emptied it out for his singular invention, the Etherium Capacitor.

The capacitor drew in power from the universe itself, just like runewrights did to power their magic, but on a much larger scale. Once absorbed, the magical energy was converted into electrical power and broadcast over the island, like radio waves. Anything with a special copper coil in it could receive the wireless power, including magelights, elevators, vacuum cleaners, heaters, and a host of other electrical appliances. Older appliances were simply plugged in to the existing wiring of buildings that now had their own receivers. The only real limitation to Barton's capacitor was its range. From Empire Tower, the broadcast could only cover Manhattan itself, and the further you got away from the tower, the worse your power reception got. Many homes, businesses, and apartments in the Outer-Ring were still wired to Edison Electric, just like the rest of the city.

Alex could almost feel the energy radiating from the tower when the black sedan pulled up in front.

"Mr. Barton's steward will meet you inside," the driver said as the other man opened the car's rear door.

"Thanks," Alex said as got out, hefting the wooden crate of glassware. Neither man had spoken during the trip to Empire Tower and Alex was in no mood to force the issue. He was glad that Iggy had helped his tremors, but wondered how he would pay for costly and ongoing treatment, even with Iggy's help.

"This way," the big man said, shutting the door behind Alex and moving toward the front doors.

Since the tower was no longer a commercial building, the front had been redone with only a single pair of double doors leading inside. Alex didn't see any security, but supposed they were inside.

He was wrong.

When the big man reached the door, he grabbed the ornate handle to open it and Alex fell his skin prickle. Some sort of magical ward recognized the big man and the door opened when he pulled. It wasn't a rune-based ward, but rather the vastly more powerful magic of sorcerers and the energy it gave off made the hairs on Alex's arms stand on end.

Alex followed the big man inside, through a long, elegantly-decorated marble hallway to a pair of elevators at the back. A half-dozen doors led off the hall to offices that were dark and shuttered. The entire building seemed empty except for Alex and the big man.

Above the elevators at the end of the hall was a massive bronze relief of Empire Tower itself, stretching up over a full story. Art Deco rays of power radiated out from the top of the tower, circling it like a halo. Alex had read a story about the tower in a magazine once that said the elevator symbol pre-dated Barton's purchase of the tower. It had been that very symbol, the article claimed, that had inspired Barton to use the tower in the first place.

Each elevator had a shining steel door with a simpler relief of the tower on them, power rays and all. His guide pushed the elevator's call button and another hair-raising burst of magical energy washed over Alex. The simple amount of power used just to make sure the right person pushed an elevator button made Alex jealous. If he had that kind of magical power, he reasoned there wasn't anything he couldn't do.

Before he had time to dwell on that, a chime sounded, and the doors slid open. The big man leaned in and pressed a button inside the car, then moved back so Alex could enter.

"Someone will meet you up top," he said.

A LONG ELEVATOR RIDE LATER, Alex stepped out into an elegantly appointed waiting room. There were couches and tables laden with the latest fashion and engineering magazines scattered tastefully around. A bank of phones, in dark wood privacy booths, stood along one wall, and a bar of the same dark wood stood opposite. A dapper young man in a red-velvet waistcoat stood behind the bar, polishing a glass, while dozens of bottles of liqueur lined shelves behind him.

Hallways exited the area to the right and left and Alex could hear the staccato rhythm of typewriter keys being struck emanating from the right side.

At the far end of the waiting area was a single elevator door. Next to it was a wooden podium like a maître d' might stand behind when greeting guests at a high end restaurant. A black telephone stood on the podium and a man in a black tuxedo stood behind it.

"Bickman?" Alex said as he approached.

Gary Bickman, formerly Ernest Atwood's valet, stood with a wide smile on his face.

"I really owe you one, Alex," he said, shaking Alex's hand. "I never would have thought you had such friends in high places. The Ice Queen...uh, that is, Ms. Kincaid knew Mr. Barton was looking for a new steward so she got me on here. I can't thank you enough."

"That's great," Alex said.

Bickman's face went a little sour and he didn't release Alex's hand.

"I, uh, I won't get paid till the end of the week," he said, his voice quiet. "Even then, the missus and I have got to get new lodgings, so it might be some time before I can pay you."

Alex hadn't expected Bickman to get a job this fast in the first place, so he just smiled and patted Bickman on the shoulder.

"I know you're good for it," he said.

"I did recommend you to Mr. Barton, though" he said. "He needed a detective and I thought the job would get you through till I can pay up."

Alex had wondered why the Lightning Lord had wanted to see him. He'd seen the man once, or rather his image, when Sorsha warned him about the plot to kill four of the New York Six, but Barton hadn't seen him. As far as Andrew Barton knew, Alex didn't exist. He'd thought maybe the article in the Sun had something to do with it, but he seriously doubted a man like Barton read tabloids.

"Thanks, Bickman," Alex said with a genuine smile. "I appreciate that."

Gary smiled back at him and then straightened up, tugging his coat to make sure it was in place.

"Right," he said. "Mr. Barton said to bring you up as soon as you got here, so right this way."

He stepped to the elevator and pressed the call button. Once again a burst of magic radiated out and the doors slid open immediately.

This time, Bickman rode the elevator with Alex, and a few moments later they emerged directly into a magnificent office. Towering glass windows filled the north wall, rising up over two stories and looking out over the city and the park. Bookshelves, cabinets, and cases lined the left wall with a massive mural of the history of the industrial revolution leading up to the modern age on the right.

A desk that was longer than Alex's office was wide stood beneath the massive windows and was covered in papers, rolled blueprints, mechanical models, and bits of equipment. Two long couches sat facing each other over a low table in the center of the room and a truly impressive rollaway bar stood beside them.

Behind the desk, an older man with silver hair and a handlebar mustache paced back and forth with the receiver to a telephone pressed to his ear. He wore a gold-colored waistcoat over a white shirt with the sleeves rolled up. In his free hand, he held a lit cigarette, waving it around as he punctuated his conversation.

"I don't care about other thefts," he was saying. "Things get stolen all the time, but not from me."

He paused and kept pacing.

"No," he almost yelled. "You go down there personally and tell whatever desk jockey they put on this to get his ass out there and find my motor."

With that he slammed the receiver down into the phone's cradle and took a long drag on his cigarette.

"Idiots." He said the word like a curse. "What do they think I pay taxes for?"

Bickman cleared his throat forcefully and Barton looked up.

"It's about time," the sorcerer said. "Where were, you? Brooklyn?"

Alex wasn't sure how to answer that, so he just put on his most genial smile and shrugged.

"If you wanted to get hold of me, you should have just called my office."

Barton scowled, the ends of his mustache turning down.

"I did," he said. "Your secretary said you'd gone home."

He made a point of looking up at a massive clock hanging over the bookcases, it read four-forty-five.

"Those are some banker's hours you keep," Barton went on. "Is that your idea of a work ethic?"

Alex bristled at that. Most days he was on the job till late and some days he didn't get any sleep at all. Still, it was never a good idea to bait a sorcerer, so he just froze his smile in place.

"I had to pick up some things for a client," he said, holding up the wooden crate of glassware as evidence. "I was on my way to deliver this when your men located me."

"Gary," he said to Bickman. "Call a courier up here for Mr. Lockerby's delivery."

"Don't worry about it," Alex said, setting the crate down on the richly carpeted floor. "It's something I need to handle myself. Now, what can I do for you, Mr. Barton?"

The sorcerer cast a critical eye over Alex for a long moment. He lingered on Alex's snowy white hair before moving on. Finally he nodded to himself, obviously making up his mind.

"Gary here tells me you're a damn good private eye," he said, nodding at Bickman. "Seems to think you can help me."

"I guess that depends on your problem, Mr. Barton," Alex replied.

Barton laughed at that.

"You aren't willing to commit to anything until you know the score," he said, nodding. "Smart. Irritating, but smart. I like that."

He picked up a silver cigarette case with a green, tortoise-shell inlay on it. He flipped it open with his finger and offered one to Alex.

"I like a man who knows his business," Barton said as Alex took a cigarette. He flipped the case closed and set it back on the desk as Alex reached into his pocket for his matchbook. Before he could complete the gesture, Barton pointed his index finger at Alex and a spark of blue energy snapped between the outstretched finger and the end of the cigarette.

"My business is electricity, Mr. Lockerby," he said, picking up one of the mechanical models from his desk. It was roughly rectangular and seemed to have a lot of delicate parts. "This is a scale model of my new Etherium Capacitor, the Mark V. When it's built, it'll be about the size of a delivery van."

Barton paused as if he were waiting for Alex to ask him a question, but Alex just nodded attentively. He'd learned a long time ago to keep his mouth shut when he had no idea where a conversation was going.

"The Mark II generator is what powers Manhattan," Barton went on. "It takes up five full floors of the tower, and there are twelve of them."

Alex whistled. He was starting to see why the newer, smaller capacitor was a big deal.

Barton put the model back on his desk and turned to look out the window at the city beyond.

"This entire building is a prototype, Mr. Lockerby," he said. "I plan to make cheap, radiant power available to the whole city in the next five years."

He turned back and picked up another model, this time of a crawler.

"Right now, I'm working with Rockefeller to extend the crawler network all over the city."

"How?" Alex asked, forgetting to keep his mouth shut. Crawlers were faster than cars and rode better; their only problem was that they lost power if they left the radiant field of Empire Tower. As a result, they mostly served the Core and the Inner and Middle-Rings, leaving a huge chunk of the population outside their operating area.

Barton smiled at Alex's interest.

"We thought about putting an electric rail along the ground, but it was too hard to shield it. Anyone could just walk up and electrocute themselves. So we're going to raise the rail up above the street and add a second one. Rockefeller's marketing a new crawler that will run along the rails, right over the top of the traffic. It'll be even faster, and we'll tie the rails directly to the tower here, so there won't be any power problems."

As he spoke, Barton's words got faster and faster, like a kid explaining his favorite show at the pictures.

"Sounds great," Alex said. "What's the problem?"

Barton's exuberance faded and he sighed.

"Nothing with that," he said. "We'll have the new line to Brooklyn running by New Years. My problem is that I'm dreaming much bigger than that, Mr. Lockerby. I'm not just going to send crawlers out into the city, I'm going to power it all. Everything."

He picked up the model of his Mark V generator.

"These generators aren't cheap to build," he said. "This is my company, but I still have a board and investors to answer to. People who were with me in the beginning."

"And they don't want you providing cheap power?" Alex asked.

"It's not that," Barton said. "I can put sixty-four of these capacitors in the space of one Mark II. That means I can power the entire state, maybe multiple states, right from here."

He set the model back on his desk.

"I just have to prove the Mark V works...and I have to have a factory that can build a lot of them." He picked up a roundish model with gears visible through a cutout and tossed it to Alex. "For that to happen, I need someone else to order a whole bunch of my Mark V Etherium Capacitors."

"And that's what this is for?" Alex asked.

"That is a model of a traction motor," Barton said. "It's a special kind of electric motor that's designed to pull trains."

Now that Alex knew what it was for, he still didn't see how it could pull a train. It took enormous, coal burning boilers to build up enough steam pressure to move something so large and heavy.

"The B&O railroad has been experimenting with these," Barton explained. "They hook them up to enormous diesel engines. They generate the electricity needed to move the wheels. It's powerful enough, but you still have to carry your fuel."

"And you want to put one of your new Etherium Capacitors on the train instead," Alex said, figuring out where Barton was going.

"Sorsha said you were smart," Barton said. "There's a contest next week down in Baltimore," he went on. "A bunch of companies will be showing off their traction motors to the B&O and the winner gets a million-dollar prize."

"And you need the money to build your capacitor factory?"

"I don't give a fig about the money," Barton said. "The winner will get to build the new diesel engines for the B&O railroad. It's the contract I want. My Mark V capacitor isn't ready yet, but in a year, it will be. If I'm the guy building the diesel locomotives, it will be easy to convince the railroads to convert to my new capacitor. If GE or some other company gets it, they aren't going to cut me in and by then they'll have already built hundreds of diesels."

He took the traction motor back from Alex and held it up.

"This electric motor is twice as strong as anything my competitors can make, and it's ready right now."

"But it was stolen," Alex said, remembering Barton's phone conversation.

"Right off a truck at my factory," Barton fumed. "I need you to find it, Mr. Lockerby. I need you to find it yesterday. All my plans for the future, cheap power for the state, everything, depends on me winning that contest and getting the contract with the railroad. If I get orders for the Mark V capacitor I can build Etherium towers all over the world. No one will be without electricity. No one will freeze to death in winter because they couldn't afford coal to heat their houses. Think about it."

"So you're just a misunderstood altruist?" Alex said, managing to keep the sarcasm out of his voice by sheer force of will.

Barton actually laughed at that, a hearty, genuinely amused laugh.

"Of course not," he said. "I said cheap power, not free. Even at one or two percent profit, I'll be richer than Solomon inside ten years. That's business, kid. The world gets limitless electricity and I get rich."

"So why are you telling me all this?" Alex asked.

Barton actually looked surprised at that.

"Isn't that how finding runes work?" he asked. "The more you know about the missing object and the people and causes it's connected to, the better the rune works?"

That was exactly how finding runes worked but Alex was surprised that Barton knew it. Most sorcerers dismissively referred to alchemists and runewrights as *Lessers*.

"All right, Mr. Barton," Alex said. "I'll find your missing motor for you. I'll need to get my kit."

"You don't have your tools of the trade with you?" Barton asked with an admonishing tone.

Alex pointed to the wooden crate of glassware still sitting on the carpet.

"I was on a different case when your boys picked me up," Alex said, pulling a piece of chalk out of his trouser pocket. "But don't worry, this and a bare patch of wall are all the tools I need."

Barton perked up at that; apparently he knew about runewright vaults too. He showed Alex out into a hallway off the office where several secretaries were busily transcribing documents and filling out the mountain of paperwork that kept large businesses running. Alex saw Bickman's wife, Marjorie, among them and he waved at her.

When Alex opened his vault, Barton insisted on being shown around and spent ten minutes poking into all the shelves and cupboards, asking about the various tools, inks, powders, and oils used in the runewright trade.

"Fascinating," he said when Alex finally closed the steel door and it melted away, leaving only the wall and the chalk outline behind.

With a grin, Barton reached into thin air and pulled a white cloth into his hand. He passed it to Gary Bickman and then repeated the move with a bottle of cleaning solution. Alex couldn't help but be jealous. He'd first seen sorcerers do this when Sorsha had pulled a notebook from the empty air when she interviewed him about the

Archimedean Monograph. She'd done it casually and without fanfare, yet it was more than Alex could do on his best day.

"Showoff," he said with a grin.

"Make sure that chalk outline is completely gone, Gary," Barton said, handing the cloth to Bickman. "I don't think Mr. Lockerby could use it to gain entry to my office, but there's no sense taking chances."

Despite the explanation, Alex knew full well that Barton had done it to emphasize the difference between their relative abilities. Still, Alex took some pleasure in the fact that Barton needed him and his finding rune to get his motor back.

Iggy's finding rune, he reminded himself.

BACK IN ANDREW BARTON'S cavernous office, Alex cleared off a large space on the desk. A lot depended on this finding rune, so he took his time setting up. He took the green powder and the beeswax candles from his kit, pouring out a thin line of the powder in a hexagonal shape. He added a candle to each joint of the hexagon, then put a ceramic tile with another rune carved in it in the exact center.

Pricking his finger, Alex added a drop of his own blood to the rune on the tile and he felt it activate.

"What's all that?" Barton asked.

"Stabilizing rune," Alex explained. "It helps the finding rune get a clear connection."

That done, Alex carefully laid out the map of New York City on top of the stabilizing rune, then put his battered compass in the center.

"Is this model accurate?" he asked, picking up the little traction motor.

"Exactly accurate," Barton said.

Alex took out one of Iggy's finding runes from his jacket pocket and folded it up, then laid it on the compass with the model of the motor on top of it. He took a breath to focus his mind and then ran through everything Barton had explained about his plans and how they all rested on the missing traction motor. Flicking the ashes of his cigarette into an ashtray on the desk, Alex lit the flash paper.

The rune exploded to life, flipping the little model off the compass. The orange rune hung in the air, spinning like Alex expected. Gradually it slowed, and the compass needle began turning, catching up to the rune and matching it. Alex waited, but the rune didn't fade, it just hung there in the air with the compass needle spinning lazily in parity with it. There wasn't a spinning ring orbiting the map this time, but that was the only difference.

"What's wrong?" Barton wondered, reading the look on Alex's face.

"It isn't making a connection with the motor," he said.

"So it didn't work?" Barton said, annoyance creeping into his voice.

Alex shook his head.

"No, it worked," he said. "But something is preventing the rune from linking the compass to the motor."

"Preventing?" Barton said. "You mean like a shielding spell?"

Alex wasn't sure how that would work. Masking runes, like the kind Iggy had put on the brownstone, would have caused the finding rune to fail outright. They completely blocked any attempt to magically find something inside their filed of influence.

"I don't think so," Alex said. "It might be inside a lead-lined room or underground; that would block the signal. How big is the actual motor?"

"About three feet long and two and a half feet around," Barton said. "And it weighs around six hundred pounds."

"So, whoever took it won't have an easy time moving it," Alex said. "I'm afraid they may have damaged it. Maybe broken it in pieces or taken it apart. That would explain the rune."

He indicated the spinning compass.

Barton swore and slammed his fist down on the desk, sending sparks out from his hand.

"See Gary," Barton said, turning back to the window. "He'll pay you for the rune."

"With all due respect, Mr. Barton, that's not it," Alex said. "Detectives have been finding stuff for a long time and most of them don't have finding runes to help out."

Barton turned back to Alex with a twinkle in his eye.

"So, you think you can find my motor the old-fashioned way, do you?"

Alex nodded.

"You bet," he said.

"Why should I throw good money after bad, Lockerby?" he said. "If you're right, my motor's probably in pieces by now anyway. I'm going to have to make a new one and can only hope it gets done before the contest, so why should I pay you to find a lost cause?"

"Because," Alex said with a knowing smile. "If whoever stole your motor took it apart, they did that to keep you out of the contest. If I find the guys who stole it, and they give up the name of their employer..."

Alex let the sentence fade away, giving Barton an expectant look.

"If you can prove that one of the other contestants tampered with my motor to keep me out of the contest," Barton said, picking up Alex's train of thought, "then they'll have to let me compete, even if it takes another week to put a new motor together."

"And whoever is behind this will be out for sure," Alex pointed out.

Barton was grinning now, a wide, predatory grin that made the tips of his handlebar mustache point upward. In that position, Alex realized that they formed little lightning bolts.

"I like it," he said, his eyes sparkling with eager energy. "You know I almost didn't bring you here after that bit in the tabloids," he said. "But Gary and Sorsha were right, you are clever."

"So, I'm on the job?" Alex asked.

Barton nodded.

"The contest is next Wednesday," he said. "I'll give you till Tuesday to find the men who stole my motor."

"Don't you want the name of their employer?" Alex asked, packing up his gear.

Barton's predatory grin turned absolutely feral.

"Don't concern yourself with that, Lockerby," he said, sparks of energy beginning to dance in the blue of his eyes. "Just bring me the men responsible. I'll find out who paid them. I can be very persuasive."

8

THE ALCHEMIST

I t was ten to six when Alex left Empire Tower with the crate of glassware and fifty dollars in his pocket. Barton had paid him for his rune and given him a day's fee plus cab money. Even if he caught a cab right now, Alex knew he'd never get to the alchemist's place before six.

Fifty dollars would pay a week of Leslie's salary and he owed her that.

That and more.

So Alex decided to save the cab fare and catch a crawler. If he was lucky, he'd only be ten minutes late. Maybe Ms. Kellin would still be there.

The crawler dropped him two blocks from the alchemist's address so by the time he walked there, it was almost six-thirty. The shop of Iggy's alchemist friend was in an upscale, Inner-Ring house on the north side of Central Park. A sign in the yard bore the alchemy symbol, a stylized bottle with green liquid in it, and the name *Andrea Kellin*. The house was a neat, two story brick number with a wide porch in front and a dark red front door with matching shingles. A tall painted fence stretched out from each side of the house, closing off the back yard, and a neat walkway ran from the sidewalk to the front door. Below Andrea's name on the yard sign was the word *open* done in neon. As Alex walked up, the sign was off.

With the shop in a house, it usually meant that the proprietor lived on the premises. Since he'd come this far, Alex decided to try his luck and mounted the porch to the red door. A heavy brass knocker hung in the center of the door and Alex shifted the crate into his left arm so he could knock.

The sound of the knocker boomed and echoes bounced back from inside the house. Alex waited a minute, then tried again but nothing stirred inside.

With a sigh, Alex turned and descended the stairs back to the little walk. As he reached it, the creak of a hinge came from his left and he turned to find the gate to the back yard ajar. A woman stood there with a cigarette in her hand. She looked to be in her thirties, with a broad face, rounded cheeks and dimples. Her makeup was sparse, but expertly applied, with liner adding an exotic look to her green eyes, and lipstick that matched the deep red of her hair. A long, Chinese robe was draped over her shoulders, white with dragons done in red that ended at her knees revealing bare legs below and house slippers. A green scarf encircled her neck, bound with a silver clasp. Her lips were turned up in a sly smile and one of her eyebrows was raised as she looked at Alex.

"We're closed," she said, her voice sultry but not deep. "What's the matter, mister?" she asked when Alex didn't reply. "Can't you read?"

"Andrea Kellin?" Alex asked, making a mental note to chide Iggy for keeping this delicious creature to himself.

The smile widened and became even more mocking.

"That's Dr. Kellin," she said. "And no, she's gone out for the evening. I'm Ms. O'Neil, Dr. Kellin's apprentice."

Alex raised his own eyebrow at that.

"Aren't you a bit old to be an apprentice?" he asked.

If Miss. O'Neil took offense at his jibe, she gave no sign.

"Protégé then," she said.

"If the shop's closed, then what are you doing here, Ms. O'Neil?"

"Jessica," she said. "And why I'm here is none of your business." She took a drag and blew out a cloud of smoke. "So, what is your business?"

It took Alex a moment to follow what she meant, then he held up the crate.

"I've got a delivery from Dr. Ignatius Bell."

Jessica's eyebrow shot up again and she considered Alex for a long moment.

"Dr. Bell usually brings his deliveries himself," she said. "Who are you?"

Alex took off his hat with his free hand.

"Alex Lockerby," he said. "I'm Dr. Bell's protégé."

Jessica's smile got a bit wider at that.

"You're a doctor?"

"Runewright," Alex said. "And a private detective."

She looked impressed, but Alex wasn't entirely sure it was genuine. The fact that he couldn't read this woman intrigued him.

"I didn't know Dr. Bell was a detective too," she said.

"He used to consult with Scotland Yard during his navy days."

She considered that while she puffed on her cigarette, then she smiled with a mischievous look.

"I'm not sure I believe you, Alex." She took a step back and began to close the gate. "I think you'd better come back when Dr. Kellin is here."

"I have a message from Dr. Bell," Alex said, putting his hat back on his head and pulling Iggy's note from his pocket. "See for yourself."

Jessica O'Neil paused, then opened the gate wide enough to reach out and take the paper. She read the note at the bottom with its long Latin formula, then scrutinized Alex again. Finally, she pushed open the gate and stepped back.

"Thank you," Alex said, stepping through into the back yard.

Jessica closed the gate and bolted it before leading Alex along the side of the house. As she walked, her hips swayed, making the dragons on her kimono rise and fall.

Alex reminded himself that he was a trained detective, which was why he noticed that.

The path from the gate was paved with flat stones and sloped downward so that by the time they reached the rear of the house, the basement was level with the ground. In the back yard, the peaked roof of a shed looked like it had been just laid on the ground. Alex managed to tear his gaze away from Jessica's hypnotic hips long enough to notice a ramp cut out of the ground that led down to the underground building.

"What's that?" he asked.

"Fermentation shed," Jessica replied. "Lots of elixirs and brews have to age before they reach full potency."

They rounded the corner of the house and she led him to a simple door in the back wall of the basement. At this level, the door led straight into the lower floor. A long bank of windows ran along the entire back and Alex could see an alchemist's laboratory beyond.

"This way," Jessica said, opening the back door and passing inside.

When Alex followed her, he found himself in a small mud room with doors leading off into the main lab, which had some kind of isolated workstation. Wooden tables stood everywhere, lined with stoppered vials, glassware, rubber tubing, and gas burners. Many of the setups were working, with jars of colored liquids steeping over a low flame and others boiling off into distillation apparatus. Every table had a clipboard full of writing hanging from it and the air was full of steam and the acrid smell of chemicals.

"Put that down on the workbench," Jessica said, indicating a mostly empty table. As Alex moved to comply, she crossed the room and opened a door on the far wall. Alex could see a bed, nightstand, and an oriental screen through the opening. This seemed to be where Jessica lived.

"I'll have to mix up that elixir Dr. Bell wants," she said. "Excuse me for a moment. I can't go around mixing potions like this. It's not decent."

She stepped behind the screen and a moment later the kimono was tossed over the top. A few minutes later, Jessica emerged from the screen wearing a simple green blouse, a black skirt with a wide leather belt and dark flats.

"That's better," she said, returning to the lab and shutting the door to her room.

Alex waited for her, leaning against the workbench.

"Weren't you worried I might come in there?" he asked with a grin. "I mean, you don't even know me."

Jessica chuckled at that, deliberately slinking over to where he stood.

"You like my nail polish?" she wondered, showing him her fingers. Each nail had a dark red coat on it that reminded Alex of the color of the shop door. He hadn't noticed before, but it wasn't the same shade as her lipstick.

"It's different," he said.

"That's because it's made up of a contact poison," she said, touching the front of his shirt and dragging the nails down and over his waistcoat. "One scratch and you'll be paralyzed in two seconds. You suffocate after that."

"You'd better be careful with that," Alex said, smiling down at her upturned face. "If you get an itch, you're likely to kill yourself."

Jessica smiled back at him and shook her head, dragging her fingers back up to his shoulder. Despite her warning about the danger her nails posed, Alex didn't want her to stop.

"Working with alchemical solutions is a dangerous business," she said. "I drink a general antigen every day when I wake up, so I can scratch all I want."

"Convenient," Alex admitted. He looked around at the lab with its tables and glass. "What is all this?"

Jessica stepped back from him and wrapped her arms around herself as if she were cold. She sighed as she looked around the room.

"Alchemy is a harsh mistress, Alex," she said. "Basic potions and elixirs can be brewed up in a few hours, but the powerful stuff takes longer."

"How long?"

She walked over to one corner where a long table full of bottles, vats, tubes, condensers, and burners held liquid that was bubbling happily. At one end, clear liquid went in, was boiled off, then the steam was condensed into a different colored liquid. By the time it reached the end, a tiny drop of glowing teal potion fell out into a small bottle.

"This one takes a year and a day to brew," Jessica said. "Every eight hours it has to be checked and specific numbers of drops of specific agents have to be added along the way from those bottles." She pointed to a row of brown bottles in a small box.

"You mean you have to watch this stuff every day?" Alex was dedicated to his work, but this seemed a bit excessive.

She chuckled and nodded.

"Alchemy isn't like writing runes," she said. "You can't just do it whenever you have some spare time, it's a round-the-clock job."

"Which is why you're here now?" Alex said. "Dr. Kellin has the day shift, and you get swing."

"Yes," she said. "Each of us tends the lab for ten hours every day."

"When do you have time for your lessons?"

"In the morning," Jessica said. "Now, let me see your hands."

Alex held out his right hand and Jessica took it. Her hands were smooth and warm as she expertly turned his hands this way and that. The movements reminded him of Iggy's examination.

"Are you a doctor too?" he asked.

"No," Jessica said. "But Andrea teaches me what I need to know."

She let go of his hand and opened a nearby cabinet, taking out a small, wooden stick with red paint on the end.

"More poison?" he asked, and she laughed.

"Open your mouth."

He hesitated, and she grinned at him.

"Don't you trust me?" she asked, barely able to keep from laughing.

Alex opened his mouth and stuck his tongue out at her. She used the opportunity to jam the stick in his mouth and maneuver it under his tongue before pulling it back out again.

"What was that for?" he demanded as she compared the paint on the end to a chart on the wall. Alex could easily see that the color on the stick had changed.

"Dr. Bell's formula isn't quite right," Jessica said, adding a drop of something from a sealed bottle to the stick and checking it again.

"Uh," Alex said, not sure what to make of that. He would trust Iggy's skill with his life, and had. "Are you sure Andrea shouldn't look at that?"

Jessica raised an eyebrow at that, giving Alex a scathing look.

"If you had to make some basic runes, would you wait for Dr. Bell to do it for you?"

"No," Alex admitted. "Sorry."

"You should be," Jessica said. "I know what I'm doing."

She put on a white apron, then removed a glass bottle with a rubber stopper from a shelf. Taking it to a large tank with a spigot at its bottom, she filled it a little over halfway.

"What's that?" Alex asked.

"Alchemical base," Jessica said. "All elixirs use it as a foundation; now quit asking questions or I'll never get done."

She went to a shelf with large jars of various liquids and began adding carefully measured amounts to the base until the bottle glowed a faint yellow color.

"This will do the trick," she said, setting it on the workbench beside Alex. "You need to take a swig of this when you get up in the morning, one at noon, and one around five. Don't take any after that or it will keep you up all night."

Alex picked up the bottle and looked at it.

"I'm supposed to carry this thing around with me?"

Jessica rolled her eyes.

"Men," she said, going to a closet and rummaging around for a moment. When she emerged, she held a metal hip flask. "What would any of you do if you didn't have a woman around to fix your problems?"

She took a small metal funnel from a rack of tools on the wall and filled the flask.

"There you go, cowboy," she said, tucking the flask into the inside pocket of his coat. "Just like the old west."

She looked up at him and winked, and Alex felt a sudden urge to simply lean down and kiss her.

Must be the fumes in here, he lied to himself.

"Thanks, doll," he said, putting his hat back on as Jessica moved to one of the brewing tables. "I appreciate you're doing this."

"I'm sure you can show yourself out," Jessica said, leaning against the table with her sardonic smile in place. "You need to come back tomorrow, though so I can check on you."

Alex raised an eyebrow and Jessica smirked.

"To make sure the mix is right," she explained with exaggerated patience.

"Sure," Alex said, picking up the bottle with the rest of the yellow elixir. "I'll probably be able to come by around noon."

Jessica shook her head.

"You need to come after seven, so I can see you," she said.

"Can't wait to get me back?" Alex said.

She chuckled at that and shook her head.

"It needs to be at least twelve hours after you take the first dose tomorrow morning," she said, picking up the clipboard for the elixir brewing on the table. "You can count to twelve," she looked back over her shoulder at him. "Right?"

"I guess I'll see you tomorrow," he said.

"Tomorrow then."

IT WAS dark by the time Alex got home. Iggy chided him for missing the appointed, seven o'clock dinner hour, but had set aside a plate of poached salmon for him, under a cover to keep it warm. As he ate, Alex told Iggy about his meeting with Andrew Barton, his missing electric traction motor, and the third failure of a finding rune.

"Are you sure my magic isn't getting weaker?" Alex asked over a mouthful of fish. He tried to sound nonchalant, but the thought still scared him. "Maybe whatever is happening is affecting my mind and that's why the rune can't make the link."

He thought Iggy would rush to tell him he was off base, but his mentor just sat sipping his tea and thinking.

"No," he said at last. "You haven't been having any more problems you aren't telling me about, though? Forgetting things or getting confused?"

"Not any more than usual," Alex said.

"You sleeping all right?"

Alex picked up his dishes and moved to the sink.

"It's been harder lately," he admitted.

"Maybe you're tired," Iggy said.

"You ever have to work tired in the navy?"

Iggy chuckled at that.

"All the time," he said. "Still, maybe you should turn in early tonight. A good night's sleep wouldn't go amiss in any case."

Alex didn't want to admit Iggy was right, but the moment the old man suggested bed, he felt bone weary. It was if the very idea made him tired.

"All right." he agreed, filling the sink with soapy water. "I'll go as soon as I'm done here."

Iggy slapped him on the shoulder.

"Good lad."

He looked like he wanted to say more, but was interrupted by the door bell. Iggy went to answer the door, but he was back in a moment.

"Lieutenant Callahan is back," he said. "I left him in the library."

Alex dried his hands and found the big lieutenant standing in front of the bookcase to the left of the fireplace. He was scanning titles on the books and Alex watched as his eyes slid over a green leather-bound book and the thin red volume next to it. Both books had powerful runes on them that caused people to overlook them. The green book possessed them because Alex had hollowed it out to keep his emergency stash of money, and the red book because it was the most powerful and dangerous rune book ever written — the Archimedean Monograph.

"Is this a social call, Lieutenant?" Alex asked as he entered the room, "or has our ghost struck again?"

Callahan turned from the shelf and he didn't look happy.

"That was some stunt you pulled at Central Office," he said.

Alex smirked and shrugged his shoulders.

"I figure it was that or let Detweiler throw me in the cooler," he said.

"I don't give a damn if you spend the night in the tank," Callahan growled. "Don't you ever use my name to get yourself out of a jam, you hear me? I have to work with Detweiler and now his beef with you is splashin' on me."

Alex held up his hand in a gesture of peace. He knew when he pitted Detweiler against Callahan's reputation earlier that the Lieutenant wouldn't be happy about it. Still, from his perspective it was better than testing the limits of how long Detweiler could hold him without charging him with a crime.

"I read you, Lieutenant," Alex said.

Callahan considered that for a moment, then nodded his acceptance.

"Is that why you came by?" Alex asked.

"No," Callahan growled. "Thanks to your little stunt, Detweiler's been beefing to Captain Rooney. Now you're officially persona-non-grata at the Central Office. Rooney ordered me to come down here and tell you to stay the hell away from this case."

Alex shrugged at that.

"That's okay, Callahan," he said. "Detweiler may not be quick on the uptake but he's just got to find out how your victims are connected. I'd just be in the way."

Callahan gave Alex a long hard look but didn't say anything.

"What?" Alex asked.

"I thought you were smarter than that, Lockerby," Callahan said. "Sure, Detweiler's going to get off the widow as a suspect soon, but how many more people are going to die before he gets on the right track? I didn't become a cop for the glamour, scribbler, I did it to protect people."

Alex hadn't considered that. It wasn't his job to keep maniacs from running amok in the streets, after all. People hired him, and he did what they paid him for. If he did his job right, no one usually got killed.

"Talk to the Captain if you feel that way about it," Alex said. "Fifth Division is the best he's got and he knows it. Have him give the ghost case to you."

"I can't," Callahan growled. "Detweiler's wife is Rooney's favorite niece. The Captain gives him all the breaks."

Alex nodded, starting to see Callahan's problem.

"And while Detweiler is stumbling around in the dark, the ghost is free to go on killing."

Callahan nodded.

"So, what can I do about it?" Alex asked. "According to the Captain, I'm off the case."

"The Captain can't stop you from helping David Watson's widow."

"She won't be a suspect much longer," Alex said. "She probably won't want to pay me once the police are officially looking for her husband's killer."

"Persuade her," Callahan said.

Alex sighed. This ghost killer business had already ruined his link to the police and made him look ridiculous in the tabloids. If he pursued it and didn't catch the ghost, he'd have egg on his face in front of the whole city. The tabloids would make him a laughing stock.

On the other hand, if he got the guy, he'd be a hero. The tabloids would print his name in big letters and make him out to be the best detective since Sherlock Holmes. That would bring in business.

"All right, Lieutenant," he said with a resigned sigh. "I'll go see Anne Watson tomorrow and get going, assuming I can find her."

"She's staying at the Waldorf," Callahan said.

That explained why Leslie hadn't been able to find Anne; the Waldorf was in the Core, and very expensive. Alex told Leslie to look at Inner-Ring hotels, figuring Anne wouldn't want to spend the money on one in the Core. Apparently he was wrong.

"Well, at least she can afford my fee," Alex said without humor. "She can get me access to her place, but what about the other crime scenes? Can you get me any of the files?"

Callahan scoffed at that.

"I'm risking my job the longer I stand here," he growled, putting his hat back on. "You're supposed to be some hot-shot detective — so detect."

He moved to the vestibule and opened the door, looking back at Alex.

"It goes without saying that if you find anything, I'm your first phone call."

"Scout's honor, Lieutenant," Alex said. He didn't bother to mention that he'd never been a scout.

9

THE LEGWORK

I t was a quarter past nine in the morning when Alex got off at the crawler station across from the Waldorf hotel. He'd gone to bed early, just like he promised Iggy, but he felt like he hadn't slept a wink.

The way his day was shaping up, he needed that sleep. Since the Waldorf wasn't too far out of his way, Alex decided to stop there first. As he entered the sumptuous lobby, he remembered that he still had Leslie calling hotels looking for the widow Watson.

A row of phone booths stood against the side of the lobby and Alex made for them. When he fished a nickel out of his pocket, his hands shook badly enough that he had trouble dropping it in the slot. It was then he remembered Jessica and the flask of elixir.

"How could I forget her?" he asked himself, pulling the flask out of his jacket pocket and taking a swig. A moment later he wished he *had* forgotten. Jessica's elixir tasted like dishwater.

Shuddering as he forced it down, Alex capped the flask and put it back in his pocket. He was supposed to take another shot at noon and he was already dreading it.

In the time it took him to put the flask away, the trembling in his hands had subsided and he easily dropped the nickel for the call into the phone's slot.

"Lockerby Investigations," Leslie said after the operator connected them.

"It's me," Alex said. "I wanted to—"

"It's about time," Leslie interrupted in a harried whisper. "Where are you?"

Alex explained about his visit from Callahan and going to see Anne Watson.

"So I called to tell you not to look for her anymore," he finished.

"I haven't been looking," Leslie said, her voice indignant. "Do you have any idea what's been going on here?"

Alex admitted that he didn't; in fact, he had no idea why she seemed so upset.

"I have an office full of people here," she said. "And those are just the ones that insisted on waiting for you."

"What do they want?"

"They all read that story in the tabloids about the Runewright Detective," Leslie explained. "They're all here to get charms or wards to protect them from the ghost. One woman claims the ghost is living in her attic and wants you to drive him out."

Alex laughed. He couldn't help himself.

"Oh, real funny," Leslie growled at him in a dangerous voice.

"Sorry, doll," he said, managing to put on a straight face. "Tell you what, how would you like to close the office for the morning?"

"I can't," she said. "There might be some paying customers who come in and I'd like to eat next week."

Alex remembered the money Andrew Barton had given him, patting his pocket to make sure it was still there.

"Don't worry about that," Alex said. "I need you to go over to the library and look up everyone the ghost has killed. All but one of them are society swells so they'll be in Who's Who."

"What about eating?" Leslie wondered.

"I've got fifty bucks in my pocket right now," Alex said. "Swing by the Waldorf on your way downtown and pick it up. I'll leave it at the front desk for you."

There was a long pause on the line.

"You on the level?" she asked.

Alex was shocked. Leslie had never questioned whether he was telling her the truth before. He was really going to have to make all this up to her.

"My word as a gentleman," he said.

"Try again."

"I swear on a bottle of twelve-year-old scotch?"

"Aw, you do care," she said, her voice returning to its playful self. "How'd you dig up that much cash?"

Alex told her about his visit to Barton and his missing traction motor.

"When are you going to work on that?" she asked.

Alex sighed.

"Right after I figure out who kidnapped Leroy Cunningham and catch a murdering ghost," he said.

"Good luck then. I'll be at the library."

Alex hung up, then went to front desk and got an envelope from the clerk. He slipped the fifty dollars into it, sealed it, and wrote Leslie's name on it before leaving it with the man.

THE WIDOW WATSON looked much better when she answered the door. Her dark eyes weren't red, and her makeup wasn't running. Alex had been right, she was quite pretty when properly made up.

"I was beginning to worry," she said, inviting Alex in. "I thought you weren't going to come."

"I'm sorry about that," Alex said, taking his hat off. "No one told me where you were."

Anne apologized for that and invited Alex to sit down. The hotel room had a parlor that was separate from the bedroom, with elegant couches, a writing desk, and a fireplace.

"Would you like a drink?" she offered.

Alex accepted and noticed that she poured herself one as well.

"I don't know what to do with myself, Mr. Lockerby," she said, sitting on the couch opposite the one Alex occupied. "It seems like some horrible dream, like I'm going to wake up any minute and everything will be fine. Like David will come walking in through that door."

Alex didn't know what to say. He'd heard that same sentiment, more or less, from dozens of people over his career. He'd felt it himself when Father Harry died; still, there just weren't easy words that would make everything better.

"I think that the police won't be bothering you much longer," Alex said.

"What if they come to arrest me?" Her voice was fearful and small.

"If that happens, call your lawyer. He'll take care of you."

She wrapped her arms around herself as if she were cold, and nodded.

"Do you have someone who could come here and stay with you?" Alex asked.

"Yes," she admitted.

"Good," Alex said, finishing his drink and setting it aside. "Call them up. I don't think you should be alone right now."

Anne nodded, and she looked more hopeful.

"Do you still want me to find whoever killed your husband?" Alex asked.

"Yes I do," she said, without hesitation. "It's clear I can't count on the police and I want whoever did this punished."

"All right," Alex said, rising and indicating the writing desk. "Then I need you to write out a letter giving me permission to be in your home and to search your husband's business files."

"I gave you one of those," she said.

"This one needs to say specifically that I can come and go at your house whenever I want and that I can go through your husband's files," Alex explained. "The police might still be there, and I don't want trouble."

Anne rose and crossed to the desk.

"Why do you want to look into David's business?" she asked as she began writing.

"Because whoever killed him killed those other people the same way. There must be a connection between them."

"I can't imagine what it would be," she said. "David's been retired for almost ten years."

"Let me worry about that," Alex said.

Anne finished writing the letter, blotted the ink dry and handed it to Alex. She also reached into her pocket and withdrew a twenty.

"Is this enough to get you started?" she asked. "I ran out of the house without much cash and I haven't had a chance to go to the bank."

"This will do fine," Alex said, accepting the money. "I'll call you as soon as I know anything."

THE ARCHITECTURAL FIRM OF MILTON & White was located on the twenty-second floor of a skyscraper in the south side Mid-Ring. It was a large open area where men at drafting tables worked. Displays with models of buildings were spread throughout the room, mostly professional buildings with a few houses. No one here seemed like the kind of person anyone would kidnap.

"I don't know what I can tell you, Mr. Lockerby," Phillip Milton told Alex. He was a tall slender man in his fifties wearing a pinstripe suit that had the unfortunate effect of making him look even thinner. "Leroy Cunningham is one of my best people, but he hasn't been here all week. If he was kidnapped, as you say, then why haven't the police been here?"

"They've got their hands full with that ghost thing," Alex said. It was quicker than explaining the ins and outs of how the police handled missing persons cases, which was that they didn't unless the person missing had an Inner-Ring or Core address. "Is there anything Leroy was working on that a kidnapper might want to know about?" Alex went on, "a bank building or something like that?"

"No, nothing like that," Milton said. He took off his spectacles and nervously cleaned them with his handkerchief. "We mostly do small commercial buildings. I mean, we have done a few fancy homes, but there's nothing unusual in their design."

"Would you mind if I looked at whatever Leroy has been working on?"

"Not at all."

Milton led Alex to a drafting table with what looked like the design for a train station on it.

"Leroy is designing this?" Alex asked.

"Oh, no," Milton said. "Leroy is an apprentice draftsman." He picked up a paper with numbers and math written out on it. "These are the specifications that Leroy is using to draw out the plans."

"Did you know he was going to school to become an architect?" Alex asked.

Milton brightened up at that.

"Of course," he said. "The firm is paying for his schooling."

Alex was impressed; for a company to pay for their employee to go to school meant they really liked him.

Unless they didn't.

"Is he doing well?"

"Oh, yes," Milton said. "He makes excellent marks. Of course he was already a good draftsman when we hired him. I do hope you find him."

Something about that tickled at Alex's mind, but he couldn't put his finger on exactly what.

"Is there anything else I can do for you, Mr. Lockerby?" Milton asked, picking up the drawing and the papers from Leroy's desk. "I've got to get this work to someone else to finish and we're really quite busy."

"No, go ahead," Alex said. "Thanks for your help."

Milton moved to a nearby desk and began explaining the train station drawing to a bespectacled draftsman with a pencil mustache.

"One more thing, Mr. Milton," Alex said. "Could I look at Leroy's résumé paper?"

"Uh, yes," Milton said over his shoulder. "Just ask our receptionist."

Alex thanked him and made his way back to the little blonde at the front of the office. She had a round face and frizzy hair that blossomed over her head like a halo.

"Done with the boss?" she asked, smiling when Alex walked up.

"Yes, he was a big help. He said you'd be able to get me Mr. Cunningham's résumé?"

She smiled and nodded, then went to a filing cabinet against the wall and dug through it.

"Here you go, honey," she said, handing Alex a paper folder with the name Leroy Cunningham printed on it.

Alex paged through it slowly. According to Leroy, he had learned drafting as the Assistant Safety Engineer for the Coaldale Mining Company. That matched what his wife Hannah said. There was a drawing Leroy had done of what looked like the machinery for an elevator as well. Alex didn't know anything about drafting but the elevator looked competently done.

"What does an Assistant Safety Engineer do?" he said out loud.

"No idea, honey," the receptionist said.

Alex's stomach rumbled at him and he looked up at the big clock over the blonde's head. It read twelve-fifty-three. He'd missed breakfast, it was past lunch, and he'd forgotten his elixir again. The thought of facing the elixir without something in his stomach made him queasy, though.

"Is there a café or a lunch counter near here?"

"Sure," the receptionist said. "Down in the lobby there's a good place."

"Thanks," Alex said, handing Leroy's folder back to her.

———

ALEX CALLED his office a half hour later and was surprised when Leslie picked up.

"Back from the library so soon?" he asked.

"If you didn't think I was here, why did you call?" she noted.

He heard the click of the touch-tip lighter on her desk and the sound of her inhaling. She'd used her money to buy cigarettes. He'd just spent most of his pocket money on a dry sandwich and this phone call.

For a long moment, he was jealous. He still had the twenty dollars from Anne Watson, he reminded himself. Of course he needed that to pay Leslie, so he couldn't very well use it to buy smokes.

"Did you find out anything about the ghost's victims?"

"Yeah," she said. "The ghost's first victim was Seth Kowalski; he made a killing selling farmland out in Suffolk County to rich people wanting to build summer homes."

"The Hamptons?"

"Yep," Leslie said. "You see, he was the County Assessor up there for years, so he knew the whole area. When the rich and famous started looking for a place to build mansions, he bought up everything he could get his hands on and made a killing."

"Interesting," Alex said. "Mr. Watson was a builder and there was surveying equipment in his display case in his den."

"I don't know about that," Leslie said, "but you'll never guess where Watson's company built their first house?"

"Suffolk County?" Alex guessed.

"Got it in one."

"How about the others?" Alex asked.

"So far they don't seem to have any connections to Watson or Kowalski," Leslie said. "Betsy Phillips was killed second. She had money of her own, but I can't tell where it came from. Her husband, George, is a stock broker."

"One of the survivors," Alex said.

"Last was Martin Pride," Leslie read off her notes. "Get this, he died poor, but he used to be rich. Lost his money in the market crash."

Alex nodded as he made notes, even though Leslie couldn't see him through the phone.

"So they were all rich at one point," Alex said. "So if they're connected, it must be before Pride lost all of his dough. Is there anything else?"

"Nope," Leslie said, puffing loudly on her cigarette to rub it in. "That's all I could find this morning. Now I'm back here in the circus."

"Are we still getting people wanting magic charms?"

"Yes," Leslie said, tension returning to her voice. "Some of them are very insistent. I think you should just make up a rune and sell it to them for a buck."

Alex laughed.

"Oh, Lieutenant Detweiler would love to be able to pick me up for selling snake oil," he said.

"Well you need to wrap this case up quick, then," Leslie said. "I'm not going to be able to get much done, what with it's being Grand Central Station in here."

That gave Alex an idea.

"Speaking of Grand Central," he said. "I need to find out if Kowalski and Watson knew each other when Kowalski was County Assessor."

"You want me to call over to the Suffolk County Hall of Records and find out?"

"I don't see how that's going to help," Alex said. "What I need is for someone to go out there and talk to the current assessor, ask around town, that sort of thing."

"Are you asking me to get out of the city and go upstate?" Leslie purred through the line.

"You'll have to spend some of that scratch I got you," Alex warned.

"It'll be worth it," she said. "I'm looking up the train schedule right now. You want me to go first thing in the morning?"

"No," Alex said. "Go today and you can and stay the night. That'll give you time to ask around. Call Iggy if you find out anything urgent," Alex said.

"What about the circus?" she asked.

"Take down everyone's name and what they want and we'll figure it out once the rest of this is wrapped up."

"You're the boss."

Alex wished her Godspeed and hung up. This Suffolk County thing felt like a lead. It was too coincidental that two of the victims had been involved in land deals up on the Captain back in the day. Still, he was going to have to pay for Leslie's trip, lead or not.

"Time to track down the Lightning Lord's missing motor," he said.

THE BUILDING from which Barton's motor had been stolen turned out to be an unassuming building in the west side's Mid-Ring. Inside it, men labored at a wide variety of machines, turning out strange-looking parts that were then taken to one of several large areas where machines were being assembled.

Alex recognized a nearly-complete Mark V Etherium Capacitor in one corner. As close as it appeared to completion, however, no one seemed to be working on it. All the activity seemed to be directed in another space where over a dozen men were assembling parts for something that had yet to take shape.

"You Lockerby?" a big-shouldered man in a brown suit asked when he noticed Alex watching.

Alex pulled out one of his business cards and handed it over. The big man had dark eyes and hair with a square jaw and bushy eyebrows. His skin was browner than simply being in the sun could account for, marking him as being of Latin descent. The accent, however, was all Jersey.

"Mr. Barton said you'd be coming by," he said. "I'm Jimmy Cortez, floor manager here at Barton Electric. The boss told me to take ya around and answer any questions you have."

He stuck out a massive paw of a hand and Alex shook it.

"What are they building here?" Alex asked, pointing at the rush of activity.

"That's the new traction motor, to replace the one that got pinched," Jimmy said. "Between you and me, Mr. Lockerby, I hope you find the old one real soon. I'm not sure we can get this done in time."

Alex watched as a man in coveralls finished grinding a curved piece of metal and hurried it over to a man with spectacles and rolled-up shirt sleeves. The bespectacled man tuned the part over in his hands, then consulted a blueprint that had been unrolled over a table and weighed down with bits of scrap metal. After a moment with the blueprint, the man placed the curved bit next to a neat row of parts on the floor. By the time he was done, another man in a coverall had another bit for him.

"Looks like you've got it well in hand," Alex said, turning back to Jimmy. "Barton said this motor weighs about six hundred pounds, is that right?"

Jimmy thought about that for a second, then nodded.

"Give or take," he said.

"How did a thief manage to steal it then? I mean that would take time and a crew, right?"

"Ordinarily, yeah," Jimmy said. "There's always people here, day and night, and we've got security guards in the warehouse area and the loadin' dock."

"You didn't answer my question though," Alex said. "How was the motor stolen?"

"The guy was good, Mr. Lockerby," Alex said. "He walked right into the dock just as the motor was loaded on a truck and drove it away."

"Where were the driver and the security guard?"

"Once the trucks are loaded, the driver has to inspect the load and sign out the truck," Jimmy explained. "He was in the office doing that when the truck drove away, and the guard was at the other side of the dock walkin' his route."

That seemed like exceptionally good timing on the part of the thief.

He must have watched the dock, figured out the pattern, and then waited for his opportunity.

"Who knew your shipping schedule?" Alex asked.

"You mean when the motor was goin' out? Just me and the dock manager," he said. "Oh, and Mr. Barton, of course."

"Mind if I take a look at the loading dock?" Alex asked.

Jimmy escorted him over to the other side of the building to where a cement dock stuck out from a set of carriage doors. A small shack stood on the far side and Alex could see a man working at a desk inside.

"That's Bill Gustavsen," Jimmy said. "He runs the loadin' dock."

The lot beyond the dock was paved and enclosed by a high fence. It was large enough to accommodate parking for several trucks. One bearing the name Barton Electric on the door was parked up against the fence on the far side. To the left was an opening big enough for a truck to exit that led out to the street.

"Did your security guard report seeing anyone loitering around in the days leading up to the theft?"

Jimmy shook his head.

"No. We sometimes have to run drunks or vagrants out, so he checks when he goes by. But he didn't see nobody."

Alex thanked him, and Jimmy returned to overseeing the building of Barton's replacement motor. Alex stood on the dock for five minutes before he crossed to the other side and knocked on the open door of the little shack.

"Yes?" Bill Gustavsen said, looking up from his desk. He was older, in his fifties if Alex had to guess, with white hair and a skinny frame. He wore trousers and a white shirt with a tie. His sleeves were rolled up and held in place by garters with his suit coat draped over the back of his chair in the August heat.

Alex introduced himself, and explained why he was there.

"I don't know what more I can tell you," Gustavsen said. "I was in here signing out the truck to the driver when it just drove away. It was the damnedest thing I've ever seen."

"I was outside for quite a while," Alex said, jerking his thumb over his shoulder at the dock. "I didn't see your security guard come by at all."

Gustavsen chuckled at that.

"No more deliveries are due today," he said. "The guard only patrols when we're working here at the dock. Otherwise he comes by every half-hour."

"How often do shipments go out of here?"

"Out?" Gustavsen said. "Every other day or so. We ship out receivers for wireless power along with replacement parts for the Etherium Capacitors and anything else Mr. Barton might need."

"Doesn't seem like enough work for a full-time dock manager?"

Gustavsen bristled at that.

"Shows what you know," he said. "We get deliveries every single day. It's my job to inspect everything, inventory it, and make sure it's stored properly. I also make sure all our outgoing shipments are right." He puffed up like a toad and thumped his chest. "In the twenty years I've been here, there's never been a bum shipment...not until the motor was stolen."

Alex asked him who knew about the shipments in advance, and he gave the same answers Jimmy had.

"Is that the truck that was taken?" Alex asked, pointing to the lone vehicle in the lot.

"No," Gustavsen said. "That's the spare. The police have been looking for the truck, but it's still missing too."

Alex wondered if there were any way to use the finding rune on the missing truck and find the motor that way. Unfortunately he'd need something connected to the truck and everything that fit that bill was likely to be on the truck itself.

"What about the driver?" he asked. "Does he usually drive the missing truck?"

"No," Gustavsen said. "We have a contract with the Teamsters. They provide our drivers."

Foiled, Alex thanked Gustavsen and descended the stairs to the paved dock. He walked up to the opening in the fence and looked both ways.

The lot emptied onto a side street that ran between the factory and a clothing mill next door. There wasn't a good vantage point to watch the loading dock from anywhere on the street, no place that the security guard wouldn't have seen.

There was a narrow alley between the mill and whatever was behind it. Alex crossed the street and peered down the space. It ran along the mill until it intercepted the next side street. Boxes and crates were stacked behind some of the buildings on the opposite side and trash was strewn along the ground.

Alex examined the ground around the entrance, looking for signs of surveillance. If anyone had been watching the Barton Electric loading dock, they cleaned up after themselves. There were no cigarette butts or apple cores to be found.

He was about to leave, but suddenly wondered, *What if the surveillance might have been a team? The crates just up the alley would be a perfect place to sit while your partner watches the dock.*

He walked down the alley to the crates and examined the ground but found nothing tell-tale there either. Cursing, he straightened up and shook his head. At this rate he'd never find Barton's motor, and that meant he couldn't pay for Leslie's trip upstate. He had a feeling that the widow Watson wouldn't want to pay either if he didn't find the ghost.

Turning back to the street, Alex wished he had found some cigarette butts; after all, one of them might be long enough to smoke.

He was chuckling grimly at his own dire circumstances when a shot rang out and a bullet slammed into his back. It hit him on the lower right side, near the kidney and the sudden impact caused him to stumble.

As Alex tried to catch his balance, three more shots rang out. Two hit him in the upper back and he lost his balance. The third shot skimmed his hip as he went down and distracted him enough that instead of catching himself, he landed on his face.

The impact stunned him and he was vaguely aware of someone rolling him over and ransacking his pockets before taking his red-backed rune book and running off.

10

THE ENGINEER

Alex's pocketwatch showed two-thirty when he used it to open the door to the brownstone and limped inside. The shield runes he'd written on the inside of his suit jacket had saved his life, slowing the bullets enough that they wouldn't penetrate. That said, he still felt like someone had worked him over with a Louisville Slugger.

His hip was another story.

The bullet had hit below the protection of his jacket, scraping a trough out of his flesh. Fortunately it had only grazed him, but he still bled like a stuck pig. By the time he got home, his pant leg was wet with blood and the handkerchief he was pressing against the wound was saturated.

"Iggy," he called from the tiled floor of the brownstone's vestibule. "I'm bleeding, bring your vault rune."

Even though Alex knew how to write cleaning runes now, he didn't want to waste them on the Persian carpets that covered the floor between the vestibule and the kitchen if he didn't have to.

"What happened?" Iggy said, hurrying down the stairs from the direction of his room. He was dressed for the evening in just his shirt and slacks with a smoking jacket over top and slippers on his feet.

"Somebody took a shot at me," Alex said, holding up his blood-soaked handkerchief. "Several shots, in fact."

"How bad?" Iggy said, tracing a door on the wall with a piece of chalk he took from the pocket of his smoking jacket.

"I took three in the back, but the shield runes stopped those. One took a bite out of my leg but it doesn't look too deep."

"It's bleeding enough to be serious," Iggy said, lighting a vault rune. "You feeling light-headed?"

"No."

Iggy opened his vault and motioned Alex inside.

"What happened to your face?" he asked as he directed Alex to the table in the middle of his operating theater room.

Alex touched his forehead and felt the bump there. He'd forgotten about that.

"The shots took me by surprise," he admitted. "I fell on my face. Damn near knocked me out."

"Can you take off your trousers?" Iggy asked as he rummaged through one of his cabinets full of potions.

Alex unbuckled his trousers and let them fall to the floor. It was better than letting Iggy cut them off as it would take less magic to repair.

"Here." Iggy handed him a small vial of red liquid.

Alex drank it and handed back the container.

"And this for that black eye," he said, pressing a small square of flash paper to Alex's eyelid. "Hold still," he said, taking out a cigarette case and his lighter. A moment later he touched the smoldering end of the cigarette to the rune paper. It flashed and Alex resisted the urge to jerk back. He felt a tingling spreading out over the right side of his face and he knew the rune was taking effect.

Iggy examined the gash in Alex's hip.

"Not too bad," he said, getting out his sewing kit. "Now, lie on the table and tell me what happened."

"I was looking into Andrew Barton's missing motor," Alex said, laying on his side with his hip in the air. "It was stolen from the loading dock of his factory right after it had been put on a truck."

"Convenient," Iggy said, using a cotton ball to dab an ice-cold liquid on the wound. Alex winced as he began sewing it up, but the cold had penetrated into the gash and he couldn't feel the needle.

"That's what I thought," Alex said. "Whoever did it had a window of about a minute to get in and get out with the truck. I figured they were watching from the alley across the street, so I checked it out."

"Find anything?"

"Nope," Alex said. "From what I can tell you can't even see the loading dock from that alley. I was just about to leave when someone shot me in the back and stole my rune book."

"It's probably a good thing you fell on your face then," Iggy said. "If the man who shot you had realized you weren't really hurt, he'd have shot you in the head for good measure."

Alex hadn't considered that. His clumsy stumble might just have saved his life.

"Did you see the back-shooting coward?" Iggy asked, washing the stitches with iodine.

"Just his arm," Alex said. "The rest was a bit...blurry."

"You were dazed. Was there anything distinct about the shooter's arm? What did his footsteps sound like when he ran? Did you smell anything?"

Alex searched his memory. He hadn't heard the shooter approach. The first sign of his presence was when he turned Alex over. His face swam, blurrily into Alex's minds-eye but the only detail he could clearly see was a mop of black hair.

"What happened next?" Iggy probed as Alex recounted the memory.

"He searched my jacket pockets. I remember seeing his arm. His skin was brown."

"Asian maybe, or Latin," Iggy said.

"He had a mark on his wrist," Alex said, struggling to remember. "A tattoo."

"What did it look like?"

"It had a face looking up toward his body."

"Was it a person?"

Alex shook his head.

"No, it was...it was square," Alex said, focusing on the image in his mind. "Like something from the funny papers."

"Was it colorful?" Iggy asked.

"No, it was in that blue ink most tattoo artists use." Alex shook his head and the vision vanished. "That's it."

Iggy picked up Alex's sopping trousers and wrapped them in a towel.

"I'll let you handle these," he said, handing the towel to Alex.

"I lost my rune book."

Iggy gave him an unamused look.

"If you haven't taken the simple precaution of preparing a spare, then go to my table and write a cleaning rune and a restoration rune. I'd like to see how steady your hands are."

Alex sighed and left the bloody towel on the operating table. He moved to Iggy's runewright lab, with the doctor in tow, and sat down at the writing table.

"So, who do you think shot you?" Iggy asked as Alex drew a minor restoration rune.

"Someone who doesn't want Barton to get his motor back," Alex said, showing the rune to Iggy for approval.

"Yes, yes, you can draw simple runes," he said, setting it aside. "Now the cleaning rune if you please."

Alex set to work on the much more complicated of the pair.

"You said the prize for this railroad contest is a million dollars, right?"

"Yeah," Alex muttered, concentrating.

"Well, men have certainly killed for much less. How did the shooter know you were investigating?"

"Well," Alex said, his hand moving slowly as he traced in the delicate details of the cleaning rune. "I'm guessing someone at Barton's warehouse called them when I showed up there." He remembered Jimmy Cortez saying that Barton had called and told him to expect Alex. "Maybe before."

"So you think the theft was an inside job?"

"The timing was exact," Alex said. "The thief walked into the dock just as the driver and the security guard were out of sight. That's much easier when someone tips you off."

"I agree," Iggy said as Alex finished. He held up the rune to the light for a long minute. "Good enough," he said, passing it back to Alex. "You need more practice, though."

"Maybe someone will shoot me tomorrow," Alex said with a sardonic smile.

"Perish the thought."

Alex and Iggy left the vault and went through the kitchen to the door that led to the brownstone's tiny, walled-in back yard. Once there, Alex stuck the cleaning rune to his trousers and held his breath as he activated the rune. Blood and dirt burst into powder and swirled away down the alley, leaving his pants still torn, but clean.

"Adequately done," Iggy said once Alex had come back inside. "Practice and you'll be able to work the restoration rune and the cleaning rune together. Saves time."

Alex ignored him, setting the towel aside and sticking the restoration rune to the tear in his trousers. He lit the rune and the torn fabric wove itself back together as if it had never been damaged.

"So how goes the case of the missing husband?" Iggy said as Alex put his pants back on.

"I went by his work this morning," Alex said, describing his conversation with Leroy's boss. "It doesn't sound like whoever grabbed Leroy wants him for his drafting abilities, and they don't do any confidential work there."

"You're sure he's not heir to some secret fortune?" Iggy asked, tapping his cigarette into an ashtray on the kitchen table.

"Not likely," Alex said. "He grew up in a coal town in West Virginia." He sighed and sat down next to Iggy. "The only thing I can figure is that whatever the kidnappers want, it must be something from Leroy's past. There just isn't anything in his present."

"Well," Iggy said, puffing on the cigarette. "I've always said that if you remove the impossible, whatever is left must be the truth."

Alex rubbed his face, which felt better already. Iggy's cigarette was bugging him, though. He wanted one pretty badly.

"I hate it when you quote yourself."

Iggy chuckled, taking another puff as if to spite Alex.

"Be that as it may, what will you do now?"

Alex looked at the clock. It was after three, but there was still plenty of daylight left.

"Do you know what an Assistant Mining Engineer does?" he asked.

"No," Iggy admitted. "What's that?"

"Leroy's job back in Coledale."

"Well, if that's a mining job, there must be someone here in town that can tell you. Maybe someone in the coal industry or a supplier of mining equipment."

"Not a bad idea," Alex said. "I'll call Leslie and have her...oh."

"What is it?"

"I sent Leslie out to Suffolk County to run down a lead in the ghost case." Alex thought for a moment, then got up and went to the phone. "Ralph's Building Supply," he told the operator. Alex had helped Ralph deal with some vandals a few years ago and now Ralph gave him tools or hardware at cost.

"Ralph, it's Alex," he said once the operator connected them. "No, I don't need any tools this time, but I've got a question for you. Is there anyone in town who makes gear for mining?"

A few minutes later Alex hung up, having scribbled the address of a mining supply manufacturer in his notebook.

"How many shield runes are left in your coat?" Iggy asked as Alex headed for the door.

"Three," Alex said, putting on his hat.

"Try not to get shot again."

MASTERSON TOOL and Die was on the south side in a four-story office building attached to a factory and warehouse. A perky receptionist with black hair in a pixie cut greeted him when he entered the lobby and asked, very politely, what she could help Alex with.

"I need to see somebody that knows about coal mining," he said.

"Did you have specific questions about our tools?"

Alex handed her his card.

"It's about someone who's been kidnapped," he said. "I just need a few minutes with someone who knows about mining."

She looked at Alex as if she wasn't sure if he was serious, but decided after a minute that he was. She picked up the phone and spoke into it for a minute.

"Mr. Sanderson is our lead engineer," she said. "He'll be down in a minute if you care to wait."

Alex thanked her and took a seat in one of the overstuffed chairs in the lobby. Almost exactly one minute later, the elevator door opened and a large man with short brown hair got off. He wasn't just tall, he had a bigness about his frame that spoke of an athlete's body gone soft. His hands were rough, the hands of a man who'd done physical work. His face was lined, with a strong, Roman nose and brown eyes.

"Mr. Sanderson?" Alex said, standing up.

"What's this about?" Sanderson said, sticking out his massive hand.

Alex explained about Leroy Cunningham and his life in Coaldale.

"Could someone have grabbed Leroy because they needed help digging a tunnel?"

Sanderson thought for a moment, then shook his head.

"If he was the engineer, maybe," he said. "All the assistant safety engineer does is keep the records of the inspections and draw out where the tunnels go."

"So that's where he learned how to be a draftsman," Alex said. "But he wouldn't know anything about how to dig a mine."

Sanderson shrugged.

"He might," he said. "If he worked in the mine before he became the assistant engineer."

"How much could he really know?" Alex asked.

"At his age, not much," Sanderson said. "If whoever took him needed to understand mine safety reports, he'd be the guy."

"Well, thank you for your time, Mr. Sanderson," Alex said, sticking out his hand.

Sanderson shook it.

"Good luck finding Leroy," he said. He started to turn away but stopped and turned back. "Let me know if you find him."

Alex promised that he would, then put his notebook in his pocket and headed for the street. It just didn't make any sense, someone grabbing Leroy. He wasn't worth any money, he didn't design banks, and he knew virtually nothing about mining beyond the safety reports.

It didn't track. The people who took him had a reason, but he just wasn't seeing it.

HALF AN HOUR LATER, Alex opened his vault on the wall of his office. He took off his coat and draped it over his writing desk. On the inside, running down the back on either side of the seam, were three shield runes. Each one was formed from a triskaidecagon with a triangle on the top point and circles and diamonds alternating the rest of the way around. The circles had symbols in them defining resistance while the diamonds bore radiant symbols. Inside the center was a rune that looked a little like a fountain wearing a hat.

Each construct was done in silver ink with diamond ink for the rune at the center and alternating sapphire and gold ink for the symbols inside circle and diamond shapes.

Alex laid out the inks and the special pens needed to use them, then paced around his vault, going over the process for writing the complex construct in his mind. One of the reasons he'd come here, to his office, was that he didn't want Iggy kibbitzing while he worked. The rune was already one of the most complex he knew.

He checked his hands and found them shaking a bit, though whether that meant the elixir was wearing off or he was just nervous was impossible to tell. Taking the flask out of his pocket, he took a shot of the noxious stuff and put it back.

"All right," he said out loud. "Time to get to work."

He was grateful a moment later when the phone on his desk rang.

"Lockerby Investigations," he said once he'd reached it.

"Hey, I'm glad I caught you," Leslie said. "I found something you're going to want to hear."

Alex perked up immediately.

"Give it up," he encouraged.

"Not only did David Watson and Seth Kowalski know each other, but Watson worked as a surveyor in the assessor's office when Kowalski ran the place."

That was a definite connection.

"Great work, doll," Alex said, finally feeling like he was getting somewhere with the ghost.

"There's more," Leslie said. Alex could hear the mischievous energy in her voice. "I had Randall, he's the current assessor, look through their employment records and you'll never guess what he found."

"Randall?" Alex said with a smirk he was sure Leslie could hear. Leslie was a serious beauty and she had a bad habit of wrapping men around her little finger, especially when he wanted them to do boring things like comb through records for her.

"Yes, Randall," she purred. "Now are you going to guess what he found or not?"

"Watson's not the only one who worked for Kowalski?"

"Got it in one," Leslie said. "Betsy Phillips was Kowalski's clerk back in the day."

"How much do you want to bet if Randall looks for the name Martin Pride, he'll find him too?"

Leslie laughed.

"No bet," she said.

"While he's digging, have your beau look up the names of everyone who worked in that office when Kowalski ran the place. Five will get you ten that some of those people are on our ghost's hit list."

"I'll take care of it in the morning," Leslie said. "Right now Randall and I are going to dinner."

"Have fun," Alex said before hanging up.

Now he had a definite connection between most of the ghost's victims. Whatever these killings were about, it had to do with the Suffolk County Assessor's Office.

"Now all we have to do is find out who hated Kowalski and his crew enough to still want to kill them thirty years after the fact."

11

THE LUNCH BOX

Alex sat at the massive oak dining table in the brownstone's kitchen sipping his third cup of coffee.

It wasn't helping.

"You look terrible," Iggy said. He was dressed in his heavy dungarees and a work shirt, his usual attire for puttering with his orchids in the greenhouse.

"I didn't sleep a wink," Alex muttered. "None of these cases make any sense and if I don't solve at least one of them, I won't be able to pay Leslie. She'll quit and then everything will go straight to Hell."

"Don't forget that if you don't solve this ghost business, the police will never work with you again," Iggy chuckled. Alex gave him a sour look but then nodded.

"And if I don't find Leroy in the next few days, he's probably a dead man," Alex said.

Iggy's smile disappeared, and he sighed, looking weary himself.

"Steady on, lad," he said. "Work your leads and I dare say you'll figure it out."

"What if I don't?" Alex said, setting his empty cup aside. "How am I going to tell Hannah Cunningham that I let her husband die?"

Iggy patted him on the shoulder.

"If we reach that bridge, we'll find a way to cross it," he said. "Until then, Leroy is alive and you have a chance to keep him that way. What's your next move?"

Alex shook his head and shrugged.

"I have no idea," he said. He told Iggy about his conversation with Sanderson, the mining expert. "If there's a valid reason to kidnap Leroy Cunningham, I don't know what it is."

Iggy nodded, stroking his mustache, something he always did when he was thinking.

"Well, what do you know?" he asked at last.

"Nothing about Leroy."

"What about your other cases?" Iggy prodded.

"Someone at Andrew Barton's factory was in on the theft of his motor," Alex said.

"Start there."

"How does that help Leroy?"

"It doesn't," Iggy said. "Not directly, anyway. But it gets your mind working and once that happens, you might just think of something about Leroy that you haven't before."

Alex sighed and stood.

"Work the problem," he said.

Iggy nodded and patted him on the shoulder before turning toward his greenhouse.

"Work the problem," he echoed. "But have another cup of coffee before you go, you look like the very devil."

TWO MORE CUPS of coffee and a long crawler ride later, Alex walked onto the work floor of Barton Electric. The replacement traction motor looked virtually the same as it had yesterday, though Alex noticed that some of the piles of parts had been assembled into incomplete-looking shapes.

"Back so soon, Mr. Lockerby?" Jimmy Cortez said, spotting Alex. He stuck out his hand and Alex shook it. "It's something ain't it?" he said, indicating the bits of the motor.

"Yes," Alex agreed. "Still think you won't finish on time?"

"Between you, me, and the wall, it'll be done next Tuesday," Jimmy said. "That's if everything goes right."

"When's the contest?"

"Wednesday."

"That's pretty close," Alex admitted.

"Too close," Jimmy said, with a worried look. "What can I do for you, Mr. Lockerby? Are you here to talk to Mr. Barton?"

Alex was taken aback at that.

"Is he here?"

Jimmy shook his head.

"Not yet, but he's coming in to supervise the motor personally. I have to admit, I'm kinda glad. If there are any screw ups, he can't blame me."

"Well, I'll get out of your hair," Alex said. "Just point me at your personnel department."

Jimmy pointed at a second-floor office with a metal stair running up to it.

"Good luck," he said.

Alex crossed the floor and climbed the stairs to the office. An elderly secretary brought him a stack of folders for everyone who was working on the day of the theft, and directed Alex to an empty office. One by one he went through the employee files, but nothing jumped out at him. There was one man who had asked for a raise several times in the last few months, but a quick check of his time card showed that he'd been given the requested raise a week before the theft.

If there was someone in the factory that had a beef with Barton or the company, there wasn't any evidence in the files. Alex sighed and shut the last folder, dropping it back on the stack.

"That bad?"

Alex looked up to find the Lightning Lord himself leaning on the frame of the open door. He was dressed casually, in a white shirt and dark slacks with a burgundy vest. The ends of his lightning bolt mustache were turned up in a smile.

Alex didn't know how long Barton had been there watching him. It spoke to how tied he felt that he didn't notice the man arrive.

"No," Alex said. "Just not as easy as I'd hoped."

"What have you learned?"

"I'm pretty sure someone here tipped off the thief."

Barton's easy demeanor vanished.

"How dare you makes such an accusation?" he fumed. "Where is your evidence?"

Alex wasn't prepared for this response. Barton seemed to be taking the suggestion that one of his employees was in on the theft rather personally.

"I don't have any evidence," Alex said. "Not yet, anyway." He explained about the timing and how the thief must have known the loading dock schedule down to the second in order to get in and steal the truck at exactly the right moment.

"It points to an inside job," Alex explained.

"That's the easy explanation," Barton admitted, his voice still full of resentment.

"There's also the guy who took a shot at me yesterday," Alex said. "I was across the street, checking out the alley just down from the loading dock. I wanted to know if someone could have watched from there and learned your schedule, but it turns out you can't. When I went to leave, someone shot me in the back and stole my rune book. They probably thought it was my notebook."

"You don't look like a man who got shot in the back," Barton said.

"Shield runes," Alex explained. "I do find it interesting, though, that someone was waiting for me in that alley. How did they know when I'd be here?"

The anger in Barton's eyes abated a bit.

"You think someone here called the gunman and tipped him off?"

Alex nodded.

"Who knew about the shipment the day the motor was stolen?"

Barton thought for a moment, then raised an eyebrow.

"Only Jimmy Cortez, Bill Gustavsen, and myself," he said.

"What about the men who loaded it on the truck?"

"Jimmy would have called them in to load the motor, but they wouldn't have known beforehand."

Alex leaned back in the chair and thought for a moment.

"What about Gustavsen's log book? Could someone have looked in there and seen the shipment?"

"No," Barton declared with certainty. "He didn't know when it was supposed to be shipped out until that day. I called him in the morning."

"So the only people who had time to tip anyone off were Cortez, your floor manager, or Gustavsen?"

"The idea is preposterous," Barton said, his indignant tone coming back. "I've known both of them for years! They're loyal men."

Alex held Barton's gaze for a long moment, the shook his head.

"There is one other possibility," he said. "But you're not going to like it either."

"I'm listening," Barton said.

"If no one here tipped off the thief, then maybe this was a crime of opportunity."

Barton laughed out loud at that.

"You came highly recommended, Mr. Lockerby, but I must say I'm not impressed. Why would someone take the motor if they didn't know what it was?"

"They just wanted the truck," Alex explained. "I noticed that you have spaces for two trucks to park in your loading dock, but there's only one there now. The other truck is still missing, isn't it?"

Barton tacitly admitted that it was.

"If the thief only wanted the truck, then they might have just dumped the motor. If they dropped it in the river, that would explain why the rune can't connect to it."

Barton's expression didn't soften one bit.

"There's just one hole in your theory, Lockerby," he said, darkly. "If the theft of the motor was a crime of opportunity, then who shot at you in that alley? Assuming you were telling the truth about that."

He had a point. The idea that some random person had shot Alex in the back and then stolen his rune book didn't seem likely.

"People in my business make enemies, Mr. Barton," Alex said. "It's possible one of them followed me here from somewhere else and just waited for me to leave before jumping me."

"Well, I can understand how someone might want to shoot you,"

Barton said. "If you're guessing right, there's very little chance I'm going to get my motor back. To make matters worse, there's no conspiracy by my competitors so there's no chance I can get the deadline extended." He clenched his fists and Alex could hear a humming noise like an electric motor under a load. "I suppose I need to put all my efforts into making sure the new motor is ready on time, then."

Barton reached into his trouser pocket and pulled out a roll of cash that had a thousand-dollar bill on the outside. He opened it and peeled off a twenty and a five, handing them to Alex.

"Your daily rate, I believe," he said. "I won't be needing your services any longer."

Alex accepted the money.

"There's still a chance," he said as Barton turned away. "Give me till Saturday to find your motor."

Barton looked back and shook his head.

"I never throw good money after bad, kid," he said.

"Are you a betting man, Mr. Barton?"

Barton's handlebar mustache turned up in a smirk.

"You're speaking my language," he said. "What do you have in mind?"

"You give me till Saturday, double or nothing," Alex said.

Barton considered him for a moment, looking Alex up and down.

"For someone who seems to be right out of clues, you seem awfully confident," he said, then he stuck out his hand and Alex shook it. "Done then," he said. "You have till Saturday to find my motor. Good luck."

With that, Barton turned and swept down the hall and out onto the metal stairs that led to the factory floor.

"COFFEE," Alex told Doris as he dropped his hat on the stool in front of *The Lunch Box* counter. "And some poached eggs on toast." She smiled and nodded at him, laying out a cup and saucer.

Alex moved to the pay phone on the wall and dropped a nickel in the slot. He didn't know if Leslie would be back from Suffolk county yet, but he gave the operator his office number anyway. The phone rang for a long time until Leslie's voice came on.

"How was your trip?" Alex asked.

"Divine," she said with a smile Alex could hear. "I'm not even mad at the mass of people already here who want anti-ghost runes."

"Wow," Alex said. "Is Randall as happy as you are?"

"You're just jealous."

"So, do you have anything for me? Other than gloating I mean."

"Be nice," Leslie said. "Randall worked late last night and we found twenty-three names of people who worked for Seth Kowalski."

"Good," Alex said. "I'm at *The Lunch Box* right now, but I'll come by as soon as I eat, and we can go over it."

"That's great, but there's more," Leslie absolutely purred. "I *convinced* Randall to look for any suspicious activity during Kowalski's tenure."

"Did he find anything?"

"Not yet, but he's going to call me this afternoon if he finds anything."

"You must have made quite an impression on him."

"What can I say? I'm very good at my job."

"See if you can run down any of the names on that list and I'll see you soon," Alex said.

"Wait," she said before he could hang up. "Did you find the guy who was kidnapped?"

Alex sighed. He didn't want to talk about Leroy. Despite Iggy's assurances, he didn't have any better idea how to proceed now than he had at breakfast.

"You need to call the wife right now," Leslie admonished when Alex explained his situation. "She must be going crazy, Alex."

He sighed again. Leslie was right, of course. He'd been a heel to make Hannah wait by the phone for any word on her husband. The news wasn't good, but she ought to know the truth.

"All right," he said. "I'll call right now."

He said goodbye, then dropped another nickel in the slot. Pulling out his notebook, he gave the operator the number for Hannah Cunningham's apartment.

"I'm sorry," the operator came on a few minutes later. "Your party doesn't answer."

Alex thanked her and hung up, being sure to retrieve his nickel from the return slot. He'd try her again after he'd finished his eggs.

"You look like hell," Mary said, setting down Alex's plate. She winked at him as he came back to the counter. "You need to eat better," she said. "Come by more often."

"Sorry," Alex said. "I've been up to my neck in impossible cases."

Mary opened her mouth to ask him about it, but right then a half dozen people came in and she had to vanish back to the kitchen. Alex hated to admit it, but he was grateful not to have to talk about his frustrations, even to Mary.

It felt good to just sit and eat and not have to think.

"Hey, where are you?" Danny's voice suddenly cut through his thoughts.

Alex looked up from his empty plate and was surprised to find his friend sitting next to him. He checked the clock on the wall and found that nearly three-quarters of an hour had gone by.

"Sorry," Alex said, finding it difficult to focus. "I guess I was lost in thought."

"I'll say," Danny said with a concerned look. "I was talking to you for a couple of minutes before I noticed that you'd punched out."

"You here for lunch?"

"As I tried to explain, Leslie told me where to find you," Danny said. "I was wondering if you could help me with all these thefts. The Captain is leaning on Callahan and he's leaning on me and I don't have any idea where to look next."

"Join the club," Alex said.

"What?"

"I don't know if I can help," Alex said. "I've been officially forbidden from helping the police."

Danny gave him a steady look.

"When has that ever stopped you before?" he asked. "Besides, I really need your help."

Alex rubbed his eyes. He could feel a headache coming on.

"All right," he said after a long minute. "Come by the brownstone tonight and bring your case file. We'll go through it and see if there's anything you missed."

Danny slapped him on the back and Alex winced. The spots where the bullets hit him were still bruised and tender.

"Thanks, I really appreciate it," Danny said, oblivious to Alex's discomfort.

Alex nodded and stood.

"Where you off to now?" Danny asked.

"I've got a lead on your ghost killer," Alex said, heading for the phone. "Need to run it down."

Alex called Hannah one more time with the same result. As he hung up, her absence bothered him. Why would a woman whose husband was missing leave her phone unattended? He should have thought of that before. It didn't feel right.

Dropping the nickel back in the phone, he called Leslie.

"Did Hannah Cunningham call you recently?" he asked once Leslie picked up.

"No, but I was out most of yesterday and all of this morning, remember?"

"I've tried her twice with no answer."

Leslie started to respond but stopped, picking up on Alex's tone.

"You think something's wrong?"

"I don't know," he said, surer now that there was. "I'll be by as soon as I can, but I'm going to go by Hannah's apartment first."

"Be careful," she said. "Remember somebody out there took a shot at you."

"You've been talking to Iggy," Alex accused.

"Just be careful," she said with a sigh. "It's starting to look like you might actually get paid soon."

"You're all heart," Alex chuckled.

12

THE TAIL

Hannah and Leroy Cunningham lived in a six-story apartment building of stained, brown brick on the Outer-Ring side of Alphabet City. Alex left the crawler station two blocks away and turned south. The streets were lined with beggars and the lucky few who had boxes of apples or newspapers to sell. Since the market crash large parts of the city were overrun with the desperate, the drunk, and the vagrant.

Alex felt for them as he passed, ignoring their entreaties for money. He had a roof over his head and enough to stay fed, but he couldn't even buy his own cigarettes. He chuckled humorlessly at the thought that he was only about a week away from joining these ragged souls.

When Alex reached Hannah's building, he checked the address written in his notebook. The building wasn't very far into the outer ring, but no outer ring building would have an elevator, so of course, Hannah's apartment number was sixty-four.

A few minutes later, Alex reached the sixth-floor landing, sweating in the sweltering August heat. He pushed for a moment to catch his breath, then moved down to door sixty-four and knocked.

No sound came from inside, so he knocked again.

This time, a door across the hall opened and a middle-aged woman with a plump face, black hair, and too much perfume peered out.

"Do you know if Mrs. Cunningham is home?" Alex asked, putting on his friendly smile.

"You get out of here," the woman hissed, closing her door so that only her eyes were visible. "I'll call the cops this time."

Alex held up his hands in a gesture of peace.

"Easy there," he said. "I don't know who you think I am, but I'm a private detective. Mrs. Cunningham hired me to look for her husband."

"Well she don't want to talk to anybody," the woman growled. "Not after last time. You better get lost."

With that, she slammed the door and Alex could see her setting the bolt on the other side.

He wasn't sure what had happened, but it wasn't nothing. Concerned, he pounded on the door again.

"Hannah," he called. "It's me, Alex."

"Go away," a ragged voice came from inside. Alex barely recognized it as Hannah's. She was hoarse and clearly scared.

"I'm not going anywhere until you talk to me," Alex said, firmly. "Now open up before I get the superintendent."

A long pause followed and then he heard the bolt on the door being drawn back and the lock clicked. The door opened and Hannah stood inside, huddled as if she were cold. Alex could see that she had a black eye and a bruise on her cheek.

"Please," she gasped. "They said they'd kill him if I talked to anyone."

The apartment beyond the door was disheveled, with a broken chair leaning against the dining table and a trash can overflowing with shards of broken dishware. Alex pushed the door open and Hannah shuffled back.

"Please," she said, holding out her arm. "They'll know."

Alex took her by the wrist and gently turned her arm so he could see the underside. A symbol had been burned there, as if Hannah had been branded with an iron. The symbol was rectangular with a rounded square on top of three curled shapes below. Inside the square was a cartoonish pair of eyes in a rounded head, with what looked like a stone on top. The stone had one large hole in the center and three to each side.

It reminded Alex of a television screen with an octopus staring out of it, its legs dangling down and a clay ocarina on its head.

He didn't have to break out his ghostlight to tell it was magical; he could feel the power in the symbol when he ran his thumb over it. Hannah winced when he did and Alex noticed that the skin around the mark was still pink. Whoever had done this to her and busted up her place had done it recently.

"Someone told you to stop looking for Leroy?"

She nodded, tears streaming down her face.

"They barged in yesterday," she said. "They told me they'd killed you. They even showed me your red book."

She squeezed her eyes closed, forcing the tears out onto he cheeks.

"They said if I talked to anyone else, they'd kill Leroy."

"They told you if you kept quiet, that they'd let him go?" Alex guessed.

She nodded.

"Then they put this paper on my arm and it burned me," she wept. "They said if I talked to anyone, they'd know. That this," she nodded at the symbol. "That they'd use this to kill me."

Alex looked closely at the octopus symbol. From Hannah's description, it worked just like a rune. There were three schools of runes: the Geometric school, which Alex used; the Kanji school that used Oriental characters; and the Arabic school which favored artistic, flowing script.

"I've never seen this kind of rune," Alex said. "But I know runes. This isn't complex enough to kill someone. They did this to keep you quiet."

It was mostly true. Alex suspected the rune could very easily be a tracking rune, so whoever they had watching Hannah's place could follow her if she gave them the slip. He leaned back out into the hall and checked up and down the corridor. So far as he could tell, they were alone. Whoever was watching, and he was sure now that someone was, they must be outside.

Alex stepped back into Hannah's apartment and shut the door behind him, pausing to set the bolt.

"Hannah," he said, looking her straight in the eyes. "I know you're scared, but I need you to listen to me, okay?"

She took a deep shuddering breath and nodded.

"Whoever did this is trying to scare you, to keep you quiet while they do whatever it is they took Leroy to do. Whoever they are, they're not going to just let your husband go once they're done. He knows who they are by now — he's been with them almost a week."

Hannah gasped, and her trembling got worse. It was clear she was moments away from simply breaking down.

"There's good news, though," he went on. "Doing this," he took hold of her wrist and turned her arm to reveal the rune. "This means they've got someone watching you, making sure you don't leave this building."

"How is that good news?" she wanted to know, her eyes darting to the door to make double sure Alex had bolted it.

"It's good news because it gives us a way to find Leroy, but you'll have to be very brave for it to work."

To her credit, Hannah stopped shaking and stood up straight.

"What do I have to do?" she asked with only a hint of controlled fear in her voice.

"You need to do exactly what they're afraid you'll do," Alex said. "I want you to go down to the station and catch a northbound crawler. Go straight to my office. Stay at the station when you change crawlers and don't stop along the way, understand?"

She nodded, her eyes a bit wild.

"But how will this help find Leroy?"

"Because," Alex said with reassuring smile. "When you leave here, whoever is watching is going to follow you. They're going to want to know where you're going."

Hannah shuddered and wrapped her arms around herself.

"Don't worry about that," Alex said. "He won't bother you until he knows where you're going. I'm going to go out the back and get a cab. Once I see that you're safely on the crawler, I'll go back to my office.

I'll find a good place to wait and watch for you. When you get there, I'll be able to see who's tailing you."

Hannah thought about this and nodded. It looked like she was trying to convince herself rather than simply agreeing.

Alex dug a folded vault rune and his lump of chalk out of his pocket. He quickly drew a door on the wall of Hannah's apartment and opened his vault. He still hadn't made a backup rune book but there wasn't time for that now. He needed his 1911 and his knuckle duster.

Once he had slipped the brass knuckles into his jacket pocket and put on his shoulder holster, Alex closed the vault. Next he used Hannah's phone to call Iggy. He explained about the strange rune and asked the doctor to meet Hannah at his office, and to bring his silver pocketwatch. His preparations complete, Alex hung up the phone and turned back to Hannah.

"All right then," Alex said with a nod. "I want you to wait five minutes after I leave, then go straight to the crawler station. Don't worry, I'll be watching."

"What are you going to do once you find the man watching me?"

Alex shrugged.

"Once I get the drop on him, I was thinking of tying him to a chair and beating your husband's location out of him. Unless you have a problem with that sort of thing," he added.

Hannah looked around at her ransacked apartment and then at the burn mark on her arm.

"No," she said. "No problem at all."

TWENTY MINUTES LATER, Alex stood just inside the window display at a five and dime near his office. It was positioned perfectly in the block between the crawler station and his office on the opposite side of the street.

For the fifth time, Alex brushed his hand against the slight bulge under his left arm, feeling the 1911's reassuring bulk. He didn't have to remind himself that the man following Hannah was in league with whoever tried to kill him yesterday. There was a real chance he might try to kill Hannah before she could get to Alex's office.

He took a puff on his cigarette and tried to calm his nerves. He knew it was an indulgence, but he'd bought a pack of smokes from the five and dime to help with the waiting.

As refreshing as it was to have cigarettes again, it really wasn't helping calm his nerves.

At least Jessica's potion is working, he thought, looking at his steady fingers.

He swore.

Jessica.

He was supposed to go back and see her yesterday and he'd completely forgotten.

Getting shot will do that.

Smoking his cigarette down to the nub, Alex resolved to see Jessica tonight, if he had time. The idea wasn't unpleasant, of course, but he had to find Leroy first.

As if on cue, Hannah came hurrying by on the far side of the street. She walked purposefully, but to her credit, she wasn't running.

Alex moved to the door and looked out through the glass. A moment later a man in a gray suit walked by with his hands in his pockets. He didn't seem to be following, but his steps were quick, much faster than his nonchalant demeanor would suggest. Of course, he had to walk fast if he didn't want to lose Hannah.

Slipping out of the five and dime, Alex turned up the street and began walking parallel to the man in the gray suit. Once Hannah ducked into the lobby of Alex's building, gray suit crossed the street, heading for an alley between two buildings just a little ways up.

With Hannah safely in his office, Alex turned the corner of the street and broke into a run. He circled the block, reaching the other end of the alley where Hannah's tail had vanished and peeked around the corner.

At the far end of the alley, the man in the gray suit was smoking a cigarette and watching Alex's building.

Taking care to be quiet, Alex moved carefully along the alley. The man in the gray suit never took his eyes off the building across the street. He clearly wasn't expecting trouble.

Alex reached inside his coat and tugged his 1911 free.

"Hold it," he said when he was only a few feet away.

The man jumped but froze when he saw the gun. He almost jumped again when his eyes darted up to Alex's face.

"Bet you weren't expecting to see me?" Alex said with a grin. "Was it you who shot me in the back yesterday?"

The man's face hardened into a mask, but Alex didn't care; his reaction had told the story.

Alex looked the man over carefully. There was a tell-tale bulge in the right pocket of his jacket. He looked young, in his twenties, with tanned skin and dark hair. His face was blocky and angular with a prominent nose.

Indian heritage, Alex thought.

"You want to tell me where the girl's husband is now, or does this have to get ugly?"

"Don't look at me," the man said with a shrug. He had a sullen, Jersey accent that tended to slur his words. "I just get paid to follow the girl. I don't know nothin' about any missing husband."

"A liar and a back-shooter," Alex said. "Your mother must be so proud."

The man's face curled into a sneer for an instant, then he relaxed.

"You shouldn't meddle in things that aren't your business," he said with an easy air.

"Like what, for instance?"

He just smiled and shook his head.

"It's your funeral," Alex said, nodding toward the street. "Let's go. I'm sure Hannah will want to talk to you."

"You should worry about yourself," he said, turning to face Alex squarely.

The move was odd, but Alex didn't think anything of it, he had a .45 caliber semi-automatic pistol pointed straight at the man, after all.

Gray suit opened his right hand and let the cigarette he was holding fall to the ground. Alex's eyes followed it for half a second and he didn't see the symbol burned into the man's palm.

He felt the rune activate before he saw it, then a wave of force hit him and knocked him off his feet. Alex rolled into a ball to avoid hitting his head on the ground but ended up flat on his back nonetheless. Pain exploded through his side when he tried to rise.

Broken rib.

At the end of the alley, gray suit was clutching his arm. He hadn't been braced when the force rune or whatever had been on his hand went off. The way he was holding it, the backlash had broken his wrist. He scrambled with his left hand to get the gun in his right pocket, finally jerking it free, then he rushed down the alley toward Alex.

Alex didn't hesitate. He raised the 1911 and fired twice. The first bullet hit gray suit in the shoulder but didn't slow his charge one bit. The second hit him square in the center of the chest and he faltered. Taking a stumbling step, he collapsed next to Alex, his gun skittering away on the concrete.

Rolling onto his knees, despite the screaming pain in his side, Alex pointed the pistol at gray suit's prone form, but the man didn't move. He put the barrel of the 1911 against the side of the man's head, then checked for a pulse with his other hand, ignoring the protestations of his ribs.

Dead.

Looking around, Alex tucked his 1911 back into its shoulder holster. Two gunshots were bound to bring the police to the scene and Alex did not want to be nearby when they arrived. He was already on Detweiler's short list and he didn't want to give the man any more leverage.

Working quickly, Alex turned out Gray Suit's pockets. In the inside jacket pocket he found his own red rune book, and a black baked book filled with strange picture runes in it. Pocketing both, he kept looking. The dead man's pants pockets yielded a ring of keys and a brass compass whose needle pointed right at Alex's building.

Something tickled against Alex's senses. He'd felt the same thing right before the force rune had cracked his rib and put him on his back. Standing up as quickly as he could, Alex backed away from the body. Magic erupted from the dead man and a sudden flash of fire burned a hole in his shirt front from the inside. Fire spread from the hole, enveloping the body in seconds.

Alex was forced to move back as waves of intense heat assaulted him. Shielding his face, he nearly tripped over the burning man's revolver.

Alex bent down and picked up the gun, shoving it in his own jacket pocket. His side burned where the force rune had hit him, but his attention was focused on the immolating body.

In less than a minute, the flames died down and burned out, leaving nothing behind but a pile of ash, a scorch mark on the ground, and the rank odor of burnt flesh.

13

THE BREAKDOWN

Police sirens were wailing in the distance when Alex knocked on the locked door of his office.

"It's me," he said.

A moment later, Iggy opened the door and let him in.

"Are those sirens for you?" he asked.

"Not anymore," Alex said.

Hannah sat on one of the beat-up couches along the wall with Leslie holding her hand. Both looked up as he came in.

"Did you find him?" Hannah said, her voice urgent.

Alex hated to dash the hope in her eyes. He wanted to say something soothing, but nothing came to mind. In fact, he had a splitting headache and he couldn't move his left arm without searing pain.

"Yes," he said.

"We heard gunshots," Iggy said, looking out into the hall to make sure no one was with Alex. "And what was that flash in the alley?"

Alex moved to Leslie's desk and put the dead man's book, gun, keys, and compass on it.

"I got the drop on him real slick," Alex said. "But he had some kind of force rune on his hand. Knocked me down."

"He got away?" Hannah squeaked.

Leslie had her arm wrapped tightly around the girl's shoulders and Alex wondered if that was the only thing keeping her up.

"No," Alex said, his headache suddenly flaring up to a thumping inside his skull. "He...he rushed me, and I put two bullets in him."

Leslie gave him the once-over, clearly looking for wounds.

"What's wrong with your arm?" Iggy asked, noticing that Alex was holding his left arm across his body.

"Force rune hit like a truck," he said.

"What happened to the other fellow?" Iggy said, moving to probe Alex's side.

"Ow!" Alex winced as Iggy pressed one of his ribs.

"I'll say it hit hard," the doctor said. "This rib is broken." He pulled his chalk from his pocket. "Don't move while I get a sling and some bone restorative."

"But, what happened to the man who was following me?" Hannah insisted.

"He's dead," Alex replied. "Second shot took him right in the heart."

"Did you stash the body in your vault?" Iggy asked, drawing a door for his own on the back wall of the office.

Alex shook his head.

"He had some kind of magic on him," he said, struggling to remember what he felt when it activated. "It burned his body to ash in about a minute."

Iggy paused at that.

"Was it a rune or a device?"

Alex picked up the black rune book. "He might have had one of these," he said, tossing it to Iggy. "The symbols in there look like the one he had on his hand and the one on Mrs. Cunningham."

Hannah touched her wrist unconsciously as Iggy paged through the book.

"Ever see anything like that?" Alex asked.

"No," Iggy admitted, closing the book and passing it back to Alex.

"What are we going to do then?" Hannah gasped. Her voice was strained, and she looked back and forth from man to man in a near panic.

Alex didn't know what to tell her. Without the dead man, he was back to square one with finding her husband. He didn't have the heart to tell her that, but for some reason he couldn't think of a better lie.

"Don't worry," he said. "We've got the stuff from his pockets."

Alex picked up the keys from Leslie's desk.

"These go to something," he said. "We can use them to...to track down...your husband."

Alex shook his head. For some reason he couldn't remember the girl's husband's name. He picked up the compass. It was pointing right at Hannah.

"Where's your pocketwatch?" he asked Iggy. "The silver one. I did ask you to bring that, didn't I?"

"Of course you did," Iggy said. He reached into the pocket of his waistcoat and passed the watch over before entering his now open vault.

Alex turned the watch over and pressed the crown, flipping the silver cover open. Inside, the guts of the watch had been removed and replaced with five stacked disks of glass. Each disk was covered with intricate runes, their geometric shapes filling the center with delicate runic script ringing the edges. As soon as Alex opened the lid, the runes began to glow, and his ears felt pressure, as if he were underwater.

Setting the watch aside, Alex checked the compass. Now that the masking rune in the watch had been activated, the compass needle pointed north. Its connection to Hannah had been broken as the masking field expanded from the watch. Fully extended, the runes in the watch would keep location magic from working in a radius of about twenty feet.

"Alex?" Hannah said.

He looked up to see her staring at her wrist. The burned symbol had faded, leaving only a pink mark where her skin had been singed.

"I'll get you some ointment for that in a minute," Iggy said, returning from his vault. "Pull up your shirt," he said to Alex.

Alex moved to comply, but his side erupted in pain when he tried to raise his arm.

"You'd better do it," he said with a groan.

"Help me with this," Iggy said to Leslie.

Alex sat down on Leslie's desk as she tugged his shirt-front loose and pulled it up so Iggy could slather something cold on Alex's chest. He grunted as his muscles contracted involuntarily.

"Easy," he said.

"Be quiet and drink this," Iggy said, shoving a shot glass into his hand.

Alex downed the shot and nearly choked. It was alcohol of some kind but mixed with something noxious.

"Steady, lad," Iggy said. He pressed a sheet of flash paper against the ointment on Alex's chest, then lit it with his lighter.

Alex's rib twanged like a guitar string as the magic infused the break.

"Damn it," Alex grunted, his teeth clamped together. Finally the sensation eased to a dull ache. "Thanks Iggy," he said.

Leslie rolled her eyes at him. She'd never approved of Alex calling Dr. Bell 'Iggy.'

"What do we do now?" Hannah asked. She seemed calmer, but her voice was still strained and she sat ramrod straight, every muscle in her body seeming to strain against stillness.

"Now," Alex said, getting up from Leslie's desk. "I'll use a...a rune to find...your husband."

He pulled out his red book and began paging through it. It didn't look like the dead man had removed any of the pages, but he couldn't be sure.

"What am I looking for?" he asked. The book was his, but the runes inside didn't seem right.

"Sit down," Iggy said, suddenly appearing beside him.

"I'm all right," Alex said.

Iggy gave him a shove and Alex fell back onto Leslie's desk. If the doctor hadn't reached out and grabbed him, Alex would have gone all the way over.

"Look at me," Iggy said, his voice seeming to echo. "Focus!"

Alex forced his eyes to obey him and pointed them at Iggy. The old man held up a finger and moved it back and forth in front of him. It seemed to flicker and jump, moving like it wasn't fully attached to Iggy's hand.

Iggy turned and said something to Leslie and the other girl, but Alex couldn't make out the words. Then Iggy sank toward the floor and Alex found himself looking at the ceiling.

ALEX STARTLED AWAKE, gasping for air like a drowning man. He tried to sit up, but the second the muscles in his neck contracted, his head exploded with pain. Groaning, he lowered his head back down.

"Yes," an unfamiliar voice said. "Let's not do that again."

Alex opened his eyes and found himself staring at the ceiling of his office. The back of his waiting room couch rose up on his right, so he slowly turned his head left.

The window behind Leslie's desk showed the pale light of evening beyond, and his secretary was nowhere to be seen. Her desk had been cleared off and a wooden case sat open, pivoting on a hinge down its center so its contents could be easily accessed. An alcohol burner sat in front of the case, under a metal stand that supported a glass beaker with a triangular base and a narrow neck. A viscous, sludgy liquid the color of mud churned and bubbled within the glass.

As he lay, watching the muddy liquid, a woman entered his field of view. She wore a knee-length blue skirt with a white blouse and a jacket that matched the skirt. She looked to be in her late sixties with white hair bound up in a bun behind her head. Her face was lined and a bit severe, but she had blue eyes that sparkled with an element of mischief.

"W-who are you?" Alex asked. His mouth felt dry and his words were a bit slurred.

The woman walked over to him and held a monocle up to her eye.

"So you're back among the living finally," she said with a raised eyebrow. "It's about time."

"Didn't answer..." Alex swallowed hard, but his mouth still felt like it was full of cotton. "My question," he finished.

"My name is Dr. Andrea Kellin," she said, squinting through the monocle. Alex remembered the name, she was the alchemist he was looking for when he met Jessica.

"Dr. Bell asked me to come have a look at you. It's a good thing I did," she added.

Alex felt somewhat exposed under the doctor's gaze as she scrutinized him through the little glass. As he observed it, however, Alex noticed that instead of a proper spectacle lens, the monocle had some kind of gemstone in it.

"What's that?" he croaked.

Dr. Kellin smiled and took the monocle away from her eye.

"You're just like Ignatius," she said. "He doesn't miss a detail either. This is a Lens of Seeing."

Alex had no idea what that meant.

"It's actually a salt crystal," Kellin said, holding it close enough for Alex to see it clearly. "I grew it over the course of six months in a vat filled with the philter of true sight."

"Very patient of you," Alex managed.

Dr. Kellin laughed. Her smile was a bit crooked, but it was warm and genuine, and Alex decided he liked her.

"The philter of true sight is one of the most difficult concoctions in alchemy," she said. "I spent the better part of a decade learning to brew it and the batch I used to make this," she held up the monocle, "took me two years of work."

Alex opened his mouth, but she put her finger on his lips to silence him.

"The lens allows me to read your energy," she explained. "I can see where you are hurt." She touched his side where his broken rib was, and he felt a twinge even from that gentle contact. "I can also see what you need to get better."

Alex chuckled at that. He doubted very much that even the formidable doctor could cure him of having spent the majority of his life-force.

Kellin's face turned sour when Alex laughed.

"Yes," she said, giving voice to Alex's thoughts. "I can also see the terrible price you've paid for your magic. I hope whatever power you sought was worth it."

"Seemed like a good idea at the time," Alex croaked. "Can you tell how much—"

"No," the doctor said, anticipating his question. "I only know what's left isn't much."

Alex felt a cold knot of fear in his guts. He'd successfully suppressed that emotion for months by the simple trick of not thinking about it. He wouldn't have changed what he did if he could go back, but he didn't want to die any more than the next guy.

"Thanks anyway," he said.

"Enough questions," Kellin said, turning and walking to the bubbling container on Leslie's desk. She extracted a small brown bottle with a dropper in the lid. As Alex watched, she carefully added one drop of red liquid from the dropper to the muddy sludge. Instantly it began to roil and churn like a living thing until it burst into a pale yellow light that pulsed out like burning phosphorus. A moment later the light subsided, leaving a clear, yellow liquid behind that looked, to Alex, like a beaker full of urine.

Dr. Kellin picked up the alcohol burner from under the beaker and blew out its flame. That done, she produced one of the shot glasses Alex usually kept in his desk and poured two fingers of bourbon from the bottle Leslie kept in her desk, Alex's bottle being empty. To this, she added an equal part of the yellow liquid and swirled them together in the glass.

"I want you to sit up," she said, walking back to the couch. "Slowly," she cautioned.

Alex moved and the pain in his head nearly blinded him. Taking the Doctor's advice, he slowly levered himself up into a sitting position.

"I want you to sip this," she said, handing him the shot glass. "It's hot."

Alex raised it to his lips and just touched the hot liquid to his tongue. It tasted sweet and the moisture was welcome in his mouth.

"Jessica told me about you," Kellin said as Alex took another sip. "I must confess, I'm surprised that you didn't go back to see her yesterday as she instructed. Usually young men find the prospect of her company more than enough inducement for them to visit."

"Someone shot me yesterday," Alex said between sips. "It was a busy day."

Dr. Kellin eyed him as if she wasn't sure she believed him, then put the monocle back over her eye. She looked him up and down, twisting the monocle as if she were focusing a telescope.

"How did you stop the three that hit you in the back?" she asked.

"Shield runes."

If Kellin was surprised by this answer she didn't show it; she just shrugged and put the monocle away.

"If you had seen Jessica yesterday, she'd have tested your blood and seen that the mixture of the nerve tonic was off."

"Is that why I fainted?" Alex asked.

"No, you fainted because you have a concussion."

"What?"

"Dr. Bell said you were hit by a blast of magical force that broke your rib," she said. "It hit your head just as hard. That gave you a concussion."

"Is that serious?"

"Very," Kellin said. "Untreated it can cause brain injury and even death."

"What do I do for that?"

"Death?" Dr. Kellin smirked. "Nothing. To treat the concussion," she tapped the shot glass of yellow liquid, "keep drinking your medicine."

As Alex continued to sip the hot liquid, Dr. Kellin went back to her portable chemistry set on Leslie's desk. She picked up the silver flask that Jessica had given him and opened the top. Taking several bottles from her case, she added drops and splashes to the flask, then capped it again and shook it vigorously.

"I can't say it will improve the taste," she said, picking Alex's coat up off the foot of the couch and slipping the flask back into the inside pocket. "But this will stop the tonic from keeping you up at night."

Alex finished the shot glass and Dr. Kellin took it. He put his feet on the floor in preparation to stand up, but the doctor put her hand on his forehead.

"Stay there a while," she said. "You shouldn't stand until you've had a bit more rest. Give your brain a chance to heal."

Alex nodded and leaned against the back of the couch.

"Where is everyone?" he asked. The last thing he remembered, Iggy, Leslie, and Hannah had still been there.

"Dr. Bell thought that Mrs. Cunningham would be safer at your secretary's apartment, so he escorted them over there. I expect him back at any moment."

Alex closed his eyes and laid his head back on the back of the couch. He could hear Dr. Kellin packing up her alchemy equipment and it briefly occurred to him to help, but he didn't feel like he could lift his head again, much less stand.

A few minutes later a key scraped in the lock and the door opened. Alex looked up to see Iggy enter.

"Excellent," he said, seeing Alex. "I see Andrea's got you patched up."

"Mmm," Alex mumbled noncommittally.

"He'll be all right in a few more minutes," Dr. Kellin said. "Will you see me out?"

"Of course, my dear," Iggy said.

Alex opened his eyes again and watched Iggy pick up the doctor's heavy case and offer her his arm.

"Make sure you go see Jessica tomorrow," she admonished Alex as they passed. "I want her to check you over."

"Didn't you just fix the tonic?"

She grinned and winked at him.

"I want her to have the experience," she said. "It will be good for her. Now don't forget."

"No, ma'am," Alex promised.

Iggy led her out into the hall and Alex could hear the sounds of their shoes on the stairs fade away. A few minutes later, Iggy returned, shutting and locking the door behind him.

"You had me worried, lad," he said, offering Alex a hand up off the couch. "You've gotten into a bad habit of doing that."

Alex eased himself up off the couch with Iggy's help and took a deep breath. His rib hurt when he did that, but not as much as before.

"Are you sure Leslie and Hannah are going to be okay?" he asked.

"Of course," Iggy said. "I gave them my silver pocketwatch so no one can trace Hannah there, and I gave Leslie that .38 you took off the dead man." He put a reassuring hand on Alex's shoulder. "They'll be fine."

Alex wasn't sure about Hannah, but he could well believe that Leslie would be fine now that she had a gun.

"We need to trace those keys," Alex said, remembering what he was doing before he fainted.

Iggy nodded and produced one of Alex's New York Maps from the first of the three file cabinets on the wall. Alex picked up his coat and found his rune book back in the inside pocket, opposite the flask. He quickly navigated to one of the new finding runes he'd written and tore it out.

"In my office," he said as Iggy began laying the map out on Leslie's desk. Alex still wasn't sure about the finding rune and he wanted to take advantage of the stabilizing rune under his office carpet.

A few moments later, Alex struck the metal match from his desk lighter and ignited the finding rune. It flashed, throwing the key ring off and leaving the orange, glowing rune in its place.

With a sinking feeling in the pit of his stomach, Alex watched the rune and the compass needle spin in lazy circles without managing to latch onto the location of the lock that went with the keys.

"Maybe there are too many keys," Iggy suggested.

Alex picked up the ring and took off all but one.

"I hope this is the right one," he said, tearing out another rune and resetting the key ring on top of it.

This time when he lit the flash paper, the ring flew further as a result of having less weight, but that was the only substantive difference. The rune and the compass behaved exactly as before.

"Wherever this goes to must be shielded," Iggy said.

Alex looked at him with disbelieving eyes.

"Everything seems to be shielded these days," he said. "Or maybe they're underground, or under water."

"I doubt very much that the lock that these keys open is underwater," Iggy said, rolling his eyes. "But you're right about something blocking the rune."

"What am I going to tell Hannah?"

"Tell her you're still working on it," Iggy said.

"What if I don't find him in time?" Alex didn't want to admit it, but this fear had been growing in him every day since he promised Hannah that he'd find Leroy. Her husband couldn't last forever; sooner or later whoever took him would be done with whatever they were doing, and when that happened, Leroy Cunningham was a dead man.

Iggy took the black book with the strange runes out of his jacket pocket.

"Let's go home," he said. "You need some sleep and I need time to study this. With any luck, things will be clearer in the morning."

Alex sighed. So far the only luck he'd had on this case was bad luck and it didn't look like that was going to change. The thought of sleep, however, made him instantly tired. And, if he was honest with himself, he really had no idea what to do next.

14

THE LIST

I t was almost nine when Alex managed to drag himself out of bed
the next morning. He usually had trouble waking up, but today it
felt like his eyelids had been glued shut and he had that same
cotton feeling in his mouth as last night. A suspicious man would have
suspected that the good Doctor had put something other than medicine in that urine-colored cocktail.

Alex was a very suspicious man.

He hoped Iggy had the coffee pot still on the stove but was disappointed when he finally managed to get dressed and down to the
kitchen. The only thing waiting for him was a handwritten note from
his mentor saying that he was going out to the museum to get a line on
the strange pictogram runes.

The Lunch Box didn't open till noon, so Alex rode the crawler all the
way to his office before stopping by the lunch counter of the five and
dime across the street. Four cups of black coffee later, he climbed the
stairs up to his office.

"There you are," Leslie said, looking exasperated. "I've been calling
your place for half an hour."

Alex looked her up and down for any sign of something amiss, but
found none.

"Having a lodger seems to disagree with you," he observed.

"Hannah was a delight," Leslie said, giving him a stern look. "This, however," she said, picking up her copy of the morning paper and dropping it on her desk so Alex could see the front page. "This is a problem."

So Called Ghost Killer Claims Another Victim, the headline screamed. Alex perused the article but there were precious few details, other than the victim's name, Paul Lundstrom.

"I take it Mr. Lundstrom is on your list?" Alex asked, putting the paper back on the desk.

Leslie nodded and handed Alex a folded piece of paper. He opened it and found a neatly-written list of about thirty names. Four had been crossed off — the names of the ghost's previous victims. As Alex read down the list, he found the name Paul Lundstrom.

"This is it," he said, slapping the paper with the back of his hand. "This is the connection the Police have been looking for."

Leslie grinned at him.

"And we found it."

"It doesn't matter," Alex said. "Or at least it won't matter to the cops. I'll be lucky if they don't throw me in the cooler, but he's got to see this."

Leslie looked shocked.

"They wouldn't arrest you after we did all the work for them?"

"Oh, wouldn't they," Alex laughed. "I bet Detweiler would arrest me if I brought in the ghost himself, wearing handcuffs with a signed confession."

"I'm thinking you should give this to Callahan," Leslie said. "Oh, and if you're going to get thrown in the slammer, I'm going to need bail money."

Alex pulled the money Barton had given him out of his pocket and handed it over. He was tempted to keep back the twenty that Anne Watson had paid him, but with a sigh he passed that over as well. He had no idea how much the train had cost Leslie to the Hamptons, though he was relatively sure he didn't need to reimburse her for dinner.

"Wow," Leslie said as he piled bills in her hand. "I need to go out of town more often. That's quite a haul."

Alex explained about the Lightning Lord's missing motor and Anne Watson's insisting that he find her husband's killer. Leslie listened as she logged the cash into the strongbox, then reimbursed herself for the trip. Before she finished, Alex took two bucks and the loose change out of the box.

"I've got a lot of running around to do today," he explained, tucking the money into his pocket.

"That's enough to get my landlord off my back," Leslie said, locking the box and putting it back into the desk's bottom drawer. She smiled wistfully. "Just not enough for cigarettes."

Alex sighed and took the pack he'd bought yesterday out of his pocket. He dumped about half of them out onto his hand and passed them over.

"Thanks, kid," Leslie said, dropping the cigarettes and the cash into her purse. "You're a doll."

"Remember that if you have to bail me out later," he said. He tucked the list Leslie had given him in his shirt pocket, brushing against the flask. Remembering that he hadn't yet had any this morning, he checked his hands. They weren't trembling badly, but they were trembling.

He swore under his breath and took a swig from the flask. Grimacing, he agreed with Dr. Kellin's assessment from the night before — she hadn't improved the taste.

Replacing the flask, he checked his hands, but nothing seemed to have changed. He knew that alchemical concoctions took time to work, but it was human nature to look anyway.

Pushing his shaking hands from his mind, he checked his rune book. It looked like all of his runes were there, as well as the note Anne Watson had written him, giving him permission to go through her husband's records.

Alex felt guilty for not remembering his promise to Anne, but Leroy and the people on the ghost's hit list were literally on borrowed time.

"All right," he said, putting on his hat. "I'm off to get arrested. Hold down the fort till I get back."

"I hate to bring this up," Leslie said in a voice that clearly indicated that she didn't mind bringing it up at all. "But what are you going to do to find Hannah's husband?"

Alex paused, then shook his head.

"I'm up against a wall with that," he admitted. "I still don't know what the people who took Leroy want with him. If I can figure that out, I can find him, but right now I've got nothing."

"Well, think about it while you're on your way to the police station," she said, giving him a supportive smile. "And try not to get shot today," Leslie called as he stepped out into the hall.

Good advice.

A GAGGLE OF REPORTERS, all clamoring for information on the ghost, clogged the cavernous lobby of the Central Office of Police. Alex used the commotion to get to the elevators without anyone paying particular attention to him.

Lieutenant Callahan's office was to the right off the elevator and then down a hall that ran along a set of offices. Alex had never been to Detweiler's office, and he hoped he wouldn't pass it on his way.

Callahan's office was a glassed-in room with file cabinets along one side, a couch at the back, and two chairs sitting in front of a squat, plain desk. Piles of folders and loose papers covered the desk along with a new model telephone with both the speaker and the receiver in one handset. A stained coffee cup sat atop a stack of papers and brown rings revealed that this was the cup's usual spot. The only thing missing from a quintessential policeman's office was the man himself.

Alex considered venturing out into the bullpen to look for Danny, but he didn't want to run the risk of encountering any of Detweiler's people before he had a chance to talk to Callahan.

The couch in Callahan's office was up against the hall-side window, so Alex laid down on it to wait. This made it impossible for anyone to see him from the hall.

"What are you doing in my office, Lockerby?" Callahan's voice startled him. "You know that if the Captain sees you in here, he'll have me lock you up on an obstruction charge."

Alex hadn't intended to doze, but he must have, since he didn't hear the big Lieutenant come in. He made a mental note to speak to Jessica about the power of her mentor's sleeping draughts.

"Lieutenant," he said, sitting up on the couch. "I was beginning to wonder if anybody worked around here?"

"Funny," Callahan said, dropping into the chair behind his desk. "I'm not surprised you managed to get up here," he said, shuffling papers around on his desk until he found what he was looking for. "You always manage to turn up in the damnedest places."

Alex grinned at him and moved from the couch to one of the two chairs in front of the big man's desk.

"You say the sweetest things, Lieutenant," he said.

Alex hadn't noticed it before, but up close, Callahan's face was drawn and his eyes were bloodshot. Apparently Alex wasn't the only one who hadn't been sleeping well.

Till now, he reminded himself.

"Cute," Callahan said, closing the folder he'd been looking through. "We'll see how cute you are when Detweiler catches you skulking around. Word has it he's offered a bounty for anything he can use to lock you up."

"You know me, Lieutenant," Alex said, dropping the folded-up list of names on his desk. "I love to make an impression."

Callahan rolled his eyes as he reached for the paper.

"The only impression around here is going to Detweiler's size nines on your butt. What's this?"

"That's a list of people the ghost has targeted for death."

Callahan raised an eyebrow and perused the list.

"Okay," he said, dropping it on his desk. "What makes you think the ghost is after these people?"

"Seth Kowalski," Alex said.

"The first victim, so?"

"He was the County Assessor for Suffolk County from eighteen-ninety-seven through aught-nine."

Callahan picked up the paper again and held it up.

"And that relates to these people how?"

"Everybody on that list worked for Kowalski when he ran the Assessor's office."

Callahan looked the list over again.

"Where did you get this?" he asked. "You sure it's legit?"

"I got it from the current Assessor out in Suffolk County," Alex said. "Name's Randall Walker. He can confirm it."

Callahan stared at the list for a long time before speaking.

"This could be a coincidence," he said, clearly playing devil's advocate.

Alex didn't think for a minute that someone as sharp as Callahan believed in coincidence. He shrugged and decided to play along.

"Maybe it is," he said. "But if I didn't give this list to you and someone on there got bumped off, I could be up for a complicity charge. And if I gave the list to you, and you didn't do anything and someone on that list got killed..."

"Yeah," Callahan said after a long minute. "Remember that explanation. I have a feeling you're going to need it."

He picked up the phone on his desk.

"Tell Detweiler I want to see him," he growled into it.

Alex sat back in the chair, crossing his legs and lighting a cigarette. He knew he'd just delivered information that might make Detweiler's career, but he didn't put it past the Lieutenant to have him arrested just for spite. He took a long drag on the cigarette to calm his nerves.

The door opened behind Alex and he turned. Detweiler in his rumpled jacket stood in the doorway, the stump of a cigar clutched in his teeth. He looked like an unmade bed, with hair flying wildly and bloodshot eyes. The ghost case was clearly running him ragged.

"What is it, Callahan?" he said. "Some of us have work to..." He stopped short when he caught sight of Alex and his tired face turned red. "I thought I told you I'd arrest you if I caught you up here," Detweiler sneered, reaching for his cuffs.

"Sit down, James," Callahan growled.

Detweiler looked like he was about to tell Callahan exactly where to put that remark, but as he looked up at his counterpart, something made him stop.

"All right, Callahan," he said in an easy voice. "I'll give you one minute to convince me why I shouldn't run in your boy here and report you to the Captain."

"Take a look at this," Callahan said, handing the list of names over.

"Where'd you get this?" he asked after looking it over.

"From Randall Walker," Alex explained. "He's the Assessor for Suffolk County."

"And he knew all four victims?" Detweiler said. "Is he connected to these other people?"

"No," Callahan said. "All of these people worked for Seth Kowalski back when he was the Suffolk County Assessor."

Detweiler looked at the list again, more critically this time.

"So, you think the ghost is after these people," he said at last. "That the fact they all worked for the first victim, Kowalski, isn't just a coincidence."

"That's how I figure it," Callahan said.

Detweiler looked up from the list with a suspicious expression and turned to Alex.

"You get this list from your friend at *The Midnight Sun?*"

Alex almost burst out laughing, but managed to control himself. Laughing at the exhausted Lieutenant was a surefire way to get locked up.

"No," Alex said, being careful to keep his voice friendly and snicker free. "I dug this up myself."

"I thought I told you to drop this case," the portly Lieutenant sneered.

"You did," Alex said, puffing on his cigarette. "But then I remembered that I don't work for you."

Detweiler's face turned red and he reached for his cuffs again.

"It's a good thing Alex kept digging," Callahan interjected in his take-charge voice. "If the ghost is going after people on that list, not only can we protect them, but we've got a good chance to catch this maniac."

"Oh sure," Detweiler said, turning his anger on Callahan. "I notice you didn't go to the Captain with this yourself. You want me to take charge of this so if it blows up I'll look like a monkey."

"What are you talking about?" Callahan said. "I gave it to you because it's your case."

Detweiler slammed the paper down on Callahan's desk.

"Are you telling me that you didn't do this because the name Nancy Sinclair is on this list?"

"Who?" Alex and Callahan said at the same time, leaning over to see the name at which Detweiler pointed.

The portly Lieutenant looked back and forth between them before throwing up his hands.

"You know, for a couple of smart guys, you dummied up pretty quick," he growled. "Nancy Sinclair. Now called by her married name, Nancy Banes."

"Wife of Mayor Claude Banes?" Callahan said with raised eyebrows.

"The same," Detweiler confirmed.

"That's why you thought the list came from that hack at the Sun," Alex said, finally understanding. "His paper's been trashing the Mayor's wife for months."

"And you expect me to believe you didn't know?" Detweiler said, glaring at Alex. "If I run with this, we'll have to put extra guards on the Mayor. The papers will have a field day and I'll be public idiot number one if nothing happens."

"Or," Alex pointed out, "if you ignore the list, the Mayor will make sure you rot if his wife gets killed."

Detweiler crumpled the paper in his hands.

"It's a nice box you've put me in, the both of you," he growled. "If this is a bum steer and I end up looking the fool, I'll make sure they put you away, Lockerby. I'll make sure they throw away the key."

"You're welcome, Lieutenant," Alex said with an easy smile. "Just don't forget to mention my help when the mayor gives you the key to the city."

Callahan struggled to hide a smirk so hard he looked like he might pop his collar button. He managed to master himself before Detweiler looked back at him.

"Callahan," he said, nodding at the big man, then he turned toward the door but stopped. "If you find out anything else about this case, scribbler," he growled at Alex, "I'd better be your first call. Got me?"

Alex put his hand over his heart with a wounded expression.

"Of course, Lieutenant," he said. "My word of honor."

Detweiler looked like he wanted to comment on what Alex's honor was worth, but he apparently thought better of it and stormed out of the office.

"You'd better run while you can," Callahan said to Alex once Detweiler was gone.

Alex had a sneaking suspicion he was right.

"Can't," Alex said. "I promised Danny to look over that list of thefts and see if anything pops."

Callahan dug through the folders on his desk for a moment, then extracted a thick one and opened it.

"Here," he said, handing Alex a single sheet of paper. "That's a list of everything missing and where it was taken from," he said. "I'll have Danny call your office when I see him; now get going. I don't want to have to explain to that secretary of yours why you've been locked up. She's scary."

Alex chuckled at that. Leslie had managed to get information out of cops for him before, mostly by being gorgeous. When that didn't work, however, she'd use the force of her considerable, take-no-prisoners personality.

"Terrifying," Alex agreed, folding up the paper and tucking it into the back of his red rune book. "I'll make sure Danny gets this back to you."

"Go," Callahan said as a commotion erupted at the far end of the hall.

Alex skipped the elevator and made for the stairs, disappearing through the exit door just as Detweiler and a pair of uniforms rounded the far corner of the hallway, heading for Callahan's office.

15

THE TRUCK

The lobby of the Central Office of Police was still mobbed with reporters when Alex emerged from the stairwell. He didn't want to spend any more time in the lobby than he had to; after all, he wouldn't put it past Detweiler to come down after him. Still, he was at a dead end with all his current cases, and it was far too early to go see Jessica.

He resolved to go to Anne Watson's house and dig through her husband's files. It probably wouldn't yield anything, but now that he had a list of the ghost's potential victims, maybe he'd find a further connection.

"Hey," a voice said, loud in his ear.

Someone grabbed his shoulder, and Alex tensed, fearing that Detweiler's men had caught up to him. When he turned, however, he saw the face of a man in his mid-twenties. He had a broad smile under a narrow nose in the middle of a boyish face. A dimple in his left cheek increased his youthful look and his eyes were brown and inquisitive. He wore a brown suit that looked made for hard wear and a tag had been stuck into the band of his trilby hat that read, *Press*.

Alex suppressed a sneer when he saw the press card. He knew a couple of decent guys at the Times, but most reporters treated P.I.s like bumbling incompetents or outright competition.

"No comment," Alex said, yanking his shoulder free and turning back toward the door.

"Wait," the man said. "You're that consultant, Lockerby. The runewright detective. Is it true that you're working with the cops to find the ghost?"

"I said no comment," Alex said.

"Aw, come on, pal," the reporter pressed. "The whole city is scared to death over this thing. I mean, he seems to be mostly killing rich folk, but there was that one guy in Harlem. People are scared."

Alex looked back at the man with his boyish grin.

"I was never working this case with the police," Alex said. "I under-stand Lieutenant Detweiler is running the investigation. If you want information, you'll have to take it up with him."

With that, Alex pulled away and maneuvered through the crowd to the big glass doors at the end of the lobby.

"Thanks for nothing, mac," the reported called after him.

TEN MINUTES and a short crawler ride later, Alex pushed open the gate to the Watson home. He was surprised to find it locked and empty. There wasn't even a squad car on the street.

Detweiler must have called off the investigation into Anne when Paul Lundstrom was murdered.

Alex hadn't anticipated being locked out of the house, but he came prepared. Taking out his rune book, Alex paged to the back. He passed a green and gold rune that would open the lock magically, but the components of that rune cost forty dollars. Alex preferred a much cheaper method of entry.

He tore out a vault rune and, taking a bit of chalk from his jacket pocket, drew a chalk door on the wall of the porch. A moment later he was back on the porch with the beat-up leather doctor's bag that held his kit.

Alex paused for a moment to wipe away the chalk outline before he opened his kit. Anne Watson was his client after all; no sense in leaving her porch untidy. He took out an ornate pencil case that held the various writing instruments he might need on the job. The case was made of wood with a slender, mahogany tray and a cherry cover. Turning it upside down, Alex pushed his thumb along the bottom of the mahogany tray and a concealed panel slid sideways, revealing a hidden compartment. Inside were several tools for picking locks.

The Watsons' lock was the newer kind that took a small key with multiple teeth. Setting his kit and the pencil case aside, Alex selected a slim tool with an undulating end and an L-shaped tension tool. It had been a while since he'd been forced to pick a lock, but Iggy kept saying it was like riding a bike. Alex had never ridden a bike, so he wasn't sure that was true, but the lock clicked open after only a few moments of manipulation.

Feeling quite self-satisfied, Alex replaced the tools inside the hidden compartment of the wooden case, picked up his kit, and went inside.

TWO HOURS LATER, Alex sat at David Watson's enormous desk. It was no longer a shrine to neatness and order. Piles of file folders were stacked from one end to the other and his immaculately organized file cabinets stood open and mostly empty.

With a sigh of disgust, Alex closed the file he'd been reviewing and dropped it on a stack to his left. He'd been through almost every land deal for which David Watson had records, and none of them involved anybody on the ghost's list. There were many records from Suffolk County, mostly houses David had built.

Alex stood up and went to the wet bar he'd found concealed behind a folding door. Locating a bottle of single malt scotch, Alex poured himself two fingers in a shot glass and sipped it.

It was exquisite.

He closed his eyes and enjoyed the aroma and the taste of the liquor. On his budget, the best he could do was bourbon. Occasionally Iggy would break out the good stuff from his liquor cabinet, but that was a rarity. He reserved that for important conversations and deep contemplation.

"I could get used to this," Alex said, taking another sip. He looked around the office at the wall with the glass-enclosed shelves. Watson's old surveyor's transit and other equipment were there, showing his humble beginnings. The next case held blueprints and photographs of houses, detailing the man's years as a builder and finally a developer. According to the files, Watson had built some of the biggest houses on the north shore.

Alex took another sip of the whiskey, but it didn't go down as smoothly this time. Something about Watson's wall bothered him.

Setting the drink aside, Alex moved back to the desk. Each of the folders had a label on it listing the date of whatever transaction the files detailed. He began stacking them up by year and returning them to the file cabinets where he'd gotten them. After an hour of this, the clock on the wall read one o'clock; he was ravenously hungry, but he had a small stack of folders left on the desk.

These folders represented Watson's work as a surveyor. None of the files detailed his work for the Assessor's office; those records would be in storage in Suffolk County. The files on the desk represented Watson's independent work. There were seventeen of them. The eighteenth file, in chronological order, had been the first building Watson had ever built, a glassed-in tennis court for a wealthy family.

As far as Alex could tell, David Watson had only been a surveyor for two years after he started working for himself. Alex had no idea when Watson had quit working for the assessor's office, but he felt sure it was before the man started in the building trade.

Alex went back to the wet bar and refilled the empty shot glass with single-malt.

Watson had kept meticulous records. That was what was bothering Alex. In two years he went from being a surveyor to being a builder, but there was no record of his ever learning the building trade. He hadn't apprenticed or gone to school, he just stopped surveying and started building for some of New York's richest families. All in the space of two years.

Alex knew enough about building to know that Watson could

never have pulled off a glassed-in tennis court with his surveyor's knowledge. That meant he'd hired someone who did have the experience to run his crew. Add to that all the materials he would have to buy up front and it added up to a tidy sum. Watson would have needed that money *before* he put up the first glass panel in that tennis court.

"Where did he get the money?" Alex asked the stack of folders.

It was possible, of course, that someone had fronted him. A silent partner who believed in Watson enough to set him up.

Alex shook his head. That wouldn't work. The folders contained every detail about the builds Watson did, and there was no payout to any partner. All the expenses were listed and catalogued.

"So where did the money come from?" he asked again. "There's no way he saved that kind of scratch on a county surveyor's salary."

Alex's stomach rumbled, and he sighed. If he wanted to make any more progress on this, he was going to need something to eat.

He picked up the telephone on Watson's desk and gave the operator his office number. A few moments later, Leslie answered.

"It's me, doll," he said. "I'm over at Anne Watson's house looking into her husband's business dealings. I think I'm on to something, but I wanted to know if you've heard anything from lover boy?"

"I'll say," Leslie said, her voice positively bubbly. "He had a lovely bouquet delivered here for me."

Alex chuckled.

"Not exactly what I was hoping for," he said.

"Randall did send a card," Leslie explained. "He said he didn't find anything out of the ordinary in the files, but he'll keep looking. Apparently there's a lot of records to go through."

With tax assessments on each property in the county required every year, and every land sale documented, Alex could well believe it was a mountain of paperwork.

"Well, if you talk to him, tell him to keep on swinging," Alex said. "I'm going to grab a bite and then head over to the hall of records. I want to check some of Watson's information against the permits he had to file with the state. Maybe I'll find something there."

"Before you do that, Danny called," Leslie said.

Alex rubbed his forehead and stifled a curse. He'd forgotten about his promise to help his friend and he hadn't even glanced at the lost property statement Callahan had given him.

"All right," Alex said. "Call him back and tell him to meet me at *Gino's*. I'll go over his case while I get lunch."

"Will do," she said and then hung up.

Alex picked up the seventeen folders that encompassed David Watson's surveying career, along with the ones for the first five builds he'd done, and slid them into his kit bag. The room looked pretty much as he'd found it except for the empty shot glass on the desk.

Thinking it would be rude to leave that out, Alex took it back to the wet bar, refilled it, drained it again, then rinsed the glass out in the sink.

GINO'S WAS a little hole in the wall diner with a short counter and a half-dozen booths. They catered to the beat cops who came in to grab a sandwich or a bowl of chowder. Alex was never one to be picky where food was concerned, and he liked that the proprietor, an older woman named Lucy, never skimped on the meat in her sandwiches.

"Two hot pastramis on white," he ordered once he sat down at the counter.

Lucy wore a floral dress under a stained apron and her white hair was bound up behind her in a bun. She looked to be about fifty with a lanky, slender build and a rough but smiling face. Nodding at Alex, she took two ready-made sandwiches from a cooler and dropped them on a buttered grill.

"Cup of joe?" she asked, picking up the steel coffee pot from the far side of the griddle.

Alex checked the handful of change in his pocket before nodding.

The bell on the door jingled behind Alex but he was too hungry to care.

"There you are," Danny's exasperated voice assaulted him. A moment later them man himself was pulling on his sleeve. "I've been looking all over town for you."

Alex picked up his coffee cup and sipped it, relishing the energy it was giving him.

"Well, you found me," he said. "Pull up a stool."

That was meant to be a joke as the stools were bolted to the floor and therefore, immovable.

"Get up," Danny said, still pulling on his sleeve. "We've got to go."

"What?"

Danny's usually smiling face showed irritation and excitement in a fairly equal mix. He wore his gray suit with his gold detective's badge clipped to the outside breast pocket. Danny was very proud of his status as a police detective.

"There's a break in the case," he said, still tugging at Alex's sleeve, "but I need you and your bag of tricks."

The empty pit in Alex's stomach started to churn. He remembered his recent string of failures with finding runes. He hadn't had one that actually worked since Hannah Cunningham came to his office three days ago and he definitely didn't want to crap out in front of Danny.

"Can I at least eat?" he stalled. "I'm starving."

Danny pinched the bridge of his nose and sighed.

"You remember how I told you that the stuff that was stolen was taken off delivery trucks?" he said, clearly not wanting to have to stop and explain.

Alex shrugged noncommittally. He hadn't been sleeping well before last night and he wasn't sure if Danny had told him that or not.

"Well, we caught a break. They found one of the missing trucks," he said. "It broke down in the Outer Ring by the rail yards."

"Was the stolen stuff still on the truck?"

Danny's face split into a wide grin and he shook his head.

"No," he said. "That means that the thieves unloaded it somewhere."

Alex was nodding along now, seeing the way Danny's line of thought was running.

"So as long as they don't move that truck, I can use it as an anchor and track it back to where it's been," he said.

Danny slapped him on the shoulder again.

"I told them to hold the tow-truck until I got there," he said. "But they won't wait forever, let's go."

Alex downed his coffee as fast as the hot liquid would allow then motioned to Lucy.

"Looks like I need those pastramis on white to go out," he said.

ALEX HAD FINISHED both his sandwiches in the half hour it took Danny to drive from *Gino's* to the rail yards. When he finally pulled off the road, Alex saw a rather dilapidated-looking truck built from the frame of a Model A. It didn't have any paint or signage on it indicating who might have owned it and Alex wondered how a patrolman managed to recognize it as one of the missing trucks.

A half dozen beat cops stood around looking at the vehicle. A disgruntled looking man with a tow truck was arguing with one of the uniforms but the cop waved him off when he saw Danny pull up.

"It's about time, Detective," the officer said. "We need to get this off the street and down to impound."

"Send the tow guy home, Johansson," Danny said. "We can't move this truck till my friend here works his magic."

Johansson looked dubious but, to his credit, he didn't argue. The tow truck operator wasn't so genial, and Alex heard him yelling at Johansson as he put his kit on the curb.

"What was this truck delivering?" Alex asked as he examined the bed.

"Rolls of denim fabric," Danny said, checking his note pad. "They were on their way to a factory in the Garment District that makes dungarees."

Alex circled around the truck but didn't see anything out of the ordinary. Whoever stole it might have left fingerprints inside, of course, but they'd be impossible to tell from the dozens of others left by people who had access to the truck. He decided he'd let the police sort that mess out.

"All right," he said to Danny. "When was this truck stolen?"

Danny checked his notes again.

"A week-and-a-half ago."

"Damn," Alex swore. "I was hoping I could use the truck to track its cargo to where the thieves unloaded it, but I don't think that's going to work."

Danny looked dismayed.

"Why not?"

"Fabric is easy to sell," Alex said. "I'm sure they've gotten rid of it by now."

"There must be something you can do," Danny said.

Alex thought about it. What he needed to do was to find out where the truck had been before it had broken down.

"When was the last time it rained?" Alex asked.

"Uh, Sunday," Danny answered.

"Perfect," Alex said, setting his kit on the bed of the truck and pulling out his multi-lamp and oculus.

"Why is that perfect?" Danny asked.

Alex pointed to a tin bucket in the bed of the truck.

"If the truck had been here on Sunday, there'd still be some water in that," he explained. "That means the thieves kept it somewhere before it broke down here."

"And you can use a rune to locate that place?"

Alex shrugged as he clipped the amberlight burner into his multi-lamp.

"Not exactly."

He lit the burner, then pulled the oculus over his head, settling the telescope-like lens over his right eye.

Amberlight was one of the lesser used magics in Alex's kit. It was essential for reconstructing a crime scene because if you shone it on an object, it would show you where that object used to spend its time. If you shone it on a discarded book, the amberlight would reveal a ghostly trail up to the shelf where the book had been stored.

Alex adjusted the colored filters on the oculus' lens until he could see the caramel-colored light. The fact that it was early afternoon and the sun was high in the sky didn't make it easy to see, but he'd manage.

As he looked at the truck, Alex could see almost invisible lines coming away from it and going back up the street the way he and

Danny had come. They showed how the truck had moved to get her from wherever it had been.

"This way," he said, holding his lamp out in front of him. "And grab my bag."

ALMOST AN HOUR LATER, Alex followed the faint lines of the truck's passing along a waterfront street on the south side of the rail yards. The path had led them into the Middle Ring, to a hardware supply shop, then back out toward the Hudson. Now, as Alex walked along the street, the faint lines turned and flowed up against a carriage door set into the side of a dark warehouse.

Alex closed his right eye and opened his left, looking up at the building. There was no sign that anyone worked there. No doors were open, no windows were lit, and there was no noise or commotion.

"I think this is it," Alex said over his shoulder.

Behind him, Danny and the six beat cops had been following in Danny's car. He pulled over and they piled out.

"Check the door," Danny told Johansson.

The big, blond cop walked over to a service door in the side of the building and tugged on the handle.

"Locked," he said.

Alex tried the carriage door and it budged a little.

"I think this one's open," he said, putting his shoulder against it and pushing. A moment later he wished he hadn't as his still cracked rib exploded in pain. Alchemy could speed up healing, but it still took time.

"Ah! That was stupid," he gasped, clutching his side and stepping back so that Johansson and two other officers could take his place.

"What's wrong?" Danny asked, stepping up beside Alex.

"Bad guys," Alex said, giving their long established code phrase. They both knew there were parts of Alex's job that a straight arrow police detective was better off not knowing about. Now, anytime Alex was involved in something that might put his friend in an awkward position, like being the victim of attempted murder, Alex blamed it on bad guys and Danny let the matter drop.

The doors of the warehouse creaked as the officers pulled it open, revealing a cavernous space beyond. Light streamed in from third-story windows, revealing an open floor with blocks and bolts and concrete pads arranged in rows that must have once supported machines on an assembly line. Whatever this factory had been, however, someone had turned it into a garage. No less than twenty trucks of all different shapes and sizes were parked inside. They sat, silently in four rows of five, just gathering dust. Other than the trucks, the warehouse was completely deserted.

Danny stepped up beside Alex and whistled.

"Would you look at that," he said. "Why would people steal all those trucks and then just leave them sitting here?"

Alex shook his head.

"I have no idea," he said, stepping into the cool space beyond the carriage door. He moved over to the first truck in line and pulled open the back door. The inside space was empty except for some tools and a broken crate.

Moving to the next one, Alex pulled the rear doors open. This time the truck wasn't empty. A row of full crates lineed one side of the delivery truck's cargo space and there were tied bundles of something that looked like cotton.

"Danny," Alex called. "You'd better take a look at this."

The detective and several of the officers came hurrying over. Danny took off his hat and stared at the nearly full truck.

"Check the other trucks," he said to Johansson. The officers each took a truck and soon they began calling out their findings. When they were done, only six of the trucks were empty, and the rest had cargo left in them. Some of them had obviously not been touched.

"I don't get it," Johansson said, scratching his blond head. "I mean I'd get it if the guys who stole all this stuff wanted to use the trucks, but why steal a truck and just park it with everything still in it?"

Alex had a thought and pulled out the list Callahan had given him. Scanning through it, he found the rolls of denim, bales of cotton, cans of lamp oil, a crate of cast iron toy cars, paper napkins, and other things that didn't seem to have any real value. There were, however, some things that stuck out. A dozen spools of heavy gauge copper wire, a truckload of magelights, assorted construction equipment, and building supplies.

Folding up the list again, Alex walked along the rows of trucks, looking at the company names. He stopped when he got to one labeled, *Masterson Tool & Die.*

Consulting the list again, he saw that the truck from Masterson had been carrying drill bits for a mining machine that were to be shipped by train to a site in Colorado. Walking around to the back of the truck, Alex opened the rear door. He already knew what he'd see there, but it was nice to have his hunch confirmed by the site of the empty cargo space.

"I know that look," Danny accused, stepping up beside him. "You've figured something out."

Alex put the folded list of stolen goods back into his shirt pocket and shook his head.

"Maybe," he said. "It's just a hunch right now."

"Care to share?"

"Not yet," Alex said, patting Danny on the shoulder. "Let me make a few calls first. I wouldn't want to send you off on a wild goose chase."

Danny looked like he might object but finally nodded.

"Okay," he said. "Let's go find a phone. I've got to call this in anyway."

16

THE HALL OF RECORDS

The diner Danny found to make his phone call from was the kind of place you didn't want to sit down in, much less eat at. That didn't seem to matter much to their clientele of burly workmen in coveralls that smelled faintly of blood. It was located across the street from a slaughterhouse and cannery, an enormous brick building that filled an entire block.

The rumble of the massive engines that drove the slaughterhouse and the cacophony of terrified pigs as they were lifted up from their pens to their doom carried all the way to the diner. Danny had to cover his free ear to hear what Callahan was saying on the other end.

Alex looked around at the men who sat eating, paying the two men in suits no attention. Despite their obviously being out of place, no one wanted to attract the attention of a police detective.

"Your turn," Danny said, handing over the telephone's earpiece.

Alex pulled Bill Sanderson's card from the pocket in his rune book and gave his number to the operator. A moment late the line connected, and Alex strained to hear the engineer's voice.

"Sorry," Alex said. "It's noisy here, there's a slaughterhouse across the street. I was calling to tell you that the police found your missing truck."

Sanderson was glad to hear that but asked about the shipment of boring bits.

"Those are still missing," Alex said. "I was wondering, though, could those be used to dig a tunnel?"

"I assume you mean here in the city," Sanderson replied. "They are made to dig tunnels, after all."

"Yes," Alex confirmed. "Like maybe under a street to get into a bank vault."

"I doubt it," Sanderson said. "Mines have big diesel engines mounted on rails to drive the bits. That would make about as much noise as your slaughterhouse. Then there's the exhaust; anyone wanting to drill under a building would have to vent the engine to the outside or it would kill them. Somebody would notice that for sure."

Alex thought about what the tool engineer had said. It made sense: if there was a big motor rumbling away in the basement of some shop or professional building, people passing by on the street would hear it.

"You're thinking that's why that guy was kidnapped," Sanderson guessed. "The Assistant Mining Engineer."

"Yeah," Alex admitted. "I thought it fit pretty good, what with your missing bits and all, but I guess you're right."

"Well I'm glad you found our truck," he said. "But I'm sorry I couldn't help you with your case."

"That's all right," Alex said. "The police should contact you later about the truck."

Sanderson thanked him and hung up.

"So," Danny said once they were back in his car. "You think these thefts are about a bank job?"

"I did," he said with a shrug. "But I guess it couldn't be. The work needed to tunnel under a city street would make too much noise."

"What made you think my thieves wanted to tunnel into a bank?"

Alex pulled out the paper and showed Danny the list of stolen items, pointing out that if you ignored the nonsense things taken, you were left with the kind of gear needed for a robbery. Then he explained about Leroy.

"But you said he doesn't know anything about digging tunnels," Danny pointed out.

"Maybe the people who took him don't know that," Alex said. "Maybe he's just going along so they don't kill him."

Danny sat in the driver's seat for a long minute, then pulled out a cigarette and lit it.

"What if you're right about the robbery, just wrong about the target?" he pondered. "Maybe they're not after a bank, but something around here." He gestured at the slaughterhouse. "Nobody would hear someone drilling a tunnel over that."

Alex considered it but shook his head.

"There's nothing out here that you'd need to dig a tunnel to steal," he pointed out.

"Well, I'm still going to mention it to Callahan," he said. "You're right about the list of things stolen — a lot of that stuff would be useful in a robbery. Maybe they're not digging a tunnel at all, maybe it's something else."

"Then how does Leroy fit in?"

"He doesn't," Danny said, puffing on his cigarette. "You're trying to make him fit, but if there's no tunnel, there's no reason for him to be involved."

Alex didn't like it, but Danny had a good point. One of Iggy's first lessons in being a detective was not to get attached to any one theory. As his famous detective said, it leads to twisting fact to suit theories, instead of theories to suit facts. He'd been letting his need to find Leroy shoehorn into Danny's case.

He sighed and took out a cigarette of his own.

"I guess that's it then," he said. "Can you drop me at a crawler station?"

Danny nodded and started the car.

As they drove, Alex racked his brain over Leroy. Nothing about his kidnapping made sense. He didn't know anything a group of kidnappers would need and he had no money or family connections. The only thing that had any logic to it was the tunnel idea, but Sanderson had put the kibosh on that notion pretty effectively.

It was frustrating, and he angrily flicked the stub of his cigarette out the window. He was pretty sure Leroy Cunningham was going to die sometime in the next few days, and as things stood now, there wasn't a damn thing he could do about it.

THE HALL of records was an imposing building of white marble that always reminded Alex of a public library. In reality it was quite like the library except that people visited the library for fun. No one visited this monument to government red tape unless they had to.

Alex made his way inside and went downstairs to where he knew the permit records were kept. He only had an hour and a half until the office closed at five, but he'd only brought twenty-two of David Watson's files, so it shouldn't be hard to look up the permits for just those.

"Can I help you?" a white-haired man said from behind a raised desk. He was thin to the point of being gaunt, though the sagging skin around his jowls indicated that he hadn't always been so. Alex couldn't tell if the dark circles under the man's eyes were a sign of lack of sleep, or just the stark lighting in the basement. He looked to be in his sixties, but seemed worn down, probably by too many years working for the government.

"I need to see some building permits," Alex said, passing over a list of the permit numbers he'd copied from Watson's files.

The man's hand trembled when he took the paper and he had to put it down on the desk to read it properly.

"That's a lot of records, young man," he said, giving Alex an appraising eye. "Are you looking for something particular?"

"I'll let you know when I find it," Alex said with a shrug.

He lit another cigarette, leaving him only four more, while he waited for the old fellow to get the files. He came back after about ten minutes with five folders under his arm.

"We can only let out five at a time," he said. "This will get you started." He opened a register book and wrote down the numbers of the files he had, then turned the book around for Alex to sign.

"I'll pull the rest and have them here for you, Mr..." He squinted at the name in the book. "Lockerby."

"Thanks," Alex said, picking up the folders.

"My name is Edmond Dante," the old man said. "Let me know if you need anything else."

Alex took the files to a nearby table and spread them out in front of him. The first one dealt with a piece of farmland Watson surveyed so that a mansion could be built on it. Alex was about to set it aside when he noticed that Watson's wasn't the only survey attached to the permit.

It turned out that the building permit encompassed six different parcels of land, only one of which had been surveyed by Watson as a condition of its sale to *North Shore Development*. It wasn't anything major, but Alex wondered why the company used different surveyors for the other parcels.

"It's because each parcel was surveyed as a condition of sale," Edmond explained when Alex posed the question to him. "When this company bought the land, they had to get it surveyed. They used whoever was available."

"Thanks," Alex said, happy to have the mystery explained but not any closer to finding any meaning in the files.

He paged through each new file, looking for something, anything, that might explain why David Watson had been murdered, but nothing seemed improper or out of place. It was almost five when he opened the last folder and quickly looked through it. This one was for a large property owned by a wealthy family who wanted to build a home on it.

Alex checked the information on the parcel and found that, like most of the others, it had been put together from several smaller parcels.

That tickled something in Alex's brain.

He picked up the folders on the desk and found the one he wanted. Opening it, he confirmed that this survey was for a five acre parcel of land. Like the first file he looked at, there were other parcels that made up the lot being built on, Watson had only surveyed that five-acre piece. The difference was, when aAlex checked Watson's file, it said that he'd done the work for a woman named Martha Gibbons, not for North Shore Development.

"She probably got him to do it so she could sell the land," Alex said, shutting the folder.

He collected the folders and took them up to Edmond at his desk. Something about Martha Gibbons was bothering him but he couldn't put his finger on it.

"Do you have land sale records here?" he asked Edmond.

The old man shook his head and Alex noticed that he was sweating.

"Sale records would be in the assessor's office of whatever county the land was located in," he explained, panting as if he were out of breath.

"You okay, Edmond? Alex asked.

"Nope," Edmond said with a mischievous grin that revealed a dimple in his cheek. "Doc gave me the long face. Leukemia, he said. Gave me six months."

Alex's mouth dropped open. Leukemia explained a lot, especially the weight loss, the shakes, and the sweating.

"I—" he began but Edmond waved him off.

"That was five years ago," he said with a chuckle. "I suppose it'll get me eventually, but not today."

"Well, stay healthy, my friend," Alex said.

Edmond thanked him, and Alex headed upstairs as the security guards began to sweep through the building before it closed. He felt like he should have said something more to Edmond, but what was there to say? The man had outlived his doctor's dire prediction by years; nothing Alex could add would change that reality. He did resolve to be more like Edmond, though. After all, his days were just as numbered. It would do him good not to think about it and just live his life.

A row of phone booths lined the wall by the front entrance to the building and Alex stopped to check in with Leslie. He still had some time before Jessica would be in, so he wanted to make sure he didn't have anything else on his plate.

"Hey, boss," Leslie said once they were connected. She sounded even more chipper than before if that was possible.

"What's the good word?" he asked.

"Randall is coming in to town on Saturday and taking me dancing," she said.

Alex laughed at that.

"Of course he is," he said.

"He just called me," she went on, ignoring Alex's dig.

"Well call him back for me, will you? I want him to look up a property owner named Martha Gibbons." He gave her the parcel number and she wrote it down.

"Do you need this tonight?"

Alex thought about that.

"No," he said. "Tomorrow is soon enough. I just need to know if there's anything unusual about her land."

Leslie promised that she would, and Alex was about to hang up.

"Hey," she said, trying to catch him.

"Yeah?"

"I talked with Hannah this afternoon, just checking up on her. She's doing fine, by the way."

"I never doubted you," Alex said.

"She said that when Alex worked for the Coledale mine that the safety engineer broke his leg and was laid up for six months."

Alarms went off in Alex's head.

"Who did his job while he was laid up?"

"Hannah didn't know, but I was thinking—"

"What if it was Leroy?" Alex finished her thought. "That would explain everything. Thanks, doll, you did great."

"Remember that when it's time for my Christmas bonus," she teased.

Alex promised to remember and hung up.

"Lobby's closing, Mister," a flat-faced security guard said, waiting politely for him to finish.

Alex absently thanked the man and made his way outside. If Leroy had done the safety engineer's job then he would know how to shore up a tunnel. That explained everything, the stolen tools and construction equipment, Leroy's kidnapping, even why the finding rune couldn't link to him. Wherever Leroy was, he was likely underground.

That had to be it.

"But how are they going to use those big drill bits?" Alex checked himself. "Sanderson was right, they'd need a big, noisy engine."

He thought about it as he walked down the bock toward the crawler station. The target had to be a bank; no one else had anything valuable enough to make such a big job worthwhile. But all the banks were in the Middle and Inner rings, far too quiet for the noise of tunneling.

The crawler station was empty when Alex reached it. He must have just missed one. Trying to shake his mental gears loose, he walked down to a news stand and bought a copy of the Times. He and Iggy hadn't had dinner together in a few days, so he was certain the old fox would want to discuss the news tonight.

As Alex handed a dime to the man at the stand, he caught sight of the screaming headline on the afternoon edition of *The Midnight Sun.*

Runewright Detective Cracks City Wide Theft Ring, Ghost Still at Large.

Alex scooped up the paper and began reading the story.

"Hey, Mac," the newsman said. "This ain't a library."

"Sorry," Alex said, dropping a nickel on the man's counter.

According to the story, famous runewright detective, Alex Lockerby had been observed by reporters leading police on a wild trip through the city. At the end of the journey, he'd revealed a stash of stolen trucks hidden in an abandoned west side factory.

Alex felt sick to his stomach. Danny wasn't likely to believe that Alex had given this story to the tabloids, but Detweiler was going to blow his top, and Callahan too. The way the story read, the department was a bunch of idiots who needed Alex to solve all their cases, literally leading them around by the nose. In the end, the writer wondered why Alex wasn't on the ghost case and openly accused the police of putting the city at risk.

Alex flipped back to the front page and read the by-line. It was Billy Tasker, the same reporter who'd outed Alex's involvement with the Watson killing case in the first place.

"What is it with this guy," Alex growled, tucking the tabloid under his arm. The death of Paul Lundstrom was the lead story on the cover of the Times, but with far less salacious details than *The Midnight Sun.* Alex flipped the paper over and read the articles below the fold while he waited for the next crawler. There wasn't much interesting, some tax bill the legislature was considering, and a political scandal in Washington D.C. A sidebar article mentioned a successful test of the first section of Andrew Barton's elevated crawler line, which ran from Empire tower north and along Central Park West.

Alex nearly dropped the paper.

"Hey, buddy," he yelled at the newsman. "Where's there a phone around here?"

The man pointed to a bar on the corner of the next block and Alex ran the whole way.

"Get me Danny Pak," he told the police operator once he reached the Central Office switchboard.

"I'm sorry," the voice came back a moment later. "Detective Pak doesn't answer."

"Take a message for him, please."

"Go ahead," the voice said after a moment.

"Tell him to call Alex Lockerby at home as soon as he can. I need to know if one of the trucks he found today is from Barton Electric."

The police operator said she would give him the message and hung up.

17

THE CHECKUP

Alex wanted to go home and wait for Danny's call, but he still had to go see Jessica. As much as he felt he was on to something, going home wouldn't make Danny call any faster, and he definitely didn't want his tremors coming back.

It was just after six when Alex walked up to the brick, two-story house with the alchemist sign in the yard. This time he didn't bother with the front door, opening the gate to the back yard instead and following the paved path around to the back.

He peered in the long bank of windows next to the door and saw Jessica moving from table to table in the back of the dimly lit lab. She'd pick up a clipboard on one table, make adjustments to the equipment or add things to the various jars, then make notes and move on. The lab was mostly dark, with hanging lights over each table, and Jessica's red hair would shine as she moved beneath them. Alex watched her for a few moments, then knocked on the glass. Jessica was so startled she nearly dropped the clipboard she was holding.

Alex took off his hat and waved at her as she made her way through the maze of tables to the mud room and the back door.

"You startled me," she said, a little flushed.

"Sorry," he said with a smile.

Jessica smiled back. She wore he work apron over a cream-colored dress, and she had her green scarf around her neck. Alex assumed she liked to accent the green of her eyes.

"Well, no harm done." She held open the door so Alex could come in, then shut it behind him.

"I was disappointed that you didn't come see me on Tuesday," she said in a voice that implied that Alex should be sorry too.

"I got shot," he said with his best, *trust me* smile.

She raised an eyebrow while running an appraising eye over him, looking for any signs that his statement was true.

"It was a busy day," he said.

"I'll bet," Jessica said, leading the way back into the lab. "Since you're early, you'll have time to tell me all about it while I make my rounds."

She walked over to the table where she'd been standing when Alex knocked on the window and picked up its clipboard.

"What are you doing?" Alex asked.

Jessica showed him the clipboard. It might as well have been written in Chinese for all the good that did. The paper on the board was covered in columns with each one headed by a time. To the right of that were some pre-written notes and some blank spaces.

As Alex watched, Jessica noted the time from a clock on the wall, then checked it against an alarm clock on the table. The clock on the wall was elaborate and ornate, with carvings of animals all around it and a large set of counterweights hanging from it. A brass pendulum hung from it as well, rocking gently back and forth while emitting tick-tock sounds. Alex had seen clocks like this before; they were prized for their accuracy and very expensive.

Finding that the clocks matched, Jessica wound the alarm clock and set it to go off at eight-thirty.

"What's that for?"

"This is when I need to stir the solution," she said, putting a check mark in an empty column next to the printed time of eight-thirty.

"So you set the clock to remind you," Alex said, nodding with understanding. He looked around the lab at the almost two dozen tables and their glassware and burners. "Do you have to do that with all of them?"

Jessica laughed, or rather giggled. The sound was girlish and held none of her usual, sultry tone. She covered her mouth as if she were embarrassed, but Alex knew she was smiling behind her hand.

"Of course I do," she said. "That's what I do here, make sure the major potions are done right."

She put down the clipboard and moved to the next table. This one didn't have a light hanging above it, so she moved back into the light of the previous table with the new clipboard.

"Why is it so dark in here?" Alex asked. Most of the room's lights had shades and hung directly over their tables. "Magelights are relatively cheap."

"Some potions are sensitive to light," she explained, putting the clipboard down and bringing a sealed can and a ring of measuring spoons from the dark table. She carefully measured out some brown powder from the can, then added it to a jar of liquid bubbling away in the dark.

"You're stalling," she said, moving on to the next table. "You're supposed to be telling me about how you got shot, and why you think that's a good excuse for missing our appointment."

Alex signed and began relating the story of his looking into Andrew Barton's stolen motor and how he'd been shot in an alley outside the Lightning Lord's factory.

"Is he handsome?" Jessica asked with her half-smile in place.

"Who?" Alex asked, surprised by the question.

"Barton," Jessica said, as if the answer were self-evident.

"I suppose he's handsome enough," he said. "He's worth over a million, and most people find that more than attractive enough."

Jessica smirked at that.

"Indeed most people would," she said, setting another alarm clock. "So did you find the Lightning Lord's motor?"

"Not yet," Alex said.

He started explaining the kidnapping of Leroy Cunningham and how the man that shot him was involved. She listened attentively, asking the occasional question as she worked her way along the tables to the far back of the room.

"Done?" Alex asked as she hung up the clipboard on the final table.

"Not quite," she said, nodding to a heavy door set in the wall. It had a large, new-looking brass lock above the handle.

Alex hadn't seen inside this room, but it was next to Jessica's room, so it was likely to be the same general size.

"What's this?" he asked as she pulled out a small key ring.

For a brief moment a frown crossed her lips, but she replaced it almost instantly with her sardonic smile.

"This is the reason I'm here," she said, inserting a key in the lock. She turned it and pushed the door open. "Don't touch the handle," she said, reaching inside to switch on a magelight. "It's got a needle coated in a nasty contact poison hidden inside it."

Alex raised an eyebrow at her, but she just shrugged.

"What?" she said. "Don't you have security measures around your valuables?"

Alex thought about his vault. The contents of it were probably worth several Gs but it wasn't like anyone could break in and steal it. Still, storing his gear in an extra-dimensional room was pretty extreme as security measures went.

"I suppose I do," he said, being careful not to get near the door as he entered.

Inside the room was another table and what looked like an alcohol distillery. A complex series of burners, beakers, tubes, evaporators, and valves filled the table, and Alex could see several different colored solutions at the various stages. A rack of various jars, cans, and stoppered bottles was mounted on one wall along with a clipboard and a thick notebook. There was another alarm clock on the table, and Jessica carried it outside to check it against the big clock on the wall.

"You still haven't said what this is," Alex said when she returned.

"My best friend is named Linda Kellin," Jessica said.

"Any relation to the Doc?"

Jessica nodded.

"Her daughter." She took a deep breath as if steadying herself. "Linda has polio," she said.

Alex felt a knot in his stomach. Not everyone died from polio, but it could leave people crippled or worse.

"So you're trying to develop a cure," Alex guessed.

"Yes," Jessica said. "It's why I came to work with Dr. Kellin."

"So, how is it going?"

"Linda...she's in an iron lung upstate," Jessica said, fighting to control her emotions. "We think we're making progress, but it's really just trial and error at this point."

She turned her head away and wiped her eyes furiously with the back of her hand. Alex wanted to reach out and hold her, tell her it was going to be all right, but he had no idea if that was true. At best it would have been a comforting lie.

"Is that why Dr. Kellin took you on as her protégé?" he asked, desperate to fill up the sudden-yet-terrible silence. "I thought alchemists usually only passed on their knowledge to family."

"I could ask you the same thing about Dr. Bell," she said. "But yes, Linda is Dr. Kellin's only family, so she had no one to pass her recipe book on to. When I told her I'd do anything to help Linda, she started training me."

"How long ago was that?"

"Six years now," Jessica said.

Alex was stunned at that.

"You've been living this way, sleeping during the day and brewing potions all night, every night for six years?" hee wondered. "When do you have time to go to dinner or catch a picture?"

"Why, Mr. Lockerby," Jessica said, her smirk returning and mischief in her eyes. "Are you asking me out?"

Alex hadn't meant that, not at all, but he was a trained observer and a man of action.

"Of course I am," he lied. "Unfortunately, you don't seem to have the time."

She broke into her girlish giggle again.

"It's true I have to mind the lab," she said. "But there are long stretches when I don't have anything to do. Usually, I read, but I can make...exceptions." She stepped close to him so they were almost touching, and looked up into his eyes. "As luck would have it, there's a three-hour window opening on Saturday night at seven. You can take me to dinner, someplace nice, since as you pointed out, I don't get out much. Pick me up here?"

"I will," Alex said, without bothering to wonder if he even had the time. For a woman like Jessica, he'd make the time.

"Now give me a minute," she said. "And then I'll check your nerve tonic."

She turned to the experiment and began taking measurements and adjusting mixtures. At every step, she noted down what she had done in the book from the shelf, then checked off some things on the clipboard.

"So," she said, pulling the door shut once she was done and re-locking it. "You shook off four bullets the other day?"

"Isn't that supposed to be poisoned?" Alex asked, pointing at the doorknob.

"If you turn it, a needle will pop out and stick your palm," Jessica said, her voice easy as if what she'd said were the most normal thing in the world. "I'm careful, but I forget every now and again. It stings like the dickens, but, as you might remember, since I told you last time you were here, I'm immune."

Alex had forgotten about Jessica and the poison paint job on her nails. He glanced down and found them the same off-red color they had been before. Maybe the color was a result of the toxin.

"Now," Jessica said, leading him over to the workbench by the windows at the front of the room. "Take off your jacket and roll up your sleeve. I need some blood."

Alex's face soured at that and she laughed at him.

"What's the matter, tough guy," she said, actually leaning against his chest. "You aren't afraid of a little needle, are you?"

Alex had to take a breath before answering. Her presence that close was about as intoxicating as David Watson's single-malt.

"In my experience, it's never a little needle," he said, only half-joking.

She smiled and patted his face.

"Don't worry," she said, her lips drawn up in an adorable pout. "If you're a good boy, I'll get you a lollipop."

Alex took off his jacket and laid it on the table before rolling up his shirt sleeve. Jessica motioned him onto a wooden stool, then put down a syringe with a needle that looked about the diameter of a swizzle stick. He knew his mind must be exaggerating it, but he decided he didn't want to find out. As she tied a rubber hose around his arm, he resolved to look the other way until she was done.

"Okay," she said, a few pain-filled moments later. "All done. Hold this on your arm."

She gave him a cotton ball and he pressed it over the puncture wound in the crook of his arm. Jessica moved to the next workbench down and squirted some blood from the syringe into a glass dish. She added some chemicals from various bottles, then heated the dish over a burner for a few seconds.

"I think I like Dr. Kellin's method better," Alex said, checking to see if the bleeding had stopped.

"She cheats," Jessica said. "This would be a lot easier with a Lens of Seeing, though."

"Can't you just make your own?"

Jessica snorted at that.

"Dr. Kellin says I'm not ready yet." She swirled a toothpick into the blood mixture in the dish. "So, I do things the old-fashioned way."

Jessica pulled the toothpick out and Alex noticed that the end had turned a lime green color. She held it up to a chart with various colors on it and nodded.

"I see the problem," she said at last. "You've got the wrong kind of blood."

Alex had no idea what to make of that.

"Well, it's the blood I came with," he said, a little defensively.

Jessica flashed him her sardonic grin.

"I mean the wrong kind for the tonic," she explained. "You have O-negative blood. That's fairly rare."

"Is that bad?"

Jessica shook her head, sending her red hair flying.

"Usually it's a very good thing. Your blood can be used on someone with any blood type. It means you're a universal donor. The problem is that while this tonic is fine for most people, it has a strange reaction with you O-negative types."

Alex reached inside his folded jacket and pulled out the little flask Jessica had given him days earlier.

"So is this going to work now that Dr. Kellin adjusted it?"

"Yes," Jessica said, moving back to him and examining the needle mark on his arm. The bleeding had indeed stopped so she pulled a Band Aid from the pocket of her apron and stuck it over the wound. When she was done, she leaned down and kissed it.

Alex could feel the silky touch of her lips even after she'd raised her head back up.

"There you go," she said, looking into his eyes. "All better."

That urge to kiss her was back and Alex wondered if he should bother to fight it. It turned out not to matter since his second of hesitation was enough for Jessica to step back and move away toward another workbench.

Alex rolled his sleeve back down and buttoned it, then slipped on his jacket. He had just resolved to go kiss her anyway, despite the moment having passed, when one of the alarm clocks on a workbench in the back began ringing. The sound echoed off the stone floor, filing the space with its cacophony.

He looked at Jessica and for the briefest moment; she looked annoyed. Her sardonic mask came back a moment later and she turned to him.

"You'd better go," she said. "This will take a while."

Alex really hated that alarm clock.

"Saturday then?" he verified.

"Seven sharp," she said, sauntering toward the back of the lab, her hips swaying. "Don't be late."

"Wouldn't dream of it," Alex said, picking up his hat.

18

THE RUNE BOOK

Alex opened his battered pocketwatch and the runes inside flared to life. He couldn't see the magic, of course, but he felt the faint tingling sensation of their power as they activated. It was comforting. He'd spent most of the week wondering if his magic was waning, if the sacrifice he'd made to save the city was stealing his very identity.

He knew what Iggy would say, what he had said, that magic was a part of him, that it didn't fade with age. Still, people went deaf and blind with age, wasn't magic just another sense?

He was a good detective, of course, but the world already had good detectives. It was his magic, the things he could do and see that others couldn't, that set him apart. He'd never have found Danny's missing trucks without it. Would anyone need another detective if he lost what made him unique?

The feel of the runes in his watch was like a musical chord, ringing in his mind. He smiled as he detected a slight sourness to the sound, as if one of the notes was not quite on pitch. Experience told him that one of the runes etched into the watch's back cover was beginning to fade. He'd have to redo it soon if he wanted to continue being able to open his front door.

Taking hold of the handle, he turned it, smiling at the memory of Jessica's poison-snared door handle. Iggy's runes on the front door and entryway were a far better and less deadly deterrent. No one without the proper rune combination could enter, and only a runewright could activate the runes in Alex's watch. Only once the runes were active would the constructs on the brownstone release the door.

Alex turned the handle and pushed. Then the smile ran away from his face.

The door didn't move.

He checked the runes, certain that they were working, and tried again with the same result.

He felt his heartbeat spike. Normally he'd have been sure that the slight sour note of the weakening rune wouldn't affect the properties of the pocketwatch, but what if he was fooling himself?

What if he'd already lost enough of his ability that he missed the difference between a weakening rune and a defective one?

He closed his eyes and willed his heartbeat back down. One thing he knew from being a detective was not to let a first impression dictate the direction of a case.

Sufficiently calm, he reached up and pulled the chain that rang the door bell. He noticed that his hands were trembling and quickly took a shot from the flask, hoping that was the reason.

A long minute passed and he was about to ring again, when he heard the inner door to the vestibule open. Iggy's silhouette, dressed in his red smoking jacket, appeared blurry through the frosted surface of the door's stained glass window. A moment later, Alex heard the thunk of the door bolt being drawn back and the door opened.

"What's the matter?" Iggy said, taking in Alex's appearance with a single glance. Before Alex could answer, his concerned look turned to one of embarrassment.

"I'm sorry, lad," he said, reaching out to take Alex by the arm and pull him inside. "I was looking through the...the Textbook, so I set the deadbolt."

Alex had to hold his hands together to keep them from shaking in pure relief. The deadbolt was an extra security measure that they only used when Iggy took the Archimedean Monograph down from its place on the bookshelf. When it was locked, an extra construct of powerful protection runes activated. To hear Iggy describe it, with these runes in place, the brownstone could survive a bomb.

As Alex stepped inside, Iggy closed the door and reset the dead-bolt. From this side, Alex felt the protection construct activate. If the construct in his watch had been a chord, this sound washed over him like the crescendo of something written by John Phillip Sousa. It wasn't a physical sound, of course, but that didn't stop the hair on his arm from rising nonetheless.

"You had me worried there," Alex said, finally having the presence of mind to close his pocketwatch and return it to his waistcoat.

Iggy cast him an appraising look.

"Still on with that nonsense about losing your magic," he said. It was not a question; the old man knew Alex well enough to make that deduction. "I told you it doesn't work that way."

Alex wanted to believe him, more than he was willing to admit, but Iggy had trained him as a detective. He knew that all the doctor had to go on was his own intuition. He'd never actually met someone who'd traded the majority of his life energy for power. Not until Alex did it, anyway. There was no way the old man could really be sure.

Still, Alex reminded himself, he could sense the runes activating in the door and in his pocketwatch, and he wouldn't be able to do that if he'd lost his magic.

It wasn't an airtight theory, but Alex decided not to poke any holes in it.

"I suppose you're right," he said to Iggy. "So," he went on, changing the subject, "why are you reading the Monograph?"

Iggy's face grew troubled.

"Follow me," he said, turning and heading for the kitchen.

Alex hung up his hat on the row of pegs along the foyer wall, then headed after his mentor. In the kitchen, Iggy had a half-dozen books laid open on the massive oak table. Each book seemed to have several pieces of torn paper sticking out of it, marking various pages. A notepad filled with Iggy's spidery script lay on the table, held open by an ashtray. In the center of this storm of reference material, lay two books; one squarish, thickish, and bound in black cloth...and the other tall, thin, and covered in red leather.

Alex could feel the presence of the Archimedean Monograph the moment he entered the room. It was a collection of the most powerful runes known to man, handed down from the most famous and clever runewrights in history. Iggy had found it around the turn of the century and had kept it carefully hidden ever since. Even that precaution wasn't enough though; he'd been forced to leave his home and his family, fake his own death, change his name, and flee to America because of it. Alex knew first-hand that the legend of the Monograph drove many dangerous, desperate, and unscrupulous people to seek it. People willing to do anything to obtain it.

Alex had learned of its existence a year ago when he managed to unravel the secret of its deadly finding rune. He'd been stunned that the book had been hiding on Iggy's bookshelf the whole time. Iggy had been prodigiously proud of Alex for finding it, promising to reveal the book's secrets to Alex in time. Then he had promptly forbidden him from opening it without his permission.

So far, Alex had kept that promise.

The smaller black book was the one Alex had taken off the dead-and-burned kidnapper. Several of the pages had been torn out and laid around the open books, their face-like symbols staring out from the papers.

"I take it you didn't have any luck at the museum," Alex said, picking up a rune that looked like a man with an enormous nose looking to the left.

"Not entirely," Iggy said, picking up the rune book and turning to the last page. "No one knew what these were at first, but then I showed their senior Egyptologist this drawing."

Iggy turned the book so Alex could see. On the last page, a runic construct had been carefully drawn. Or, at least Alex assumed it was a construct; the form seemed familiar at least. It was round and made up of concentric rings. Each ring had symbols like the strange runes on it. In the center was a large circle with a grotesque caricature of a man's face, with his tongue sticking out. Almost all the runes in the rings looked like they were depicting creatures of some kind. Alex recognized birds, animals, and a few men, along with others that he assumed were mythological.

"So what is it?" Alex asked, not able to make heads or tails of the construct.

Iggy grinned at that, causing his mustache to rise up.

"The Egyptologist sent me to a Dr. Hargrave, he's an expert on ancient languages," Iggy said. "As it turns out, this is a calendar used by the ancient Mayans."

Alex knew the Mayans used to live in South America and they made pyramids like the Egyptians, but that was the extent of his information.

"So the runes are Mayan?"

"The linguist couldn't be sure," Iggy said. "He'd never seen symbols like the ones in this book, but the calendar is exactly like one at the museum."

"So what does all this mean?" Alex asked, tracing the rings of the calendar with his finger.

"Dr. Hargrave wasn't sure," Iggy said with a sigh. "Mayan is a dead language."

"Then how do they know this is a calendar?"

Iggy laid the book back on the table and pointed to the innermost ring.

"These are months," he said. "Days, then years." He moved his finger out to each of the other rings.

"But the linguist has no idea what these say," Alex said, picking up one of the symbols Iggy had torn out of the rune book. It looked the head of snake with a string of pearls around its neck and too many teeth.

"Even if he could read Mayan, I doubt he'd understand these," Iggy said. "It's clear that these are runes, and from a school I've never heard of. That concerns me."

"So you're going through the Monograph to see if there's any mention of other schools?"

Iggy nodded.

"All the known schools are mentioned," he said. "All the writers seem to believe that Archimedes was the first runewright, and that the

Kanji and Arabic schools are offshoots of that. But I'm starting to doubt it."

"How could ancient Mayans have copied from Archimedes work?"

Iggy shrugged.

"It's technically possible," he admitted. "Archimedes died around two hundred B.C. and the Mayans existed until about the seventeen-hundreds."

"Assuming someone knew how to get from Ancient Greece to South America," Alex felt compelled to add.

Iggy didn't respond, just shrugged and stared at the strange runes scattered around the table.

"That's not what's worrying you, though," Alex guessed. "Is it?"

"No," Iggy said, picking up the Monograph. "This book has been legendary for the better part of a century," he said. "I always believed it was the pinnacle of runic lore. A collection of the most powerful and dangerous runes ever created."

Alex nodded, seeing where Iggy was going, and he picked up the black book.

"But now there's a new game in town," he said. "And we have no idea what they can do."

The thought was sobering. Alex realized that if he thought enough about it, it would probably be terrifying.

He resolved not to think about it.

"So far," Iggy said, beginning to stack up the reference books, "the runes we've seen have been fairly straightforward. Tracking, force, fire, that sort of thing."

"But how did they activate that rune that burned the dead man?" Alex asked.

"And burn that rune into Mrs. Cunningham," Iggy agreed. "They've definitely got a few tricks over on us." He indicated the black book. "I'd feel better if I knew what any of these glyphs did."

"Glyphs?"

"That's what Mayan writing is called."

Alex set down the glyph book and picked up the Monograph. Just holding it in his hand, he could feel its power. Normally, the book was shielded by powerful obscurement runes, but they didn't work when it was open.

"I take it there's no rune in here for translating languages," he said.

Iggy took the book and closed it, setting it back on the table.

"Actually there is," he said, "but I wouldn't try to use that on an unknown magic. What if it activated the rune? That'd be fine if it was a light rune, but what if it was something more deadly?"

"Point taken," Alex said.

Magic was a great tool until it wasn't. Iggy was always telling him that there weren't any shortcuts when it came to being a detective. Still, Alex seemed to always be doing things the hard way. It would be nice if something came easy, every once in a while.

Alex helped Iggy clean up, putting the Archimedean Monograph back on the bookshelf in the front room. The shelf and even the space where the book sat were covered in invisible runes that drove the viewer's eye to look anywhere but at the book. Alex knew it was there and still had problems looking right at it once it was back in its place.

"I'm hungry," Iggy said once Alex was done.

"Don't look at me," Alex said. "Dinner is your department." He hadn't been paying attention, but now that Iggy brought it up, his stomach rumbled.

"I was busy learning about glyphs so we can hopefully find your missing draftsman," Iggy said. "What did you do to help?"

A slow smile spread across Alex's face but he didn't answer.

"You figured it out?" Iggy guessed, sounding impressed. "You know why these glyph runewrights took Cunningham."

"Not yet," Alex said. "But I've got an idea. That reminds me, did Danny call for me?"

Iggy shook his head.

"It's too late to cook," he said, heading for the stairs. "I'll get my coat and we'll walk down to the diner for a bite. While we eat, you can tell me all about your solution to the kidnapping."

Alex's stomach grumbled again but he shook his head.

"I can't," he said. "I need to be here in case Danny calls."

Iggy looked at the big grandfather clock standing in the corner of the front room. It was already pushing eight o'clock.

"By the time we get back, Danny is sure to be home," he said. "You can call him then. Now let me get my coat and we'll go."

Iggy went up the stairs and down the hall to his bedroom to remove his smoking jacket and put on his suit coat. Alex waited impatiently. That feeling that he should be doing something more to find Leroy kept coming back.

If he was right about why the glyph runewright and his friends had taken Leroy, Alex would need the help of the police to find him. Right now Alex was not their favorite person. If he wanted to have a chance of getting Leroy back to his wife alive, he would have to play a very careful game. He needed proof, or at least seriously compelling conjecture, in order to get the cops on board.

Of course, standing in the foyer waiting for Iggy, there wasn't a single thing he could do about it.

It was frustrating, but Alex took a breath and resolved to wait for the evidence he needed. If he moved too soon, if he couldn't convince the police that he was right, it would cost Leroy his life.

19

THE CONNECTION

Alex woke the next morning to his phone ringing. He knew that sound meant something important, but he couldn't seem to wrap his head around it. Finally he managed to work up the energy to roll over and pick it up.

"Lo?" he slurred.

"Alex?" Danny Pak's voice came out of the receiver at what seemed like an excessive volume level.

Alarms started going off in Alex's head, but try as he might he couldn't put together why he thought hearing Danny's voice was important.

"You called me," Danny reminded him. "About a missing Barton Electric truck?"

Synapses started firing and Alex sat up.

"I need a minute," Alex said, then set the receiver down and poured himself four fingers of bourbon from the bottle on his nightstand. Downing it in one go, he felt the liquor burn its way down to his stomach.

Normally that would do the trick, but his head still felt like it was stuffed with wool. Whatever Dr. Kellin had done to the nerve tonic, it was making him sleep a little too soundly.

Alex forced himself to stand and staggered to the bathroom to splash cold water on his face. He tried not to look in the mirror at the dark circles under his eyes and the unkempt mop of white hair hanging down into his face.

You're a train wreck, he thought.

Train!

Alex jumped as if he'd been jolted by a bolt of lightning. Tearing back into his bedroom, he scooped up the receiver and pressed it to his ear.

"Danny?" he said, trying not to yell.

"I'm still here," his friend's voice announced. "Were you asleep when I called?"

"Yeah," Alex admitted, picking up his alarm clock and pressing it to his ear. The time read eight o'clock, but he couldn't believe that was possible. The ticking of the clock told him it was.

"Rough night?"

"Rough week," Alex said. "Did you find out about that truck? I expected you to call last night."

"I got your message last night," Danny said, "but I had to wait till this morning to contact the sergeant in charge of evidence at the abandoned factory. I just got off the phone with him and he said that there is a truck in there from Barton Electric."

"Is it empty?" Alex asked.

"Yeah," Danny said.

Alex let out a pent-up breath. So far, everything was lining up perfectly. If he was right, he might just have a chance to save Leroy, help Danny solve his case, and get paid double his fee. Not a bad day's work.

"I didn't have a Barton Electric truck on my list of stolen property," Danny said. "How did you know about it?"

Alex started pacing, fully awake now.

"Andrew Barton asked me to find a stolen electric motor for him," Alex said.

"But why did you think my thieves took it?"

"I'll explain it all to you at the Central Office," he said. "You've got to run this by Callahan as soon as possible. Can you meet me there in an hour?"

"Do you have a death wish?" Danny said with no trace of humor in his voice. "After that tabloid article yesterday, Detweiler has you on his shoot-on-sight list, and Callahan's not far behind."

Alex groaned. He'd forgotten about Billy Tasker of *The Midnight Sun*. Something would have to be done about that guy, but now wasn't the time.

"That's why I need you," Alex said, thinking quickly. He had intended to let Danny bring his solution to Callahan and take the credit. Tasker burned that plan and now Danny might be risking his own career by helping. Alex hesitated for only a moment before continuing. "I need you to sell this to Callahan. Someone's life is at stake, I can't afford for the Lieutenant to give me the brush off."

"Whose life is at stake?" Danny asked. "What aren't you telling me?"

"Leroy Cunningham," Alex said. "I promise I'll tell you the whole story at the Central office. Meet me in the lobby at a quarter to nine."

To his credit, Danny didn't ask if Alex was putting him on. He just sighed and agreed to the meeting. Alex hung up with only a little trepidation. If his hunch proved out, Danny would get a very big notch in his belt. If he was wrong, though, he might lose his badge.

It was a tough spot in which he was putting his friend.

"Can't be helped," he said out loud, more to convince himself than anything. He peeled off his nightshirt and headed for the shower.

"I wonder if Danny would like to be a partner in a private detective agency?" he asked his reflection as he waited for the hot water.

He didn't need his reflection to answer, he already knew. Danny would hate it.

Alex decided he would have to work extra hard not to get his best friend fired.

FIFTEEN MINUTES LATER, Alex was showered, shaved, and dressed. Iggy had gone out again, leaving him a note saying he'd gone back to the museum to talk to Dr. Hargrave, the linguist, about the glyph runes. Since Iggy usually made breakfast, and coffee, it was irritating to have him gone two days in a row, but there was no helping it. If Danny couldn't make the police listen, the glyphs were the only lead Alex had left.

He was about to head out the door and try to grab a cup of coffee from a dog wagon somewhere near the Central Office when the house phone rang.

"Glad I caught you," Leslie's voice chided him when he picked up. "You all right?" she prodded when Alex mumbled a barely intelligible greeting at her.

"Tell you later," he said. He didn't want to go into it and he really didn't have the time. "I'm on my way over to the Central Office. I think I know how to find Leroy, but I'm going to need the cops' help to do it."

There was a long pause.

"Okay," she said finally.

Alex knew that meant she was worried. She would make jokes and try to bully him if she thought everything was okay.

"Don't worry," Alex said, trying to sound more confident than he felt. "Danny's with me on this one."

"Do not get that nice boy in trouble," she said.

Alex smiled at her bullying remarks. He'd said the right thing to calm her fears.

"What did you need?" he pressed. "I need to get going."

"One thing," she said. "Randall looked up Martha Gibbons like you wanted. She owned that land for years, but she fell behind in the taxes."

"What happened?"

"She died and the land was passed to a relative named Duane King."

"Okay," Alex said, taking out his notebook and writing King's name down. "I'll try to look him up at the Hall of Records after I'm done with the cops."

It wasn't much, but he felt like he was one step closer to figuring out why David Watson was killed.

"There's more," Leslie said with a sly grin Alex could hear. "When Randall looked into it, he found that the land was sold at a tax sale."

Alex had no idea what that meant.

"What's a tax sale?"

"Apparently, if you don't pay the taxes on your land for five years, the state will sell your land at auction to cover them."

"Didn't Mr. King have the money to pay the taxes?" he asked.

"Randall didn't know. All he could find out from the report was that the land value had gone down in the year before it sold."

"That doesn't sound right. I thought land on the North Shore was valuable."

"That was before the big push for millionaires to build houses in the Hamptons," Leslie said. "Randall said that land does lose value sometimes. He figures King didn't want to pay the taxes on land that wasn't worth that much to begin with."

"Well if this is all so normal, why did Randall bother telling it to you?" Alex was starting to get irritated. He knew very well why Randall would want to keep Leslie on the phone but why would she pass useless information on to him?

"There might have been a detail he found interesting," Leslie said. Alex could tell from the teasing shift in her voice that she was annoyed that he'd gotten short with her.

"I'm sorry," he said. "What did Mr. Wonderful find so interesting?"

"The tax sale for that land was moved to a new location on the day of the sale," she said. "Randall said that tax sales are announced to the public in advance. Moving it would make it hard for people to find."

Alex nodded, starting to see where this was going.

"Do you know who won that auction?" he asked.

"North Shore Development."

"Well that's not suspicious at all," Alex said, making quick notes in his book. If Seth Kowalski or someone in his office changed the auction's location to make sure North Shore got the land, then maybe one of the losers was the ghost.

That's a long time to wait to take revenge for a bad land deal, his logical brain reminded him.

It wasn't a concrete motive, but it wasn't nothing. Alex needed to find Duane King.

"Thanks, doll," he said, tucking his notebook back in his pocket. "Call your beau back and see if he's got an address for Mr. King. I'll run the rest of this down as soon as I'm done with the police."

"If I haven't heard from you by dinner, I'll come by with bail money," she promised, then wished him luck and hung up.

———

THANKS to his call with Leslie, it was nine-fifty when Alex got off at the crawler station across from the Central Office. At the corner of the block there was a vendor selling hot dogs and sandwiches. Alex noticed the bullet shape of a coffee percolator and he headed that way instead of crossing the street.

He wasn't sure that he could get the police to help him recover Leroy, even with Danny's assistance. He needed to get his head clear. The way things were going, this might be his only chance to find Hannah's missing husband.

He decided that in addition to clearing his head, he needed something for his nerves. He took out one of his two remaining cigarettes and lit it.

"I thought I might find you here," Danny's said when Alex stepped up to the dog wagon.

Alex must have needed the coffee more than he thought. Danny stood back from the street, leaning against the corner of the building. He wasn't hidden at all and yet Alex had missed him.

"Coffee," he told the man working the dog wagon.

"Are you going to tell me what this is about now?" Danny asked as Alex paid for his drink.

"Remember my theory from the other day," he said, sipping the scalding liquid as fast as he dared.

Danny nodded.

"You thought my thieves were actually bank robbers trying to tunnel into an underground vault."

"I was right."

Danny raised an eyebrow at that.

"As I remember it," Danny said, pulling out his notebook and flipping it open, "you called an expert on mining who told you that my thieves would need a special mining engine to make that work. One that would make far too much noise and probably asphyxiate the people using it."

Alex nodded. He hoped it didn't sound that impossible when Danny told Callahan.

"That's where the Barton Electric truck comes in," he said. "That truck was carrying an experimental electric motor that Barton developed to pull trains."

Danny didn't seem sure what to make of that.

"So," he said after a long silence. "You think the thieves are using the Lightning Lord's motor to turn the boring bits to dig a tunnel."

"Think about it," Alex said. "Electric motors are quiet and they don't have exhaust. Whoever stole all that stuff has everything they need to tunnel from the basement of one building into a bank vault. Even one across a street."

Danny hesitated, flipping to his notes on the things that had been stolen.

"It's crazy," he said after a moment. "But you're right, whoever stole the trucks has everything they'd need to dig a tunnel. Callahan is not going to like this."

Alex knew Danny was right, but he pressed on anyway.

"He's going to like a Manhattan bank getting robbed a whole lot less," he pointed out.

"True," Danny said, flipping his notebook closed.

"So, are you with me on this?" Alex asked with a smile.

Danny rolled his eyes and shook his head.

"I must be out of my mind."

"ARE YOU OUT OF YOUR MIND?" Callahan roared at Alex. The usual look of casual disdain he wore when Alex was around had been replaced by something perilously close to naked hatred. "It's bad enough you're sneaking around behind Detweiler's back and feeding information to the tabloids, but now you drag my detective in here to sell me some cock and bull story about a bunch of penny-ante gangsters tunneling into a bank? Get out of my office."

"Lieutenant," Danny began but Callahan silenced him with a look.

"If you keep listening to this guy, he's going to drag you down with him. I'm not going to let that happen to me."

Alex forced himself not to blush under Callahan's tirade. Truth be told, he did worry that sooner or later he'd steer Danny wrong and cost his friend his job. Or worse, his life.

"Lieutenant!" Danny interrupted. "I know how this sounds, but you should know by now, I wouldn't have brought this to you if I didn't think there was something to it."

Callahan swelled up with fury and Alex wondered if he'd pop his collar button. After a long, pregnant moment, however, he sat back in his chair and folded his hands in front of him.

"Do you have any idea what bank these guys are planning to hit?" he asked, his voice calm and even.

"No," Danny admitted.

Alex just shook his head when Callahan looked at him.

"Do you know how many banks there are in Manhattan?"

"No," Danny was forced to admit.

"Do you know?" Alex asked, speaking before he thought better of it.

Callahan glared at him.

"I know it's more than fifty," he said. "And since you don't know which bank is the target of this master plan, you're asking me to send out officers to look in the basement of every adjacent building for some lowlifes digging a tunnel."

Alex had to admit, it sounded crazy when put like that.

"Forget the fact that the Captain will never go for this," Callahan said. "Just tell me how, in your little scenario, these bank robbers are going to power that electric train motor?"

"Most of the banks worth all this trouble are in the Inner and Mid-rings," Danny said. "Power shouldn't be a problem."

"Except when you dig a tunnel, you do it underground," Callahan said. "Radiated power doesn't do well underground, that's why mage-lights have to be wired to the building in most basements."

"Very good, Lieutenant," Alex said. "The field generated by Empire Tower is based on magic and magic doesn't penetrate the ground well."

"I don't care how big Barton's missing motor is," Callahan said. "It's not going to drill anything without power."

Alex turned to Danny.

"Can I borrow your notebook?" he asked. "I think I can narrow down the search for your boss."

Callahan ground his teeth loud enough for Alex to hear as Danny passed over the notebook. Alex flipped to the page where Danny had catalogued all the stolen items that were missing from the recovered trucks.

"See here, Lieutenant," he said, putting the notebook down on Callahan's desk. "Three one-hundred-foot spools of heavy copper wire were stolen."

"So?"

"So," Danny said, picking up on Alex's train of thought. "All the robbers have to do is patch the wire into the building's etherium receiver and run it to the motor."

Callahan looked like he wanted to object but couldn't find a flaw in that argument.

"And," Alex jumped in, eager to maintain what little momentum he'd garnered. "The only buildings you need to search are ones adjacent to banks with underground vaults."

Callahan jumped up out of his chair and got right in Alex's face.

"It doesn't matter how many banks have underground vaults," he growled. "What matters is that if I manage to convince the Captain that there's something to this and it turns out to be a bust, I'm going to be jackass of the century around here. And that's if they let me stay on as janitor or something."

"What happens if it's not a bust but you don't look?" Alex pointed out, locking eyes with Callahan. "These guys have spent too much time planning and digging to waste that effort on some little, no-name bank. They're going to hit the biggest, fattest target they can find, and what happens when they do?" Alex picked up a newspaper from the Lieutenant's desk with an article about the ghost killer. The headline declared that the city was in panic.

"You think people are panicking now," he said. "Wait until there's a run on a major bank because all their money's gone."

"He's right, Lieutenant," Danny said. "One run is likely to cause others. They'll be rioting in the streets before it's done."

Callahan swore and flopped down in his chair. Alex could tell that the Lieutenant was facing the reality that he really didn't have any choice. Alex's evidence was circumstantial, but it fit, and Callahan couldn't afford to let a major bank get cleaned out. Alex resisted the urge to smile out of sheer relief.

"You told me you became a cop to protect people," Alex reminded him. "Now's your chance."

Callahan chuckled and shook his head.

"If this blows back on me, Lockerby, then you're done," he said in a cold, even voice. "You'd better leave the state, because if I catch you, I'll make sure you get twenty years breaking rocks, you got me?"

Alex nodded.

"That's fair," he said. "One more thing, though. When you have your boys search for our tunnel diggers, tell them that one of them is a hostage. A guy named Leroy Cunningham."

"Hostage?"

"Yeah, they grabbed him because he used to work in a mine and they think he knows how to shore up a tunnel."

"Does he?" Callahan asked.

Alex shrugged.

"Maybe," he said. "In any case, tell your men it's probably best if they stay out of any tunnels they might find."

"That's just great," Callahan sighed. He stood up and put on his suit coat.

"You're with me, Pak," he said to Danny. "You," he said, waving his finger in Alex's face. "Get lost, and don't come back till this is over, got me?"

"Loud and clear, Lieutenant."

20

THE COMPANY

"Back again, Mr. Lockerby?" Edmond said from behind the reception desk of the Hall of Records. He looked better today; the dark circles under his eyes seemed faded and his hands weren't shaking. He'd even slicked back his white hair. He wore a broad smile that showed off a dimple in his left cheek and straight, if yellow, teeth.

"They've got you working up here today?" Alex asked.

"No," Edmond said with a laugh. "I'm just filling in for our receptionist while she's at lunch. We all have to chip in around here."

His smile was easy and friendly. Alex was surprised the man remembered him. Most government desk jockeys couldn't be bothered to remember anyone. It was refreshing.

"I can take you downstairs if you need some more permit records," Edmond continued. "It's not very busy during the lunch hour."

"That's okay," Alex said, leaning on the counter. "I'm looking for business records today."

Edmond looked thoughtful for a moment, then shook his head.

"You need to have record or application numbers if you want to look up business records," he said. "We don't store permit records by business name."

"I'm not looking for permit records," Alex explained. "I need the paperwork a company has to file in order to do business in the state."

Edmond's brows furrowed for a moment. Alex had hoped someone in the office would be able to tell him exactly what he was looking for. He knew companies had to file paperwork so they could open a bank account and pay taxes, but he'd never had to do it himself.

"Is there someone here who can help with that?" he asked.

Edmond's look of concern melted away and he began smiling and nodding.

"You want to see their articles of incorporation," he said, then he shook his head. "For a minute, I couldn't remember what they were called." He looked around as if he were suddenly afraid of being over-heard and leaned in, conspiratorially. "I must be getting old," he said with a wink.

Alex laughed at that.

"So companies have to sign articles?" he asked. "Like pirates."

He'd read Treasure Island enough to know that pirates did that. It seemed eerily coincidental that companies had to do it too.

Edmond laughed.

"Just like pirates," he agreed. "You want the office of business filings." He pointed at the vaulted ceiling. "Third floor."

"Thanks," Alex said, starting to turn away.

"Wait," Edmond said, reaching out to grab his sleeve. "They're at lunch."

Alex wasn't really surprised; it was a government office after all.

"If everyone's at lunch, why are you still here?" he asked. "Why not just hang a gone-to-lunch sign on the door like everyone else?"

Edmond laughed. His smile was infectious, but Alex noticed that there were dark spots on his gums where they met his teeth. No doubt a symptom of his illness. Alex had almost forgotten that the vital man across the counter was under a death sentence.

Just like me.

Alex reminded himself that if Edmond could soldier on with a smile on his face, so could he.

"Too many politicians come in here on their lunch break," Edmond explained. "They get cranky if they have to wait, so half the building goes to lunch at noon, the other half at one."

Alex pulled out his pocketwatch and checked the time. It was over half an hour until one.

"I guess I'll go get some lunch myself, then," he said, replacing his watch. As he slipped his hand into his pocket, however, he remembered that he only had about two bits on him and he needed that for crawler fare.

"On second thought," he said with a sheepish grin. "Maybe I'll just wait here."

"Oh you don't have to wait," Edmond said, looking around with his conspiratorial grin. "I can help you."

"What if someone comes in?"

He shrugged and pulled up a paper tent from under the counter that read, *back in ten minutes*.

"The only people who come in at this hour are either lost or they're the politicians I was talking about. They know their way around plenty good enough."

Edmond led Alex past the wide stairway that led up to the second floor, down a hall to the elevator.

"You'll have to pardon me," he said, pushing the button to call the car. "I'm not up to two flights of stairs these days."

Alex mimicked his conspiratorial grin.

"Me neither," he said in a low voice.

The car was one of the new kind, without an operator, so Alex pushed the button marked three.

The Office of Business Filings was enormous, taking up the entire north wing of the building. Edmond simply twisted the handle of the darkened door and opened it. Alex filed away the knowledge that the clerks didn't lock the office during lunch for possible later use.

Inside there was a large waiting area with tables under magelights that lit up when Edmond flipped a switch by the door. A long counter ran along one side of the area with rows and rows of shelves running off into the dark behind them. A ticket dispenser stood on one end of the counter, and a sign invited patrons to take a number, just like at the deli.

"You know how to find things in that?" Alex asked, pointing to the towering shelves stuffed with file folders, boxes, and folios.

"Sure," Edmond said, lifting up a hinged part of the counter to step behind it. "It's just like downstairs except things are filed alphabetically by company name instead of by permit number. So what are you looking for?"

"Anything you can give me on North Shore Development," Alex said, leaning on the counter.

Edmond turned back toward the files, but stopped after a step, leaning heavily on a desk.

"Are you okay?" Alex asked, lifting the hinged counter and moving to where Edmond stood. Before he could grab the older man's arm and help him to a chair, Edmond waved him off.

"It catches up with me every once in a while," he said. "I'm all right."

Alex wanted to ask if he was sure, but Edmond straightened up to his full height. All traces of the weakness that had affected him a moment before were gone.

"Go wait out there," Edmond said, pointing back to the waiting area. "I'll catch hell if anyone sees you back here."

Alex wasn't happy about leaving, but Edmond was a proud man and Alex didn't want to insult him.

Retreating to his side of the counter, Alex lowered the moving piece into place and leaned on it. He considered smoking his last cigarette. Since he had a dinner date tomorrow, he resolved to save it for then.

Absently he wondered where he would take Jessica. He supposed there were still a few dollars of emergency money in his safe, the hollowed-out book he kept on the shelf right next to the Archimedean Monograph. If they went to a diner, he might have enough for a decent meal, but what would Jessica think of that? She'd told him to take her somewhere nice. He suddenly realized he didn't have the faintest clue what she might like to eat.

Some detective you are, he chided himself.

"Here you go," Edmond said, coming back with a heavy looking folio. He dropped it on the counter, kicking up some dust from inside, then took out a handkerchief and mopped his brow. He looked paler than he had before.

"You should go home," Alex said, turning the folio around and removing the elastic band covering the cardboard flap on top. "Spend time with your family."

Edmond smiled at that, but it was wistful rather than happy. He didn't have any family. Alex instantly felt like a heel.

"Don't be sorry," Edmond said, reading Alex's expression. "My wife and I had a good run before she passed."

"No kids?" Alex knew he shouldn't ask, but his curiosity got the better of him.

"A son," Edmond said with undisguised pride. "I lost him in the war."

Alex had heard that story before. A lot of people lost sons in the war, but it never got easy to hear about it.

"I'm sorry," he said.

"And I said don't be," Edmond admonished. "I miss my family, but I'm grateful for the time I had with them. Besides, I'll be with them soon enough."

Alex looked down at the folio. He missed his father, of course, and now Father Harry, but he still had Iggy and Leslie. If he played his cards right, he might even have Jessica in his life. He couldn't imagine what it would be like to lose them all. To be alone.

"You got lucky," Edmond said.

"What?"

The old man pointed at the paper tag on the outside of the folio.

"According to that, North Shore Development went out of business about ten years ago," he explained. "These records are scheduled to be moved to storage in a couple of months."

"Yeah," Alex said, talking just to ensure the awkward silence didn't come back. "Lucky."

He opened the folio and pulled out an inch-thick stack of papers. Some were stapled together into packets, but others were loose and none of them seemed to be in any kind of order.

"Here it is," Edmond said, reaching into the stack as Alex fanned them out on the counter. He pulled out a yellowed packet of papers that had been stapled together. The cover had the name North Shore Development on it and several official-looking stamps.

Alex turned to the front page and found a mass of legal phrases and clauses. Skipping that, he turned to the back and found what he was looking for.

A slow smile spread across his face as he read down the list of names of the partners in the company. There were eleven all total. All were names that Alex recognized.

He laughed out loud and Edmond looked confused.

"Something funny?" he asked.

"No," Alex said, still grinning. "Definitely not funny."

He copied down the names, then wrote down the index number on the folio.

"That's all you needed?" Edmond asked, somewhat incredulous. "Who are those people?"

"If I'm right," Alex said, stacking the papers neatly and returning them to the folio, "they cheated someone out of a fortune a long time ago."

Edmond looked shocked, then sad.

"Some people," he said. "Did they get away with it?"

"For a while," Alex said with a sigh. "But as near as I can tell, the man they cheated is killing them one by one."

"So, you're going to stop him?" Edmond wondered. "The killer I mean."

"That's the plan."

"What about the people who cheated him? Are they going to keep getting away with what they did?"

Alex gave Edmond a determined smile.

"Not if I can help it," he said.

ALEX WALKED Edmond back to the reception desk, then went to the pay phones near the door.

"It's me," he said as Leslie picked up. "Did you get an address for Duane King?"

"Yes," Leslie said in a worried voice, "but we've got bigger problems. Did you see today's issue of *The Midnight Sun?*"

Alex groaned.

"Don't tell me," he begged.

"They printed that entire list of names you gave the cops," she said, ignoring Alex's entreaty. "That Lieutenant over the case called here and raised hell. He wants you to call him right away."

"Do me a favor," Alex said. "If he calls back, stall him. Tell him you haven't heard from me."

"You on to something?" There was hope in her voice.

Alex grinned.

"Get this," he said. "The company that bought King's land at the tax sale, well it turns out the assessor wasn't just working with them. North Shore Development was entirely made up of Seth Kowalski and ten people who worked for him."

Leslie whistled.

"And you think Duane King is the one killing them?"

"Makes sense," he said. "But I'll need more evidence if I want to get Detweiler off my back. I'm going to go by King's address and see if he still lives there."

Leslie gave him an Inner-Ring address and he wrote it in his notebook.

"What do I do if Detweiler sends cops here?" Leslie asked.

"Just don't let them answer the phone."

DUANE KING'S address turned out to be for an elegant brick home a block from the park. If he could afford to live here, he had the money to pay off the taxes on the land he inherited. As Alex stood looking at the tidy home, he wondered if he might be wrong about who was killing former members of North Shore Development.

Steeling himself for disappointment, Alex opened the gate and walked up to the heavy door. It was stained dark and had polished brass hardware and an enormous knocker to match. Alex rapped smartly with the knocker, then took a step back from the door.

"Yes?" An older woman said as she pulled the heavy door open. She had brown hair and thick glasses, and peered at him through the lenses.

"I'm sorry to bother you, ma'am," Alex said, quickly taking off his hat. "But does Duane King live here?"

She smiled and shook her head.

"No," she said. "I've lived here for thirty years."

That would have meant she moved in around the time King let the land go to the tax sale. Maybe he was having money problems after all.

"Mr. King lived here about thirty years ago," Alex said.

The woman's face brightened and she smiled.

"Oh, yes," she said. "King was the name of the man we bought the house from, my husband and I."

"You don't happen to know where he went after he sold you the house, do you?"

"He moved to Florida," she said. "A town called Boca Raton, there was a doctor there."

"He was sick?"

"His wife," the woman said. "Poor thing, she had tuberculosis."

Alex had never heard of Boca Raton but if there was a doctor there who specialized in treating TB, it shouldn't be too hard to track them down. The doctor would undoubtedly have more information on the Kings.

"Anything else you can remember about Mr. King or his wife?"

"I'm sorry," she said, shaking her head. "It's been a long time since I thought about them. I hope she got better."

Alex thanked her and headed back to the street. TB wasn't always fatal; there was a good chance that if the mysterious doctor helped her, then Mrs. King might still be in Boca Raton.

The problem was that in order to find out, he would have to go home. Since he didn't have a fist-full of nickels, Iggy had the only phone he could use to call long distance. It was a risk, with Detweiler looking for him. Alex wouldn't put it past the man to have a few cops staking out the brownstone.

He sighed and put his hat back on. If he wanted to get Detweiler off his back, it was a risk he was going to have to take.

WHEN ALEX REACHED the brownstone that afternoon he didn't see anyone staking out the place, but he went around to the alley behind the house just in case. The door to the tiny, walled back yard was protected just like the front door, but Alex's pocketwatch let him pass without any trouble.

Once inside, he found that Iggy was still out. One of the lessons the old man had taught him about being a detective was that it was often better to ask for forgiveness rather than permission. With that in mind, Alex crossed the kitchen and picked up the telephone receiver.

"Get me Boca Raton, Florida," he said once the operator came on. Five minutes later he was connected with the operator in Boca Raton.

"I'm looking for a doctor who lives in town," he told her.

"That would be Dr. Harrison, sugar," the operator said in a thick Georgia accent. "Would yew like me to connect ya?"

"Is he the only doctor in town?"

"Only doctor for miles and miles."

"Then go ahead and connect me, please," Alex said.

Alex wondered how big Boca Raton really was, especially when, a moment later, the doctor answered his own phone.

"I'm sorry to bother you," Alex said. "I'm calling from New York. Are you the doctor who specializes in tuberculosis?"

There was a long pause on the line and Alex thought maybe the doctor couldn't hear him. He was just about to shout his question when the man spoke.

"I'm sorry, but I think you mean Doctor Gardner."

"Is he available?" Alex wondered. "It's kind of important."

"Doctor Karen Gardener was an alchemist who lived here. She was the doctor before I moved in. I seem to remember she had a treatment for TB," Dr. Harrison said. "But she died twenty-five years ago."

It was all Alex could do not to swear. If he didn't have bad luck, he wouldn't have any luck at all.

"Did you pick up her patients?" he asked, grasping at straws.

"Most of them, yes."

"Can you tell me if you're treating a woman named King for TB?"

he asked.

"What's this about?" Dr. Harrison said, his tone suddenly suspicious.

"I'm with the assessor's office here in New York," Alex lied. "It's come to our attention that a man named Duane King may be the legal owner of some land up here and I was told that he moved down there to get care for his wife. She had TB."

Alex crossed his fingers. The trick to a really good lie was to make it as close to the truth as possible, that way it sounded believable and you could keep the details straight if anyone questioned you later.

"I'm sorry to tell you, but Mrs. King died a long time ago. Her husband, Duane, is the one who murdered Dr. Gardner. He claimed she sold him a phony cure. King got twenty years at the state pen."

"Does he have any family in the area?"

"Used to," the doctor said. "His boy. Duane King lived with him for a while, but the boy got a local girl in trouble and skipped town."

"You said King got twenty years for a murder twenty-five years ago? So King is out?"

"I reckon so," Dr. Harrison said. "Before you ask, though, I know everyone in town and he didn't move back here."

"Did you know Dr. Gardner before she died?" Alex asked. "Is it possible she sold Duane King a phony cure?"

This time the silence on the line was palpable.

"Why do you want to know?" Harrison asked. "What does this have to do with King inheriting land?"

Alex thought fast.

"Sometimes in old wills there's a clause about the recipient being of good moral character. I'm just trying to gather as much information as I can."

"It's possible," Harrison said after another pause. "Dr. Gardner was a fair doctor but her alchemy skills weren't the best. Of course no one knew that until we got a really talented alchemist in town a few years ago."

"Thank you, Dr. Harrison," Alex said. "You've been very helpful."

Alex hung up and went to the table to scribble notes in his book as fast as he could. He knew there were alchemical treatments for TB, but they were very expensive. King probably heard that Dr. Gardner had a cheaper formula. Then he sold his house to save his wife and ended up losing her to a quack. Just thinking about it made Alex mad; he had no idea how angry Duane King had been.

Well, he had some idea.

Alex closed his notebook and sat there at the table for a long minute. He dreaded what was going to come next, but putting it off wouldn't make it go away. With a sigh, he got up, crossed back to the phone, and called the Manhattan Central Office of Police.

"Detweiler," the pudgy lieutenant's voice announced once the police operator connected him.

Alex took a deep breath and wished he had more than one cigarette.

"I hear you've been looking for me," he said in his most eager voice.

"Is that you, Lockerby?" he sneered. "You just cost me a five-spot. I bet Callahan that I'd have to drag you in wearing cuffs."

"Now what would you want to do that for?" Alex asked, pouring on the innocence.

"Don't get cute with me," Detweiler snarled. "You've been talking to that muckraker at the Sun. You gave him that list of the ghost's targets and now the Mayor's involved."

Alex closed his eyes and banged his head against the wall. He'd forgotten that the Mayor's wife was one of the people on the list. Worse, someone at the tabloid had it out for her.

He needed to make this go away. Quickly.

If the mayor got involved, Alex could lose more than just his P.I. license, he could do hard time. Taking a deep breath, he put on a smile. Iggy had taught him years ago that your voice changes when you smile. It makes people want to believe you, even if they can't see you.

"Well then, Lieutenant, I've got good news for you," he said.

"Don't try to talk your way out of this, scribbler. I warned you that I'd lock you up if you interfered in this case and I'm going to do just that."

"You might want to hear what I have to say, first."

The line went silent and Alex tried to remember one of the prayers Father Harry had drilled into his head as a youth.

"You've got one minute," Detweiler said. "Impress me."

Alex grinned at that. Detweiler had used that one-minute thing on him before, so he'd gotten his explanation down to forty seconds.

Iggy had told him time and again that preparation was everything.

"I know who the ghost is," Alex said. "I know that he's only targeting specific people on that list I gave you. I know who those specific people are, and I know why he's killing them."

Detweiler growled on the other end of the line. Alex had to cover his mouth to keep from laughing at the mental image of Detweiler trying to decide if he wanted to arrest Alex or catch the ghost. The former would be immensely satisfying for him, while the latter would get his name in the Times instead of the tabloids.

"Fine," he said, choosing his career over personal satisfaction. "You come down here and tell me what you know."

"I'll be right over."

"Be warned, scribbler," Detweiler said, his voice dangerous and calm. "If this doesn't pan out, the Mayor is going to be calling for your head and I'll be only too happy to give it to him."

Alex hung up and dialed Leslie.

"That was fast," she said. "Is this your one phone call?"

"No, but that may be coming soon," Alex said, only half joking. "I'm on my way over to the Central Office to give Detweiler everything I've got on Duane King. In the meantime, I want you to run over to the library and look up everything you can on that tabloid reporter, Billy Tasker."

"You want the whole works?"

"Everything you can find," he said. "I need this guy off my back."

"All right," she said. "Just remember why I won't be here if you need someone to bail you out."

Alex hadn't thought of that, but shrugged it off. He really didn't want the Mayor coming after him and if that meant he had to miss his date because he spent the weekend in jail then so be it. Jessica would understand.

You hope.

"Wish me luck then," Alex said, then he hung up and went to meet his fate.

21

THE CHIEF

The late afternoon sun lit up the Central Office of Police as Alex approached it for the second time that day. This time he wasn't going to meet Danny, or even Callahan. Callahan disliked P.I.s but still held a fair amount of respect for Alex and his work. Detweiler, on the other hand, viewed Alex as a bungler who was making his job harder through incompetence and leaking to the press. He'd never believe that the information in the Sun had come from a different source.

The only way Tasker could have learned about the list of names Alex had given the police was from a cop. The Sun obviously had a source inside the Central Office, but Alex knew he'd never be able to sell that idea. Detweiler simply wouldn't believe it. If it came down to a choice between Alex being a rat or one of his own, Detweiler would blame Alex every time.

Taking a deep breath, Alex savored what might be his last moments of freedom for the foreseeable future. He wouldn't put it past Detweiler to lock him up just out of spite.

He needed a plan.

The man's married to the Captain's favorite niece, Alex thought. *And the*

Captain is a political appointee. He's concerned with his image. Two-to-One Detweiler's cut from the same cloth.

Alex needed to appeal to the Lieutenant's ego.

It wasn't a great plan, but it wasn't nothing. Alex crossed the street and entered the lobby. The crowd of reporters seemed to have lessened from the other day, but there were still a half dozen or so sitting in the waiting area.

Alex caught sight of the young reporter with the brown suit that had accosted him the other day. Not wishing a repeat performance, he hurried across to the elevators.

When he reached the fifth floor, Alex found a uniformed officer leaning against the wall just outside the door.

"You Lockerby?" he asked in a bored voice.

Alex felt a twinge of fear. He didn't think Detweiler was dumb enough to throw him in a holding cell without hearing him out first. After all, Alex had given him good information before. That said, the Lieutenant might want to let Alex cool his heels for a few hours just out of spite.

"That's me," Alex said, pasting a friendly smile on his face.

"Detweiler said to bring you upstairs," he said, nodding for Alex to get back on the elevator.

That took Alex by surprise. The Detectives for Manhattan all worked out of the fifth floor. Above them were several floors of clerks, functionaries, interview rooms, and, at the top, the higher ups. Captain Rooney had an office there, as did the Chief of Police, though the Chief spent most of his time in a satellite office in city hall.

It wasn't likely that Detweiler wanted Alex in an interrogation room; he could grill Alex just fine in his own office. In fact, that would be better for him as his detectives would get to see him dressing down a meddlesome P.I. Going upstairs could only mean one thing — the Captain wanted in on whatever Detweiler had in mind.

Alex felt his hands shaking, but didn't dare take a swig out of his flask. The cop escorting him would think it was a sign of weakness and tell Detweiler. Alex didn't want to give the Lieutenant anything he might be able use against him.

The elevator dinged and Alex and the cop got off on the tenth floor. The Captain's Office was down the hallway to the right; Alex had been there before the previous year. That time the Captain wanted to hang the murder of a customs inspector on him.

Before Alex had time to wonder what Rooney would accuse him of this time, the cop escorting Alex turned left.

"Where are we going?" Alex asked, falling into step beside him.

"Keep walking," the cop said in a bored voice.

Alex didn't have to wonder long. At the end of the hallway they turned again, and the cop opened an ornate door of dark wood with a brass plaque in its exact center. The name *Arnold Montgomery* was engraved on the plaque.

Arnold Montgomery was the Chief of Police for New York City.

Alex wondered about the plaque. Most men would have had their title engraved on it along with their names. Chief Montgomery was either so arrogant that he simply expected everyone to know that he was chief, or so humble that such accolades didn't matter.

As he stepped inside the office Alex wondered which.

A humble man could be appealed-to, mistakes would be seen as human. An arrogant man would have to be told he was right, that he was smart, that mistakes were the fault of lesser, unimportant people.

Alex could work it either way.

Chief Montgomery's office was surprisingly sparse. His desk was ornate, but clear of debris: only a phone and a note pad occupied it. A couch sat against the side wall with three comfortable chairs facing the desk. A sideboard filled with various awards and bric-a-brac sat against the back wall, and an enormous window behind the desk looked out toward Empire Tower.

There were five people in the room.

A slender man with black hair that was going gray at the temples and a pencil mustache sat behind the desk. He wore a dress blue police uniform with a gold shield and a white braid encircling his right arm. The buttons on his coat were polished brass and his gun belt had a leather strap that ran up and over his left shoulder. The leather gleamed with polish.

This could only be Montgomery, though Alex couldn't tell if his immaculate appearance was due to respect for the job or if it was, itself, a demand for respect.

Detweiler and Rooney stood in front of the desk. It had been a while since Alex had seen the Captain, but he hadn't changed appreciably. He reminded Alex of a puppy because the man's hands and feet seemed disproportionally large for his body, only to be outdone by his nose. Due to his pale complexion and red hair, the nose always looked a bit red, as if Rooney were a hard drinker.

Alex didn't know the other two people, though he recognized the man immediately. His name was Claude Banes. He was slender and big shouldered, with a handsome face, brown hair, and a cleft in his pointed chin. Alex was surprised a man that ruggedly handsome hadn't already gone off to Hollywood, but he suspected being Mayor of the greatest city in the world had other charms.

The woman next to Mayor Banes was a study in contrast to her husband, as she could only be his wife. She stood with her shoulders slumped, looking down, like a schoolgirl anticipating a scolding. Alex knew from the list of potential ghost victims that her name was Nancy. She was pretty in a small-town girl kind of way, with delicate features, blue eyes and dark hair. She wore a dress with short sleeves and her bare arms came down in a V before her where she kneaded her hands together nervously.

"Thank you, Officer Thomas," Chief Montgomery said, dismissing the officer. Once he left and the door was shut, Rooney looked at the Mayor.

So, Banes is running this meeting.

"I'd like to know just what you think you are doing, Mr. Lockerby," Banes said angrily. "You can't drag my wife's name through the mud and expect to get away with it." He was shouting now, and his wife cringed with every syllable. Alex couldn't tell if she was embarrassed or afraid. "I'll have your license—"

Montgomery stood up and the Mayor seemed to recover his temper.

"The last time I heard your name, Lockerby," Montgomery said, stepping out from behind his desk to take over this interrogation. "Captain Rooney here was telling me how it was your fault that this department staked out the customs warehouse over at the Aerodrome for no good reason. Now I hear you're giving highly sensitive information to a tabloid reporter," he walked around Alex as he spoke, sizing him up. "As you heard, the Mayor is quite upset, to say nothing of Mrs. Banes."

He stopped directly in front of Alex and looked him right in the eyes. Alex noticed that his eyes were a deep brown, almost black. His face was a mask, halfway between amusement and condescension. Alex was very glad he didn't have to play poker with the man.

"Would you care to explain yourself?" he said.

It sounded like an invitation, a chance for Alex to tell his side of the story, but Alex recognized it for the trap it was. If he admitted to anything, it would be used at the roasting everyone was here to watch.

"I'm sure you got a report from Ms. Kincaid and the FBI about my part in stopping the attack on the city last year," he said.

Alex caught Captain Rooney's flinch out of the corner of his eye, but he kept his gaze on Montgomery. The Chief gave no outward sign that Alex had scored a point, but Alex detected a slight shift in his posture. He leaned away slightly. That probably meant that Alex was on the right track.

"As for Mrs. Banes," Alex said, looking at her. She had been watching him, but when he looked up, her blue eyes darted away. "I haven't been talking to any reporters about her or this case."

Her eyes darted up to meet his. They looked soft and grateful, then they darted away again. Montgomery opened his mouth to retort.

"And," Alex cut him off. "There wouldn't be anything for that hack to print if it wasn't for my work. I made the connection between the victims. I found out who the ghost was likely to be after, and that reporter didn't print any of that stuff until after I gave it to you."

"That doesn't prove anything," Rooney growled.

"No," Alex agreed. "It doesn't, but if I wanted my name in the paper, I'd be down at the Sun right now telling them who the ghost really is and why he's killing, instead of up here having my integrity impugned."

Rooney looked like he might explode, but Montgomery's expression hadn't shifted one bit. He paused for a long moment, letting the silence in the room stretch out. Alex knew better than to speak now. He'd said his piece and baited the hook, the next person to speak would likely be the loser.

Montgomery smiled, and Alex realized that the Chief knew this game. Worse, he knew how to play.

"Lieutenant," he said to Detweiler. "Do you have any detectives working for you who would stoop to talking to the press?"

Detweiler was grinning like a child who suddenly found himself in an unattended candy shop. Alex didn't want to tell Chief Montgomery how to run his department, but Detweiler was giving away the game.

"Wait," Mayor Banes said before the Lieutenant could speak. "You know who the ghost is?"

Alex nodded, looking the Mayor right in the eye.

"And I can prove that your wife is just an innocent bystander in all of this. The ghost isn't after her at all."

Nancy Banes gasped as if she'd suddenly been allowed to put down a heavy load and the Mayor put his arm protectively around her shoulders.

"I don't think—" Rooney began.

"No one's asking you to think, Patrick," Mayor Banes said. "I for one want to hear what Mr. Lockerby has to say."

Montgomery raised an eyebrow, then gave an almost imperceptible nod, acknowledging the point, but most definitely not the game.

"I guess you'd better tell us what you think you know, Mr. Lockerby," he said, returning to his seat behind the desk.

Alex took out his notebook and tore out a page, dropping it onto Montgomery's desk.

"The ghost is a man named Duane King," he explained as Montgomery picked up the paper. "He's killing people who were once owners of a company called North Shore Development. Seth Kowalski and ten of his employees at the Suffolk County Assessor's office formed the company so they could buy up land cheap, then sell it to rich people looking to build summer homes in the Hamptons."

"Why do you think he's the ghost?" Montgomery asked.

"Because," Alex said. "King's wife had tuberculosis, and treatments for that are expensive. He sold his house to get the money to pay an alchemist in Florida, but his wife died anyway. Kowalski and the people involved in North Shore undervalued his property so they could buy it at a tax sale auction cheap. They cheated King out of tens of thousands of dollars, money that would have saved his wife."

"Mr. Kowalski did that?" a fragile voice interjected. Nancy Banes looked directly at Alex but she didn't look away this time.

"I was his secretary for a year when I got out of school," she said. "I was never part of any land company."

"I know," Alex said. He leaned over Montgomery's desk and pointed to a number written on the paper. "This is the file number for their articles of incorporation, and Lieutenant Detweiler can check it."

"We believe you," Montgomery said, though Alex suspected that was only for the Mayor's benefit. Detweiler would be double-checking everything Alex said; he might be an ass, but he wasn't stupid.

"What makes you think the ghost is actually Duane King?" Montgomery asked again. "If Kowalski and his friends cheated him, it's a cinch they cheated others."

"This is about King's wife," Alex explained. "Think about the murders. Two stab wounds to the chest, one through each lung. The victims would drown as their lungs filled up with their own blood."

"The same way his wife would have died from tuberculosis," Detweiler said.

"Very good, Lieutenant," Alex said.

Rooney cleared his throat and all eyes turned to him.

"If King thought these people were responsible for his wife's death, why did he wait so long to take revenge?"

"That's a very good question," Chief Montgomery said, turning to Alex.

Alex allowed himself to smile. Montgomery blanched a little when he saw it, but to his credit, he kept his poker face in place. He knew Alex was about to win their game.

"He was in prison for twenty of those years," Alex said. He turned to Detweiler. "Ask me why?"

The Lieutenant sighed but played along.

"Why?"

"Because he murdered the doctor who had been treating his wife," Alex explained. "She sold him a phony cure."

Chief Montgomery raised his eyebrows, then nodded again, conceding the game.

"Where is Mr. King now?" he asked.

"I don't know," Alex admitted. "But I imagine the Florida prison system knows. They wouldn't tell me, of course, but they'll be happy to tell you."

Montgomery looked over his shoulder at the Mayor and something unspoken passed between them.

"You'll keep this information to yourself for the moment," the Chief said to Alex.

"Unless you *want* me to leak it to the Sun," he said. The Mayor's face turned dark and angry, so Alex rushed on. "I'm sure they'd love to hear that Mrs. Banes is no longer a potential target."

Montgomery laughed at that.

"I'll see to that myself," he said. "As for you, this information of yours had better pan out."

"I know," Alex said, putting up a hand to stop the Chief. "Or you'll bury me in a hole and throw away the shovel."

"Something like that," his voice was as smooth and calm as it had been the whole time, but Alex detected a slight note of irritation. He'd misjudged Alex. Bringing the Mayor here had been a bit of theater. Chief Montgomery intended for the Mayor to see him lay the blame for his department's inadequacies at Alex's feet. By not letting them set the narrative, Alex had turned the Mayor's presence to his own advantage.

He wasn't sure if Chief Montgomery was impressed or angry, but either way he wouldn't be forgetting about it. The next time Alex was in this office, he'd need a much bigger trump card if he had any hope of coming out without handcuffs.

"Well," Montgomery said, rising. "His honor and I have things to get back to." He handed the paper from Alex's notebook to Detweiler. "Run this down and double the guard on the remaining five members of North Shore Development. The ghost may try again, and I want him caught this time."

"What about the officers we've got guarding the others?" Captain Rooney asked.

Montgomery thought about that for a moment.

"Better keep them in place until we're sure Mr. Lockerby's information is good." He turned to Alex. "I'm sure you can find your own way out."

Alex thanked him and fled in as dignified a manner as possible. He took the stairs down two at a time, worrying the whole time that Detweiler would come chasing after him.

When he finally reached the street, he walked to the side of the building and turned down the alley between it and the next one. He sat down on the bare dirt and took a swig from his flask. He'd been prepared for Detweiler, even Rooney, but the Mayor and the Chief were in a whole other league. One word from either of them and he'd be rotting in a cell without bail.

He sat there, resisting the urge to throw up and squeezing his hands together until the tremors subsided. Finally, he got up, brushed himself off, and headed across the street to the crawler station.

22

THE CALM

lex trudged up the stairs to his fourth floor office, pausing on the landing as he caught sight of his door. *Lockerby Investigations* was written on a frosted glass panel in gold paint. Down in the bottom right corner, the ink-pot and quill symbol was painted as well, announcing that the office offered runewright services in addition to detection. It wasn't an elegant office, or particularly well appointed, but it was his. The sight lifted his spirits.

A sign hung on the door handle that read, *closed for the day.*

Taking out his key, he let himself in, but left the sign on the door. He had work to do, and with Leslie gone, he didn't want to be interrupted by potential clients. That hurt a bit, but it had to be done.

Locking the door, he went straight to his office. A stack of notes sat there, all from Leslie. Thanks to the story in the Sun, a lot of people had come in seeking his services.

There were a few legitimate cases among the notes, mostly missing valuables, cheating spouses, and even a lost dog. They'd be easy money provided he could get his finding rune working. With a sigh and a wish for a better class of cases, he set them aside.

Many of the people in Leslie's notes wanted runes done. Even though the runewright symbol was on his door, he almost never sold runes from the office. Simple barrier and mending runes could be bought from runewrights who sold their wares in shops or off carts. Most people who came in here wanted Alex's finding rune — but that came with his services.

With a sigh, Alex read through the list of desired runes. It would take several hours to write them all, and he simply didn't want to do it. That didn't change the fact that he needed the money, by tomorrow if he wanted to take Jessica somewhere nice for dinner, and selling the runes for which he had orders would make that happen.

The thought of money made him check his pocketwatch. If Danny and Callahan found the bank robbers today, he could collect double his fee from Barton. That would be one hundred and fifty clams, enough to catch up Leslie's salary.

Of course there was a good chance that the cops wouldn't find the tunnel until tomorrow. If that happened, Alex's double or nothing bet with the Lightning Lord would roll over to nothing.

Time to take another gamble.

Alex picked up his phone and gave the operator Barton's number.

"Yes," Gary Bickman's voice answered.

"This is Alex Lockerby. I need to talk to your boss."

"One moment."

If Bickman was glad to hear Alex's voice, he hid it well. Of course he was a professional valet, dispassion was probably in the job description.

"Lockerby!" Barton's voice rolled down the line like thunder. "I was beginning to lose faith in you. What's the good word?"

"I found your truck," he said. "It was part of a group of vehicles that have been stolen in recent weeks."

"Is the motor intact?" Barton's voice was eager, almost desperate. Alex guessed that the new one wasn't coming along as quickly as Barton had hoped.

"The motor was missing," Alex said.

"I'm not paying you to find trucks, Lockerby," he growled. "I need that motor."

"Take it easy," Alex said. "I know why the thieves took your motor."

"I don't care why they took it, I just need it back."

Barton's voice was angry now. Absently, Alex wondered if the Lightning Lord could electrocute him through the telephone line.

"And the police are looking for it right now," Alex said in as soothing a voice as he dared. "The people who took it want to use it to help them rob a bank."

There was a long pause.

"How would my motor help anyone rob a bank?" he asked, his voice now intrigued.

Alex told him about the thefts and the kidnapping of Leroy Cunningham, and how that added up to a robbery.

"I never thought about using my motor in mines," Barton said. "That might be a whole new industry. You say the cops are searching for these kidnappers right now?"

"There are a lot of buildings they'll have to search, but they'll find your motor sooner or later."

"I appreciate the update, Lockerby, well done."

"I was hoping I could get some consideration for that well done work," Alex said, trying to keep his voice calm and even.

"Like what?"

"One more day on our bet," he said. "The cops will find your motor by then and it's a cinch the thieves didn't take it apart, so it'll be ready to show off to the railroad. Based on what we thought at the start, it's the best possible outcome."

"You've got brass," Barton said, amusement in his voice. "All right, one more day, double or nothing. But only because I like you."

With that, Barton hung up.

Alex slumped back in his chair, letting out an explosive breath he didn't realize he'd been holding. Now all he needed was for the cops to find the bank robbers. They wouldn't want to release the motor, since it was evidence, but Alex had no doubt that once Andrew Barton got involved, that wouldn't be a problem.

He opened the desk drawer where he kept his liquor bottle and found it empty. He'd forgotten that he'd emptied it when Hannah Cunningham had come to see him. That seemed so long ago.

Tossing the empty bourbon bottle into his waste basket, Alex got up and moved to the wall where his vault door had been painted in neat lines on the otherwise blank sheet rock. Taking a vault rune from his book, he activated it to reveal the heavy door, then opened it with the ornate skeleton key on his key ring.

Inside, he had another bottle of bourbon on the file cabinet next to his writing table. This one was almost empty too.

He poured himself a shot and downed it.

Looking at his angled writing table, Alex decided that he might as well start writing the runes he needed. He'd done all he could for Leroy and Barton, and it was up to the cops to catch the ghost.

He set the bottle aside and turned to make his way back to his office where the list of runes awaited him, but paused as a thought struck him. He walked to the secretary cabinet where he kept his important papers and a duplicate investigation kit. Opening the writing table, he rummaged through the drawers until he found an ornate paper card with a red border and gold Chinese dragons in the corners. The name, *Lucky Dragon*, had been printed in the same gold lettering across the top over a single line of handwritten text.

Mister Lockerby and party are my guests.

It was signed, Chow Duk Sum, though Alex knew there was no such person. The name was an alias for Shiro Takahashi, Danny Pak's father — leader of the Japanese Mafia in New York.

Alex had gotten Danny in some trouble about a year back and had to appeal to Shiro for help getting Danny out of it. Apparently Alex's work met with the man's approval, because that card arrived in the mail a week or so after the fact. It was inside a folded sheet of paper with a single word written on it.

Impressive.

Alex had worried that the obvious invitation was some kind of set up, but in the year that passed, no further communication had been received. It was probably safe. Besides, the *Lucky Dragon* was swanky, located in the inner-ring. Jessica should be suitably impressed.

Making up his mind, Alex put the card in the back of his rune book, then walked back to his office and scooped up the list of needed runes. He had just turned back to the open vault door when his phone rang.

Hoping it was Danny with good news, he scooped it up eagerly.

"Hey, handsome," Leslie's voice greeted him. "I tracked down the reporter you wanted."

"Just a second," he said, pulling out his notebook and sitting down at the desk. "Go ahead."

"William 'Billy' Tasker, born in Georgia and studied English at Duke University. He graduated in twenty-nine and got a job with the Miami Herald. He won an award for some exposé he wrote about corruption in the state senate. After that he got hired at the *New York Times*."

"He what?" Alex was shocked. "How did that muckraker go from the Times to a rag like the Sun?"

"I couldn't find out," Leslie said. "I don't know why he left the Times or when he got hired by *The Midnight Sun*. I did find a story by him in the Sun that's two years old, so he's been working for the tabloid at least that long."

"Anything else?"

"Yeah, I talked with Hannah. She wants to know how you're doing."

"Tell her the police are on it now and we should know something in a day or two," Alex said. "How is she holding up?"

"She's great," Leslie said, a trace of sarcasm in her voice. "But she's eating me out of house and home. I hope you get paid soon."

"Sorry," Alex said. "She must be a nervous eater."

"No," Leslie said. "I suspect she's in a family way. She threw up this morning. Blamed it on her nerves."

Alex's head dropped down on the desk. He'd been feeling the pressure to find Leroy, to get him home to his sweet wife, but that had mostly vanished now that he had the police involved. With the news that Hannah was likely pregnant, that weight dropped right back on his shoulders.

"Leroy will be thrilled," he said, not bothering to hide the weariness in his voice.

"Just find him, kid," Leslie said. "For both our sakes."

"Are you coming back here?"

"No," Leslie said. "It's after five, I'm headed home."

Alex thanked her and hung up.

Despite Hannah's condition, there wasn't anything Alex could do to speed Leroy's recovery along, so he pushed them out of his thoughts.

Turning to his notes, he couldn't believe that Billy Tasker, the tabloid hack, had worked for the Times. A while back he'd made a friend of their sports editor, a man named Jared Watson. Alex resolved to give him a call, then remembered Leslie saying it was after five. Sports reporters didn't work late, so he'd have to call in the morning.

With a sigh, Alex put away his notebook and picked up the discarded rune list. Making his way back into his vault he assembled the pens, paper, and inks he would need and set to work. He started with the hardest ones first. It was an old habit he'd picked up from Father Harry.

Always do the hardest jobs first, he would say. *Then when you get down to the end and you're tired, the work is easy.*

It had been a year since Father Harrison Clementine had died. As Alex thought of it, he was ashamed. In all that time, he hadn't been back to the grave once since the funeral.

Resolving to go on Sunday made him feel better, and he set to work on a complicated cleaning rune that someone wanted for a painting that had been damaged by smoke. He kept going, rune after rune, until he found himself drawing a circle inside a square then adding a symbol that looked like a lighthouse being attacked by a steam shovel.

Once the minor restoration rune was done, he did it three more times, then crossed it off Leslie's list, last of all, and set his pencil aside. His back ached and his hand was cramping, so he poured himself another drink, then got up to pace around a bit and get his blood flowing.

Since the vault had no windows, he had no idea how much time had passed, but a quick glance out into his darkened office told him it must have been a few hours. He checked his watch and found it was seven-thirty.

"Iggy's going to be mad that I'm late," he grumbled, heading back to the drafting table. He picked up the stack of runes he'd drawn and carried them out of the vault, shutting off the light and locking the door after him.

Leslie had their mostly-empty cashbox in her desk drawer and Alex locked the runes in there, leaving a note on the desk telling her where to find them. In the morning she'd call the people who ordered them and, hopefully, get paid.

He had just put on his hat when the phone in his office rang. A wave of weariness flooded him, but the thought that it might be Danny with good news impelled him back into his office.

"Lockerby," he said, picking it up.

"Alex," Iggy said.

"I know I'm late," Alex said with a smile. He was surprisingly glad to hear the old man's voice. "I had a few things to finish up here. I'm just on my way home."

"Stay there," Iggy said. "There are policemen here looking for you."

Alex felt a surge of adrenaline burn away his exhaustion. Had the Mayor or Chief Montgomery changed their minds and loosed Detweiler on him?

"I'm sending them over to you now," Iggy went on before Alex could ask why cops wanted him.

Iggy wouldn't tell the cops where he was if they intended to lock them up, that much was sure.

"What's going on?" he asked.

"Get your kit together," Iggy said, his voice heavy and serious. "The ghost has killed again."

23

THE SEAL

It was pouring down rain when the police cruiser that picked up Alex pulled up in front of an Inner-Ring address. The Wentworth Building was a luxury high-rise, strictly upper crust. Alex remembered seeing the building listed as the address for one of the members of North Shore.

"The Lieutenant's waiting for you inside," the officer who picked up Alex said. He wore a sadistic grin indicating that his pulling up on the far side of the street in the pouring rain was no accident.

"Thanks," Alex said. He pulled out his rune book and tore out a barrier rune, licking it and sticking it to the brim of his hat.

"What's that?" the driver's partner asked.

Alex didn't answer, just lit the paper with a match.

"Hey," the driver protested as the flash paper burned away, filling the interior with light and smoke.

"Thanks, fellas," Alex said as the air around him distorted for a moment. The feel of the rune taking effect was so subtle that he wouldn't have noticed it if he hadn't been paying attention. He hadn't realized it before, but he'd grown so used to the sensation of magic that he'd begun to tune it out. With the week he'd been having, he resolved to savor every bit of magic he could.

As the cops continued to protest, Alex picked up his kit and stepped out of the car into the pouring rain. The world around him seemed to shimmer as the barrier rune repelled the rain, sending it spattering away from him. It was only a dozen yards across the street and he'd certainly been wet before, but he didn't want to show up at a crime scene looking like a drowned rat.

Detweiler would like that, after all, and Alex wanted to deny him any such pleasure.

He dismissed the rune during the elevator ride up to the thirtieth floor. The man operating the elevator was short and built like a fireplug, with a square jaw and big hands. He wore a tuxedo and maintained an air of quiet dignity despite having to ferry cops and P.I.s up to a murder scene.

"The Gordons' apartment is to the right," he said when they reached their destination.

Alex stepped off the elevator and found himself in a short hallway with only three doors. One was the door that accessed the stairs. The other two were for the apartments on this floor. That idea made Alex shake his head. How big were these apartments?

At the right end of the hall, a policeman in a blue uniform stood guard at an open door. Alex could see many more officers moving about inside.

"Lieutenant Detweiler sent for me," Alex told the man at the door.

"You Lockerby?"

When Alex nodded, the man stepped aside.

"There you are," Detweiler growled as soon as Alex came in. "It's about time."

"Sorry Lieutenant," Alex said, keeping his voice and expression neutral. "Your boys went to my apartment, but I was at my office."

"Spare me the details," he said, clearly in a foul mood. "I need you to look over this crime scene."

Alex looked around. At least half a dozen officers and detectives that Alex could see were milling around. The apartment was enormous. From where he stood, Alex could see a sitting room, formal dining room, a solarium, and what looked like a library in the distance.

The elevator man had said the crime occurred at the Gordon residence. Marcellus Gordon was one of the names on the North Shore Development articles, and Alex knew from the research Leslie had done that he was married.

"Where is Mrs. Gordon?"

"She was in hysterics," Detweiler said. "I had some of the boys take her over to the hospital."

"Is there a back way out of this apartment?" Alex asked.

"There's a back door that goes out to a stairwell, but it's locked and barred from the inside."

"Did you double the guard here like the Chief said?"

Detweiler's face turned red and his eyebrows knit together.

"I didn't bring you here to ask stupid questions," he exploded. "Of course I did. There were two uniforms in the lobby and three up here, one outside the door and two in the apartment."

Alex wanted to find fault with that just to be a contrarian but he had to admit, five officers should have been plenty.

"What did your men say happened?" he asked.

Detweiler looked like he wanted to stay angry, but his color faded and he sighed.

"Come with me," he said, then headed off through the parlor to the formal dining room. A huge table of light wood with gold art-deco inlays occupied this room, with seating for six. A mahogany sideboard held a full service of gleaming silver and a china cabinet opposite shimmered with dishware.

To the left a door on a swinging hinge led into the kitchen. It was bigger than the dining room with massive countertops, an electric stove and range, and a cold box big enough to keep a side of beef. In the center of the room was a simple dining table with four chairs around it. A tea service had been laid out on the table and Alex saw four cups and saucers along with bread and butter and the teapot. There were scuff marks on the tile floor around one of the chairs.

"So your men were here, having tea with Mrs. Gordon when it happened," Alex stated, assessing the scene.

Detweiler's face went red again, but Alex held up a placating hand.

"Just an observation, Lieutenant," he said. "No judgement."

"Mr. Gordon went upstairs to his office," Detweiler explained. Alex wondered just how big this apartment was that it had an upstairs. "About five minutes later, the officers report that they heard him fall down."

The Lieutenant led the way through a door on the far side of the kitchen and into a long, paneled hallway. This ran down to a spiral staircase that led up to a small sitting room. Another door and short hall later let them to Mr. Gordon's office. It was quite the most elegant office Alex had ever seen, with a small mahogany desk, comfortable-looking chairs, a gas fireplace, and bookshelves on the side walls. Frosted glass sconces lined the walls, radiating white light, but reflecting purple light back on the walls through a bit of colored glass. The only thing out of place in the room was Mr. Gordon's corpse.

He lay face up next to a thick pool of his own congealing blood. Alex could smell the tang of iron in the air. There was far too much blood for the ghost's usual stab wounds. On top of that, a red line of spatter ran up the wall near the body.

"Our ghost was in a hurry," Alex guessed.

"That's the way we figure it," Detweiler said, nodding at the body. "His throat's been cut."

"You kept your men out," Alex said, noticing that the carpet was mostly undisturbed.

"Once my men called it in, yeah," Detweiler said.

Alex looked at him with a raised eyebrow.

"There are only two ways into this apartment, Lockerby," he said. "Through the front door and the back stairs. I checked the door to the stairs, it's locked and bolted. That means that the ghost got in here past five alert policemen." He shook his head. "I don't buy it. Unless this King fellow is really a ghost, he must be using magic. That's your department, so get in there and find out how this maniac is doing his disappearing act."

Alex set his kit down on the floor and took out his multi-lamp, ghostlight burner, and oculus.

"What's that for?" Detweiler asked Alex as he readied his gear.

"This lets me see magical residue," Alex explained. "If someone used magic to get in here, this should reveal it."

"How would someone do that?" the lieutenant asked. "I mean if it was a sorcerer doing this, they'd just turn these guys into toads or something, right?"

Alex agreed. This didn't seem like something a sorcerer would cook up. With their power they could exact much more painful and personal revenge without leaving a trace. Whoever was doing this was getting the best revenge they could manage.

So, Alex thought, *if I wanted to murder someone to avenge my dead wife, how would I do it?*

"A powerful runewright could do it," Alex said, sweeping his lantern carefully over the body. "There's a thing called a linking rune that allows a runewright to connect a person with an anchor."

"And that lets you walk through walls?"

"No," he admitted. So far there were no traces of magical residue on the body, so he expanded his search to the room. "But when the rune is activated, it moves the recipient from where they are to wherever the anchor is."

"Like when sorcerers teleport?" Detweiler said.

"Exactly like that."

"What?" Detweiler almost yelled. "You knew that all along, but you didn't say anything until now? That would explain everything."

"No, it wouldn't," Alex corrected him. "King might be able to use it to escape from the murder; runewrights even call these things escape runes. That said, how did he get in?"

"The same way," Detweiler said, as if it were obvious.

"In order for that to work," Alex explained, "King would have had to get into this room at some point and draw an anchor rune in here to connect the spell." Alex swept the ghostlight around the room. "If there was an anchor rune in this room, it would have left magical residue that would be obvious. Think of it as the magical equivalent of a scorch mark."

"That would still work," Detweiler said. "King got in through the back stairs, then locked and bolted the door. He kills Gordon and uses one of these escape runes to get away."

"There are two problems with that," Alex said. "The first is that escape runes are powerful, they're expensive, and there aren't many runewrights who can make them."

"That doesn't mean that King didn't get his hands on enough to get his revenge," Detweiler said. "What's the other problem?"

"Escape runes are fueled by the user's life energy. That means that every time King used one, he'd be burning a year or more off his own life. The spell could very well kill him at any time."

"You said that King's wife died, his son disgraced some skirt and disappeared, and he spent twenty years in prison," Detweiler pointed out. "Sounds to me like he's a man who doesn't have anything to lose."

Alex hated to admit it, but the Lieutenant had a point. He and Iggy had ruled out using escape runes, but that was before he knew about Duane King and his story. Detweiler was right, King was a man with very little to lose, one who might be willing to trade years of his own life for revenge.

"Do me a favor, Lieutenant," he said. "Go ask the men you had stationed here if they checked the door to the back stairs when they came on duty. Also ask them if they swept the apartment."

"Why?"

"Because," Alex said. "If it was locked and bolted when they got here, and they cleared the apartment, then we still have the problem of how the ghost got in."

Detweiler grumbled, but headed back down the hall and down the spiral stair. Alex ground his teeth together. He'd swept the entire room with his ghostlight and the only magic he found were three alchemical bottles on a shelf. One potion was to regrow hair, one was for indigestion, and one was for virility.

That one looked well used.

Alex blew out the burner and replaced it with the silverlight. This time the room lit up with bluish-purple marks, mostly fingerprints. Alex examined the blood on the floor. There was cast-off spatter from the knife, indicating that the killer was left-handed.

As Alex examined the spatter on the wall he wondered why there didn't seem to be any voids.

The killer must have come up behind him, which means he's right-handed, not left-handed.

The killer being behind Gordon explained the lack of any voids where the dead man's blood would have landed on the killer, but what about the knife? It was unlikely that the killer had a rag handy to wrap up the bloody knife, so it must have dripped on the ground.

Kneeling down, Alex examined the floor carefully. There were a few drops of blood outside the pool. That explained it — the blood pool was obscuring the cast-off from the bloody knife.

Standing up, Alex mimed coming up behind Gordon and cutting his throat. He would have had to step back when the body fell.

Turning his light on the floor again, Alex found a tiny stain out and away from the body. It looked like it had been obscured by someone walking on it, either the killer or one of the policemen who found the victim. After a minute of searching, he found another near Gordon's desk.

The waste basket next to the desk was made of a tightly woven wire. As Alex examined it, he found one last drop of blood on the top of the narrow rim.

Excitedly, he picked it up and emptied its meager contents onto Gordon's immaculate desk. He doubted the dead man would mind.

"Bad news," Detweiler said, coming back into the room. "Both the officers say they checked the door and it was locked and bolted. They also said they cleared the apartment."

"So Duane King wasn't already hiding in here when they arrived," Alex said. It was starting to look like King had access to some magic that Alex didn't know.

A sudden chill ran through him and he wondered if the ghost was somehow connected to the glyph runes. After a moment he gave up the idea as a long shot.

None of the crumpled papers or the banana peel that made up the contents of Marcellus Gordon's waste basket looked important, but Alex was starting to feel a little desperate. He changed burners back to the ghostlight and inspected the trash again.

This time something glowed.

Alex did a double take, focusing his lamp on a tiny fragment of a paper. It looked like the corner of something and it had definite magic residue on it.

"Find something?" Detweiler asked.

"Maybe," Alex said, taking off his oculus so he could better inspect the tiny paper fragment.

It was a heavy gauge paper with a residue on the front that was tacky. On the back was some kind of label. It was the label that glowed under the ghostlight, so Alex examined it closely.

"There's a rune here," he announced.

"Is it one of those escape runes?"

Alex shook his head. Escape runes were difficult and complex, and this rune was far too simple. What he could see of it anyway.

"It's torn," he said. "There's only about half of it left, but it does confirm that there was magic in this room at some point."

"Lieutenant," someone yelled from down the hall.

"Figure it out, Lockerby," Detweiler said, turning back to the hall. "I want Mr. King behind bars before he has a chance to kill again."

The half of the rune on the torn paper wasn't much, but it was the only clue available. He didn't recognize it, but then he had no way of knowing how much was missing. It was a rune of the geometric school, which let out the glyph runewrights, but that didn't make him feel much better.

Taking out his notebook, he copied the half-rune as exactly as he could. Later he'd go home and draw it bigger; maybe then he'd recognize it.

"Lockerby!" Detweiler shouted, his tromping footsteps coming up the hall. "Get out here!"

Alex had no idea what the Lieutenant was upset about, but he didn't want to be caught flat footed, so he blew out his lantern and dropped it and the oculus into his kit.

"What's the matter, Lieutenant?"

Detweiler rounded the corner with a crumpled paper clutched in his hand. His face had gone red again and his teeth were bared.

"Duane King is not the ghost," he shouted, throwing the crumpled paper at Alex. "That telegram just arrived from Florida. King died in Miami six months ago."

Alex unfolded the paper and read the neat typewritten words. According to his parole officer, King had been killed in a fire in boarding house. His body was buried in a common grave in the city cemetery.

Alex read the telegram again, just to make sure he'd actually read it right. He wanted to say something reassuring, something that would make this information make sense, but nothing came to mind.

"That's it," Detweiler said, somehow angrier at Alex's bewilderment. "You've been messing this case up from the start, leading us around by the nose, leaking to the press, and generally making me look the fool."

"Lieutenant," Alex began but Detweiler cut him off.

"I've had enough of your antics," he shouted. "Preston, get in here and arrest this meddler."

24

THE COOLER

The basement of the Central Office of Police was a series of rooms, cages, and holding cells known collectively as *the Cooler*. After Officer Preston had put Alex in handcuffs, he'd been driven to the Central Office and thrown unceremoniously into a large open cage with a few drunks and a sullen-looking pickpocket.

The police had confiscated all his possessions, including his suit coat with its shield runes. Apparently they'd dealt with runewrights before and had procedures for handling them.

There wasn't a clock anywhere, so Alex had no idea how long he'd been there. Not that it mattered. He'd been so sure that Duane King was the killer. As far as Alex could tell, he was the only person with a real motive.

That you know of, he reminded himself.

Seth Kowalski and his confederates at North Shore Development probably swindled dozens of people out of their land, buying up small farms and scrubland before anyone knew rich people were looking to build their summer homes in the area. Seth and his friends probably made millions before anyone knew better. There could be hundreds of people who wanted them dead.

No, the contrarian part of his brain protested. *Word would have gotten around fast that rich people were buying up land. Even if North Shore wanted to swindle people, they really didn't have the time.*

Alex thought about the building permit North Shore filed for the parcel of land that included Duane King's property. That permit had been filed just a few weeks after the tax sale.

Duane King's five acres of land was right in the middle of the twenty-two acre parcel. North Shore wouldn't have been able to sell the parcel if they hadn't gotten King's piece. That had to be it, they were desperate. That permit was one of the first they filed; if that deal had fallen through because they didn't have King's land, they'd have probably lost everything. That sale gave them the capital they needed to buy up the next bit for the next fat-cat looking for a beachfront home.

Alex had already figured out the rest. They told Duane King the land was worth less than what was owed for the taxes, so he'd let it go to tax sale, and then manipulated the sale to be sure they got it.

"So unless there's another phony tax sale on the books, King is probably the only person they actually swindled," Alex said out loud.

"What?" the nearest drunk mumbled looking up. "You know a king? Really?"

"Go back to sleep," Alex told him, then got up and started pacing around the cage.

None of this made sense. Everything pointed to Duane King, but that simply wasn't possible. If the ghost was using escape runes to leave the scenes of his murder, he'd be purchasing his revenge with his own life. Who, other than Duane King, would be motivated to pay that kind of price?

And yet, King was dead. Dead and buried in a pauper's grave.

Alex sat down angry. He tried to sleep, lying down on the wooden bench with his hat over his face, but his mind was too active for that. He kept seeing the rune fragment he'd found in Marcellus Gordon's wastebasket. The police took his notebook along with his other possessions, but Alex remembered the fragment well enough.

It wasn't an anchor rune, that much he knew: it wasn't complicated enough for that. It kind of reminded him of a shield rune, but it wasn't complicated enough for that either.

Frustrated, he got up and began pacing again.

"You look rested," Iggy's voice interrupted him several miles later.

"Iggy," Alex gasped. "You found me."

The old man wore his tweed suit with a bowler hat and looked as tired as Alex felt. Iggy smiled. He looked relieved, like he'd expected to find Alex in solitary confinement.

"When you didn't come home by midnight I started asking around," Iggy said. "That's the one," he said, turning to a uniformed policeman with a large ring of keys that moved up from behind him.

The officer unlocked the cage and held the door so Alex could step out.

"How'd you manage this?" Alex asked as he breathed in the free air again. "I figured Detweiler would hold me for at least a day while he figured out some bogus charge against me."

"Later," Iggy whispered. He nodded at the officer who was closing the door to the cage. With a wink, he led Alex away, toward the elevators. A wall with a locked cage door separated the Cooler from the elevators and there were two armed officers on the inside, in case of trouble. Both of them eyed Alex with a mixture of curiosity and disdain as Alex picked up his coat, rune book, notebook, matchbook, flask, and the few loose coins he'd had in his pocket when Officer Preston brought him in. His kit bag was there as well, and he picked it up without bothering to inspect its contents.

Discretion, he'd learned, was definitely the better part of valor. Especially since Iggy seemed to think that the order for Alex's release could be rescinded at any minute.

"Okay," Alex said, once they were safely outside the Central Office and into a taxi. "How did you pull that off?"

"When you didn't call, I knew something was amiss, so I went over to the Gordons' home to find you."

"How did you know where the crime scene was?"

"Those officers Detweiler sent to the brownstone to fetch you weren't exactly tight-lipped," Iggy said with a grin.

Alex should have known better. The old fox would have had the whole story off them before he told them that Alex wasn't there.

"So," Iggy continued. "Once I got there and learned what had happened, I spoke to Detweiler." His smile faded for a moment. "He told me about Duane King, and that's a problem, I grant you, but I convinced him not to charge you."

Alex couldn't believe that the Lieutenant had rescinded his order to arrest Alex, no matter what Iggy had said. The old man must have called in a major favor to pull that off.

Alex got a chill as he realized the most obvious leverage Iggy could get was to call Sorsha. Alex already owed her for getting Bickman a job with Andrew Barton; he didn't like the idea of owning her further. He didn't want to admit it, but he disliked the idea of her knowing he'd been thrown in jail, too.

"Give me some credit, lad," Iggy said, reading Alex's expression. "I just reminded the Lieutenant that they wouldn't know who the ghost was targeting or why without you. I also pointed out that if I were to mention that to that nice Tasker fellow over at the Sun, it would sell a lot of papers."

Alex barked out an explosive laugh.

"And make Detweiler into a citywide chump," he said.

"He decided to put off bringing any charges against you for the moment," Iggy said, lighting up a celebratory cigar despite the lateness of the hour.

Alex sat back against the seat and closed his eyes, letting out a long sigh. That could have gone very badly for him if Detweiler had actually filed a charge.

"Thank God for paperwork," he said.

"Now," Iggy said, slapping him on the knee. "Tell me where we are with the case."

Alex sighed again and shook his head.

"We're nowhere," he said. "Turns out I was wrong about Duane King."

"What makes you say that?"

"He's dead."

Iggy puffed his cigar in silence for a moment.

"Well, that certainly is a setback," he said.

"Setback?" Alex laughed. "That's the whole game." He leaned back in his seat again. "I was so sure it was him."

"Me too," Iggy said. He was stroking his mustache in the manner Alex knew meant his incredible brain was working overtime. "Everything you found points to King. The victims, the motive, even the method of the murders."

"You think someone did that on purpose?" Alex asked.

Iggy shook his head.

"Why?" he pointed out with a shrug. "It's too easy for the police to find out he's dead."

"True," Alex admitted.

"Is there anyone else involved with this business who could be involved?" Iggy asked.

"Not that I could find," Alex said.

"What about Duane King's son, the one who impregnated that girl and then ran away?"

"Nobody knows where he is," Alex said. "Besides, if he wanted to avenge his mother's death, why wait this long? The delay only makes sense for Duane because he was in prison for twenty years."

Now it was Iggy's turn to sigh. It actually made Alex feel a little better: if the mind of the great Sir Arthur Conan Ignatius Doyle was stumped by this, what chance did he have?

"I did what you said," Alex said, speaking just to fill up the silence that had descended. "I eliminated the impossible so that whatever was left should have been the truth, right?"

Iggy chuckled at that, but it wasn't a dry, ironic chuckle of agreement, this was amusement. Alex looked over to find the old man grinning behind his mustache, his teeth clenched on the cigar, and his eyes shining in the glow of a passing streetlight.

"Thanks, lad," he said. "You just reminded me that there's a corollary to that formula."

Alex sat up, interested.

"If you eliminate the impossible and nothing remains," he said, taking his cigar out of his mouth and considering it.

"Yes?" Alex prompted.

"Then some part of the impossible, must be possible."

"Well, I'm sure Duane King's ghost isn't committing these murders," Alex said. "So where does that leave us?"

"Think about it," Iggy said puffing on his cigar again. His shining eyes and wide grin told Alex that he'd already come to a conclusion.

Alex thought about it, turning the problem this way and that in his head. There really was only one satisfactory answer.

"Duane King didn't die in that fire," Alex said. "Either the cops messed up or King made sure they thought it was him. Either way, he's still alive, and he's still the killer."

"That's my read on it," Iggy said, finally sitting back against his seat.

"Okay, I'll tell Detweiler in the morning," Alex said, so tired he couldn't even remember what day it was.

Iggy sat back up and gave him a withering look.

"Detweiler isn't going to believe a word you say," he said. "You're going to have to find King yourself and bring him in before the lieutenant will take your word for anything. And, if you go to him with something less, he'll press those charges, tabloid or no."

"Great." Alex rubbed his temples. How was he going to find one not-as-dead-as-reported ex-con in New York City?

"So," Iggy said, his senior-detective voice firmly in place. "What are you going to do to find our ghost?"

Alex thought about that for a long moment.

"I have to find out how he haunts," Alex said. "I'm pretty sure he's using an escape rune to get away from the crime scenes. It's the only thing that makes sense after Marcellus Gordon. If he'd left any other way, the cops would have seen him."

"I agree," Iggy said, nodding. "He's killing for revenge, so he doesn't care about spending his own life."

"So that leaves the question of how he's getting into the crime scenes. The cops watching Gordon's place swore the place was locked up tight." He rubbed his chin. "Is it possible King could have used an escape rune to get in?"

Iggy shook his head.

"There are only two ways to link an escape rune to a location," he said. "One..."

"Draw the link rune on the spot you want to land on," Alex supplied. That's how the second part of his own escape rune worked. If he triggered the rune, he and anyone within ten feet would be teleported to a spot about one hundred feet above the North Atlantic, then he would be teleported again, landing right on the rune he'd carved into the floor of the brownstone's library.

"And two..." Iggy prodded.

"Use latitude and longitude in the escape rune itself," he said. That was how the first part of his rune worked. The coordinates of the spot over the North Atlantic were coded right into the rune tattooed on his left forearm. It was, of course, horribly imprecise, but that didn't matter when the point of it was to dump a ten-foot radius worth of bad guys into the ocean. It would never be precise enough to allow someone to teleport to a specific room.

"Any chance King snuck into all those homes a month ago and carved link runes under their desks to get ready for this?" Alex asked.

Iggy didn't dignify that with an answer.

"I don't suppose King inherited a bunch of money while he was in prison, so he could afford a couple dozen unlocking runes?" Alex asked.

Unlocking runes could have gotten King through the locked and bolted door at the Gordons, but that was about one hundred and fifty dollars' worth of runes. An ex-con wouldn't have that kind of cash on hand, so that was out.

Something twitched in his brain. Something about carving link runes under the murdered people's desks, but he was too tired to suss it out. Besides, he knew that there weren't any runes in those rooms, under the desks or otherwise.

Or were there?

"Wait a minute," he said, digging out his notebook. "I completely forgot to tell you, I found a fragment of a rune in Marcellus Gordon's trash."

He flipped open to the page where he'd drawn what had remained of the rune and passed it to Iggy. The old man flicked his gold lighter and held it up to see what Alex had drawn.

"I don't know what it is yet," Alex began, but Iggy handed him back the book.

"It's an obfuscation rune," he said. "Write out a document, then draw the rune with the same ink and the text becomes unreadable. Some business men put them on important papers and contracts."

"What use is a contract that no one can read?" Alex asked.

"Use the ink to draw the rune on a glass lens and anyone looking through the lens can read it," Iggy explained. "They also have a side effect of blocking any kind of linking rune."

"Watson must have used it on some business papers," Alex said. He hadn't found any unreadable papers, but since the rune was in the trash, it was likely Watson destroyed it.

With a sigh, Alex closed the notebook and put it back in his pocket.

Another dead end.

The cab eased to a stop in front of the brownstone, and Iggy paid the cabbie while Alex got out. He had no idea what time it was, but he needed to get to bed. Not because he was exhausted, but because tomorrow he had to find a dead man, recover a motor, and save a kidnap victim all in time to have a date with an angel.

Cheer up, he thought as they mounted the stairs to the front door. Tomorrow couldn't possibly be worse.

25

THE SEARCH

Despite his going to bed well after midnight, Alex was up and at his office at nine sharp. In the detective business, he didn't get many customers at that hour, but the time was useful to tackle the various tasks that needed to be done to finish cases and keep his business running.

"Wow," Leslie said as he entered the office. "Things must be worse than I thought if you're here on time."

"You have no idea," Alex said. He'd managed, with the aid of three cups of Iggy's strongest coffee, to wake up and take the crawler to the office, but his mind was still fuzzy. "Please tell me there's coffee," he said.

Leslie stepped over to the little table that sat beside the filing cabinets and picked up a steel coffee pot sitting on a tick square of cork. Moving past Alex, she went into his office and then into the little bathroom attached to it, filling the pot with water. The office didn't have a stove and the radiator connected to the boiler in the basement was off for the summer, but there were other ways to brew coffee, especially in New York. When Leslie returned, she put the pot back on the cork pad and opened the slender drawer in the front of the side table. Inside lay a decorative wooden box with paper flames of red and orange lacquered to its sides and top. Opening the box, Leslie took out a small, brown rock that pulsated with red light from somewhere deep inside. The light gave Alex the impression that the stone was breathing.

The rock was a boiler stone, the invention of Sorcerer Malcolm Henderson, one of the New York six. By itself the stone was an unremarkable, if slightly creepy, rock, but submerge it in water and it became hot enough to boil that water. Most buildings in the city had their boilers converted to use boiler stones instead of oil or coal. Alex was grateful that they could also be used to make coffee.

"Things aren't really that bad, surely?" she asked, dropping crystals of instant coffee into the pot as the water began to boil. Before Alex could protest, she added a second scoop. Leslie knew his habits almost as well as he did.

"Well, I almost got arrested last night," he said

"How does someone *almost* get arrested?" Leslie asked.

"Remember Duane King?""Yeah. The guy who the old Suffolk County Assessor cheated out of his land." Leslie nodded.

"Well, I told Lieutenant Detweiler that he was the ghost killer."

"Let me guess," she said, refilling Alex's cup. "He has an alibi."

Alex nodded, as he drank deeply again.

"Real good one," he said. "He's dead."

"Ouch," Leslie said, a pained look on her face. She picked up the coffee pot by its wooden handle and refilled Alex's cup. "I'm guessing the Lieutenant didn't take it well. So what now?"

Alex accepted the cup and took a long sip of the scalding liquid. It burned his tongue but he didn't care.

"Now, I have to prove that King faked his death and is actually the killer."

Leslie raised her eyebrow at that.

"It sounds like I've got a full morning ahead of me," she said. "Did you get those runes written that I asked for?"

"Last night," Alex said, finishing his second cup. "They're in the lockbox, but what does that have to do with your morning?"

Leslie smiled sweetly at him and sauntered around behind her desk.

"Because," she said, "I either have to get these runes to the people who ordered them, or I've got to go out and find a job that can pay me."

"I made up two weeks of your back pay," Alex said in a hurt voice. It was a game they played. He knew that Leslie wouldn't just quit, she'd go down swinging. So would he for that matter, but her bringing it up meant they were still in danger.

It seemed like they were always in danger.

"Well, you've got your work and I've got mine," he said, after a long silence.

"What about the Lightning Lord's missing engine?" Leslie asked.

"Motor," Alex corrected. "And I don't know. I talked him into giving me another day to find it, but if I don't hear from Danny or Callahan today, that's a bust."

Leslie reached across the desk and put a hand on his arm.

"You'll get it done, kid," she said, despite the fact that she was only ten years older than him. "You always do. Now get to it. I've got people to call and money to collect."

Alex met her gaze and nodded, passing silent thanks to her. She knew him well enough to see he was on the ropes. He wondered again why he never made a pass at her; she was amazing, after all. Theirs was more of a kid brother and big sister relationship and to be honest, Alex liked it that way. He could be himself around Leslie without the pressure of a relationship making him watch what he said or how he said it.

"Good luck," he told her, and headed for his office.

THE FIRST THING he did was to call Anne Watson at her hotel and give her an update. Detweiler had already informed her that she wasn't a suspect, but she was glad to hear that Alex was still on the case. He told her the story of Duane King and why he might want revenge on her husband.

"I don't know if I can believe that, Mr. Lockerby," she said, voice and manner somewhat cold. He had just accused her husband of fraud, after all.

"I'm sorry to have to tell you, Mrs. Watson," Alex said, meaning every word. "But I figured you deserved the truth. I can't prove that King is still alive or the one responsible, but I'm going to keep digging until I know who killed your husband for sure."

Anne paused for a moment, then sighed.

"Thank you for not lying to me," she said. "Part of me wishes you had, but I appreciate the truth. Call me when you know for sure."

Alex promised that he would, then hung up. He sat at his desk, paging through his notebook, searching for something, some bit of information he'd overlooked that would help him find Duane King. Alex felt sure Iggy was right, and King was still alive. The question was, how to prove it? He didn't have any better idea now than he had last night about how King was stalking his victims.

"But he is stalking them," Alex said out loud. "He would have had to, in order to know when they'd be home."

If King had been loitering in Inner-Ring neighborhoods or Core apartment buildings, someone would have noticed him. And however he got into the houses, he would have started outside.

Reaching for the phone on his desk, Alex intended to call Anne Watson back. Since picking the front door lock in broad daylight was risky, he'd need her house key to get back in and look for King's means of entrance. Everyone had been so focused on what happened in the locked rooms, Alex hadn't searched the rest of the house.

King had been careful not to leave any traces at the murder, but had he been that careful getting inside in the first place?

Alex grabbed the phone's receiver, but it rang before he could pick it up.

"Lockerby?" Andrew Barton said.

Alex wondered if he'd heard from the police about his motor. Danny would be sure to call him once they found it, but Alex expected to get a call first.

"I've got good news and bad news," Barton continued. "Which do you want first?"

"Let's have the good news," Alex said, needing some this morning.

"I called around and that idea you had about using my traction motor for mining was a damn good one. It's perfect for their needs. I'll have a prototype for them in a month."

"I'm happy for you," Alex lied. "What's the bad news?"

"I don't think those bank robbers could be using my motor the way you think they are."

Alex felt a sinking feeling in his gut and he wished he'd eaten breakfast.

"Why not?"

"That motor weighs six hundred pounds," he said. "It's smaller than a normal traction motor because it's a prototype, but it's still capable of pulling a locomotive."

"I don't see the problem," Alex said. "They've probably got enough men to move it."

"But how are they going to power it?" Barton asked. "A motor that size pulls a few thousand volts, even to do light work like turning a mining drill. You can't just plug that in to a light socket."

Alex wasn't sure exactly what the problem was, but if Barton was right, it would mean that Danny and Callahan were looking for a tunnel that might not exist.

"They have a couple hundred feet of heavy gauge copper wire," Alex said. "I figure they've patched in to the fuse panel of whatever building they're tunneling from."

Barton thought about that for a moment.

"Well, the wire could certainly carry the current, but if they were pulling that much voltage through a building, no one inside would be able to run a toaster."

Alex thought about it. He hadn't considered the traction motor's power requirements. That didn't mean he was wrong, but maybe he was wrong about where the kidnappers were digging their tunnel.

"What about the Edison Electric lines?" he asked. While Barton powered most of Manhattan from Empire Tower, the rest of the city was wired to the power grid, owned by Thomas Edison's company.

"They have the same problem," Barton explained. "If someone pulled that much power off one of their poles, the nearby buildings would notice. They'd have gotten calls before now."

"Even if they're drilling at night?" Alex asked.

"You know this city doesn't sleep," he said. "I'm sorry, Alex, but I don't think the police are going to find my motor in the basement of a building next to a bank. Not unless the people who took it are using it as an enormous paperweight."

Alex rubbed his eyes with his free hand. Callahan was not going to take this news well. In less than two days, he'd managed to burn every bridge he had with the police. He'd be lucky if they called him to consult on mugging now.

"Thanks, Mr. Barton," he said, smiling to make his voice cheery. "I'll call the police and let them know this is probably a wild goose chase."

"Sorry to be the bearer of bad news," Barton said, "but I thought you'd want to know. Cheer up though, you've still got the rest of the day to win our bet."

Promising to get right on that, Alex hung up. He opened his desk drawer before he remembered that he was out of bourbon. Deciding he needed to be calm when he called Danny, he took out his last remaining cigarette and lit it.

The more he thought about his predicament the angrier he got, until he cocked his hand back to throw the cigarette across the room. He didn't, of course. He couldn't afford a new one. That thought just made him angrier.

"What's wrong?" Leslie's voice came from the doorway.

Alex hadn't heard her open it; he must have been madder than he'd thought.

"What makes you think anything's wrong?" he asked, trying to force a smile onto his face.

She raised an eyebrow at that.

"Never kid a kidder, Alex," she said. "I heard you grinding your teeth all the way back at my desk."

Alex took a deep breath and related his call with Barton.

"To make matters worse," he concluded, "the only thing I can think to do about finding the ghost is to go back to the Watson house and try to figure out how he got in."

"And you have to call Danny and warn him that you were wrong," Leslie said. Alex had conveniently left that particularly unpleasant task out of the story.

"And I have to call Danny," he admitted.

She looked him in the eye for a long moment.

"I guess you better get started," she said in her matter-of-fact voice.

Alex knew she was right, but he really didn't want to admit it. She just held his gaze for another moment, then turned to go back to her desk.

"Keep swinging, kid," Leslie said. "You're bound to hit one sooner or later."

"Thanks," Alex said, crushing out the stub of his cigarette and reaching for the phone.

He called back Anne Watson and arranged to meet her and get her house key. He didn't have any new ideas about how to find Leroy Cunningham, but he could at least go after Duane King.

"And call Danny," Leslie said from the waiting room after Alex hung up with Anne.

He bit back a retort and picked up the phone. Since Danny would still be out looking for bank robbers digging a tunnel, Alex intended to leave a message with the operator, but when she tried to connect him, Danny picked up his phone.

"Hey, I can't talk right now," Danny said. His voice was tense, and he clearly wanted to get off the phone.

"I was wrong about the bank robbery," Alex said, speaking quickly. Callahan would be furious once he figured it out, to say nothing of Captain Rooney, and Alex had to make sure Danny was prepared for that.

"I know" Danny hissed. "Callahan is madder than a wet hen."

"I'm sorry," Alex said. "How much trouble are you in?"

"I'm the guy who led the search teams to half the basements in New York," he said. "Callahan's not mad at me. You, on the other hand, you'd better lay low for a while."

"I'm already on Detweiler's hit list," Alex admitted. "I'll make myself scarce for a few days. Can I call you later?"

"When I'm at home," Danny whispered, then hung up abruptly.

Damn.

Alex managed to get his friend in trouble again. Callahan was probably sending officers over to Lockerby Investigations right now to haul him in.

That thought impelled Alex to action and he stood up. Taking a moment to get his kit from the vault, he headed out into the main office.

"Callahan's probably going to send cops over to bring me in," he said to Leslie as he headed for the door. "I'm going over to the Watson place to look for clues."

"I'll hold the fort and tell the cops I haven't seen you," Leslie said with a smile.

SIX HOURS LATER, Alex had been over the Watson house from top to bottom.

Twice.

He'd had to refuel his ghostlight and silverlight burners but there was no part of the house from the cellar to the attic that he hadn't checked.

All for nothing.

Once he'd finished with the house, Alex took to the streets and talked to the neighbors. All of them knew the Watsons and even though the police suspected the widow on account of her being fifteen years younger than David, none of the neighbors believed it. They all had stories and anecdotes about the Watsons but not one of them had seen anything suspicious, and definitely had not seen anyone lurking in the neighborhood watching the Watsons' home.

If Duane King had staked out the Watsons' house, he'd done it from his invisible car.

Frustrated and angry, Alex went back inside to pack up his gear. It had been a long and fruitless day, but at least his evening would be good. He'd pick up Jessica at seven and take her to the *Lucky Dragon*. All he had to do was shower off the grime of crawling through attics and cellars, and put on a clean shirt.

As he packed up his gear, he remembered Danny's warning to lie low. He went back into David Watson's office and called Iggy, just to be sure.

"I'm glad you called," Iggy said. "Some police officers were here looking for you. There's one in a car down the street and one watching the alley. I think Detweiler might have changed his mind about arresting you."

"He might have," Alex said, "but Callahan sent these guys." He explained the call from Andrew Barton and what it meant for his theory.

"So what now?"

"Now I have a date," Alex said.

"I mean about Leroy Cunningham," Iggy said. "You can't just leave him to whatever fate is waiting for him."

"It's the same story as the ghost," Alex protested. "I know why he was taken. I know what they're doing. It's just not possible."

"Some part of the impossible must be possible," Iggy said.

"I know," Alex said softly. "But damned if I can figure out what."

Iggy sighed.

"All right," he said. "You need to clear your head, get a fresh perspective on the problem. Go have your date, then call me when you're done, and we'll sneak you back in here."

"I told Danny I'd call him later," Alex said. "I'm pretty sure I can bunk with him tonight. That's probably safer."

"Do you need anything from here?" Iggy asked. "I mean for your date, do you have money?"

"The only thing I need is a shower and a clean shirt," Alex said.

"How are you going to manage that?"

Alex actually smiled. For the fist time today, he actually had an answer.

"I've got a complete change of clothes in my vault," he said. "And I don't think Mr. Watson will mind if I borrow his shower."

Alex was about to hang up, but Iggy was quiet. He knew that meant the old man was thinking.

"I'm going to head down to the diner for a slice of pie," he said. "Why don't you swing by there on your way, and ask Mary if she's got something for you?"

26

THE OUTING

Jessica was waiting for Alex in the back yard of the alchemist shop. She stood on the little patch of grass overlooking the herb garden with her back to him. Alex knew she heard the click of the gate as he let himself in, but she didn't turn, forcing him to wait to see her until he was closer.

When he was within five paces of her she turned, flinging her long red hair around so that when she faced him, it draped over the front of her right shoulder. She wore a cocktail dress that clung to her generous figure in ways that made Alex forget all about his problems. It hung below the knee, but had a slit in the left side that rode up quite a bit. A single strap went up over her left shoulder, accented with a polished bronze clasp, and she wore a matching necklace of metal plates that reminded Alex of the ornamental collars worn by Egyptian Pharaohs.

"Hello, Alex," she said, her voice quietly amused. "You're right on time."

Alex wanted to reply, but he worried that if he spoke, the vision before him would disappear. A girl that beautiful couldn't be real. She wore just enough makeup to accent her face, with blush on her sharp cheekbones, and the dark red lipstick she favored.

"You look fantastic," he said, finally.

He held out his arm and she stepped forward, slipping her hand onto it.

"And where will we be going this evening?" There was the faintest hint of a challenge in her question, as if daring him to impress her.

"I hope you like Chinese," he said, desperately hoping she did. He didn't actually have a backup plan, or any money to pull one off. Nevertheless he fixed an easy smile on his face and held her calculating gaze.

She smiled. A dazzling display of white teeth, red lips, and raw sexuality that told Alex he could relax.

"I adore it," she said.

"Good," Alex said. He still didn't have any real money, not even enough for a taxi, so he hoped his charm and a quick story would keep the lovely Jessica from being too upset. "We've got a table at the *Lucky Dragon*," he told her.

"Oh," she cooed. "And here I thought private dicks didn't make much money."

"We don't," Alex said. "So we'll have to go by crawler."

He resisted the urge to hold his breath while she appraised him with cool eyes. She raised an eyebrow, and then a subtle smile returned to her lips.

"Sounds like fun," she said. "The *Lucky Dragon* is in the Core, right? We can take the Lightning Lord's new line."

Alex was confused for a moment, but then remembered the construction on Central Park west where the workmen were building Barton's new elevated crawler rails.

"I thought they were still testing that," he said, remembering the story he'd read in the paper.

"It opened today," she said. "It's supposed to be faster than anything in the city."

"Well," Alex said, leading her through the gate and into the front yard of the shop. "Then we simply have to try it."

He wasn't sure if her enthusiasm for the crawler ride was genuine, or if she was putting it on so he wouldn't be embarrassed. Her face was unreadable, and Alex decided then and there not to play poker with her. In either case, he was grateful for her easy, friendly, sexy manner, and he realized he was grinning like a mental patient.

Alex toned his smile down to the quirky grin that Leslie said made him look dashing. As he did so, he realized that their conversation had lagged.

"How goes the elixir brewing?" he asked and immediately felt like an ass. She was taking a much-needed break from her very demanding job, and he was asking her to bring it along.

Idiot.

"Let's not talk about that," she said, her smile never slipping. "How's it coming with the kidnapped man?"

Even as the words came out of her mouth, Alex caught a flash of chagrin in her expression. It disappeared almost instantly, but Alex could tell she'd regretted it as much as he had his own awkward question.

"Let's not talk about work at all," he said, remembering not to grin like a loon.

She smiled back at him and leaned close so that her arm and shoulder were pressed against him.

"I think I'd like that," she said.

BY THE TIME they reached the elevated crawler station a few minutes later, Alex was desperately glad to see it. So far, their non-work conversation had dealt with the weather and the few front-page stories in which Alex wasn't involved.

He really needed a better angle. It was like he was a teenager on his first date.

Kathy MacMillan. She'd thought he was an idiot too.

The station at the end of the test line for Barton's elevated crawler was a platform built over the northbound side of Central Park West, across from the museum. Two sets of shiny metal rails about four feet apart ran along the street, supported by thick steel poles every half block or so. They didn't look like the heavy square rails that trains ran on, but more like polished rods. They seemed flimsy, and Alex wondered how they could hold up a crawler in the first place. To say nothing about how a crawler could navigate them without falling off onto the road below.

As Alex and Jessica watched, a crawler came into view, speeding along the outermost set of rails. It was moving much faster than the ones Alex was familiar with and its legs weren't blue but a rather violent shade of purple. Sparks of energy crackled and popped where the hundreds of energy legs touched the rails, but the vehicle showed no signs of slipping.

"That's amazing," Jessica said with a look of wonder and delight.

"Come on," Alex said, taking her by the hand and hurrying toward the stairs that led up to the platform. A few minutes later they sat side by side on the crawler's upper deck, watching Central Park fly by at an unbelievable sixty miles an hour.

Alex had never spent much time in the park, despite the fact that the brownstone was only six blocks from the east side of it. Jessica, however, seemed to love the park and happily commented on the various points of interest as they passed.

It was strange to move so fast without the noise or vibration of machinery. Alex could hear the crackle and hum of the electrified rail that fed power to the crawler directly from Empire Tower, but that and the wind were the only sounds.

A regular crawler would have taken half an hour to get to the core from the museum, but the elevated one dropped Alex and Jessica off at the end of the line, Empire Tower, in just over ten. By the time they got there, they were both laughing and chatting happily about their experiences in New York.

"You know people used to live in there," she said, looking up at Empire Tower as they headed east toward the *Lucky Dragon*.

"Some still do," Alex said, telling her about Bickman and his wife, who now had apartments up above Barton's etherium capacitors.

"Is he as handsome as everyone says?" Jessica asked with a grin.

Alex laughed and described Barton, studiously avoiding any details that might lead to a work conversation. The talk took them three more blocks and right to the door of the *Lucky Dragon*.

The restaurant was crowded and noisy and smelled absolutely wonderful. Alex had been here once before, but never to eat. If he was being honest, he was far too nervous the last time to even think about food.

He wasn't thinking now, and his stomach grumbled just for emphasis. It had been a while since he'd eaten.

The tables at the Lucky Dragon were full of elegant food and elegant people. Jessica would fit right in, but Alex felt a little underdressed as he saw several men in formal attire. More worrying was the crowd of people standing outside, apparently waiting for a table.

"Do you have a reservation?" the hostess asked when Alex approached her. She looked him up and down, obviously taking his measure, and if her expression was to be believed, finding him wanting.

Without answering, Alex handed over the ornate, handwritten card. The hostess read it and looked uncertain.

"Just a moment," she said.

She went inside and disappeared. Alex looked at Jessica and she looked suitably impressed.

After a minute the hostess came back, all smiles this time.

"Right this way, Mr. Lockerby," she said. "Unfortunately we are booked solid tonight, but the owner said to put you at his private table."

She led the way through the dining room to the back, past an enormous tank filled with colorful fish, and pulled aside a silk curtain. Beyond was a small room with an intimate table inside and a sideboard along the wall.

"Someone will be with you in a moment," the hostess said. Alex thanked her, and she withdrew.

"Okay," Jessica said with sly grin. "I'm impressed."

Alex held out her chair and she sat. Alex sat across from her and pulled a silver lighter out of his pocket, putting it on the table.

"What's that for?" Jessica asked.

Before Alex could answer, a Chinese man in an oriental robe came in with a teapot on a tray and two handle-less cups.

"Good evening," he said in accented English. "Mr. Chow has arranged for your meal; it will be along shortly. Right now, I will perform for you the tea ceremony, an ancient custom of my people."

After the tea, more men brought in trays and bowls of all different kinds of food, including a plate loaded with the restaurant's famous dumplings. Then they departed, leaving Alex and Jessica alone.

"I don't even know what this is," Jessica said a few minutes later, "but it's wonderful."

Despite living with Iggy, Alex wasn't much for fancy food, and with his budget, he was used to eating at dog wagons and in greasy spoons. Still, he had to admit, the dumplings were excellent.

He picked up the lighter next to his plate and lit it, setting it back on the table next to a salt shaker to keep it from falling over.

"Okay," Jessica said, giving him an annoyed look. "What's with the mood lighting?"

Alex laughed at that. It felt good.

"It has to do with work," he said, "and we're not talking about that."

That earned him a raised eyebrow.

"You're deliberately being obtuse," she said. "Spill."

"Well," Alex said, not wanting to ruin the pleasant mood at the table. "Let's just say that the police are angry with me right now and, if they were to try to find me with magic, this lighter prevents that."

Her expression darkened.

"You're not in trouble, are you?"

Alex smiled at that. She wasn't worried at all that he might have done something worthy of being sought by the police. She was worried that they might catch him.

"It's just a misunderstanding, but I'd rather deal with it on Monday."

"So what does the lighter do?"

Alex picked it up and extinguished it before passing it over.

"There's an obfuscation rune scraped into the side," he said. "Iggy, that is Dr. Bell, wanted to try it."

"You call Dr. Bell, Iggy?" she asked with a smirk.

"We have an understanding," Alex said, dodging the question. "Anyway, there are better runes but they're more complicated. This is the quick and dirty solution. As long as it's lit, runes that link to other things, like finding runes, won't work."

"Well you need to get this thing with you and the police sorted out soon," Jessica said, returning to her meal. "I might be able to free up some more time, and I think we should go out again."

Alex couldn't help smiling at that.

"Maybe take in a picture?" he wondered.

"I was thinking we could go to a museum."

Alex scoffed at that.

"We could do that tonight," he said. "It's right there at the end of the new crawler line, and it's open till ten. We could stop in on the way back to your place."

"But I want to see the Almiranta exhibit," Jessica explained. "The curator said on the radio that they won't have it put back until Tuesday."

Alex wracked his brain until he remembered the story he'd read in the paper. The Spanish government had sued Phillip Leland, the explorer who found the wreck of the Almiranta, claiming the ship and its treasure were their property. The museum had to take the treasure exhibit off display during the trial.

"Spain lost their case then?" he asked.

Jessica nodded, spearing a dumpling with her fork.

"It got thrown out of court," she said. "It was on the radio."

"I guess we can go next week then," he said, trying not to sound too disappointed. He wasn't much for walking around and looking at things. That was pretty much what his job was, and museums were nothing but that. Still, Jessica would be there the whole time, so it wasn't exactly time wasted.

It was a bit of a busman's holiday, though.

It took Alex a full five minutes for his brain to start working, though whether his mental torpor was caused by the food or his company, he couldn't be sure. When at last his synapses finally did start firing, he stood up so fast he sent his chair tumbling across the private room.

Jessica just stared at him with wide eyes.

"What's the matter?"

He didn't answer, just stepped around the table, leaned down, and kissed her square on the mouth. If he hadn't been numb he imagined she would have tasted sweet.

"Thank you," he said. "I've got to find a phone."

Before Jessica could object or protest, he raced out through the curtain into the dining room.

"Is everything all right, Mr. Lockerby?" the robed man who had been serving them asked. Alex intended to ignore him but something in the man's face made him stop. He remembered who this man's boss really was, and while he doubted Danny's father cared one whit about whether or not Alex enjoyed his meal, this man didn't know that. For all this waiter knew, Alex was an important guest, and the conse-quences for failing to make him happy could be dire.

"I'm sorry," Alex said, stopping to put a reassuring hand on the man's arm. "I've just been called away to work. My companion and I will be leaving as soon as I make a telephone call."

The man's face blanched, confirming Alex's suspicions.

"Please tell Mr. Chow that the food was wonderful, the service was superb, and the dumplings were exquisite."

The man's smile bloomed back to his face and he nodded.

"Thank you," he said with a bow.

"Now, where can I find a telephone?"

ALEX MADE TWO PHONE CALLS, using up most of the change left in his pocket. The first was to Gary Bickman. Alex had to use every bit of leverage he had with the little Brit, but he finally convinced him to have Andrew Barton meet Alex at the Central Office.

His second call was to Iggy, delivering pretty much the same message. Alex did spend an extra few minutes explaining his reasoning to the doctor just to make sure he wasn't crazy.

"You're crazy," Iggy said. "Call in a tip to the cops and go back to that beautiful woman."

Iggy always could see the right of things.

"You know I can't do that," Alex said. "Just meet me there as soon as you can."

Iggy said that he would, and Alex hung up.

"That was a quick phone call," Jessica said when he returned their dining room a moment later. "You want to explain what that was all about?"

"Nope," he said, picking up his chair. "That'd be work talk, and we promised no more work talk tonight." He picked up his fork and speared a dumpling. Honestly, he was glad, after this week of failures. He didn't want Jessica to know his plan in case he failed again. Of course if he failed again the world would know because he would definitely be going up on an obstruction charge.

Or three.

"We do need to go," he said, picking up his hat and putting away the battered cigarette lighter.

Jessica just looked at him in bewilderment for a long moment, then her playful, sexy smile came back. She set her napkin aside and stood up.

"All right," she said. "Keep your secrets, but I'd better hear all about it on our date next week."

Alex promised to tell her everything, and she nodded, then stood.

"I am a bit disappointed, though," she said, fixing him with a challenging stare. "You're cutting our meal short and all you can manage by way of apology was that quick peck on the lips? I should think you'd be more gentlemanly than that."

Alex's brain was firing on all cylinders now, but it still took him a long second to sort out what she'd said. Embarrassed at the lapse, he stepped up in front of her, lifted her chin with his finger, leaned slowly down and kissed her.

Everything he'd missed in that first brief kiss exploded through him. The touch of her lips was electric, and he felt her hands slide up his arms and over his shoulders. He wrapped his arms around her waist and pulled her tightly against him.

After what seemed like an all too brief eternity, he let her go. As she stepped back, he wanted to say something, something witty or clever like the movie actors did, but nothing came to him. When she saw the struggle in his face, Jessica smiled.

"Did you smear my lipstick?" she asked.

"I'm afraid so," he said, noting that it was now spread beyond the borders of her lips.

She reached up and patted him on the cheek.

"Good boy," she said, her smile positively wicked. "Now where, exactly, are we going?"

She pulled a mirror out of her handbag and fixed her lipstick. Alex waited for her to finish, then offered her his arm and she took it.

"You are going home," he said, leading her out into the dining room. When her brows furrowed angrily, he continued. "Have you forgotten your potions?"

Her face softened a bit, but she didn't look happy.

"Iggy will meet us at the Central Office and escort you home."

"You're a real stinker," she said.

"Save that for the cab," he said. "We're in a hurry and I, uh, I need to borrow the fare."

The look she gave him was unamused.

"Iggy will pay you back as soon as he gets there," Alex promised.

Jessica gave him a sardonic smile that told him she really wasn't too angry.

"You're one hell of an interesting date, Alex," she said, bumping him affectionately with her shoulder. "I'll give you that."

"Don't count me out yet," he said, whistling for a cab. "You said you wanted to meet the Lightning Lord. Looks like you're going to get your chance."

27

THE PRIZE

H urry up and wait.

Alex looked around the cavernous room and felt like he was the only one who was anxious. Uniformed police officers sat on the floor, leaning against shelves and boxes, their hats down over their eyes. To a casual observer, it looked like they were sleeping.

Every now and then, scattered throughout their ranks was a detective in a suit, but they were just as relaxed. Most smoked quietly, the tips of their cigarettes glowing and fading in the semi-darkness.

To be fair, Alex supposed that part of a cop's life was the hurry-up-and-wait game. Stakeouts and paperwork were exercises in patience.

Alex hated patience. That was one of the many benefits, in his opinion, of being a private detective runewright. He set his own hours and if he wanted to know where someone went, he could plant a tracking stone on them and link it to his map and a duplicate stone. Then all he had to do was sit in his comfortable chair, drink bourbon, and watch the map. Which, now that he thought about it was still waiting, but in much more pleasant surroundings and with a readily available bathroom.

Sitting in the dark and waiting simply wasn't on his list of fun things. His mind kept drifting back to Jessica, to that fiery kiss that had smeared her lipstick so agreeably. Every time he smiled, however, the more cynical part of his brain reminded him of where he was, and more importantly, what was at stake.

"Lockerby," Andrew Barton whispered from his left. The sorcerer lay in a hammock he had conjured out of thin air that hung, suspended in the aforementioned air. It swung gently by itself as Barton lay with his ankles crossed and his hand behind his head.

Most of the beat cops avoided looking at the sorcerer. Everyone knew sorcerers were temperamental and used to getting their own way. Nobody wanted to run afoul of one. As a result there were only three people crouched, hidden, behind the shelf that concealed the magical hammock.

"What is it?" Alex asked.

"I'm starting to revise my opinion of you," he said.

Alex wasn't sure what to make of that.

"Thanks?" he said quizzically. "What brought that on?"

"You seem to have a real eye for beauty," Barton said. "Not to mention a way with the ladies. First, dear Sorsha, and now that luscious creature you had on your arm tonight. I'm starting to think you've made it your mission to involve yourself with all the beautiful women in the city."

"This isn't the time, gentlemen," Captain Rooney growled from the semi-darkness.

Rooney's presence was one of the things currently giving Alex heartburn. When the Captain had first heard Alex's idea, he'd wanted to run Alex out of his office on a rail. The presence of Andrew Barton, the most prominent of the New York Six, however, made him a bit more cautious. Too cautious, as it turned out. With Barton endorsing Alex's plan, Rooney wanted to come along.

It was a blatantly political move as far as the Captain was concerned. If Alex was right, he could take the credit, if Alex was wrong yet again, no one would blame the Captain for going along with a plan endorsed by the great and powerful Andrew Barton. For the Captain it was a no-lose proposition.

"Don't worry, Captain," Barton said, swinging easily in his hammock. "We aren't likely to be taken by surprise."

Rooney didn't answer that, and Alex grinned. There were some advantages to having the Lightning Lord around, though Alex wondered how the sorcerer would take it if this all turned out to be for nothing.

It won't be, he assured himself. Everything fit this time. He was right.

"What did you mean about Sorsha?" Alex asked. She'd made her feelings quite clear a year ago.

Barton chuckled.

"Some detective you are," he said. "She's still smitten with you. Won't even give me the time of day."

"As I recall, that was her position long before I met her," Alex said.

"Alex," Barton chided. "You wound me. Things with Sorsha were coming along just fine until you showed up and made her fall in love with you."

Alex scoffed at that.

"Sorsha Kincaid is not the kind of woman who would sit up in her flying castle and wait for a man to come to her," Alex said, keeping his voice low.

Barton sat up in his hammock.

"You're right," he said. "I doubt you rejected her, you're too smart for that. So," he said, turning to stare intently at Alex. "What is she waiting for?"

Alex tried not to wither under that intense gaze. He noticed a faint blue nimbus of energy glowing around the outer ring of the sorcerer's irises. It gave him a disturbing, other-worldly look.

Almost on cue a low, grinding rumble filled the room. It started faintly but in the quiet, everyone heard it.

"Get ready," Callahan growled in a voice that was soft enough not to be loud, but forceful enough to carry. "Sorenson, wake up O'Mally."

All around the storage room policemen and detectives roused themselves, checking their sidearms and crushing out their cigarettes.

"Saved by the bell, eh, Lockerby?" Barton said with a sardonic smile. He snapped his fingers and the hammock vanished, leaving him to float down to the ground as if he were no heavier than a feather.

"This is actually rather exciting," he said. He opened his hand and arcs of blue energy danced between his fingers.

"I'd rather you stayed here with me, Mr. Barton." Captain Rooney said. "The governor would have my hide if anything happened to you."

"He's got a point, sir," Callahan said. "This might get dicey and I can't have you distracting my men."

Barton closed his hand and pouted.

"All right," he said in a way that reminded Alex very much of a five-year-old. That ability to switch between corporate tycoon and petulant child seemed prevalent in all sorcerers, if the stories were to be believed. It was what made them so dangerous.

Alex smiled at the thought of Sorsha behaving that way. She simply didn't have it in her.

Maybe it only applies to men.

As the grinding sound got loud enough that Alex could feel it in the floor, he moved from his cover next to Barton and scurried up to where Danny crouched behind a box.

"You ready for this?" Alex asked.

Danny smiled and nodded.

"Looks like you were right."

Alex held his breath as the words washed over him. He'd believed he was right, he knew he was right all the way down to his core. Everything fit. But he didn't realize until that moment just how much he needed to hear someone else say it.

It had been obvious to him the moment Jessica had asked him to take her to the museum. The same museum that had stored a king's ransom in salvaged gold in its vault, thanks to a court case.

According to the papers, the treasure of the Almiranta was worth over one hundred million dollars. A far greater prize than any mere bank. On top of that, literally, was Andrew Barton and John D. Rockefeller's elevated crawler station, connected by electrified rail directly to Empire Tower. All the thieves had to do was tie the electric motor to it with the copper cable they stole, and they were in business. From there the operation was simple, dig through into the museum's secure storage room from the abandoned subway tunnels, steal the gold, and use their stash of stolen trucks to get it out of the city.

Since Alex and Danny found their trucks, they would have had to make new plans, but with the court case being thrown out, they were out of time. If they didn't move on the gold tonight, they'd lose their chance.

Alex smiled with satisfaction at figuring it all out.

Finally.

A crack appeared in the far wall of the storage room and the wall bulged out slightly.

"Douse the light," Callahan said. "Stay hidden. Nobody move until I give the word. Remember, they've got a hostage with them."

The single magelight on the ceiling went out, plunging the room into inky blackness.

Alex's smile at his own cleverness faded when Callahan mentioned Leroy. If the thieves had been delaying, looking for another way to get the gold away, they might have already finished their tunnel. If that had happened, they wouldn't need Leroy any more.

Alex figured they'd want to keep him around for the last push into the vault.

Or rather, he hoped they did.

A chunk of masonry fell out of the wall and a massive boring bit as big around as dinner plate pushed into the room. Light bled through around it, making it look like a glowing rune circle. A moment later, the bit was pulled slowly back, and light flooded into the storage room.

Alex and the police all ducked out of sight. A few minutes later they heard sounds of someone pulling debris away from the hole.

"We're in," a Jersey-accented voice said.

Alex smiled. He knew that voice, and it explained one of the few pieces still missing from this puzzle.

"Hit it again," the voice said.

A moment later a humming sound came through the hole, followed shortly by the grinding noise of the boring bit. It took a few more minutes, but it punched another hole in the back wall, sending bits of broken masonry and debris scattering across the floor.

The sounds of sledge hammers came next as the thieves broke open the hole.

"That'll do it," Jersey accent said. Alex could hear him enter through the hole. "Bring the flashlights and spread out. Focus on the small stuff and find the entropy stone."

Men began to move into the room, opening the nearest crates full of ancient American gold. Danny flexed his hand, tightening his grip on his service .38. Alex wondered if Callahan could see what was happening. He'd deployed his men well back from the wall that faced the subway tunnels, but if he let the thieves get too far in, they were bound to stumble across some of his men.

"Hands up!" Callahan's voice boomed through the room. At the same moment all the lights in the room were turned on. "Stay where you are."

Danny and the other officers and detectives rushed the room, leveling their weapons at the startled men with flashlights.

"Cops!" Jersey yelled, still in the back by the hole.

A couple of the thieves rushed the cops and gunshots erupted in the space. Jersey turned and ran.

"Where are you going, Jimmy?" Alex yelled.

The man turned back, and Alex confirmed that it was Jimmy Cortez, the big floor manager for Barton Electric. Alex had wondered how the thieves knew enough about the traction motor to steal it.

Jimmy snarled, but his eyes went suddenly wide and he darted away through the hole. An instant later a bolt of blue energy raked the wall where he'd been.

"Traitor!" Barton yelled in a voice that echoed unnaturally off the walls.

"After them," Callahan yelled, charging toward the hole at the back.

Danny took off running, with Alex right behind him. They reached the hole right before Callahan and a dozen cops, pushing through into the crude tunnel beyond. It had been dug out tall enough for a man to stand comfortably and wide enough for two men to pass each other. The walls and ceiling were supported by beams made of two-by-fours that had been lashed together and placed every four or five feet.

The tunnel ran straight for about twenty yards, then opened out into a dark space that had to be the abandoned subway.

"Which way did he go?" Danny shouted, as they neared the end of the tunnel.

"Left," Alex answered. "Watch yourself."

Danny skidded to a stop and ducked around the corner for a quick look around.

"It's clear," he shouted, running out into the tunnel.

Alex followed.

The tunnel was lit with magelights that had been hung along one curving wall. Barton's traction motor, mounted on a wheeled cart and sporting the massive boring bit, sat just outside the tunnel. Farther away to the left, Alex could see half a dozen men taking cover behind piles of dirt that they'd obviously removed when they made the tunnel.

As Alex looked for cover of his own, a man in a pair of dirty overalls stepped out from behind a stack of empty crates. Alex recognized the round magazine and forward grip of a tommy gun as the man leveled it at Danny.

"Get down," he yelled, charging forward as the gun spat fire. Alex caught Danny by the shoulder, throwing himself in front of the detective. Pain tore through his left hand and he felt the impact of bullets against his back as his shield runes did their job.

He and Danny went down in a heap and Alex put his arm up to cover his head as best he could with his reasonably bulletproof coat.

Assuming you didn't just use up all your shield runes.

"You all right?" he whispered to Danny as the tommy gun barked again, and cops behind them began to return fire.

"Not really," Danny gasped. His breathing was shallow and rapid and his face was pale.

The firing continued over their heads and all Alex could do was act as a human shield.

"Where are you hit?" he asked.

"Side," Danny gasped.

Alex tried to hold himself up, so his weight wasn't on his friend.

"Enough!" Barton's voice boomed down the tunnel.

The tommy gun fired again, but this time it was met with a crackle of electricity, and the gunman screamed. A moment later the tunnel went silent and the smell of ozone filled the air.

Alex rolled off Danny and reached for his handkerchief, intending to press it down over the spreading bloodstain on the detective's side.

He stopped when he saw the red handprint on Danny's lapel. Blood ran freely from Alex's left hand where one of the bullets from the machine gun had passed right through the back of his hand and out his palm.

Cursing, Alex tied his handkerchief around the wound, using his teeth to pull the knot tight.

"Come out of there with your hands up," Callahan roared. "Or we're coming in to get you."

"I wouldn't do that," Jimmy Cortez said. He stepped out from behind a mountain of dirt. He held a lighter in one hand and a piece of paper in the other.

"Everybody hold it," Callahan barked.

Alex pulled Danny's handkerchief from his coat pocket and pressed it down over the bullet wound in Danny's side.

"This rune is linked to another that's just over our heads," Jimmy said. "If I light it, it will blow up the tunnel and kill us all."

"Lockerby," Callahan called. "Is that possible?"

Alex looked up. Attached to the ceiling was a box with the word, *Explosives*, clearly printed on it. One of the strange, face-like glyph runes had been painted on the outside. Alex could see a bit of fuse running from inside the box into the paint that made up the rune.

"Maybe," Alex said.

"You know it is, Alex," Jimmy said. "You're too smart to doubt it. Now I want all of you to back off," he said. "Or I'll bring down the roof and kill us all."

"You gonna be all right for a minute?" Alex whispered to Danny.

Danny grunted and nodded, his breathing shallow.

"I need to go talk to the nice man who wants to blow us up," he said, digging through Danny's pockets until he found the detective's cigarettes. "I need to borrow these," he said. Then he picked up Danny's .38 and tucked it into his jacket pocket.

"Get moving," Jimmy yelled.

"Just a minute," Alex said. He was tired, sore, and hurt, and it took him a few seconds to get to his feet. "I have a few questions first."

"You think I'm kidding, Alex," Jimmy said, bringing the lighter close to the paper. "You know how this works. Once it starts, nothing on earth can stop it. Now back off."

"Just a minute," Alex said, taking a few tentative steps forward.

"Alex—" Jimmy threatened.

"Hang on," Alex said, digging a cigarette out of Danny's pack and sliding it out with his lips on account of his wounded hand.

"I mean it, Alex, stop right there." Jimmy's voice had risen a bit, he was starting to panic. Alex felt a surge of pride; he must have made quite the impression on Jimmy Cortez for him to actually be afraid.

"Lockerby!" Callahan warned. Clearly he'd heard the same notes of desperation in Jimmy's voice.

Alex stopped and slipped the cigarette pack into his shirt pocket. He held up a placating hand and tried to get into his left jacket pocket with his good right hand. Eventually, he gave up and gingerly slipped his left hand inside.

"I've really only got one question," he said, pulling out the silver lighter and passing it to his good hand. "Well, that's not true," he amended as he flicked the lighter to life and lit his cigarette. That first puff was wonderful and reminded him that he hadn't been able to smoke regularly for the better part of two months.

"First," Alex said, blowing out a long trail of smoke. "Where's Leroy Cunningham?"

"Is that what you're thinking about at a time like this?"

"His wife hired me to find him," Alex said with a shrug. "So, where is he?"

Jimmy nodded off into the darkness of a side tunnel.

"He's down there, alive," he added when Alex's look hardened. "Once we're gone, you're welcome to him. Is that all?"

"Well no," Alex said, taking the cigarette out of his mouth so Jimmy could see the grin spreading across his face. "I want to know why, if you thought I was so dangerous, you let me get this close."

Jimmy's eyes went wide as Alex flicked the cigarette right at him. It hit the paper clutched in his hand, igniting it, and the paper vanished in a puff of flame and smoke. When the flash vanished, however, there was no glowing glyph rune left behind.

Jimmy stood, staring at the explosive box attached to the top of the tunnel, his eyes wide as saucers. Alex used the time to snap the cigarette lighter closed with his left hand, extinguishing its flame and the obfuscation rune powered by it. With his good hand, he pulled Danny's gun out of his pocket.

"Now get on the ground, Jimmy," he said, pointing the gun at the man's chest. The sound of running feet grew louder behind Alex, and Jimmy put up his hands, glaring in furious disbelief. Alex just grinned back at him.

"Looks like you lose," he said.

28

THE RELATION

Danny had already been bundled into a police car bound for the hospital when Alex emerged from the museum's basement with Leroy Cunningham in tow. Cunningham was a skinny blonde kid with spectacles who looked barely out of his teens. Despite being held for a week in the old subway, he didn't seem much the worse for wear.

"I can't say enough how grateful I am, Mr. Lockerby," he said for the third time in his mild, West Virginia drawl. "I thought for sure they'd just leave me tied up in the dark when they left."

Alex didn't say it, but he didn't doubt Leroy was right. He guessed that Jimmy Cortez intended to use that box of explosives on the ceiling to cover their escape once they'd looted the vault. That would have buried Leroy under several tons of rock.

"Don't mention it, kid," Alex said, trudging across the museum lobby toward the bank of phones near the door. "How did they know about you, anyway?"

"I grew up with Benny Hanes," Leroy explained. "He's one of those guys. He worked in the Coledale mine; that's how they knew how to dig tunnels, but he didn't know much about shoring them up."

"And he knew you lived here in the city," Alex said.

Leroy didn't answer, but nodded.

That had been the last missing piece of the puzzle for Alex. With Jimmy Cortez leading the crew, it was a cinch how they'd got onto Barton's traction motor, but Alex hadn't been able to figure out how they'd picked Leroy Cunningham, draftsman, as their mining expert. It was a small detail, but Alex felt better for knowing it.

"Give me a minute," Alex said, stepping into one of the booths and fishing a nickel out of his pocket. "I need to make a call, then we'll call your wife."

"She is okay, right?" Leroy said, worry blooming in his voice. "They said they had someone watching her and that they'd hurt her if I gave them any trouble so I...I just went along."

Alex grinned at that. Leroy was a good kid, the kind who wouldn't jaywalk, and the idea of being part of a heist didn't sit well with him, even when he had no choice.

"You did the right thing," Alex said, dropping the nickel into the phone. "Hannah's fine. I got her stashed at my secretary's place for safekeeping."

Leroy closed his eyes and sighed, his body starting to tremble as the pent-up stress of the last week finally broke. Alex clapped him on the shoulder, then turned back to the phone and gave the operator the number of the brownstone.

"Iggy," Alex said when the old man picked up. "I need you to get over to the Mount Sinai Hospital quick, Danny's been shot."

"I'm sure the doctors there will take good care of him," Iggy said. "Are you all right?"

"I'm fine," Alex said. "Well, I took a bullet to the hand, but it's not too bad. Shield runes stopped the rest, but that's not the point. Danny got hit three times, twice in the side and once in the arm. Before they took him away, he said he couldn't feel his fingers."

"Possible nerve damage," Iggy said. "He'll need a major restoration rune; how long has it been since he was shot?"

"About ten minutes, so you'll need to get going."

"All right," Iggy said. "But I want you to meet me over there, so I can take a look at your hand, understand?"

Alex grinned.

"Yes, sir. I've got to let Leroy talk to his wife, and then we'll be right over."

"I'm glad you found him," Iggy said in his gruff, official-doctor voice. "I want to hear all about it later, but for now, get going."

He hung up and Alex fished his last nickel out of his pocket. He called Leslie and told her to bring Hannah over to the hospital, then passed the phone to Leroy so he could assure his wife that he was fine.

Alex couldn't help grinning as he listened to Leroy try to calm his wife. He'd dreaded the thought of having to tell Hannah that he'd been too late. Now he could feel the knots in his neck and shoulders finally loosening.

"Well, hello," a familiar voice said. "You sure seem to turn up in exciting places."

Alex looked up to see the young reporter with the dimple and the brown suit approaching.

"What happened here?"

Alex resisted the urge to roll his eyes. The last thing he wanted was to deal with the press. He'd had enough of that over the last week. Still, if this reporter was here, there were bound to be others.

"Looks like I'm not the only one who shows up where they're not expected, Mr.—?"

The young man smiled and stuck out his hand.

"Tasker," he said. "Billy Tasker."

A surge of anger ran through Alex at the name. This little punk was the reporter causing him all the trouble with the police.

"You're Tasker?" Alex said, stuffing his anger down into his gut. He shook the man's hand but couldn't manage a smile. "What'd I ever do to you?"

Tasker's smile actually faltered, like he had no idea what Alex was talking about.

"I do a lot of work for the cops," Alex explained. "You made it look like I'm some kind of crime solving genius and they're my bumbling lackeys."

A slow smile spread across Tasker's face and he shrugged.

"Isn't that pretty much how it works?" he asked in an amused voice.

"The cops get in trouble and then you lead them around town till you solve their case?"

"You followed me," Alex said, remembering when he first met Tasker. "That's how you knew about the trucks." He'd been on his way out of the Central Office to meet Danny when Tasker accosted him. Later that day, the story about his leading Danny and the cops to the factory full of stolen trucks appeared in the Sun. Tasker shrugged again.

"I saw you meeting your cop friend, the oriental, over at Gino's," he said. "When you left, you looked like you knew where you were going, so I followed. Worked out pretty good for me."

Alex wanted to strangle the smug fool, but he thought better of it. Tasker used him, but maybe he could return the favor.

"I'll tell you what," Alex said. "Not only will I tell you exactly what went down here tonight, but I'll get you an exclusive interview with someone who was on the inside."

"If—?" Tasker asked, catching the conditional nature of Alex's invention.

"Two things," Alex said, holding up his fingers. "First, you keep my name out of it — no mention of the runewright detective."

Tasker nodded.

"Your loss, but okay. What's number two?"

"You give the credit to Captain Rooney and his men."

"Rooney's a clown," Tasker said, displaying insight beyond his years.

"Those are my terms," Alex said. "Take 'em or leave 'em.'"

"All right," Tasker said with a sigh. "It won't be as much fun, but I do like scooping the Times. Now spill it."

"First, why did the Times fire you?" Alex asked, remembering the reporter's history.

Tasker looked genuinely surprised.

"They didn't like a story I had," he said.

"And they fired you?"

"I wouldn't let it go," he admitted. "Still won't."

"What story is worth that?"

"A personal one," Tasker said, attempting to change the subject.

"No, you don't get off that easy," Alex said. "What's so important that you give up a job at the Times to go to work for a rag like *The Midnight Sun?*"

Tasker looked like he was going to object again, but changed his mind.

"You're involved in the ghost killer case, right?" he asked.

"I've been asked to consult about a few things," Alex said, choosing his words carefully.

"Well you've got that case all wrong," Tasker said. "Everybody, you, the cops, the papers."

"And I suppose you know who's doing the killing and how?" Alex didn't bother to hide the sarcasm in his voice.

"No," Tasker admitted. "But I know who's behind it, the reason that the ghost is killing. The ghost is after Nancy Banes."

Alex almost laughed, but the look on Tasker's face silenced him. He still needed the young reporter's cooperation on the museum heist story.

"So you're the one who has it out for the Mayor's wife," he said. "What'd she do to you, have a cop give you a parking ticket?"

The look Tasker gave Alex told him that the young reporter had something bigger and much more personal against Nancy Banes. Without a word, Tasker reached into his jacket and came out with a folded piece of paper.

"This is a letter from Nancy Sinclair, now Nancy Banes, to a man named Duane King," he said, unfolding the papers so Alex could see official looking letterhead. "I have two more, but this is the one where she tells Mr. King that his land isn't worth the price of the taxes owed on it. She lied to him so that she could steal his land. That's why the ghost is killing people who used to work in the Suffolk County Assessor's office at the time she did."

"Where did you get that letter?" Alex asked. According to Leslie, Randall Walker hadn't found any correspondence in his records.

"My mother sent it to me a few days after Duane King died in a fire," Tasker said. "That's when I got the job with the Times and moved up here."

Alex felt gooseflesh rise on his arms as everything clicked into place.

"Tasker is your mother's name," he said. "Isn't it?"

"So?"

"So you're Duane King's grandson," Alex said. "King's son got a girl pregnant and skipped town. That girl was your mother."

Tasker raised his eyebrows at that, but nodded after a moment.

"It's not as bad as all that," he said. "My dad came back for a few years when I was a kid before he took off for good. That's when I decided to go by Tasker."

Alex could fill in the rest of the story without any trouble. Billy's dad gave the letter to his mom as proof that they were heirs to some great fortune that had been stolen from them. and then he went off to reclaim it and never came back. Tasker's mom had probably told Billy that fairy tale while he was growing up, how his dad would someday come back, how they'd all be happy and rich. Now little Billy was trying to get some justice for his mother.

"You're wrong," Alex said. "About the Mayor's wife, I mean. She didn't have anything to do with cheating Duane King out of his land."

"Her signature is on this letter," Tasker said, waving it in Alex's face.

"Of course it is," Alex said, trying to keep his voice soft and friendly. Contempt at this point wouldn't serve anyone. "Nancy Sinclair was Seth Kowalski's secretary. He was the assessor, and the man behind defrauding Duane King. All Nancy did was handle his correspondence."

"How do you know that?" Tasker asked. "You'd have to get access to the records from the assessor's office and the old bastard who runs that place doesn't let anyone see those."

"Unless you've got great legs," Alex said with a grin. He then explained about Kowalski and the others in *North Shore Development* and how they had stolen King's land and used it to build their fortunes.

As Alex talked, Tasker's face went from disbelieving to shocked and finally to confusion.

"Then who's the ghost?" he asked.

"I have no idea," Alex lied. "But if I find out, I'll let you know." Alex held up his bandaged hand. "Now, if you don't mind, I need to go to the hospital; do you have a car?"

Tasker nodded.

"You can tell me that exclusive story on the way," he said.

Alex turned to Leroy who was saying, "I love you" to his wife over and over on the phone.

"Time to go," he said. "Leslie will bring her to meet you over at the hospital."

ALEX LEFT Leroy in the lobby of the hospital with Billy Tasker eagerly taking notes on his story of kidnapping and tunneling into the museum's vault. Leslie and Hannah were on their way in, but he'd promised to go see Iggy first thing and his hand was really starting to hurt.

"There you are," Iggy's voice assaulted him when he reached the surgery floor.

Alex turned to find the doctor bearing down on him.

"What took you so long?"

"Sorry," Alex said. "I stumbled on a break in the ghost case." He held up his hand so that Iggy could examine it. "How's Danny?"

"It's not good," Iggy said. "I got here in time to use the rune but the fool doctor in charge tried to stop me. I had to get rather insistent."

Alex smiled at that. He'd seen Iggy upset a few times and the man was a force of nature.

"He's sleeping now," Iggy continued. "The doctors will keep him sedated until the nerves in his arms have time to regrow. Shouldn't take more than a few days."

Alex sighed, and his hand started to tremble from pure stress relief; he'd been under a tremendous load the last few days, and with Danny out of the woods, daylight was beginning to glimmer.

"Danny would have been much worse if it weren't for you," Iggy was saying as he peeled the bandage off Alex's hand. "That was quick thinking, getting him down like that."

"Wish I'd been faster," Alex said.

"How many bullets hit you?"

"Besides this one," Alex said, trying to wiggle his fingers and wincing at the pain it caused. "I counted four."

"Danny's lucky," Iggy said. "Four more bullets and he'd have lost too much blood before he ever got here. The surgeon who pulled the other three out of him said it was touch and go for a few minutes."

Alex just nodded with a mixture of pain and relief.

"Come with me," Iggy said, leading Alex into a small examination room.

Under the bright lights, Iggy studied Alex's wound. The hole where the bullet had hit him was still leaking blood, but he couldn't see daylight through it, so that was something.

"Does this hurt?" Iggy asked, raising Alex's ring finger.

Purple dots swam in Alex's vision and he bit his tongue to keep from screaming.

"Figures," Iggy said, shaking his head. "The shot messed up some of the little bones in your hand. I can fix that, but it will take a few weeks. A major restoration rune could have handled it, but you took too long getting here." He seemed a bit miffed about that. "Fortunately for you, bones can be regenerated."

Iggy produced a piece of chalk and drew a door for his vault on the wall. A few moments later, he had it open and was leading Alex through. He spent the next ten minutes painfully injecting Alex's hand with all manner of syringes that all seemed to have square needles and be filled with acidic liquid. While he worked, Alex told Iggy about the events at the museum.

"Did you get a look at Jimmy Cortez' rune book?" Iggy asked.

Alex shook his head.

"The cops took all that stuff," he said. "But Callahan told me I could see it on Monday at the Central Office."

Iggy pulled out his green-backed rune book and tore a standard regeneration rune from inside. Sticking it to the wet blood on the back of Alex's hand, he reached for his lighter and his face fell.

"Damn," he said. "I left it on my nightstand."

Alex chuckled and pulled the silver lighter out of his own pocket.

"This came in real handy tonight," he said, passing it over.

Iggy carefully lit the rune paper, leaving a pulsating blue rune behind, hovering in the air for a moment. It vanished suddenly in a shower of blue sparks that settled down on the back of Alex's hand. As he watched, the ragged tear began to shrink as the skin knitted itself back together. After a minute, the only sign of the wound was the blood on his skin and the ache in his hand.

"Drink this," Iggy said, shoving a vial of sickly green liquid into Alex's good hand.

Alex drank and handed it back. Surprisingly, it wasn't too bad.

"That'll keep it from getting infected," Iggy said. He took out some narrow strips of thin wood and broke them into short lengths.

"So, was Barton happy?" Iggy asked as he began to wrap Alex's hand, using the splints to keep the palm from moving.

"Yes," Alex said, his voice a bit sarcastic. "His motor was fine."

"You don't sound happy."

"The thieves didn't break through the wall until after midnight," Alex said. "That means I lost our bet and he doesn't owe me anything."

Iggy raised an eyebrow.

"He said that?"

Alex nodded.

"Said if he made an exception, everyone he did business with would think he could be played."

"Sorcerers," Iggy declared, shaking his head.

Alex agreed.

"Now don't try to use that hand for at least a week," Iggy said. He'd wrapped Alex's palm tightly using the wood splints to keep his fingers from moving, then looped a cloth sling over Alex's head.

"Thanks, doc," Alex said as Iggy went to the sink to wash up. He picked up the lighter, intending to return it to his pocket, but it slipped from Alex's fingers and clattered to the floor. Alex just sat there, staring at it.

"What's the matter?" Iggy said, returning from the sink. "Alex, are you all right?"

Alex nodded, a broad grin spreading across his face. He hopped off the exam table and picked up the lighter, stuffing it quickly into his pocket.

"I know that look," Iggy said. "What do you know?"

Alex just kept grinning. "Do me a favor," he said. "There's a reporter in the lobby talking to Leroy Cunningham, blond guy in a brown suit with a dimple in his left cheek. Go tell him that I've got another exclusive for him, and this time it's huge."

Iggy looked confused.

"What story?" he asked. "What have you figured out?"

"I know how he's doing it," Alex said, heading out of the vault and back into the hospital. "The ghost, I mean. I know how he's getting in to the houses."

Alex stopped at the door and looked back at the still-confused Iggy. He felt so good that he laughed out loud.

"I know everything," he said. "Now meet me in the lobby; I've got to find a telephone."

29

THE GHOST

Alex couldn't sleep a wink after getting home from the hospital. Despite that, he still found himself sitting in the third row at St. Mark's for Mass the following morning. He hadn't been one for church after he left the Brotherhood of Hope mission where he'd spent his teenage years. When Father Harry died, however, he took with him that anchor of faith which Alex had always taken for granted. Now he went to church every Sunday, rain or shine. He told himself that he was doing it to honor Father Harry, but in truth, he needed that connection to what Father Harry had represented. He had been there for Alex like an immovable object, a compass needle invariably pointing north. A moral surety in an ever-changing world.

Father Harry was a constant reminder that being a good man was a choice. It didn't happen by accident.

As Alex listened to the sermon, he hoped Father Harry was proud of him. He'd certainly done his share of good deeds, saving the city at the cost of decades of his own life, finding Leroy when Hannah had no hope of paying what she would owe him for the job.

It was like Iggy always told him, he thought, somewhat sourly, no good deed goes unpunished. Still, he couldn't be too cynical in church, not with Father Harry looking down on him. In that sense, Harry was still his anchor.

"How was the Mass?" Iggy asked when Alex got home.

"Turns out God wants us to be nice to our neighbors," Alex said, hanging up his hat.

"I'll alert the media," Iggy said.

"Any word from Detweiler?"

"No," Iggy said. "I've got lunch ready. It's just some cold chicken and bread for sandwiches."

Alex chuckled. It was a meager fare by Iggy's standards.

"You're slipping," he said.

"I was up late," Iggy replied, sitting down at the table. "I've been thinking," he said as Alex joined him. "What if the glyph runes are older than Archimedes?"

Alex shrugged.

"Does it matter?"

"It might," Iggy said, assembling some sliced chicken and cheese onto a piece of bread. "I mean the Mayans weren't the only ones to have a pictographic language. The Aztecs and the Egyptians did as well."

"You're wondering if some of those Egyptian hieroglyphs are actually runes or runic constructs?"

Iggy nodded, slathering his sandwich with mustard.

"I doubt if anyone has ever shined a ghostlight on any of those ancient writings."

Alex took a bite of his own sandwich, chewing absently as he thought. Iggy had invented the ghostlight, so he was pretty sure the old man war right. Something about last night kept bothering him though, something he couldn't quite identify.

"I thought maybe," Iggy continued, "we could go over to the museum and use your ghostlight on whatever Egyptian junk they've got. The odds aren't good, but you never know. We might get lucky."

Alex put down his sandwich. Last night when Jimmy Cortez had first broken into the museum's vault, he'd told his men to grab jewelry. That made sense, because jewelry would be small and worth more than just the cost of the metals of which it was made. But Jimmy had said something else — that his men were supposed to look for something specific.

"The entropy stone," Alex said.

"What?"

"When Jimmy Cortez and his crew broke into the vault, he told the others to find something called the entropy stone."

Iggy stopped chewing and set his sandwich aside as well.

"I'll be damned," he said. "The treasure of the Almiranta was gold taken by the conquistadors. It came from Central and South America. Some of it might be Mayan."

"Are they looking for the glyph version of the Archimedean Monograph?" Alex asked.

Before Iggy could answer, there was a knock on the door.

"We need to take a ghostlight over to that museum," Iggy declared as Alex headed for the door.

He was right. Whatever Jimmy and his fellow glyph runewrights had been after, it was worth finding.

When Alex opened the door, he found Lieutenant Detweiler and three of his officers on the stoop. The Lieutenant didn't look particularly happy, but he obviously wasn't there to arrest Alex, so it was a win.

He held up an envelope made of heavy-looking paper. A gold foil seal had been placed over the point of the envelope's flap. Even at a distance, Alex could see it bore an obfuscation rune.

"How did you know?" Detweiler asked.

"Come in," Lieutenant," Alex said. "We need to invite a few other people to join us and then I'll explain everything."

AN HOUR AND A HALF LATER, the brownstone's kitchen was full of people. Detweiler and his contingent of police were present along with Detective North and two more officers he'd brought along. Captain Rooney sat next to Detweiler at the far end of the oak table. The Lieutenant had strenuously objected to the inclusion of Billy Tasker, but

Alex had insisted. Now the reporter sat near the head of the table by Iggy.

"Now that everyone's here, we can get started," Alex said, standing up to address the crowded room.

"You said we should be ready to apprehend the ghost," Rooney said. "How exactly are we going to do that in Dr. Bell's home? He wasn't a member of *North Shore Development*."

"That's true," Alex said, "but the ghost is going to come here nevertheless." Alex held up the envelope Detweiler had brought with him. "Last night, I telephoned Lieutenant Detweiler."

"In the middle of the night," Detweiler grumbled.

Alex put his hand over his heart and affected his most contrite expression.

"My most sincere apologies, Lieutenant," he said. "But I was worried the ghost might strike again if you didn't act quickly."

"What did he have you do?" Captain Rooney asked, looking a bit perturbed, though whether that was because Alex was giving his men orders or because Detweiler followed them, Alex couldn't tell.

"Lockerby told me that there would be a letter waiting at one of the potential victim's homes," Detweiler said. "We searched for the envelope Lockerby described. This morning we found one on in a pile of unopened mail at the Zimmerman home."

"This envelope here," Alex said, holding it up so all could see.

"What does that have to do with the ghost?" Detective North asked.

"This is how the Ghost has been getting into his victim's homes," Alex explained. "We know he's been using an escape rune to flee the scenes of his crimes. It's a very rare type of rune that costs the user's own life to transport him to a fixed location. To use one, a runewright would have to make an anchor rune in the spot he wanted to travel to."

"So someone snuck in and put one of these anchor runes in the houses of the victims?" Tasker asked.

Alex shook his head.

"No, the anchor rune is in here." He held up the envelope. "This seal," he indicated the foil label on the front of the envelope. "This contains a special type of rune that prevents nearby runes from making a magical connection. Without a connection, the anchor rune is useless. When the recipient breaks the seal to read the letter, the anchor rune becomes active."

"And the ghost attacks," Detweiler finished.

"Just so," Alex said.

"So let's go down to the Central Office, break the seal, and throw the letter into a cell," Captain Rooney said. "Why did we have to come all the way over here on a Sunday for this?"

A rumble of assent from the assembled police circled the room.

"Because," Iggy said, standing up, "this house has special protection runes on it that prevent people from using escape runes while inside."

"That means that the ghost can use the rune to get here, but not to leave again," Alex explained. If Iggy's protection runes didn't allow escape runes in, Alex wouldn't have been able to return here when he used his own rune last year. Of course, now that they knew that it was possible to mail an anchor rune, adjustments would have to be made.

"How would the ghost know that his victim had the letter?" Tasker asked. "I mean, what if they opened it and then went to answer the telephone?"

Alex held up the envelope again.

"This envelope feels pretty heavy," he said. "I'll bet there's a long letter inside designed to keep his intended victim reading. That will give him time to attack. Now, once I break this seal, the ghost will know, so he should get here within the next few minutes."

"But because of the protection runes on the house, he'll be trapped here," Rooney concluded.

"Yes," Alex said. "Once he arrives, Captain, you and your men will have him."

Alex stepped over to the light switch and flicked it, extinguishing the magelights in the chandelier over the dining table. There was still a little light from the windows in the front library, but the table and its occupants were mostly obscured.

"I'd ask you not to move or speak until the ghost shows himself," Alex said, moving to the little hallway that connected the kitchen and the library.

He held up the envelope and tore it open with a swift motion.

Inside were several sheets of heavy paper. Alex took them out and unfolded them, turning them over to the back. As he expected, an anchor rune was neatly drawn on the back side of the last page.

Alex had wondered how the ghost was able to get the drop on his victims, but the letter explained it. Whoever opened the envelope would spend at least ten minutes reading the letter, and that gave the ghost time and proximity to strike. After he'd killed his victims, he simply took the paper with him when he left. He probably reused it and the letter, sending them to his next intended victim.

Alex felt the rune on the paper tingle where his fingers touched it.

"He's coming," Alex hissed. "Remember to wait for my signal."

A moment later the air shimmered and suddenly a short, slender man was standing in front of Alex. Without hesitation he plunged a stiletto dagger into Alex's chest.

Or rather he would have, if the fresh shield runes Alex had inked into his suit coat hadn't stopped it. Alex knew the rune would stop a blade, but he hadn't experienced it before. It felt strange to see the blade, gleaming in the light from the window, slash toward him and then stop. It felt like someone poking him hard in the chest with their finger.

The ghost looked up, staring right at Alex. Recognition bloomed on the man's face, as he realized he'd been played. He dropped his knife and his now-empty hand clamped down on his left forearm.

Nothing happened.

"I should have known," the ghost said in a tired voice. "You were far too smart."

"Hello, Edmond," Alex said. "I had hoped to invite you to my home, just under different circumstances."

"You know this man," Detweiler said.

Edmond Dante whirled around as Iggy turned on the kitchen light. He chuckled when he saw nearly a dozen people waiting there.

"All for me?" he asked.

"And who might you be?" Captain Ronny asked, rising from his chair.

"This is Edmond Dante," Alex explained. "You know him as Duane King. I met him in the Hall of Records where he's been working since moving to New York. I assume he got the job there so he could search for the names of the people who defrauded him and caused the tragic death of his wife."

"If I'd had the money that land would have brought, I could have bought a real cure for her," Edmond said, his mouth turning up into a snarl. "Their greed condemned her to a slow, lingering death. They deserved what they got, each and every one of them. I only wish I'd managed to finish the job."

Edmond turned to Alex.

"You weren't surprised when I appeared," he said. "How did you know it was me?"

"Your name," Alex said. "Edmond Dante, it's from *The Count of Monte Cristo*, only his name is Edmond Dantés. It's a story about a man who fakes his own death in order to carry out a complicated revenge."

Edmond laughed at that.

"I thought I was being clever," he said.

"You're Duane King?" a shaky voice piped up from the far side of the table.

"Yes, yes," King said, not bothering to turn around. "Try to keep up, flatfoot."

Alex shook his head at that.

"You really should pay more attention to the literary references you use as aliases," he said. "In *The Count of Monte Cristo*, Edmond discovers that he has a son he didn't know about."

"So," King said with a shrug. "My son is dead. The Army told me he died in the war."

"You're forgetting that girl he left town with," Alex explained. "She was pregnant."

King turned around and went as white as his hair when he saw Tasker.

"Like looking at an old picture of yourself, isn't it?" Alex said. "Duane King, meet your grandson, Billy Tasker."

"Sit down, Mr. King," Iggy said, pulling out a chair across the table from Tasker.

King did as he was told and within a minute was answering questions from Tasker and asking his own.

"Can we arrest him now?" Detweiler said, stepping up beside Alex.

"Give him a few minutes," Alex said. "This may be his only chance to do something good with his life."

"You don't ask for much, do you Lockerby?" he groused. "It's not like we've got all day."

Alex jerked his thumb over his shoulder at the stiletto lying on the carpet in the hall.

"You can always take charge of the murder weapon," he said. "I'm sure that'll come in handy."

Detweiler looked chagrined and hurried over to collect it.

"Neatly done, lad," Iggy said, stepping into the space the Lieutenant had vacated. "How did you know it was Edmond?"

"Look at him," Alex said. "Once I knew that Tasker was King's grandson, the resemblance was obvious. Then there's Edmond's white hair and his trembling hands. That's not leukemia, those are the signs of someone who's spent a lot of his life energy on escape runes."

"Speaking of escape runes," Iggy said, "we'll have to do something about those or he'll just trigger them once he's outside the house."

"I've got a rock hammer with a dozen spellbreakers on it in the pantry," Alex said.

"Spellbreakers are illegal," Iggy pointed out.

"We'll just tell the police that they're nullification runes," Alex said under his breath. "They won't know the difference."

"So," Iggy said after a moment. "You solved two tough cases this week."

"Three if you count Andrew Barton's traction motor," Alex said.

"And," Iggy said. "Your runes didn't work before because Leroy Cunningham and that motor were literally underground."

"What's your point?"

"That you solved all three of those cases with your brain," Iggy said. "Not with your magic."

Alex thought about that. He'd been so caught up in the idea that he might be losing his magic...as if that were what defined him. It was part of who he was, certainly, but it wasn't him. Iggy was right. If Alex had lost his magic, he could still be a detective. He could still help people.

He could still make Father Harry proud.

"Thanks, old man," he said. "I needed to hear that."

"I know you did," Iggy said with an enigmatic grin. "After all, I'm still a lot smarter than you."

Alex wanted to argue, but he wasn't sure that was an argument he could win, so he wisely let it drop.

"I'm afraid you'll have to come with us now, Mr. King," Captain Rooney said. "Mr. Tasker can visit you at the Central Office once you've been booked."

King stood up and one of the officers instructed him to remove his shirt. Alex excused himself and got his prepared hammer, then he gently tapped it on the seven remaining escape runes tattooed on King's arm. As the hammer made contact, one of the spellbreaker runes on its handle flared and the escape rune it touched faded and vanished.

Once Alex finished, King put his shirt back on and Detective North handcuffed him.

"It was nice to know you, Alex," King said, then the police led him out.

Billy Tasker stopped to thank Alex. He looked a little dazed, but also excited as he left.

"At least the story will get out now," Alex said.

"It's about time," Iggy agreed.

Alex helped Iggy put the table and the chairs back in place in the kitchen, then they both headed for the library.

"After that discussion, I have a desire to reread *The Count of Monte Cristo* again," Iggy said, selecting the book from one of the shelves.

He was about to sit when there was a knock at the door. Alex and Iggy exchanged looks.

"Are you expecting more guests?" Iggy asked.

Alex shook his head and went to answer the door.

Two men were outside on the stoop when Alex opened the door. One was a tall thin man with dark hair, a bottlebrush mustache, and the olive complexion of an Italian or possibly a Greek. He wore an expensive suit and held a derby hat in his hands.

In front of him stood another man, dressed in a plain dark suit, well-made but not extravagant, with a matching fedora in his hand. He had Oriental features with a lined face, and long, dark hair that he had tied behind his head. Alex knew him as Shiro Takahashi, leader of the New York branch of the Japanese mafia. He was also Danny Pak's father.

Shiro used the Chinese alias Chow Duk Sum when posing as the owner of the *Lucky Dragon* restaurant.

"Good evening, Mr. Lockerby," Shiro said, and his voice was smooth and cultured with no trace of a Japanese accent. Of course there wouldn't be, since Shiro Takahashi had been born in America and raised in Brooklyn. "May we come in?"

Alex got over his shock at seeing Danny's father on his doorstep and moved back, holding the door open.

"Of course," he said.

Alex shut the door after the two men, then took their hats, hanging them on the pegs just outside the vestibule.

"We have company," he announced as he led Danny's father and the tall man into the library.

Iggy set aside his book and rose.

"Doctor Bell," Alex said, pointing to Danny's father. "This is Mr. Chow."

Shiro raised his hand and Alex stopped.

"Please," he said, "there's no need for that here. I am Shiro Takahashi," he said, bowing low. "I am very pleased to make your acquaintance, Dr. Bell." He straightened and turned, indicating his companion. "I believe you already know my personal physician, Dr. Themopolis."

Greek, Alex confirmed.

Iggy gave the doctor the once-over, and his expression soured.

"Yes," he said, somewhat stiffly. "We met last night when I was trying to help your son." Shiro seemed surprised that Iggy knew of his family connection, but Iggy waved his curiosity away. "Family resemblance," he explained.

Iggy indicated the chair on the far side of the little reading table from his.

"Why don't you sit here, Mr. Takahashi?" he said, then looked at

Alex. "Please get a couple of chairs from the kitchen for yourself and the doctor."

Alex did as he was told but had to make two trips on account of his injured hand.

"How's Danny doing?" Iggy asked the doctor once everyone was seated.

"Healing nicely, thanks to you," he said.

"Doctor Themopolis tells me that you insisted on treating Daniel for nerve damage to his arm," Shiro said.

"Alex called me," Iggy explained. "He said Danny complained of not being able to feel his fingers. I'm sorry if I offended you, doctor," he said to Themopolis, "but major restoration runes are only effective if administered within thirty minutes."

"No," Themopolis said. "You were in the right, and I admit it. I'm grateful to you for your help."

"I too wish to thank you," Shiro said. "You rendered my son a great service, at no small cost. I would like to reimburse you for your time and your materials. Is five hundred enough?"

Alex expected Iggy to object but instead he inclined his head.

"Five hundred is far too generous," he said. "The rune costs me one hundred and fifty dollars in materials, plus ten dollars for my time and a dollar-fifty for the cab ride both ways. Call it one-seventy?"

Shiro took out a billfold made of alligator leather and pulled two, fresh hundred-dollar bills from it.

"Let's say two hundred," he countered. "To offer less would be to insult my son's worth."

"I wouldn't dream of making you do that," Iggy said with a smile, and he accepted the money.

Shiro bowed again, then turned to Alex. His eyes dropped for a moment to Alex's bandaged hand, then he looked up to his face again.

"Dr. Themopolis also tells me that you jumped in front of Daniel when someone started shooting with a machine gun."

"He'd have done it for me," Alex said. He wasn't trying to be humble, it was the simple truth.

"I have no doubt," Shiro said, smiling. "Still, I value my son's life very much and I am grateful that you took the risk to save him."

He stood and bowed deeply to Alex. Not really knowing what to do, Alex sat where he was.

"Last year, you came to my work to ask me a question," Shiro said, sitting back down. "I remember it very well. You'd be surprised how many people want my help and then ask stupid or foolish questions. Yours was refreshingly well thought out."

"Thanks?" Alex said, still not sure where Shiro was going.

"At the time, I told you never to return, unless you wanted dumplings."

Alex chuckled.

"I remember."

"In return for your service to my son, I am rescinding that order," Shiro said. "If you ever need my help again, I will answer one question from you, to the best of my ability."

Alex felt gooseflesh run up his arm. Shiro Takahashi had just offered him something for which other men would pay handsomely. He wondered if there were hidden strings that might come with such an offer? In any case, it was probably best if Alex only used his question in the direst of need.

"Thank you," he said, amazed.

"Well," Shiro said, standing. "I've taken up enough of your afternoon. I would like to invite you both to come and dine at the *Lucky Dragon* with me." He turned to Iggy. "Danny tells me that you are a connoisseur of fine food, so I'll have the chef make you something special. Next week, perhaps."

"Delighted," Iggy beamed.

Shiro bowed to both of them, then shook their hands and left with his doctor in tow.

"Now I'm hungry," Iggy complained once they'd gone. "You want a plate of something?"

Alex shook his head. He suddenly felt as if he couldn't keep his eyes open.

"I've had enough excitement for one day," he said. "I'm going to bed."

30

THE DAY AFTER

Despite going to bed in the late afternoon, Alex slept clear through until the following morning. Despite all that sleep, it still took him four cups of coffee to wake up enough to get to his office by nine.

Even with a head start, Leslie still managed to beat him into the office. As a result, she had a stack of work ready and waiting for him. He'd given Billy Tasker a hard time for imperiling his relationship with the police, but he had to admit, walk-in business had picked up since the stories about the *Runewright Detective* had appeared in the tabloid.

Alex spent the next few hours calling potential clients and making appointments to use finding runes or do research for clients who wanted information found. By the time his intercom buzzed, it was nearing lunch.

"You have a visitor," Leslie said, somewhat enigmatically, when he answered.

Exiting his office, Alex found Gary and Marjorie Bickman waiting for him. Both of them beamed at him.

"Thank you so much, Alex," Marjorie said, stepping up to give him the hug that her very proper British husband never could.

Alex was a little taken aback since he'd seen, and been thanked, by both of them only last week.

"Master Barton paid us an advance to help make up for the money the Atwoods absconded with," Gary said, holding out a white envelope. "Since the master provides us an apartment, we don't need very much, and we wanted to make sure you were paid."

Alex took the envelope without looking inside and tucked it into his inner jacket pocket with his rune book. He then shook Gary's hand and got another hug from Marjorie.

"If there's ever anything we can do for you," Gary said, putting his arm around his wife.

"Just tell anybody who might need some help to look me up," Alex said with a smile, then he bade them goodbye and they left, arm in arm.

Alex took the envelope out and dropped it on Leslie's desk.

"If that's the hundred bucks they owed me, it should catch you up on your back pay," he said.

Leslie picked up the envelope and pulled out a fifty, two twenties, and a ten.

"We only need twenty more to make rent," she said. "But I still have a bunch of those rune orders to collect on. With luck, we'll be all caught up in a few days."

She was about to say more when the door opened, and Andrew Barton walked in.

Leslie's jaw dropped open and she blushed, standing up quickly.

"Really, Lockerby?" Barton said, looking at Leslie. "Another beauty? I need to start keeping you around." He crossed the room and held out his hand for Leslie to take. "And who is this lovely creature?"

"Andrew Barton, this is my secretary, Ms. Leslie Tompkins."

"Enchanté," he said in French, kissing the back of Leslie's hand.

Leslie blushed harder, keeping up her million-dollar smile.

"How can I help you, Mr. Barton?" Alex asked, nudging Leslie with his hip.

"Excuse me," she said, snapping out her trance. She picked up the envelope the Bickmans had given Alex. "I need to put this away."

She stepped around the desk and busied herself pulling the lock box out of the desk drawer.

"You should write dating advice for the newspaper, Lockerby," Barton said, still watching Leslie. "You'd make a fortune."

"I'll take it under advisement," Alex said, not trying hard to hide a grin.

Barton finally tore himself away from Leslie and smiled at Alex.

"I was going over my files and I discovered something in my Operations Filing."

"What's an Operations Filing?" Alex asked, not really interested, but willing to see where the sorcerer was going.

"It's a document the state makes you file if you want to have a big company," Barton said, sounding a bit bored himself. "Anyway, as it turns out when I set up the company, I established a bounty for anyone who exposed a traitor in my organization."

"What kind of bounty?" Alex asked, his interest returning.

Barton grinned at him. He'd apparently been watching the expression on Alex's face match the wheels turning in his head.

"One hundred and fifty dollars, cash," Barton said, handing Alex an envelope that looked remarkably like the one the Bickmans had just handed him.

Alex didn't know why the government would want a paper on how a business operated, or even if there was such a thing. Barton had been right when he refused to pay Alex at the museum. Technically Alex lost that bet. If he had paid Alex after the bet expired and anyone found out, he could lose prestige and maybe leverage in negotiations. Bargaining at any level was a lot like staring down a predator — whoever blinked first usually lost.

The envelope and the story about the bounty were Barton's way around that. If anyone asked, Alex lost the bet, and Barton didn't pay him. Coincidentally, Barton paid off the exact amount he would have owed...as a bounty for exposing a traitor in his organization.

"Glad I could be of help," Alex said, accepting the envelope. "Did you get the motor back all right?"

Barton nodded.

"It's being transported to Baltimore as we speak. The kid that

Jimmy and his miscreants grabbed actually did a good job of adapting it for mining. We didn't have to do much to get it ready for the contest." Barton stuck out his hand. "I've got to catch a train," he said as Alex shook his hand. "Thanks for all your help."

"Good luck in Baltimore."

Barton winked at Leslie, then withdrew.

"Did we just get paid?" Leslie said, not trusting what she heard.

Alex dropped the envelope on her desk with a smile.

"Yes, we did," he said. "This means not only are we in the black this month—"

"But we can buy cigarettes again," she finished.

"Take a fiver across to the five and dime and pick up a couple of packs for us," Alex said.

Leslie grinned at that.

"Sure thing, boss," she said, pulling the lock box back out of the drawer. "Right after I take care of this."

AN HOUR LATER, Alex found himself in a little room in the Manhattan Central Office of Police. He'd been through the rune books taken from Jimmy and at least three of his accomplices. Most of the strange glyphs looked familiar, since Alex had seen them in the book Alex had taken off their dead colleague. A few were new, and Alex faithfully copied them down in his notebook.

He wasn't sure what he would do with them, because without knowing what they actually did he couldn't make them work...or didn't dare try. So far, Lieutenant Callahan hadn't found where Jimmy and his cohorts were keeping their lore books, either. Those would have details about writing the glyphs and what they were for, though they wouldn't necessarily enable Alex to use them himself. Each school of runes had their own methods for using magic and they didn't play well with each other. Still, Alex had to find the missing lore books to know for sure.

Once he finished, Alex returned the books, and Callahan took him down to lockup to see Jimmy.

"What do you want?" he grumbled, once a uniformed officer brought him into one of their interrogation rooms.

"Just to talk," Alex said, trying to put him at ease.

"We've got nothing to say to you, traitor."

Alex raised an eyebrow at that. How did Jimmy think of him as a traitor?

"Because I ratted out a fellow runewright?" Alex scoffed. "I don't owe you anything. Now who is *we*?"

"What?"

"You said *we*," Alex explained. "Just who is it that doesn't have anything to say to me?"

Jimmy clammed up, just staring at Alex.

"These are nifty," Alex said, paging through the glyphs he'd copied into his notes. "Where'd you learn something like this? I never heard of a Mayan glyph school of runes."

Jimmy started at that. Alex had struck a nerve. He didn't expect Alex to have figured out that the glyphs were an unknown form of rune magic.

"The Maya are an old people," Jimmy said. "Our magic is old too."

"You still haven't said who *us* is?

"The magic of the Maya is in our Talons," he said. The phrase sounded ritualistic as he said it, like a chant or maxim repeated by students.

"So what were the Talons really looking for in that museum?" Alex asked.

"Gold that belongs to our people," Jimmy said.

Alex managed to keep from laughing out loud at that. Jimmy was no altruist, that was for sure.

"What's the entropy stone?"

Jimmy's eyes went hard and flat and he crossed his arms. He was putting on a brave face, but Alex could tell that he was desperately afraid of something, or maybe someone. Alex tried to get him to say more, but he just sat there, mum.

Eventually Alex called the guard and sent Jimmy back to his cell. Whatever the entropy stone was, Jimmy had been terrified by the idea of Alex knowing about it. He thought about interviewing the other thieves, but Jimmy was probably telling them not to talk to him right that minute.

He was at a dead end.

A moment later the guard returned, this time with Edmond, or rather with Duane King.

"I thought I'd be seeing you again," he said as he sat down on the opposite side of the table. Alex smiled back at him, not bothering to hide the fact that he was glad to see him.

"They treating you okay?"

King laughed at that.

"I spent twenty years in the joint," he said. "This is fine."

"Has Billy come to see you?"

"He just left before you got here," King said. "I wanted to thank you, Alex, for finding him. I know it probably doesn't mean much coming from me, after all I did, but I'm grateful. It's like somehow I've got Beatrice back, you know?"

"I'm glad," Alex said.

"So tell me," King said with a sly smile. "Was it worth it?"

"Was what worth it?"

"Whatever you spent all your life energy on." King reached up and touched his white hair. "Same as me," he said. "And you've got the shakes too. Whatever you spent your life on, was it worth it?"

"Yeah," Alex said after a moment. "It was."

"I can feel my body breaking down," King said. His voice was sad but held no tenor of fear. "My eyesight has started to go, and every day it's harder to wake up in the morning. I bet I don't last to the end of my trial. My only regret is Billy. I won't get much time with him."

The door to the interrogation room opened, and the guard that had brought King leaned in.

"Five minutes," he said, then withdrew.

"I guess visiting hours are over," King said. "Thanks for coming to see me."

"I need to ask you something first," Alex said, leaning forward.

"Let me guess," King said with a wry smile. "You want to know where I got those escape runes?"

Alex nodded.

"He said you'd ask," King said.

"Someone said I'd ask about the runes?"

"Not you specifically," King said. "I got these runes from a guy I met in prison by the name of Sam Enderby. I told him my plans while we were inside, and he said he'd help once I got out, so I tracked him down. He was the one who came up with the idea of using the letter. He also tattooed the runes on my arm. Didn't even ask me for money to do it."

That didn't sound right. Escape runes were expensive to produce just in materials, never mind the time it took. No old prison friendship would justify that.

"And he said someone would ask about it," Alex pressed.

King nodded.

"Sam said if I got caught that whoever figured it out would want to know about those runes and where they came from. I told him I'd keep it a secret, but he said that anyone smart enough to catch me deserved to know."

"And that's all?"

"That's all," King said.

"What did this Sam Enderby look like?"

"He was a Brit, about five foot ten with dark hair and a Roman nose."

The door opened, and the officer came in.

"Anything else?" Alex pressed as the guard waited for King to rise.

"He had a tattoo," King said. "Not a rune, but some kind of arrow-head on the inside of his wrist."

King smiled as the guard led him out.

"It really was nice to meet you, Alex. Come see me again before the end."

"I will," Alex said, and then he was gone.

Alex didn't know what to think. The thought that occupied his mind the most was King's list of symptoms: not being able to wake up and failing eyesight. He already had one of those. How much time did he have left?

Shaking his head, Alex stood, forcing the morbid thoughts from his brain. Someone had given Duane King over a grand's worth of runes without asking anything in return. That wasn't right. Sam Enderby obviously had some bigger game in mind, but what?

Alex picked up his kit and left the interrogation room. It was time to call Iggy.

"I just got done at the Central Office," Alex said once Iggy picked up the phone.

"Did you find out anything about our glyph rune cousins?"

"Just that they're probably actual descendants of the Maya," Alex said. "Jimmy called them the Talons, like they were some kind of organized group."

"That might explain why we've never heard of them," Iggy said. "If they're a small group, it'd be easy for them to stay secret. Did Jimmy say anything about the entropy stone?"

"He clammed up hard when I mentioned it," Alex said. "He didn't even like me knowing the name."

Iggy laughed at that.

"I think we should look into it, then," Iggy said. "Did you talk to the curator over at the museum?"

"I did," Alex said. "He wasn't thrilled, but since he owes me one, he said we can look around after closing time. Meet me there at seven and we'll go over the place."

"Will do," Iggy said. "What about Duane King?"

Alex filled Iggy in on his conversation with the former ghost, leaving out the bit about his life rune symptoms.

"You're right," Iggy agreed once Alex was done. "I don't like this Enderby fellow. The only reason he would have to set King up with all those runes was if he wanted something out of the deal."

"Maybe he hated one of the people King wanted to kill?" Alex suggested.

"No, he didn't know who was involved in North Shore Development until after he got that job in the Hall of Records."

"Maybe he was testing that anchor rune through the mail trick."

"That's a possibility," Iggy said. "Though it seems like an awfully expensive test."

"Well, I'll think about it some more," Alex said.

"Yes, and we'll need to find out everything we can about Sam Enderby and why he was in prison," Iggy added.

"I've got to get going," Alex said, checking his pocket watch.

"What are you going to do until the museum closes?"

"I've got three family heirlooms to track down with my finding rune," Alex answered. "Then I have to see a woman about tailing her cheating husband."

Iggy laughed at that.

"Just don't be late," he said.

31

THE HIEROGLYPH

A lex spent the rest of the afternoon working through Leslie's stack of potential clients. It wasn't glamorous work, but it was work and if it kept up like this, they'd have next month covered in a week or two.

By five o'clock, Alex closed the office and took the crawler across town to the Waldorf hotel. Anne Watson didn't look much better when she let him into her suite. She listened patiently as he told the story of Duane King and her husband's involvement in *North Shore Development*.

"Thank you, Alex," she said when he finished.

Alex could see that the knowledge of what her husband had done, even though it was decades ago, weighed on her like a millstone.

"Do you think the police have enough evidence to convict the man who killed David?" she asked.

"They do," Alex assured her.

"I'm sorry," she said, as if she bore some responsibility for what had happened years before she'd even met her husband.

She paid Alex and wished him well, but it was clear that she just wanted Alex to go and hopefully take the pain of her husband's past with him.

Alex thanked her and left. He wanted to say something to help, but there really wasn't anything he could say.

———

ALEX PUFFED on a cigarette as he rode a crawler along Central Park North to the station near Dr. Kellin's shop. It had been a good day, and he hoped it was about to get better.

"What are you doing here?" Jessica asked when she answered the back door to the lab.

"I wanted to apologize again for cutting our date short," Alex said.

Jessica leaned against the door jamb, crossing her arms with a raised eyebrow.

"Okay," she said, the ghost of a smile playing across her lips. "Let's hear it."

Alex suppressed a smile of his own. Jessica wanted her pound of flesh for ditching her to solve his case. Still, if she wasn't willing to forgive him, she would have slammed the door in his face.

He told her about the museum heist and Andrew Barton's traction motor, then about Duane King and the ghost murders.

"I read about those in the papers this morning," she said. "They didn't mention you."

Alex explained about Billy Tasker and his deal with the reporter.

"How modest of you," she said.

Alex wasn't sure if she believed him or not. Jessica had a great poker face.

She had great everything.

"So," she said, her barely-visible smile shifting to a mocking one. "How will you ever make it up to me?"

Alex found himself grinning this time. He'd anticipated that question and he had a damn good answer.

"Well, if you had a few hours free tonight," he said, "the curator of the American Museum of Natural History owes me a pretty big favor. How would you like a private tour of the Almiranta exhibit with myself and Dr. Bell?"

"You're bringing a chaperone?" Jessica smirked and stepped close to him, so they were almost touching. "Do you need protection from me?"

"No," Alex said, resisting the urge to close the gap between them. "But Iggy knows a lot about this stuff, and he's an excellent tour guide."

Jessica stepped forward, pressing her body against his.

"Well," she said, her eyes boring into his. "I'll get my handbag." She leaned in and pressed her lips against his for a long moment before she pulled back.

Alex slipped his hand around her waist, preventing her from moving.

"In a minute," he said, then pulled her in again.

"So we're on a treasure hunt?" Jessica said as Alex handed her a pair of yellow spectacles.

They'd had a tour of the Aztec and Mayan gold from the curator and Jessica had enjoyed every minute, clinging to Alex's arm the whole time. Of course that wasn't the part Alex was worried about. That came when Iggy opened the doctor's bag he'd been carrying and pulled out Alex's multi-lamp. He had no idea how Jessica would react to their ulterior motive for this visit — the search for the entropy stone, or, failing that, some sign of ancient runecraft.

"That's exactly it," Iggy said.

"If you don't want to help, I'll understand," Alex said. "I can take you home."

"Don't you dare," Jessica said, fitting the spectacles on her perky nose.

"Told you," Iggy said.

Alex put on his oculus, then lit the ghostlight burner in his lamp.

"What am I looking for?" Jessica asked.

Alex pulled out his rune book and opened it to a page with a vault rune on it. He shone the green light from the lamp onto the page and the rune glowed an iridescent yellow in his oculus.

"Oooh," Jessica cooed.

"Just call out if any part of the treasure glows," Iggy said, clipping a yellow pair of pince-nez spectacles to his nose.

No bigger than the Almiranta exhibit was, they were able to search it twice in just over half an hour. When they didn't find anything, Jessica pouted adorably.

"Oh well," she said.

"What about the Egyptian exhibit?" Alex asked.

"Good idea," Iggy said. "They've got a couple of mummies here."

A quick chat with the curator, and twenty minutes later Jessica was pouting again.

"No luck," Alex said. They'd been over the mummies and the various artifacts from their tombs three times to no avail.

"There is another mummy in the basement," the curator offered. He was a little man in an expensive suit with slicked back hair and a pencil mustache. "We didn't have room for all three with the Almiranta display in the big room," he continued. "And she's not really anyone important anyway."

Jessica snaked her hand into the crook of Alex's arm.

"Can we try that?" she said. Despite having no success, she was clearly having fun. Alex had forgotten how rarely she got out.

Since he had no objection to spending more time with Jessica, Alex asked the curator to show them the mummy in storage.

There wasn't much to her, just the wrapped body in the bottom half of a wooden sarcophagus, sitting on a sturdy table. A few unimpressive-looking artifacts belonging to the dead woman were stacked neatly on a shelf nearby.

"She was some kind of priestess," the curator said. "A trusted advisor or something like that." He looked at his pocket watch, then glanced back in the direction of the stairs. "I need to check with the security office," he said. "Just meet me upstairs once you're done."

Alex tried to light the lamp, but his burner had run out of fuel.

"Ano..." Jessica said, trying to read a long Egyptian name from a card mounted on the foot of the wooden coffin.

Alex glanced at it and saw the name, Ankhesenpaaten Tasherit. He decided not to try it.

"Anox-en-pay-a-teen Ta-sher-eet," Jessica managed at last. "Priestess of Ra."

"Pleasure," Alex said, nodding toward the mummy as he replenished his burner from a glass bottle in his kit bag.

"Who's Ra?" Jessica asked.

"Egyptian god of the sun," Iggy said, pointing to a stylized eye printed on the card. "This is his symbol."

Alex relit his lamp and this time, when the green light washed over the mummy, the shelf behind it glowed.

"Look," Jessica gasped, digging her nails into Alex's arm in her excitement.

"Carful with those things," Alex said, prying her poison-tipped manicure off his arm.

"Sorry," she said with fake remorse.

"It's these jars," Iggy said, pulling one of five roundish jars about a foot and half tall from the shelf.

A glowing line ran up the side of the jar to some kind of animal head on top. As Iggy turned it, they could see more lines and shapes on the back of the jar.

"It's only on the one side," Iggy said, putting the jar back on the shelf with the glowing lines visible.

"Check the other jars," Alex said, holding the light steady.

One by one, Iggy checked the jars. Each of them had a pattern of lines and shapes on its back, but none of them looked complete.

"They form a pattern of some kind," Iggy said.

"Try rearranging them," Jessica said.

It took Iggy a few minutes, but he finally managed to put the jars in an order where the lines on one seemed to be continued on the next.

"So what is it?" Jessica asked, breathless in her excitement. "What does it mean?"

"It means that the ancient Egyptians knew rune magic," Alex said.

"As for what it's for?" Iggy said. "Haven't got a clue."

Alex pulled out his notebook and sketched the strange Egyptian glyph. Iggy did the same, and then they compared notes.

"Now what?" Alex asked.

"Now we go to work," Iggy said. "Jimmy Cortez and his Talon

friends were trying to uncover lost rune knowledge. We need to figure out what they were after and why."

"Is this part of it?" Jessica asked.

"I don't know," Iggy admitted, stroking his mustache. "I'll go thank the curator and tell him we're leaving," he went on, turning to Alex. "You take Jessica home. I imagine we've kept her from her duties long enough. Then you can meet me back at the brownstone."

Alex nodded, and Iggy headed out through the museum's vast storage basement toward the stairs.

"Well this was one hell of a date," Jessica said, leaning against a table full of wooden crates. Alex noticed that she liked to lean against things with her hip cocked. She probably thought it presented her figure to the greatest advantage like that.

She was right.

Alex grinned at her as he finished putting away his gear.

"We'll have to do it again, then," he said. He offered her his arm and began walking the same way Iggy had gone.

"Yes, we will," she said. "I am sorry about Dr. Bell, though."

"What about Iggy?" Alex asked, confused.

"Well, he seems very eager to go over all that ancient rune stuff with you," she said. She took a quick step forward and turned directly into Alex's path. He stopped short to avoid running into her. "I'm sorry because he's going to be disappointed." She leaned in, pressing herself against him like she had done before. "You see, you're not coming home tonight."

Before Alex could reply, she kissed him.

She was right. Iggy was going to be disappointed.

32

EPILOGUE

The following day a notice was set to appear on the police blotter of the *New York Times*. It was a small story about an insignificant yet baffling theft.

According to the article, a mummy had been reported stolen from the basement of the American Museum of Natural History. A security guard was suspected of the theft, since he disappeared the same night as the missing mummy. The only evidence left behind were five smashed jars that were part of the mummy's collection.

Unfortunately, that same day a brawl broke out at a Dodgers game in Brooklyn. The fight spilled off the field and out into the streets. Police were called, and dozens of arrests were made. The event was unprecedented and drove all mention of the museum theft out of the newspaper entirely.

THE END

A QUICK NOTE

. . .

You made it. You got all the way to the end, thanks so much for reading my book, it really means a lot to me. As an independent author, one thing that really helps me to get my books out to more people are the reviews I get over on Amazon. So if you would be so kind, take a moment and head over to Amazon and leave me a quick review. I'd really appreciate it. It doesn't have to be anything fancy, just a quick note saying whether or not you liked the book.

Thanks so much.

Since this is book 2 in the Arcane Casebook series, most of you will have already read book 1 and if you have, you've probably downloaded the prequel novella, *Dead Letter*. If, for some reason you haven't, however, you can get it absolutely free at www.danwillisauthor.com. *Dead Letter* is the story of how Alex met Danny and the first case they worked together. Get yours now.

So take two minutes and leave me a review on Amazon. And, if you didn't get *Dead Letter* before, grab your free copy at my website (www.danwillisauthor.com).

Also, I love talking to my readers, so please email me at dan@danwillisauthor.com — I read every one. Or join the discussion on the Arcane Casebook Facebook Group.

Look for The Long Chain: Arcane Casebook #3.

ALSO BY DAN WILLIS

Arcane Casebook Series:

Dead Letter - Prequel

Private Detective Alex Lockerby needs a break and it materializes in the form of an ambitious, up-and-coming beat cop, Danny Pack. Alex and Danny team up to unravel a tale murder, jealousy, and revenge stretching back over 30 years. It's a tale that powerful forces don't want to come to light. Now the cop and the private detective must work fast and watch each other's backs if they hope to catch a killer and live to tell about it.

Dead Letter is the prequel novella to the Arcane Casebook series.

Get Dead Letter Free at www.danwillisauthor.com

In Plain Sight - Book 1

In 1933, an unwitting thief steals a vial of deadly plague, accidentally releasing it in at a soup kitchen in Manhattan. The police, the FBI, and New York's 'council of Sorcerers' fear the incident is a trial run for something much deadlier. Detective Alex Lockerby, himself under suspicion because of ties to the priest who ran the kitchen, has a book of spells, a pack of matches, and four days to find out where the plague came from, or the authorities will hang the crime squarely on him.

Available at Amzazon.com

Dragons of the Confederacy Series:
A steampunk Civil War story with NYT Bestseller, Tracy Hickman

Lincoln's Wizard

Washington has fallen! Legions of 'grays' -- dead soldiers reanimated on the battlefield and pressed back into service of the Southern Cause -- have pushed the lines as far north as the Ohio River. Lincoln has moved the government of the United States to New York City. He needs to stop the juggernaught of the Southern undead 'abominations' or the North will ultimately fall. But Allan Pinkerton, his head of security, has a plan...

Available at Amzazon.com

The Georgia Alchemist

With Air Marshall Sherman's fleet on the run and the Union lines failing, Pinkerton's agents, Hattie Lawton and Braxton Wright make their way into the heart of the south. Pursued by the Confederacy's best agents, time is running out for Hattie and Braxton to locate the man whose twisted genius brings dead soldiers back to fight and find a way to stop the inexorable tide that threatens to engulf the Union.

Forthcoming: 2020

Other books:

The Flux Engine

In a Steampunk Wild West, fifteen-year-old John Porter wants nothing more than to find his missing family. Unfortunately a legendary lawman, a talented thief, and a homicidal madman have other plans, and now John will need his wits, his pistol, and a lot of luck if he's going to survive.

Available at Amzazon.com

ABOUT THE AUTHOR

Dan Willis wrote for the long-running DragonLance series. He is the author of the Arcane Casebook series and the Dragons of the Confederacy series.

For more information:
www.danwillisauthor.com
dan@danwillisauthor.com

 facebook.com/danwillisauthor
twitter.com/WDanWillis